THE SILENCE OF THE LAMBS

A native of Mississippi, Thomas Harris began his writing career covering crime in the United States and Mexico, and was a reporter and editor for the Associated Press in New York City. His first novel, *Black Sunday*, was published in 1975, followed by *Red Dragon* in 1981, *The Silence of the Lambs* in 1988, *Hannibal* in 1999 and *Hannibal Rising* in 2006.

'No thriller writer is better attuned than Thomas Harris to the rhythms of suspense. No horror writer is more adept at making the stomach churn'

Craig Brown, *Mail on Sunday*

'Harris is a superb writer'

Scotland on Sunday

THOMAS HARRIS

THE SILENCE OF THE LAMBS

arrow books

Reissued by Arrow Books in 2009

10

First published in the United Kingdom in 1989 by William Heinemann

This edition first published in 1990 by Mandarin Paperbacks and
reprinted 17 times.

Arrow Books
The Random House Group Limited
20 Vauxhall Bridge Road, London, SW1V 2SA

www.randomhouse.co.uk

Addresses for companies within The Random House Group Limited can be
found at: www.randomhouse.co.uk/offices.htm

The Random House Group Limited Reg. No. 954009

A CIP catalogue record for this book
is available from the British Library

ISBN 9780099532927

The Random House Group Limited supports The Forest Stewardship
Council® (FSC®), the leading international forest-certification
organisation. Our books carrying the FSC label are printed on
FSC®-certified paper. FSC is the only forest-certification scheme
supported by the leading environmental organisations, including
Greenpeace. Our paper procurement policy can be found at
www.randomhouse.co.uk/environment

Typeset by Palimpsest, Book Production Limited,
Polmont, Stirlingshire

Printed and bound by CPI Group (UK) Ltd, Croydon, CR0 4YY

To the memory of my father

If after the manner of men I have fought
with beasts at Ephesus, what advantageth
it me, if the dead rise not?

– I Corinthians

Need I look upon a death's head in a
ring, that have one in my face?

– John Donne, 'Devotions'

BEHAVIORAL SCIENCE, the FBI section that deals with serial murder, is on the bottom floor of the Academy building at Quantico, half-buried in the earth. Clarice Starling reached it flushed after a fast walk from Hogan's Alley on the firing range. She had grass in her hair and grass stains on her FBI Academy windbreaker from diving to the ground under fire in an arrest problem on the range.

No one was in the outer office, so she fluffed briefly by her reflection in the glass doors. She knew she could look all right without primping. Her hands smelled of gunsmoke, but there was no time to wash—Section Chief Crawford's summons had said *now.*

She found Jack Crawford alone in the cluttered suite of offices. He was standing at someone else's desk talking on the telephone and she had a chance to look him over for the first time in a year. What she saw disturbed her.

Normally, Crawford looked like a fit, middle-aged engineer who might have paid his way through college playing baseball—a crafty catcher, tough when he blocked the plate. Now he was thin, his shirt collar was too big, and he had dark puffs under his reddened eyes. Everyone who could read the papers knew Behavioral Science Section was catching hell. Starling hoped Crawford wasn't on the juice. That seemed most unlikely here.

Crawford ended his telephone conversation with a sharp "No." He took her file from under his arm and opened it.

"Starling, Clarice M., good morning," he said.

"Hello." Her smile was only polite.

"Nothing's wrong. I hope the call didn't spook you."

"No." *Not totally true*, Starling thought.

"Your instructors tell me you're doing well, top quarter of the class."

"I hope so, they haven't posted anything."

"I ask them from time to time."

That surprised Starling; she had written Crawford off as a two-faced recruiting sergeant son of a bitch.

She had met Special Agent Crawford when he was a guest lecturer at the University of Virginia. The quality of his criminology seminars was a factor in her coming to the Bureau. She wrote him a note when she qualified for the Academy, but he never replied, and, for the three months she had been a trainee at Quantico, he had ignored her.

Starling came from people who do not ask for favors or press for friendship, but she was puzzled and regretful at Crawford's behavior. Now, in his presence, she liked him again, she was sorry to note.

Clearly something was wrong with him. There was

a peculiar cleverness in Crawford, aside from his intelligence, and Starling had first noticed it in his color sense and the textures of his clothing, even within the FBI-clone standards of agent dress. Now he was neat but drab, as though he were molting.

"A job came up and I thought about you," he said. "It's not really a job, it's more of an interesting errand. Push Berry's stuff off that chair and sit down. You put down here that you want to come directly to Behavioral Science when you get through with the Academy."

"I do."

"You have a lot of forensics, but no law-enforcement background. We look for six years, minimum."

"My father was a marshal, I know the life."

Crawford smiled a little. "What you *do* have is a double major in psychology and criminology, and how many summers working in a mental health center— two?"

"Two."

"Your counselor's license, is it current?"

"It's good for two more years. I got it before you had the seminar at UVA—before I decided to do this."

"You got stuck in the hiring freeze."

Starling nodded. "I was lucky though—I found out in time to qualify as a Forensic Fellow. Then I could work in the lab until the Academy had an opening."

"You wrote to me about coming here, didn't you, and I don't think I answered—I know I didn't. I should have."

"You've had plenty else to do."

"Do you know about VI-CAP?"

"I know it's the Violent Criminal Apprehension Program. The *Law Enforcement Bulletin* says you're working on a database, but you aren't operational yet."

Crawford nodded. "We've developed a questionnaire. It applies to all the known serial murderers in modern times." He handed her a thick sheaf of papers in a flimsy binding. "There's a section for investigators, and one for surviving victims, if any. The blue is for the killer to answer if he will, and the pink is a series of questions an examiner asks the killer, getting his reactions as well as his answers. It's a lot of paperwork."

Paperwork. Clarice Starling's self-interest snuffled ahead like a keen beagle. She smelled a job offer coming—probably the drudgery of feeding raw data into a new computer system. It was tempting to get into Behavioral Science in any capacity she could, but she knew what happens to a woman if she's ever pegged as a secretary—it sticks until the end of time. A choice was coming, and she wanted to choose well.

Crawford was waiting for something—he must have asked her a question. Starling had to scramble to recall it:

"What tests have you given? Minnesota Multiphasic, ever? Rorschach?"

"Yes, MMPI, never Rorschach," she said. "I've done Thematic Apperception and I've given children Bender-Gestalt."

"Do you spook easily, Starling?"

"Not yet."

"See, we've tried to interview and examine all the

4

thirty-two known serial murderers we have in custody, to build up a database for psychological profiling in unsolved cases. Most of them went along with it—I think they're driven to show off, a lot of them. Twenty-seven were willing to cooperate. Four on death row with appeals pending clammed up, understandably. But the one we want the most, we haven't been able to get. I want you to go after him tomorrow in the asylum."

Clarice Starling felt a glad knocking in her chest and some apprehension too.

"Who's the subject?"

"The psychiatrist—Dr Hannibal Lecter," Crawford said.

A brief silence follows the name, always, in any civilized gathering.

Starling looked at Crawford steadily, but she was too still. "Hannibal the Cannibal," she said.

"Yes."

"Yes, well—okay, right. I'm glad of the chance, but you have to know I'm wondering—why me?"

"Mainly because you're available," Crawford said. "I don't expect him to cooperate. He's already refused, but it was through an intermediary—the director of the hospital. I have to be able to say our qualified examiner went to him and asked him personally. There are reasons that don't concern you. I don't have anybody left in this section to do it."

"You're jammed—Buffalo Bill—and the things in Nevada," Starling said.

"You got it. It's the old story—not enough warm bodies."

"You said tomorrow—you're in a hurry. Any bearing on a current case?"

"No. I wish there were."

"If he balks on me, do you still want a psychological evaluation?"

"No. I'm waist-deep in inaccessible-patient evaluations of Dr Lecter and they're all different."

Crawford shook two vitamin C tablets into his palm, and mixed an Alka-Seltzer at the water cooler to wash them down. "It's ridiculous, you know; Lecter's a psychiatrist and he writes for the psychiatric journals himself—extraordinary stuff—but it's never about his own little anomalies. He pretended to go along with the hospital director, Chilton, once in some tests—sitting around with a blood-pressure cuff on his penis, looking at wreck pictures—then Lecter published first what he'd learned about Chilton and made a fool out of him. He responds to serious correspondence from psychiatric students in fields unrelated to his case, and that's all he does. If he won't talk to you, I just want straight reporting. How does he look, how does his cell look, what's he doing. Local color, so to speak. Watch out for the press going in and coming out. Not the real press, the supermarket press. They love Lecter even better than Prince Andrew."

"Didn't a sleazo magazine offer him fifty thousand dollars for some recipes? I seem to remember that," Starling said.

Crawford nodded. "I'm pretty sure the *National Tattler* has bought somebody inside the hospital and they may know you're coming after I make the appointment."

Crawford leaned forward until he faced her at a distance of two feet. She watched his half-glasses blur the bags under his eyes. He had gargled recently with Listerine.

"Now. I want your full attention, Starling. Are you listening to me?"

"Yes, sir."

"Be very careful with Hannibal Lecter. Dr Chilton, the head of the mental hospital, will go over the physical procedure you use to deal with him. Don't deviate from it. *Do not deviate from it one iota for any reason.* If Lecter talks to you at all, he'll just be trying to find out about you. It's the kind of curiosity that makes a snake look in a bird's nest. We both know you have to back-and-forth a little in interviews, but you tell him no specifics about yourself. You don't want any of your personal facts in his head. You know what he did to Will Graham."

"I read about it when it happened."

"He gutted Will with a linoleum knife when Will caught up with him. It's a wonder Will didn't die. Remember the Red Dragon? Lecter turned Francis Dolarhyde onto Will and his family. Will's face looks like damn Picasso drew him, thanks to Lecter. He tore a nurse up in the asylum. Do your job, just don't ever forget what he is."

"And what's that? Do you know?"

"I know he's a monster. Beyond that, nobody can say for sure. Maybe you'll find out; I didn't pick you out of a hat, Starling. You asked me a couple of interesting questions when I was at UVA. The Director will see your own report over your signature—if it's clear and

7

tight and organized. I decide that. And I *will* have it by 0900 Sunday. Okay, Starling, carry on in the prescribed manner."

Crawford smiled at her, but his eyes were dead.

2

DR FREDERICK CHILTON, fifty-eight, administrator of
the Baltimore State Hospital for the Criminally Insane,
has a long, wide desk upon which there are no hard
or sharp objects. Some of the staff call it "the moat."
Other staff members don't know what the word *moat*
means. Dr Chilton remained seated behind his desk
when Clarice Starling came into his office.

"We've had a lot of detectives here, but I can't
remember one so attractive," Chilton said without getting up.

Starling knew without thinking about it that the shine
on his extended hand was lanolin from patting his hair.
She let go before he did.

"It is *Miss* Sterling, isn't it?"

"It's *Star*ling, Doctor, with an *a*. Thank you for
your time."

"So the FBI is going to the girls like everything else,
ha, ha." He added the tobacco smile he uses to separate
his sentences.

"The Bureau's improving, Dr Chilton. It certainly is."

"Will you be in Baltimore for several days? You know, you can have just as good a time here as you can in Washington or New York, if you know the town."

She looked away to spare herself his smile and knew at once that he had registered her distaste. "I'm sure it's a great town, but my instructions are to see Dr Lecter and report back this afternoon."

"Is there someplace I could call you in Washington for a follow-up, later on?"

"Of course. It's kind of you to think of it. Special Agent Jack Crawford's in charge of this project, and you can always reach me through him."

"I see," Chilton said. His cheeks, mottled with pink, clashed with the improbable red-brown of his coif. "Give me your identification, please." He let her remain standing through his leisurely examination of her ID card. Then he handed it back and rose. "This won't take much time. Come along."

"I understood you'd brief me, Dr Chilton," Starling said.

"I can do that while we walk." He came around his desk, looking at his watch. "I have a lunch in half an hour."

Dammit, she should have read him better, quicker. He might not be a total jerk. He might know something useful. It wouldn't have hurt her to simper once, even if she wasn't good at it.

"Dr Chilton, I have an appointment with you now. It was set at your convenience, when you could give me some time. Things could come up during the interview—I may need to go over some of his responses with you."

"I really, really doubt it. Oh, I need to make a telephone call before we go. I'll catch up with you in the outer office."

"I'd like to leave my coat and umbrella here."

"Out there," Chilton said. "Give them to Alan in the outer office. He'll put them away."

Alan wore the pajama-like garment issued to the inmates. He was wiping out ashtrays with the tail of his shirt.

He rolled his tongue around in his cheek as he took Starling's coat.

"Thank you," she said.

"You're more than welcome. How often do you shit?" Alan asked.

"What did you say?"

"Does it come out lo-o-o-o-nnng?"

"I'll hang these somewhere myself."

"You don't have anything in the way—you can bend over and watch it come out and see if it changes color when the air hits it, do you do that? Does it look like you have a big brown tail?" He wouldn't let go of the coat.

"Dr Chilton wants you in his office, right now," Starling said.

"No, I don't," Dr Chilton said. "Put the coat in the closet, Alan, and don't get it out while we're gone. *Do it.* I had a full-time office girl, but the cutbacks robbed me of her. Now the girl who let you in types three hours a day, and then I have Alan. Where are all the office girls, Miss Starling?" His spectacles flashed at her. "Are you armed?"

"No, I'm not armed."

"May I see your purse and briefcase?"

"You saw my credentials."

"And they say you're a student. Let me see your things, please."

Clarice Starling flinched as the first of the heavy steel gates clashed shut behind her and the bolt shot home. Chilton walked slightly ahead, down the green institutional corridor in an atmosphere of Lysol and distant slammings. Starling was angry at herself for letting Chilton put his hand in her purse and briefcase, and she stepped hard on the anger so that she could concentrate. It was all right. She felt her control solid beneath her, like a good gravel bottom in a fast current.

"Lecter's a considerable nuisance," Chilton said over his shoulder. "It takes an orderly at least ten minutes a day to remove the staples from the publications he receives. We tried to eliminate or reduce his subscriptions, but he wrote a brief and the court overruled us. The volume of his personal mail used to be enormous. Thankfully, it's dwindled since he's been overshadowed by other creatures in the news. For a while it seemed that every little student doing a master's thesis in psychology wanted something from Lecter in it. The medical journals still publish him, but it's just for the freak value of his byline."

"He did a good piece on surgical addiction in the *Journal of Clinical Psychiatry*, I thought," Starling said.

"You did, did you? *We* tried to study Lecter. We thought, 'Here's an opportunity to make a landmark study'—it's so rare to get one alive."

"One what?"

"A pure sociopath, that's obviously what he is. But he's impenetrable, much too sophisticated for the standard tests. And, my, does he hate us. He thinks I'm his nemesis. Crawford's very clever—isn't he?—using you on Lecter."

"How do you mean, Dr Chilton?"

"A young woman to 'turn him on,' I believe you call it. I don't believe Lecter's seen a woman in several years—he may have gotten a glimpse of one of the cleaning people. We generally keep women out of there. They're trouble in detention."

Well fuck off, Chilton. "I graduated from the University of Virginia with honors, Doctor. It's not a charm school."

"Then you should be able to remember the rules: Do not reach through the bars, do not touch the bars. You pass him nothing but soft paper. No pens, no pencils. He has his own felt-tipped pens some of the time. The paper you pass him must be free of staples, paper clips, or pins. Items come back out through the sliding food carrier. No exceptions. Do not accept anything he attempts to hold out to you through the barrier. Do you understand me?"

"I understand."

They had passed through two more gates and left the natural light behind. Now they were beyond the wards where inmates can mix together, down in the region where there can be no windows and no mixing. The hallway lights are covered with heavy grids, like the lights in the engine rooms of ships. Dr Chilton paused beneath one. When their footfalls stopped, Starling

13

could hear somewhere beyond the wall the ragged end of a voice ruined by shouting.

"Lecter is never outside his cell without wearing full restraints and a mouthpiece," Chilton said. "I'm going to show you why. He was a model of cooperation for the first year after he was committed. Security around him was slightly relaxed—this was under the previous administration, you understand. On the afternoon of July 8, 1976, he complained of chest pain and he was taken to the dispensary. His restraints were removed to make it easier to give him an electrocardiogram. When the nurse bent over him, he did this to her." Chilton handed Clarice Starling a dog-eared photograph. "The doctors managed to save one of her eyes. Lecter was hooked up to the monitors the entire time. He broke her jaw to get at her tongue. His pulse never got over eighty-five, even when he swallowed it."

Starling didn't know which was worse, the photograph or Chilton's attention as he gleaned her face with fast grabby eyes. She thought of a thirsty chicken pecking tears off her face.

"I keep him in here," Chilton said, and pushed a button beside heavy double doors of security glass. A big orderly let them into the block beyond.

Starling made a tough decision and stopped just inside the doors. "Dr Chilton, we really need these test results. If Dr Lecter feels you're his enemy—if he's fixed on you, just as you've said—we might have more luck if I approached him by myself. What do you think?"

Chilton's cheek twitched. "That's perfectly fine with me. You might have suggested that in my office. I

14

could have sent an orderly with you and saved the time."

"I could have suggested it there if you'd briefed me there."

"I don't expect I'll see you again, Miss *Star*ling— Barney, when she's finished with Lecter, ring for someone to bring her out."

Chilton left without looking at her again.

Now there was only the big impassive orderly and the soundless clock behind him and his wire mesh cabinet with the Mace and restraints, mouthpiece and tranquilizer gun. A wall rack held a long pipe device with a U on the end for pinioning the violent to the wall.

The orderly was looking at her. "Dr Chilton told you, don't touch the bars?" His voice was both high and hoarse. She was reminded of Aldo Ray.

"Yes, he told me."

"Okay. It's past the others, the last cell on the right. Stay toward the middle of the corridor as you go down, and don't mind anything. You can take him his mail, get off on the right foot." The orderly seemed privately amused. "You just put it in the tray and let it roll through. If the tray's inside, you can pull it back with the cord, or he can send it back. He can't reach you where the tray stops outside." The orderly gave her two magazines, their loose pages spilling out, three newspapers and several opened letters.

The corridor was about thirty yards long, with cells on both sides. Some were padded cells with an observation window, long and narrow like an archery slit, in the center of the door. Others were standard prison cells, with a wall of bars opening on the corridor. Clarice Starling was aware of figures in the cells, but she tried not to look at them. She was more than halfway down when a voice hissed, "I can smell your cunt." She gave no sign that she had heard it, and went on.

The lights were on in the last cell. She moved toward the left side of the corridor to see into it as she approached, knowing her heels announced her.

D<small>R</small> L<small>ECTER</small>'S cell is well beyond the others, facing only a closet across the corridor, and it is unique in other ways. The front is a wall of bars, but within the bars, at a distance greater than the human reach, is a second barrier, a stout nylon net stretched from floor to ceiling and wall to wall. Behind the net, Starling could see a table bolted to the floor and piled high with softcover books and papers, and a straight chair, also fastened down.

Dr Hannibal Lecter himself reclined on his bunk, perusing the Italian edition of *Vogue*. He held the loose pages in his right hand and put them beside him one by one with his left. Dr Lecter has six fingers on his left hand.

Clarice Starling stopped a little distance from the bars, about the length of a small foyer.

"Dr Lecter." Her voice sounded all right to her.

He looked up from his reading.

For a steep second she thought his gaze hummed, but it was only her blood she heard.

"My name is Clarice Starling. May I talk with you?" Courtesy was implicit in her distance and her tone.

Dr Lecter considered, his finger pressed against his pursed lips. Then he rose in his own time and came forward smoothly in his cage, stopping short of the nylon web without looking at it, as though he chose the distance.

She could see that he was small, sleek; in his hands and arms she saw wiry strength like her own.

"Good morning," he said, as though he had answered the door. His cultured voice has a slight metallic rasp beneath it, possibly from disuse.

Dr Lecter's eyes are maroon and they reflect the light in pinpoints of red. Sometimes the points of light seem to fly like sparks to his center. His eyes held Starling whole.

She came a measured distance closer to the bars. The hair on her forearms rose and pressed against her sleeves.

"Doctor, we have a hard problem in psychological profiling. I want to ask you for your help."

"'We' being Behavioral Science at Quantico. You're one of Jack Crawford's, I expect."

"I am, yes."

"May I see your credentials?"

She hadn't expected this. "I showed them at the . . . office."

"You mean you showed them to Frederick Chilton, Ph.D.?"

"Yes."

"Did you see *his* credentials?"

"No."

"The academic ones don't make extensive reading, I can tell you. Did you meet Alan? Isn't he charming? Which of them had you rather talk with?"

"On the whole, I'd say Alan."

"You could be a reporter Chilton let in for money. I think I'm entitled to see your credentials."

"All right." She held up her laminated ID card.

"I can't read it at this distance, send it through, please."

"I can't."

"Because it's hard."

"Yes."

"Ask Barney."

The orderly came and considered. "Dr Lecter, I'll let this come through. But if you don't return it when I ask you to—if we have to bother everybody and secure you to get it—then I'll be upset. If you upset me, you'll have to stay bundled up until I feel better toward you. Meals through the tube, dignity pants changed twice a day—the works. And I'll hold your mail for a week. Got it?"

"Certainly, Barney."

The card rolled through on the tray and Dr Lecter held it to the light.

"A trainee? It says 'trainee.' Jack Crawford sent a *trainee* to interview me?" He tapped the card against his small white teeth and breathed in its smell.

"Dr Lecter," Barney said.

"Of course." He put the card back in the tray carrier and Barney pulled it to the outside.

"I'm still in training at the Academy, yes," Starling said, "but we're not discussing the FBI—we're talking

19

about psychology. Can you decide for yourself if I'm qualified in what we talk about?"

"Ummmm," Dr Lecter said. "Actually . . . that's rather slippery of you. Barney, do you think Officer Starling might have a chair?"

"Dr Chilton didn't tell me anything about a chair."

"What do your manners tell you, Barney?"

"Would you like a chair?" Barney asked her. "We could have had one, but he never—well, usually nobody needs to stay that long."

"Yes, thank you," Starling said.

Barney brought a folding chair from the locked closet across the hall, set it up, and left them.

"Now," Lecter said, sitting sideways at his table to face her, "what did Miggs say to you?"

"Who?"

"Multiple Miggs, in the cell down there. He hissed at you. What did he say?"

"He said, 'I can smell your cunt.'"

"I see. I myself cannot. You use Evyan skin cream, and sometimes you wear L'Air du Temps, but not today. Today you are determinedly unperfumed. How do you feel about what Miggs said?"

"He's hostile for reasons I couldn't know. It's too bad. He's hostile to people, people are hostile to him. It's a loop."

"Are you hostile to him?"

"I'm sorry he's disturbed. Beyond that, he's noise. How did you know about the perfume?"

"A puff from your bag when you got out your card. Your bag is lovely."

"Thank you."

"You brought your best bag, didn't you?"

"Yes." It was true. She had saved for the classic casual handbag, and it was the best item she owned.

"It's much better than your shoes."

"Maybe they'll catch up."

"I have no doubt of it."

"Did you do the drawings on your walls, Doctor?"

"Do you think I called in a decorator?"

"The one over the sink is a European city?"

"It's Florence. That's the Palazzo Vecchio and the Duomo, seen from the Belvedere."

"Did you do it from memory, all the detail?"

"Memory, Officer Starling, is what I have instead of a view."

"The other one is a crucifixion? The middle cross is empty."

"It's Golgotha after the Deposition. Crayon and Magic Marker on butcher paper. It's what the thief who had been promised Paradise really got, when they took the paschal lamb away."

"And what was that?"

"His legs broken of course, just like his companion who mocked Christ. Are you entirely innocent of the Gospel of St John? Look at Duccio, then—he paints accurate crucifixions. How is Will Graham? How does he look?"

"I don't know Will Graham."

"You know who he is. Jack Crawford's protégé. The one before you. How does his face look?"

"I've never seen him."

"This is called 'cutting up a few old touches,' Officer Starling, you don't mind, do you?"

21

Beats of silence and she plunged.

"Better than that, we could touch up a few old cuts here. I brought—"

"No. No, that's stupid and wrong. Never use wit in a segue. Listen, understanding a witticism and replying to it makes your subject perform a fast, detached scan that is inimical to mood. It is on the plank of mood that we proceed. You were doing fine, you'd been courteous and receptive to courtesy, you'd established trust by telling the embarrassing truth about Miggs, and then you come in with a ham-handed segue into your questionnaire. It won't do."

"Dr Lecter, you're an experienced clinical psychiatrist. Do you think I'm dumb enough to try to run some kind of mood scam on you? Give me some credit. I'm asking you to respond to the questionnaire, and you will or you won't. Would it hurt to look at the thing?"

"Officer Starling, have you read any of the papers coming out of Behavioral Science recently?"

"Yes."

"So have I. The FBI stupidly refused to send me the *Law Enforcement Bulletin*, but I get it from secondhand dealers, and I have the *News* from John Jay, and the psychiatric journals. They're dividing the people who practice serial murder into two groups—organized and disorganized. What do you think of that?"

"It's . . . fundamental, they evidently—"

"*Simplistic* is the word you want. In fact, most psychology is puerile, Officer Starling, and that practiced in Behavioral Science is on a level with phrenology. Psychology doesn't get very good material to start with. Go to any college psychology department and look at the students and faculty: ham-radio enthusiasts and other personality-deficient buffs. Hardly the best brains on the campus. *Organized* and *disorganized*—a real bottom-feeder thought of that."

"How would you change the classification?"

"I wouldn't."

"Speaking of publications, I read your pieces on surgical addiction and left-side, right-side facial displays."

"Yes, they were first-rate," Dr Lecter said.

"I thought so, and so did Jack Crawford. He pointed them out to me. That's one reason he's anxious for you—"

"Crawford the Stoic is anxious? He must be busy if he's recruiting help from the student body."

"He is, and he wants—"

"Busy with Buffalo Bill."

"I expect so."

"No. Not 'I expect so.' Officer Starling, you know perfectly well it's Buffalo Bill. I thought Jack Crawford might have sent you to ask me about that."

"No."

"Then you're not working around to it?"

"No, I came because we need your—"

"What do you know about Buffalo Bill?"

"Nobody knows much."

"Has everything been in the papers?"

"I think so. Dr Lecter, I haven't seen any confidential material on that case, my job is—"

"How many women has Buffalo Bill used?"

"The police have found five."

"All flayed?"

23

"Partially, yes."

"The papers have never explained his name. Do you know why he's called Buffalo Bill?"

"Yes."

"Tell me."

"I'll tell you if you'll look at this questionnaire."

"I'll look, that's all. Now, why?"

"It started as a bad joke in Kansas City Homicide."

"Yes . . ."

"They call him Buffalo Bill because he skins his humps."

Starling discovered that she had traded feeling frightened for feeling cheap. Of the two, she preferred feeling frightened.

"Send through the questionnaire."

Starling rolled the blue section through on the tray. She sat still while Lecter flipped through it.

He dropped it back in the carrier. "Oh, Officer Starling, do you think you can dissect me with this blunt little tool?"

"No. I think you can provide some insight and advance this study."

"And what possible reason could I have to do that?"

"Curiosity."

"About what?"

"About why you're here. About what happened to you."

"Nothing happened to me, Officer Starling. *I* happened. You can't reduce me to a set of influences. You've given up good and evil for behaviorism, Officer Starling. You've got everybody in moral dignity pants—nothing is ever anybody's fault. Look at me, Officer

Starling. Can you stand to say I'm evil? Am I evil, Officer Starling?"

"I think you've been destructive. For me it's the same thing."

"Evil's just destructive? Then *storms* are evil, if it's that simple. And we have *fire*, and then there's *hail*. Underwriters lump it all under 'Acts of God.'"

"Deliberate—"

"I collect church collapses, recreationally. Did you see the recent one in Sicily? Marvelous! The façade fell on sixty-five grandmothers at a special Mass. Was that evil? If so, who did it? If He's up there, He just loves it, Officer Starling. Typhoid and swans—it all comes from the same place."

"I can't explain you, Doctor, but I know who can."

He stopped her with his upraised hand. The hand was shapely, she noted, and the middle finger perfectly replicated. It is the rarest form of polydactyly.

When he spoke again, his tone was soft and pleasant. "You'd like to quantify me, Officer Starling. You're so ambitious, aren't you? Do you know what you look like to me, with your good bag and your cheap shoes? You look like a rube. You're a well-scrubbed, hustling rube with a little taste. Your eyes are like cheap birthstones—all surface shine when you stalk some little answer. And you're bright behind them, aren't you? Desperate not to be like your mother. Good nutrition has given you some length of bone, but you're not more than one generation out of the mines, *Officer* Starling. Is it the West Virginia Starlings or the Okie Starlings, Officer? It was a toss-up between college and the opportunities in the Women's Army Corps, wasn't

25

it? Let me tell you something specific about yourself, Student Starling. Back in your room, you have a string of gold add-a-beads and you feel an ugly little thump when you look at how tacky they are now, isn't that so? All those tedious thank-yous, permitting all that sincere fumbling, getting all sticky once for every bead. Tedious. Tedious. Bo-o-o-o-r-i-ing. Being smart spoils a lot of things, doesn't it? And taste isn't kind. When you think about this conversation, you'll remember the dumb animal hurt in his face when you got rid of him.

"If the add-a-beads got tacky, what else will as you go along? You wonder, don't you, at night?" Dr Lecter asked in the kindest of tones.

Starling raised her head to face him. "You see a lot, Dr Lecter. I won't deny anything you've said. But here's the question you're answering for me right now, whether you mean to or not: Are you strong enough to point that high-powered perception at yourself? It's hard to face. I've found that out in the last few minutes. How about it? Look at yourself and write down the truth. What more fit or complex subject could you find? Or maybe you're afraid of yourself."

"You're tough, aren't you, Officer Starling?"

"Reasonably so, yes."

"And you'd hate to think you were common. Wouldn't that sting? My! Well, you're far from common, Officer Starling. All you have is fear of it. What are your add-a-beads, seven millimeter?"

"Seven."

"Let me make a suggestion. Get some loose, drilled tiger's eyes and string them alternately with the gold beads. You might want to do two-and-three or one-and-two, however looks best to you. The tiger's eyes will pick up the color of your own eyes and the highlights in your hair. Has anyone ever sent you a Valentine?"

"Yep."

"We're already into Lent. Valentine's Day is only a week away, hummmm, are you expecting some?"

"You never know."

"No, you never do . . . I've been thinking about Valentine's Day. It reminds me of something funny. Now that I think of it, I could make you very happy on Valentine's Day, *Clarice* Starling."

"How, Doctor Lecter?"

"By sending you a wonderful Valentine. I'll have to think about it. Now, please excuse me. Good-bye, Officer Starling."

"And the study?"

"A census taker tried to quantify me once. I ate his liver with some fava beans and a big Amarone. Go back to school, little Starling."

Hannibal Lecter, polite to the last, did not give her his back. He stepped backward from the barrier before he turned to his cot again, and, lying on it, became as remote from her as a stone crusader lying on a tomb.

Starling felt suddenly empty, as though she had given blood. She took longer than necessary to put the papers back in her briefcase, because she didn't immediately trust her legs. Starling was soaked with the failure she detested. She folded her chair and leaned it against the utility-closet door. She would have to pass Miggs again. Barney in the distance appeared to be reading. She could call him to come for her. Damn Miggs. It was no worse than passing construction crews or delivery louts every day in the city. She started back down the corridor.

Close beside her, Miggs's voice hissed, "I bit my wrist so I can diiiieeeeeeeee—see how it bleeds?"

She should have called Barney but, startled, she looked into the cell, saw Miggs flick his fingers and felt the warm spatter on her cheek and shoulder before she could turn away.

She got away from him, registered that it was semen, not blood, and Lecter was calling to her, she could hear him. Dr Lecter's voice behind her, the cutting rasp in it more pronounced.

"Officer Starling."

He was up and calling after her as she walked. She rummaged in her purse for tissues.

Behind her, "Officer Starling."

She was on the cold rails of her control now, making steady progress toward the gate.

"Officer Starling." A new note in Lecter's voice.

She stopped. *What in God's name do I want this bad?* Miggs hissed something she didn't listen to.

She stood again in front of Lecter's cell and saw the rare spectacle of the doctor agitated. She knew that he could smell it on her. He could smell everything.

"I would not have had that happen to you. Discourtesy is unspeakably ugly to me."

It was as though committing murders had purged him of lesser rudeness. Or perhaps, Starling thought, it excited him to see her marked in this particular way. She couldn't tell. The sparks in his eyes flew into his darkness like fireflies down a cave.

Whatever it is, use it, Jesus! She held up her briefcase. "Please do this for me."

Maybe she was too late; he was calm again.

"No. But I'll make you happy that you came. I'll give you something else. I'll give you what you love the most, Clarice Starling."

"What's that, Dr Lecter?"

"Advancement, of course. It works out perfectly— I'm so glad. Valentine's Day made me think of it." The smile over his small white teeth could have come for any reason. He spoke so softly she could barely hear. "Look in Raspail's car for your Valentines. Did you hear me? Look in *Raspail's car* for your Valentines. You'd better go now; I don't think Miggs could manage again so soon, even if he *is* crazy, do you?"

CLARICE STARLING was excited, depleted, running on her will. Some of the things Lecter had said about her were true, and some only clanged on the truth. For a few seconds she had felt an alien consciousness loose in her head, slapping things off the shelves like a bear in a camper.

She hated what he'd said about her mother and she had to get rid of the anger. This was business.

She sat in her old Pinto across the street from the hospital and breathed deeply. When the windows fogged, she had a little privacy from the sidewalk.

Raspail. She remembered the name. He was a patient of Lecter's and one of his victims. She'd had only one evening with the Lecter background material. The file was vast and Raspail one of many victims. She needed to read the details.

Starling wanted to run with it, but she knew that the urgency was of her own manufacture. The Raspail case was closed years ago. No one was in danger. She had time. Better to be well informed and well advised before she went further.

Crawford might take it away from her and give it to someone else. She'd have to take that chance.

She tried to call him from a phone booth, but found he was budget-begging for the Justice Department before the House Subcommittee on Appropriations.

She could have gotten details of the case from the Baltimore Police Department's homicide division, but murder is not a federal crime and she knew they'd snatch it away from her immediately, no question.

She drove back to Quantico, back to Behavioral Science with its homey brown-checked curtains and its gray files full of hell. She sat there into the evening, after the last secretary had left, cranking through the Lecter microfilm. The contrary old viewer glowed like a jack-o'-lantern in the darkened room, the words and the negatives of pictures swarming across her intent face.

Raspail, Benjamin René, WM, 46, was first flutist for the Baltimore Philharmonic Orchestra. He was a patient in Dr Hannibal Lecter's psychiatric practice.

On March 22, 1975, he failed to appear for a performance in Baltimore. On March 25 his body was discovered seated in a pew in a small rural church near Falls Church, Virginia, dressed only in a white tie and a tailcoat. Autopsy revealed that Raspail's heart was pierced and that he was short of his thymus and pancreas.

Clarice Starling, who from early life had known much more than she wished to know about meat processing, recognized the missing organs as the sweetbreads.

Baltimore Homicide believed that these items appeared

on the menu of a dinner Lecter gave for the president and the conductor of the Baltimore Philharmonic on the evening following Raspail's disappearance.

Dr Hannibal Lecter professed to know nothing about these matters. The president and the conductor of the Philharmonic testified that they could not recall the fare at Dr Lecter's dinner, though Lecter was known for the excellence of his table and had contributed numerous articles to gourmet magazines.

The president of the Philharmonic subsequently was treated for anorexia and problems related to alcohol dependency at a holistic nerve sanitarium in Basel.

Raspail was Lecter's ninth known victim, according to the Baltimore police.

Raspail died intestate, and the lawsuits among his relatives over the estate were followed by the newspapers for a number of months before public interest flagged.

Raspail's relatives had also joined with the families of other victims in Lecter's practice in a successful lawsuit to have the errant psychiatrist's case files and tapes destroyed. There was no telling what embarrassing secrets he might blab, their reasoning went, and the files were documentation.

The court had appointed Raspail's lawyer, Everett Yow, to be executor of his estate.

Starling would have to apply to the lawyer to get at the car. The lawyer might be protective of Raspail's memory and, with enough advance notice, might destroy evidence to cover for his late client.

Starling preferred to pounce, and she needed advice and authorization. She was alone in Behavioral Science and had the run of the place. She found Crawford's home number in the Rolodex.

She never heard the telephone ringing, but suddenly his voice was there, very quiet and even.

"Jack Crawford."

"This is Clarice Starling. I hope you weren't eating dinner . . ." She had to continue into silence. ". . . Lecter told me something about the Raspail case today, I'm in the office following it up. He tells me there's something in Raspail's car. I'd have to get at it through his lawyer, and since tomorrow's Saturday—no school—I wanted to ask you if—"

"Starling, do you have any recollection of what I told you to do with the Lecter information?" Crawford's voice was so terribly quiet.

"Give you a report by 0900 Sunday."

"Do that, Starling. Do just exactly that."

"Yes, sir."

The dial tone stung in her ear. The sting spread over her face and made her eyes burn.

"Well, God fucking shit," she said. "You old creep. Creepo son of a bitch. Let Miggs squirt *you* and see how you like it."

Starling, scrubbed shiny and wearing the FBI Academy nightgown, was working on the second draft of her report when her dormitory roommate, Ardelia Mapp, came in from the library. Mapp's broad, brown, eminently sane countenance was one of the more welcome sights of her day.

Ardelia Mapp saw the fatigue in her face.

"What did you do today, girl?" Mapp always asked questions as if the answers could make no possible difference.

"Wheedled a crazy man with come all over me."

"I wish *I* had time for a social life—I don't know how you manage it, and school too."

Starling found that she was laughing. Ardelia Mapp laughed with her, as much as the small joke was worth. Starling did not stop, and she heard herself from far away, laughing and laughing. Through Starling's tears, Mapp looked strangely old and her smile had sadness in it.

5

JACK CRAWFORD, fifty-three, reads in a wing chair by a low lamp in the bedroom of his home. He faces two double beds, both raised on blocks to hospital height. One is his own; in the other lies his wife, Bella. Crawford can hear her breathing through her mouth. It has been two days since she last could stir or speak to him.

She misses a breath. Crawford looks up from his book, over his half-glasses. He puts the book down. Bella breathes again, a flutter and then a full breath. He rises to put his hand on her, to take her blood pressure and her pulse. Over the months he has become expert with the blood-pressure cuff.

Because he will not leave her at night, he has installed a bed for himself beside her. Because he reaches out to her in the dark, his bed is high, like hers.

Except for the height of the beds and the minimal plumbing necessary for Bella's comfort, Crawford has managed to keep this from looking like a sickroom. There are flowers, but not too many. No pills are in sight—Crawford emptied a linen closet in the hall and filled it with her medicines and apparatus before he brought her home from the hospital. (It was the second time he had carried her across the threshold of that house, and the thought nearly unmanned him.)

A warm front has come up from the south. The windows are open and the Virginia air is soft and fresh. Small frogs peep to one another in the dark.

The room is spotless, but the carpet has begun to nap—Crawford will not run the noisy vacuum cleaner in the room and uses a manual carpet sweeper that is not as good. He pads to the closet and turns on the light. Two clipboards hang on the inside of the door. On one he notes Bella's pulse and blood pressure. His figures and those of the day nurse alternate in a column that stretches over many yellow pages, many days and nights. On the other clipboard, the day-shift nurse has signed off Bella's medication.

Crawford is capable of giving any medication she may need in the night. Following a nurse's directions, he practiced injections on a lemon and then on his thighs before he brought her home.

Crawford stands over her for perhaps three minutes, looking down into her face. A lovely scarf of silk moiré covers her hair like a turban. She insisted on it, for as long as she could insist. Now he insists on it. He moistens her lips with glycerine and removes a speck from the corner of her eye with his broad thumb. She does not stir. It is not yet time to turn her.

At the mirror, Crawford assures himself that he is not sick, that he doesn't have to go into the ground with her, that he himself is well. He catches himself doing this and it shames him.

Back at his chair he cannot remember what he was reading. He feels the books beside him to find the one that is warm.

6

ON MONDAY morning, Clarice Starling found this message from Crawford in her mailbox:

CS:

Proceed on the Raspail car. On your own time. My office will provide you a credit-card number for long-distance calls. Ck with me before you contact estate or go anywhere. Report Wednesday 1600 hours.

The Director got your Lecter report over your signature. You did well.

JC
SAIC/Section 8

Starling felt pretty good. She knew Crawford was just giving her an exhausted mouse to bat around for practice. But he wanted to teach her. He wanted her to do well. For Starling, that beat courtesy every time.

Raspail had been dead for eight years. What evidence could have lasted in a car that long?

She knew from family experience that, because automobiles depreciate so rapidly, an appellate court will let survivors sell a car before probate, the money going into escrow. It seemed unlikely that even an estate as tangled and disputed as Raspail's would hold a car this long.

There was also the problem of time. Counting her lunch break, Starling had an hour and fifteen minutes a day free to use the telephone during business hours. She'd have to report to Crawford on Wednesday afternoon. So she had a total of three hours and forty-five minutes to trace the car, spread over three days, if she used her study periods and made up the study at night.

She had good notes from her Investigative Procedures classes, and she'd have a chance to ask general questions of her instructors.

During her Monday lunch, personnel at the Baltimore County Courthouse put Starling on hold and forgot her three times. During her study period she reached a friendly clerk at the courthouse, who pulled the probate records on the Raspail estate.

The clerk confirmed that permission had been granted for sale of an auto and gave Starling the make and serial number of the car, and the name of a subsequent owner off the title transfer.

On Tuesday, she wasted half her lunch hour trying to chase down that name. It cost her the rest of her lunch period to find out that the Maryland Department of Motor Vehicles is not equipped to trace a vehicle by serial number, only by registration number or current tag number.

On Tuesday afternoon, a downpour drove the trainees in from the firing range. In a conference room steamy with damp clothing and sweat, John Brigham, the ex-Marine firearms instructor, chose to test Starling's hand strength in front of the class by seeing how many times she could pull the trigger on a Model 19 Smith & Wesson in sixty seconds.

She managed seventy-four with her left hand, puffed a strand of hair out of her eyes, and started over with her right while another student counted. She was in the Weaver stance, well braced, the front sight in sharp focus, the rear sight and her makeshift target properly blurred. Midway through her minute, she let her mind wander to get it off the pain. The target on the wall came into focus. It was a certificate of appreciation from the Interstate Commerce enforcement division made out to her instructor, John Brigham.

She questioned Brigham out of the side of her mouth while the other student counted the clicks of the revolver.

"How do you trace the current registration . . ."

". . . *sixtyfivesixtysixsixtysevensixtyeightsixty* . . ."

". . . of a car when you've only got the serial number . . ."

". . . *seventyeightseventynineeightyeightyone* . . ."

". . . and the make? You don't have a current tag number."

". . . *eightynineninety. Time.*"

"All right, you people," the instructor said, "I want you to take note of that. Hand strength's a major factor in steady combat shooting. Some of you gentlemen are worried I'll call on you next. Your worries would be justified—Starling is well above average with both hands.

That's because she works at it. She works at it with the little squeezy things you all have access to. Most of you are not used to squeezing anything harder than your"— ever vigilant against his native Marine terminology, he groped for a polite simile—"zits," he said at last. "Get serious, Starling, you're not good enough either. I want to see that left hand over ninety before you graduate. Pair up and time each other—chop-chop.

"Not you, Starling, come here. What else have you got on the car?"

"Just the serial number and make, that's it. One prior owner five years ago."

"All right, listen. Where most people f—fall into error is trying to leapfrog through the registrations from one owner to the next. You get fouled up between states. I mean, cops even do that sometimes. And registrations and tag numbers are all the computer's got. We're all accustomed to using tag numbers or registration numbers, not vehicle serial numbers."

The clicking of the blue-handled practice revolvers was loud all over the room and he had to rumble in her ear.

"There's one way it's easy. R. L. Polk and Company, that publishes city directories—they also put out a list of current car registrations by make and consecutive serial number. It's the only place. Car dealers steer their advertising with them. How'd you know to ask me?"

"You were ICC enforcement, I figured you'd traced a lot of vehicles. Thanks."

"Pay me back—get that left hand up where it ought to be and let's shame some of these lilyfingers."

Back in her phone booth during study period, her

hands trembled so that her notes were barely legible. Raspail's car was a Ford. There was a Ford dealer near the University of Virginia who for years had patiently done what he could with her Pinto. Now, just as patiently, the dealer poked through his Polk listings for her. He came back to the telephone with the name and address of the person who had last registered Benjamin Raspail's car.

Clarice is on a roll, Clarice has got control. Quit being silly and call the man up at his home in, lemme see, Number Nine Ditch, Arkansas. Jack Crawford will never let me go down there, but at least I can confirm who's got the ride.

No answer, and again no answer. The ring sounded funny and far away, a double rump-rump like a party line. She tried at night and got no answer.

At Wednesday lunch period, a man answered Starling's call:

"WPOQ Plays the Oldies."

"Hello, I'm calling to—"

"I wouldn't care for any aluminum siding and I don't want to live in no trailer court in Florida, what else you got?"

Starling heard a lot of the Arkansas hills in the man's voice. She could speak that with anybody when she wanted to, and her time was short.

"Yessir, if you could help me out I'd be much obliged. I'm trying to get ahold of Mr Lomax Bardwell? This is Clarice Starling?"

"It's Starling somebody," the man yelled to the rest of his household. "What do you want with Bardwell?"

"This is the Mid-South regional office of the Ford

recall division? He's entitled to some warranty work on his LTD free of charge?"

"I'm Bardwell. I thought you was trying to sell me something on that cheap long distance. It's way too late for any adjustment, I need the whole thing. Me and the wife was in Little Rock, pulling out of the Southland Mall there?"

"Yessir."

"Durn rod come out through the oil pan. Oil all over everywhere and that Orkin truck that's got the big bug on top of it? He hit that oil and got sideways."

"Lord have mercy."

"Knocked the Fotomat booth slap off the blocks and the glass fell out. Fotomat fella come wandering out addled. Had to keep him out of the road."

"Well I'll be. What happened to it then?"

"What happened to what?"

"The car."

"I told Buddy Sipper at the wrecking yard he could have it for fifty if he'd come get it. I expect he's parted it out."

"Could you tell me what his telephone number is, Mr Bardwell?"

"What do you want with Sipper? If anybody gets something out of it, it ought to be me."

"I understand that, sir. I just do what they tell me till five o'clock, and they said find the car. Have you got that number, please?"

"I can't find my phone book. It's been gone a good while now. You know how it is with these grandbabies. Central ought to give it to you, it's Sipper Salvage."

"Much oblige, Mr Bardwell."

The salvage yard confirmed that the automobile had been stripped and pressed into a cube to be recycled. The foreman read Starling the vehicle serial number from his records.

Shit House Mouse, thought Starling, not entirely out of the accent. Dead end. Some Valentine.

Starling rested her head against the cold coin box in the telephone booth. Ardelia Mapp, her books on her hip, pecked on the door of the booth and handed in an Orange Crush.

"Much oblige, Ardelia. I got to make one more call. If I can get done with that in time, I'll catch up with you in the cafeteria, okay?"

"I was *so* in hopes you'd overcome that ghastly dialect," Mapp said. "Books are available to help. *I* never use the colorful patois of my housing project anymore. You come talking that mushmouth, people say you eat up with the dumb-ass, girl." Mapp closed the phone-booth door.

Starling felt she had to try for more information from Lecter. If she already had the appointment, maybe Crawford would let her return to the asylum. She dialed Dr Chilton's number, but she never got past his secretary.

"Dr Chilton is with the coroner and the assistant district attorney," the woman said. "He's already spoken to your supervisor and he has nothing to say to you. Good-bye."

"YOUR FRIEND Miggs is dead," Crawford said. "Did you tell me everything, Starling?" Crawford's tired face was as sensitive to signals as the dished ruff of an owl, and as free of mercy.

"How?" She felt numb and she had to handle it.

"Swallowed his tongue sometime before daylight. Lecter suggested it to him, Chilton thinks. The overnight orderly heard Lecter talking softly to Miggs. Lecter knew a lot about Miggs. He talked to him for a little while, but the overnight couldn't hear what Lecter said. Miggs was crying for a while, and then he stopped. Did you tell me everything, Starling?"

"Yes, sir. Between the report and my memo, there's everything, almost verbatim."

"Chilton called up to complain about you . . ." Crawford waited, and seemed pleased when she wouldn't ask. "I told him I found your behavior satisfactory. Chilton's trying to forestall a civil rights investigation."

"Will there be one?"

"Sure, if Miggs's family want it. Civil Rights Division will do probably eight thousand this year. They'll be glad to add Miggs to the list." Crawford studied her. "You okay?"

"I don't know how to feel about it."

"You don't have to feel any particular way about it. Lecter did it to amuse himself. He knows they can't really touch him for it, so why not? Chilton takes his books and his toilet seat for a while is all, and he doesn't get any Jell-O." Crawford laced his fingers over his stomach and compared his thumbs. "Lecter asked you about me, didn't he?"

"He asked if you were busy. I said yes."

"That's all? You didn't leave out anything personal because I wouldn't want to see it?"

"No. He said you were a Stoic, but I put that in."

"Yes, you did. Nothing else?"

"No, I didn't leave anything out. You don't think I traded some kind of gossip, and that's why he talked to me?"

"No."

"I don't know anything personal about you, and if I did I wouldn't discuss it. If you've got a problem believing that, let's get it straight now."

"I'm satisfied. Next item."

"You thought *something*, or—"

"Proceed to the next item, Starling."

"Lecter's hint about Raspail's car is a dead end. It was mashed into a cube four months ago in Number Nine Ditch, Arkansas, and sold for recycling. Maybe if I go back in and talk to him, he'll tell me more."

"You've exhausted the lead?"

46

"Yes."

"Why do you think the car Raspail drove was his only car?"

"It was the only one registered, he was single, I assumed—"

"Aha, hold it." Crawford's forefinger pointed to some principle invisible in the air between them. "You assumed. You *assumed*, Starling. Look here." Crawford wrote *assume* on a legal pad. Several of Starling's instructors had picked this up from Crawford and used it, but Starling didn't reveal that she'd seen it before.

Crawford began to underline. "If you *assume* when I send you on a job, Starling, you can make an *ass* out of *u* and *me* both." He leaned back, pleased. "Raspail collected cars, did you know that?"

"No, does the estate still have them?"

"I don't know. Do you think you could manage to find out?"

"Yes, I can."

"Where would you start?"

"His executor."

"A lawyer in Baltimore, a Chinese, I seem to remember," Crawford said.

"Everett Yow," Starling said. "He's in the Baltimore phone book."

"Have you given any thought to the question of a warrant to search Raspail's car?"

Sometimes Crawford's tone reminded Starling of the know-it-all caterpillar in Lewis Carroll.

Starling didn't dare give it back, much. "Since Raspail is deceased and not suspected of anything, if we have

47

permission of his executor to search the car, then it is a valid search, and the fruit admissible evidence in other matters at law," she recited.

"Precisely," Crawford said. "Tell you what: I'll advise the Baltimore field office you'll be up there. Saturday, Starling, on your own time. Go feel the fruit, if there is any."

Crawford made a small, successful effort not to look after her as she left. From his wastebasket he lifted in the fork of his fingers a wad of heavy mauve notepaper. He spread it on his desk. It was about his wife and it said, in an engaging hand:

O wrangling schools, that search what fire
   Shall burn this world, had none the wit
Unto this knowledge to aspire
   That this her fever might be it?

I'm so sorry about Bella, Jack.

Hannibal Lecter

8

EVERETT YOW drove a black Buick with a De Paul University sticker on the back window. His weight gave the Buick a slight list to the left as Clarice Starling followed him out of Baltimore in the rain. It was almost dark; Starling's day as an investigator was nearly gone and she didn't have another day to replace it. She dealt with her impatience, tapping the wheel in time with the wipers as the traffic crawled down Route 301.

Yow was intelligent, fat, and had a breathing problem. Starling guessed his age at sixty. So far he was accommodating. The lost day was not his fault; returning in the late afternoon from a week-long business trip to Chicago, the Baltimore lawyer had come directly from the airport to his office to meet Starling.

Raspail's classic Packard had been stored since long before his death, Yow explained. It was unlicensed and never driven. Yow had seen it once, covered and in storage, to confirm its existence for the estate inventory he made shortly after his client's murder. If Investigator Starling would agree to "frankly disclose at once" anything she found that might be damaging to his late client's interests, he would show her the automobile, he said. A warrant and the attendant stir would not be necessary.

Starling was enjoying the use for one day of an FBI motor pool Plymouth with a cellular telephone, and she had a new ID card provided by Crawford. It simply said FEDERAL INVESTIGATOR—and expired in a week, she noticed.

Their destination was Split City Mini-Storage, about four miles past the city limits. Creeping along with the traffic, Starling used her telephone to find out what she could about the storage facility. By the time she spotted the high orange sign, SPLIT CITY MINI-STORAGE—YOU KEEP THE KEY, she had learned a few facts.

Split City had an Interstate Commerce Commission freight-forwarder's license, in the name of Bernard Gary. A federal grand jury had barely missed Gary for interstate transportation of stolen goods three years ago, and his license was up for review.

Yow turned in beneath the sign and showed his keys to a spotty young man in uniform at the gate. The gatekeeper logged their license numbers, opened up and beckoned impatiently, as though he had more important things to do.

Split City is a bleak place the wind blows through. Like the Sunday divorce flight from La Guardia to Juárez, it is a service industry to the mindless Brownian movement in our population; most of its business is storing the sundered chattels of divorce. Its units are stacked with living-room suites, breakfast ensembles, spotted mattresses, toys, and the photographs of things that didn't work out. It is widely believed among Baltimore County Sheriff's officers that Split City also hides good and valuable consideration from the bankruptcy courts.

It resembles a military installation: thirty acres of long buildings divided by fire walls into units the size of a generous single garage, each with its roll-up overhead door. The rates are reasonable and some of the property has been there for years. Security is good. The place is surrounded by a double row of high hurricane fence, and dogs patrol between the fences twenty-four hours a day.

Six inches of sodden leaves, mixed with paper cups and small trash, had banked against the bottom of the door of Raspail's storage unit, number 31. A hefty padlock secured each side of the door. The left-side hasp also had a seal on it. Everett Yow bent stiffly over the seal. Starling held the umbrella and a flashlight in the early dark.

"It doesn't appear to have been opened since I was here five years ago," he said. "You see the impression of my notary seal here in the plastic? I had no idea at the time that the relatives would be so contentious and would drag out the probate for so many years."

Yow held the flashlight and umbrella while Starling took a picture of the lock and seal.

"Mr Raspail had an office-studio in the city, which I closed down to save the estate from paying rent," he said. "I had the furnishings brought here and stored them with Raspail's car and other things that were already here. We brought an upright piano, books and music, a bed, I think."

Yow tried a key. "The locks may be frozen. At least this one's very stiff." It was hard for him to bend over and breathe at the same time. When he tried to squat, his knees creaked.

Starling was glad to see that the padlocks were big chrome American Standards. They looked formidable, but she knew she could pop the brass cylinders out easily with a sheet-metal screw and a claw hammer—her father had showed her how burglars do it when she was a child. The problem would be finding the hammer and screw; she did not even have the benefit of the resident junk in her Pinto.

She poked through her purse and found the de-icer spray she used on her Pinto's door locks.

"Want to rest a second in your car, Mr Yow? Why don't you warm up for a few minutes and I'll give this a try. Take the umbrella, it's only a drizzle now."

Starling moved the FBI Plymouth up close to the door to use its headlights. She pulled the dipstick out of the car and dripped oil into the keyholes of the padlocks, then sprayed in de-icer to thin the oil. Mr Yow smiled and nodded from his car. Starling was glad Yow was an intelligent man; she could perform her task without alienating him.

It was dark now. She felt exposed in the glare of the Plymouth's headlights and the fan belt squealed in her ear as the car idled. She'd locked the car while it was running. Mr Yow appeared to be harmless, but she saw no reason to take a chance on being mashed against the door.

The padlock jumped like a frog in her hand and lay there open, heavy and greasy. The other lock, having soaked, was easier.

The door would not come up. Starling lifted on the handle until bright spots danced before her eyes. Yow came to help, but, between the small, inadequate door handle and his hernia, they exerted little additional force.

"We might return next week, with my son, or with some workmen," Mr Yow suggested. "I would like very much to go home soon."

Starling was not at all sure she'd ever get back to this place; it would be less trouble to Crawford if he just picked up the telephone and had the Baltimore field office handle it. "Mr Yow, I'll hurry. Do you have a bumper jack in this car?"

With the jack under the handle of the door, Starling used her weight on top of the lug wrench that served as a jack handle. The door squealed horribly and went up a half-inch. It appeared to be bending upward in the center. The door went up another inch and another until she could slide the spare tire under it, to hold it up while she moved Mr Yow's jack and her own to the sides of the door, placing them under the bottom edge, close to the tracks the door ran in.

Alternating at the jacks on each side, she inched the door up a foot and a half, where it jammed solidly and her full weight on the jack handles would not raise it.

Mr Yow came to peer under the door with her. He could only bend over for a few seconds at a time.

"It smells like mice in there," he said. "I was assured they used rodent poison here. I believe it is specified in the contract. Rodents are almost unknown, they said. But I hear them, do you?"

"I hear them," Starling said. With her flashlight, she could pick out cardboard boxes and one big tire with a wide whitewall beneath the edge of a cloth cover. The tire was flat.

She backed the Plymouth up until part of the headlight pattern shone under the door, and she took out one of the rubber floor mats.

"You're going in there, Officer Starling?"

"I have to take a look, Mr Yow."

He took out his handkerchief. "May I suggest you tie your cuffs snugly around your ankles? To prevent mouse intrusion."

"Thank you, sir, that's a very good idea. Mr Yow, if the door should come down, ha ha, or something else should occur, would you be kind enough to call this number? It's our Baltimore field office. They know I'm here with you right now, and they'll be alarmed if they don't hear from me in a little while, do you follow me?"

"Yes, of course. Absolutely, I do." He gave her the key to the Packard.

Starling put the rubber mat on the wet ground in front of the door and lay down on it, her hand cupping a pack of plastic evidence bags over the lens of her camera and her cuffs tied snugly with Yow's handkerchief and her own. A mist of rain fell in her face, and the smell of mold and mice was strong in her nose. What occurred to Starling was, absurdly, Latin.

Written on the blackboard by her forensics instructor on her first day in training, it was the motto of the Roman physician: *Primum non nocere.* First do no harm.

He didn't say that in a garage full of fucking mice.

And suddenly her father's voice, speaking to her with his hand on her brother's shoulder, "If you can't play without squawling, Clarice, go on to the house."

Starling fastened the collar button of her blouse, scrunched her shoulders up around her neck and slid under the door.

She was beneath the rear of the Packard. It was parked close to the left side of the storage room, almost touching the wall. Cardboard boxes were stacked high on the right side of the room, filling the space beside the car. Starling wriggled along on her back until her head was out in the narrow gap left between the car and the boxes. She shined her flashlight up the cliff face of boxes. Many spiders had spanned the narow space with their webs. Orb weavers, mostly, the webs dotted with small, shriveled carcasses tightly bound.

Well, a brown recluse spider is the only kind to worry about, and it wouldn't build out in the open, Starling said to herself. *The rest don't raise much of a welt.*

There would be space to stand beside the rear fender. She wriggled around until she was out from under the car, her face close beside the wide whitewall tire. It was hatched with dry rot. She could read the words GOODYEAR DOUBLE EAGLE on it. Careful of her head, she got to her feet in the narrow space, hand before her face to break the webs. Was this how it felt to wear a veil?

Mr Yow's voice from outside. "Okay, Miss Starling?"

"Okay," she said. There were small scurryings at the sound of her voice, and something inside a piano climbed over a few high notes. The car lights from outside lit her legs up to the calf.

"So you found the piano, Officer Starling," Mr Yow called.

"That wasn't me."

"Oh."

The car was big, tall and long. A 1938 Packard limousine, according to Yow's inventory. It was covered with a rug, the plush side down. She played her flashlight over it.

"Did you cover the car with this rug, Mr Yow?"

"I found it that way and I never uncovered it," Yow called under the door. "I can't deal with a dusty rug. That's the way Raspail had it. I just made sure the car was there. My movers put the piano against the wall and covered it and stacked more boxes beside the car and left. I was paying them by the hour. The boxes are sheet music and books, mostly."

The rug was thick and heavy and, as she tugged at it, dust swarmed in the beam of her flashlight. She sneezed twice. Standing on tiptoe, she could fold the rug over to the midline of the tall old car. The curtains were drawn in the back windows. The door handle was covered with dust. She had to lean forward over cartons to reach it. Touching only the end of the handle, she tried to turn it downward. Locked. There was no keyhole in the rear door. She'd have to move a lot of boxes to get to the front door, and there was damn little place to put them. She could see a small gap between the curtain and the post of the rear window.

Starling leaned over boxes to put her eye close to the glass and shined her light through the crack. She could only see her reflection until she cupped her hand on top of the light. A splinter of the beam, diffused by the dusty glass, moved across the seat. An album lay open on the seat. The colors were poor in the bad light, but she could see Valentines pasted on the pages. Lacy old Valentines, fluffy on the page.

"Thanks a lot, Dr Lecter." When she spoke, her breath stirred the fuzz of dust on the windowsill and fogged the glass. She didn't want to wipe it, so she had to wait for it to clear. The light moved on, over a lap rug crumpled on the floor of the car and onto the dusty wink of a pair of men's patent leather evening shoes. Above the shoes, black socks and above the socks were tuxedo trousers with legs in them.

Nobody'sbeeninthatdoorinfiveyears—easy, easy, hold it, baby.

"Oh, Mr Yow. Say, Mr Yow?"

"Yes, Officer Starling?"

"Mr Yow, looks like somebody's sitting in this car."

"Oh my. Maybe you better come out, Miss Starling."

"Not quite yet, Mr Yow. Just wait there, if you will, please."

Now is when it's important to think. Now is more important than all the crap you tell your pillow for the rest of your life. Suck it up and do this right. I don't want to destroy evidence. I do want some help. But most of all I don't want to cry wolf. If I scramble the Baltimore office and the cops out here for nothing, I've had it. I see what looks like some legs. Mr Yow would not have brought me here if he'd known there was a cool one in the car. She managed to smile at herself. "Cool one" was bravado. *Nobody's been here since Yow's last visit. All right, that means the boxes were put here after whatever's in the car. And that means I can move the boxes without losing anything important.*

"All right, Mr Yow?"

"Yes. Do we have to call the police, or are you sufficient, Officer Starling?"

"I've got to find that out. Just wait right there, please."

The box problem was as maddening as Rubik's Cube. She tried to work with the flashlight under her arm, dropped it twice, and finally put it on top of the car. She had to put boxes behind her, and some of the shorter book cartons would slide under the car. Some kind of bite or splinter made the ball of her thumb itch.

Now she could see through the dusty glass of the front passenger's side window into the chauffeur's compartment. A spider had spun between the big steering wheel and the gearshift. The partition between the front and back compartments was closed.

She wished she had thought to oil the Packard key before she came under the door, but, when she stuck it in the lock, it worked.

There was hardly room to open the door more than a third of the way in the narrow passage. It swung against the boxes with a thump that sent the mice scratching and brought additional notes from the piano. A stale smell of decay and chemicals came out of the car. It jogged her memory in a place she couldn't name.

She leaned inside, opened the partition behind the

chauffeur's seat, and shined her flashlight into the rear compartment of the car. A formal shirt with studs was the bright thing the light found first, quickly up the shirtfront to the face, no face to see, and down again, over glittering shirt studs and satin lapels to a lap with zipper open, and up again to the neat bow tie and the collar, where the white stub neck of a mannequin protruded. But above the neck, something else that reflected little light. Cloth, a black hood, where the head should be, big, as though it covered a parrot's cage. Velvet, Starling thought. It sat on a plywood shelf extending over the neck of the mannequin from the parcel shelf behind.

She took several pictures from the front seat, focusing with the flashlight and closing her eyes against the flash of the strobe. Then she straightened up outside the car. Standing in the dark, wet, with cobwebs on her, she considered what to do.

What she was *not* going to do was summon the special agent in charge of the Baltimore field office to look at a mannequin with its fly open and a book of Valentines.

Once she decided to get in the backseat and take the hood off the thing, she didn't want to think about it very long. She reached through the chauffeur's partition, unlocked the rear door, and rearranged some boxes to get it open. It all seemed to take a long time. The smell from the rear compartment was much stronger when she opened the door. She reached in and, carefully lifting the Valentine album by the corners, moved it onto an evidence bag on top of the car. She spread another evidence bag on the seat.

The car springs groaned as she got inside and the figure shifted a little when she sat down beside it. The right hand in its white glove slid off the thigh and lay on the seat. She touched the glove with her finger. The hand inside was hard. Gingerly, she pushed the glove down from the wrist. The wrist was some white synthetic material. There was a lump in the trousers that for a silly instant reminded her of certain events in high school.

Small scrambling noises came from under the seat.

Gentle as a caress, her hand touching the hood. The cloth moved easily over something hard and slick beneath. When she felt the round knob on the top, she knew. She knew that it was a big laboratory specimen jar and she knew what would be in it. With dread, but little doubt, she pulled off the cover.

The head inside the jar had been severed neatly close beneath the jaw. It faced her, the eyes long burned milky by the alcohol that preserved it. The mouth was open and the tongue protruded slightly, very gray. Over the years, the alcohol had evaporated to the point that the head rested on the bottom of the jar, its crown protruding through the surface of the fluid in a cap of decay. Turned at an owlish angle to the body beneath, it gaped stupidly at Starling. Even in the play of light over the features, it remained dumb and dead.

Starling, in this moment, examined herself. She was pleased. She was exhilarated. She wondered for a second if those were worthy feelings. Now, at this moment, sitting in this old car with a head and some mice, she could think clearly, and she was proud of that.

"Well, Toto," she said, "we're not in Kansas anymore." She'd always wanted to say that under stress, but doing it left her feeling phony, and she was glad nobody had heard. Work to do.

She sat back gingerly and looked around.

This was somebody's environment, chosen and created, a thousand light-years across the mind from the traffic crawling down Route 301.

Dried blossoms drooped from the cut-crystal bud vases on the pillars. The limousine's table was folded down and covered with a linen cloth. On it, a decanter gleamed through dust. A spider had built between the decanter and the short candlestick beside it.

She tried to picture Lecter, or someone, sitting here with her present companion and having a drink and trying to show him the Valentines. And what else? Working carefully, disturbing the figure as little as possible, she frisked it for identification. There was none. In a jacket pocket she found the bands of material left over from adjusting the length of the trousers—the dinner clothes were probably new when they were put on the figure.

Starling poked the lump in the trousers. Too hard, even for high school, she reflected. She spread the fly with her fingers and shined her light inside, on a dildo of polished, inlaid wood. Good-sized one too. She wondered if she was depraved.

Carefully, she turned the jar and examined the sides and back of the head for wounds. There were none visible. The name of a laboratory supply company was cast in the glass.

Considering the face again, she believed she learned something that would last her. Looking with purpose at this face, with its tongue changing color where it touched the glass, was not as bad as Miggs swallowing his tongue in her dreams. She felt she could look at anything, if she had something positive to do about it. Starling was young.

In the ten seconds after her WPIK-TV mobile news unit slid to a stop, Jonetta Johnson put in her earrings, powdered her beautiful brown face, and cased the situation. She and her news crew, monitoring the Baltimore County police radio, had arrived at Split City ahead of the patrol cars.

All the news crew saw in their headlights was Clarice Starling, standing in front of the garage door with her flashlight and her little laminated ID card, her hair plastered down by the drizzle.

Jonetta Johnson could spot a rookie every time. She climbed out with the camera crew behind her and approached Starling. The bright lights came on.

Mr Yow sank so far down in his Buick that only his hat was visible above the windowsill.

"Jonetta Johnson, WPIK news, did you report a homicide?"

Starling did not look like very much law and she knew it. "I'm a federal officer, this is a crime scene. I have to secure it until the Baltimore authorities—"

The assistant cameraman had grabbed the bottom of the garage door and was trying to lift it.

"Hold it," Starling said. "I'm talking to *you*, sir. Hold it. Back off, please. I'm not kidding with you. Help me out here." She wished hard for a badge, a uniform, anything.

"Okay, Harry," the newswoman said. "Ah, officer, we want to cooperate in every way. Frankly, this crew costs money and I just want to know whether to even keep them here until the other authorities arrive. Will you tell me if there's a body in there? Camera's off, just between us. Tell me and we'll wait. We'll be good, I promise. How about it?"

"I'd wait if I were you," Starling said.

"Thanks, you won't be sorry," Jonetta Johnson said. "Look, I've got some information on Split City Mini-Storage that you could probably use. Would you shine your light on the clipboard? Let's see if I can find it here."

"WEYE mobile unit just turned in at the gate, Joney," the man Harry said.

"Let's see if I can find it here, Officer, here it is. There was a scandal about two years ago when they tried to prove this place was trucking and storing—was it fireworks?" Jonetta Johnson glanced over Starling's shoulder once too often.

Starling turned to see the cameraman on his back, his head and shoulders in the garage, the assistant squatting beside him, ready to pass the minicam under the door.

"Hey!" Starling said. She dropped to her knees on the wet ground beside him and tugged at his shirt. "You can't go in there. Hey! I told you not to do that."

And all the time the men were talking to her, constantly, gently. "We won't touch anything. We're pros, you don't have to worry. The cops will let us in anyway. It's all right, honey."

Their cozening backseat manner put her over.

She ran to a bumper jack at the end of the door and pumped the handle. The door came down two inches, with a grinding screech. She pumped it again. Now the door was touching the man's chest. When he didn't come out, she pulled the handle out of the socket and carried it back to the prone cameraman. There were other bright television lights now, and in the glare of them she banged the door above him hard with the jack handle, showering dust and rust down on him.

"Give me your attention," she said. "You don't listen, do you? Come out of there. Now. You're one second from arrest for obstruction of justice."

"Take it easy," the assistant said. He put his hand on her. She turned on him. There were shouted questions from behind the glare and she heard sirens.

"Hands off and back off, buster." She stood on the cameraman's ankle and faced the assistant, the jack handle hanging by her side. She did not raise the jack handle. It was just as well. She looked bad enough on television as it was.

THE ODORS of the violent ward seemed more intense in the semidarkness. A TV set playing without sound in the corridor threw Starling's shadow on the bars of Dr Lecter's cage.

She could not see into the dark behind the bars, but she didn't ask the orderly to turn up the lights from his station. The whole ward would light at once and she knew the Baltimore County police had had the lights full on for hours while they shouted questions at Lecter. He had refused to speak, but responded by folding for them an origami chicken that pecked when the tail was manipulated up and down. The senior officer, furious, had crushed the chicken in the lobby ashtray as he gestured for Starling to go in.

"Dr Lecter?" She heard her own breathing, and breathing down the hall, but from Miggs's empty cell, no breathing. Miggs's cell was vastly empty. She felt its silence like a draft.

Starling knew Lecter was watching her from the darkness. Two minutes passed. Her legs and back ached from her struggle with the garage door, and her clothes were damp. She sat on her coat on the floor, well back from the bars, her feet tucked under her, and lifted her wet, bedraggled hair over her collar to get it off her neck.

Behind her on the TV screen, an evangelist waved his arms.

"Dr Lecter, we both know what this is. They think you'll talk to me."

Silence. Down the hall, someone whistled "Over the Sea to Skye."

After five minutes, she said, "It was strange going in there. Sometime I'd like to talk to you about it."

Starling jumped when the food carrier rolled out of Lecter's cell. There was a clean, folded towel in the tray. She hadn't heard him move.

She looked at it and, with a sense of falling, took it and toweled her hair. "Thanks," she said.

"Why don't you ask me about Buffalo Bill?" His voice was close, at her level. He must be sitting on the floor too.

"Do you know something about him?"

"I might if I saw the case."

"I don't have the case," Starling said.

"You won't have this one, either, when they're through using you."

"I know."

"You could get the files on Buffalo Bill. The reports and the pictures. I'd like to see it."

I'll bet you would. "Dr Lecter, you started this. Now please tell me about the person in the Packard."

"You found an entire person? Odd. I only saw a head. Where do you suppose the rest came from?"

"All right. Whose *head* was it?"

"What can you tell?"

"They've only done the preliminary stuff. White male, about twenty-seven, both American and European dentistry. Who was he?"

"Raspail's lover. Raspail, of the gluey flute."

"What were the circumstances—how did he die?"

"Circumlocution, Officer Starling?"

"No, I'll ask it later."

"Let me save you some time. I didn't do it; Raspail did. Raspail liked sailors. This was a Scandinavian one named Klaus something. Raspail never told me the last name."

Dr Lecter's voice moved lower. Maybe he was lying on the floor, Starling thought.

"Klaus was off a Swedish boat in San Diego. Raspail was out there teaching for a summer at the conservatory. He went berserk over the young man. The Swede saw a good thing and jumped his boat. They bought some kind of awful camper and sylphed through the woods naked. Raspail said the young man was unfaithful and he strangled him."

"Raspail told you this?"

"Oh yes, under the confidential seal of therapy sessions. I think it was a lie. Raspail always embellished the facts. He wanted to seem dangerous and romantic. The Swede probably died in some banal erotic asphyxia transaction. Raspail was too flabby and weak to have strangled him. Notice how closely Klaus was trimmed under the jaw? Probably to remove a high ligature mark from hanging."

"I see."

"Raspail's dream of happiness was ruined. He put Klaus's head in a bowling bag and came back East."

"What did he do with the rest?"

"Buried it in the hills."

"He showed you the head in the car?"

"Oh yes, in the course of therapy he came to feel he could tell me anything. He went out to sit with Klaus quite often and showed him the Valentines."

"And then Raspail himself . . . died. Why?"

"Frankly, I got sick and tired of his whining. Best thing for him, really. Therapy wasn't going anywhere. I expect most psychiatrists have a patient or two they'd like to refer to me. I've never discussed this before, and now I'm getting bored with it."

"And your dinner for the orchestra officials?"

"Haven't you ever had people coming over and no time to shop? You have to make do with what's in the fridge, *Clarice*. May I call you Clarice?"

"Yes. I think I'll just call you—"

"Dr Lecter—that seems most appropriate to your age and station," he said.

"Yes."

"How did you feel when you went into the garage?"

"Apprehensive."

"Why?"

"Mice and insects."

"Do you have something you use when you want to get up your nerve?" Dr Lecter asked.

"Nothing I know of that works, except wanting what I'm after."

"Do memories or tableaux occur to you then, whether you try for them or not?"

"Maybe. I haven't thought about it."

"Things from your early life."

"I'll have to watch and see."

"How did you feel when you heard about my late neighbor, Miggs? You haven't asked me about it."

"I was getting to it."

"Weren't you *glad* when you heard?"

"No."

"Were you *sad*?"

"No. Did you talk him into it?"

Dr Lecter laughed quietly. "Are you asking me, Officer Starling, if I *suborned* Mr Miggs's felony suicide? Don't be silly. It has a certain pleasant symmetry, though, his swallowing that offensive tongue, don't you agree?"

"No."

"Officer Starling, that was a lie. The first one you've told me. A *triste* occasion, Truman would say."

"President Truman?"

"Never mind. Why do you think I helped you?"

"I don't know."

"Jack Crawford likes you, doesn't he?"

"I don't know."

"That's probably untrue. Would you like for him to like you? Tell me, do you feel an urge to please him and does it worry you? Are you *wary* of your urge to please him?"

"Everyone wants to be liked, Dr Lecter."

"Not everyone. Do you think Jack Crawford wants you sexually? I'm sure he's very frustrated now. Do you think he visualizes . . . scenarios, transactions . . . fucking with you?"

"That's not a matter of curiosity to me, Dr Lecter, and it's the sort of thing Miggs would ask."

"Not anymore."

"Did you suggest to him that he swallow his tongue?"

"Your interrogative case often has that proper subjunctive in it. With your accent, it stinks of the lamp. Crawford clearly likes you and believes you competent. Surely the odd confluence of events hasn't escaped you, Clarice—you've had Crawford's help and you've had mine. You say you don't know why Crawford helps you—do you know why I did?"

"No, tell me."

"Do you think it's because I like to look at you and think about eating you up—about how you would taste?"

"Is that it?"

"No. I want something Crawford can give me and I want to trade him for it. But he won't come to see me. He won't ask for my help with Buffalo Bill, even though he knows it means more young women will die."

"I can't believe that, Dr Lecter."

"I only want something very simple, and he could get it." Lecter turned up the rheostat slowly in his cell. His books and drawings were gone. His toilet seat was gone. Chilton had stripped the cell to punish him for Miggs.

"I've been in this room eight years, Clarice. I know that they will never, ever let me out while I'm alive. What I want is a view. I want a window where I can see a tree, or even water."

"Has your attorney petitioned—"

"Chilton put that television in the hall, set to a

religious channel. As soon as you leave, the orderly will turn the sound back up, and my attorney can't stop it, the way the court is inclined toward me now. I want to be in a federal institution and I want my books back and a view. I'll give good value for it. Crawford could do that. Ask him."

"I can tell him what you've said."

"He'll ignore it. And Buffalo Bill will go on and on. Wait until he scalps one and see how you like it. Ummmm . . . I'll tell you one thing about Buffalo Bill without ever seeing the case, and years from now, when they catch him, if they ever do, you'll see that I was right and I could have helped. I could have saved lives. Clarice?"

"Yes?"

"Buffalo Bill has a two-story house," Dr Lecter said, and turned out his light.

He would not speak again.

C H A P T E R

10

CLARICE STARLING leaned against a dice table in the FBI's casino and tried to pay attention to a lecture on money-laundering in gambling. It had been thirty-six hours since the Baltimore County police took her deposition (via a chain-smoking two-finger typist: "See if you can get that window open if the smoke bothers you.") and dismissed her from its jurisdiction with a reminder that murder is not a federal crime.

The network news on Sunday night showed Starling's scrap with the television cameramen and she felt sure she was deep in the glue. Through it all, no word from Crawford or from the Baltimore field office. It was as though she had dropped her report down a hole.

The casino where she now stood was small—it had operated in a moving trailer truck until the FBI seized it and installed it in the school as a teaching aid. The narrow room was crowded with police from many jurisdictions; Starling had declined with thanks the chairs of two Texas Rangers and a Scotland Yard detective.

The rest of her class were down the hall in the Academy building, searching for hairs in the genuine motel carpet of the "Sex-Crime Bedroom" and dusting the "Anytown Bank" for fingerprints. Starling had spent so many hours on searches and fingerprints as a Forensic Fellow that she was sent instead to this lecture, part of a series for visiting lawmen.

She wondered if there was another reason she had been separated from the class: maybe they isolate you before you get the ax.

Starling rested her elbows on the pass line of the dice table and tried to concentrate on money-laundering in gambling. What she thought about instead was how much the FBI hates to see its agents on television, outside of official news conferences.

Dr Hannibal Lecter was catnip to the media, and the Baltimore police had happily supplied Starling's name to reporters. Over and over she saw herself on the Sunday-night network news. There was "Starling of the FBI" in Baltimore, banging the jack handle against the garage door as the cameraman tried to slither under it. And here was "Federal Agent Starling" turning on the assistant with the jack handle in her hand.

On the rival network, station WPIK, lacking film of its own, had announced a personal-injury lawsuit against "Starling of the FBI" and the Bureau itself because the cameraman got dirt and rust particles in his eyes when Starling banged the door.

Jonetta Johnson of WPIK was on coast-to-coast with the revelation that Starling had found the remains in the garage through an "eerie bonding with a man authorities have branded . . . a *monster*!" Clearly, WPIK had a source at the hospital.

BRIDE OF FRANKENSTEIN!! screamed the *National Tattler* from its supermarket racks.

There was no public comment from the FBI, but there was plenty inside the Bureau, Starling was sure.

At breakfast, one of her classmates, a young man who wore a lot of Canoe after-shave, had referred to Starling as "Melvin Pelvis," a stupid play on the name of Melvin Purvis, Hoover's number one G-man in the thirties. What Ardelia Mapp said to the young man made his face turn white, and he left his breakfast uneaten on the table.

Now Starling found herself in a curious state in which she could not be surprised. For a day and a night she'd felt suspended in a diver's ringing silence. She intended to defend herself, if she got the chance.

The lecturer spun the roulette wheel as he talked, but he never let the ball drop. Looking at him, Starling was convinced that he had never let the ball drop in his life. He was saying something now: "Clarice Starling." Why was he saying "Clarice Starling"? *That's me*.

"Yes," she said.

The lecturer pointed with his chin at the door behind her. Here it came. Her fate shied under her as she turned to see. But it was Brigham, the gunnery instructor, leaning into the room to point to her across the crowd. When she saw him, he beckoned.

For a second she thought they were throwing her out, but that wouldn't be Brigham's job.

"Saddle up, Starling. Where's your field gear?" he said in the hall.

"My room—C Wing."

She had to walk fast then to keep up with him.

He was carrying the big fingerprint kit from the property room—the good one, not the play-school kit—and a small canvas bag.

"You go with Jack Crawford today. Take stuff for overnight. You may be back, but take it."

"Where?"

"Some duck hunters in West Virginia found a body in the Elk River around daylight. In a Buffalo Bill-type situation. Deputies are bringing it out. It's real boonies, and Jack's not inclined to wait on those guys for details." Brigham stopped at the door to C Wing. "He needs somebody to help him that can print a floater, among other things. You were a grunt in the lab—you can do that, right?"

"Yeee, let me check the stuff."

Brigham held the fingerprint kit open while Starling lifted out the trays. The fine hypodermics and the vials were there, but the camera wasn't.

"I need the one-to-one Polaroid, the CU-5, Mr Brigham, and film packs and batteries for it."

"From property? You got it."

He handed her the small canvas bag, and, when she felt its weight, she realized why it was Brigham who had come for her.

"You don't have a duty piece yet, right?"

"No."

"You gotta have full kit. This is the rig you've been wearing on the range. The gun is my own. It's the same K-frame Smith you're trained with, but the action's cleaned up. Dry-fire it in your room tonight when you

75

get the chance. I'll be in a car behind C Wing in ten minutes flat with the camera. Listen, there's no head in the Blue Canoe. Go to the bathroom while you've got the chance is my advice. Chop-chop, Starling."

She tried to ask him a question, but he was leaving her.

Has to be Buffalo Bill, if Crawford's going himself. What the hell is the Blue Canoe? But you have to think about packing when you pack. Starling packed fast and well.

"Is it—"

"That's okay," Brigham interrupted as she got in the car. "The butt prints against your jacket a little if somebody's looking for it, but it's okay for now." She was wearing the snub-nosed revolver under her blazer in a pancake holster snug against her ribs, with a speedloader straddling her belt on the other side.

Brigham drove at precisely the base speed limit toward the Quantico airstrip.

He cleared his throat. "One good thing about the range, Starling, is there's no politics out there."

"No?"

"You were right to secure that garage up at Baltimore there. You worried about the TV?"

"Should I be?"

"We're talking just us, right?"

"Right."

Brigham returned the greeting of a Marine directing traffic.

"Taking you along today, Jack's showing confidence in you where nobody can miss it," he said. "In case, say, somebody in the Office of Professional Responsibility has your jacket in front of him and his bowels in an uproar, understand what I'm telling you?"

"Ummm."

"Crawford's a stand-up guy. He made it clear where it matters that you had to secure the scene. He let you go in there bare—that is, bare of all your visible symbols of authority, and he said that too. And the response time of the Baltimore cops was pretty slow. Also, Crawford needs the help today, and he'd have to wait an hour for Jimmy Price to get somebody here from the lab. So you got it cut out for you, Starling. A floater's no day at the beach, either. It's not punishment for you, but, if somebody outside needed to see it that way, they could. See, Crawford is a very subtle guy, but he's not inclined to explain things, that's why I'm telling you . . . If you're working with Crawford, you should know what the deal is with him—do you know?"

"I really don't."

"He's got a lot on his mind besides Buffalo Bill. His wife Bella's real sick. She's . . . in a terminal situation. He's keeping her at home. If it wasn't for Buffalo Bill, he'd have taken compassionate leave."

"I didn't know that."

"It's not discussed. Don't tell him you're sorry or anything, it doesn't help him . . . they had a good time."

"I'm glad you told me."

Brigham brightened as they reached the airstrip. "I've got a couple of important speeches I give at the end of the firearms course, Starling, try not to miss them." He took a shortcut between some hangars.

"I will."

"Listen, what I teach is something you probably won't ever have to do. I hope you won't. But you've got some aptitude, Starling. If you have to shoot, you can shoot. Do your exercises."

"Right."

"Don't ever put it in your purse."

"Right."

"Pull it a few times in your room at night. Stay so you can find it."

"I will."

A venerable twin-engined Beechcraft stood on the taxiway at the Quantico airstrip with its beacons turning and the door open. One propeller was spinning, riffling the grass beside the tarmac.

"That wouldn't be the Blue Canoe," Starling said.

"Yep."

"It's little and it's old."

"It *is* old," Brigham said cheerfully. "Drug Enforcement seized it in Florida a long time ago, when it flopped in the 'Glades. Mechanically sound now, though. I hope Gramm and Rudman don't find out we're using it— we're supposed to ride the bus." He pulled up beside the airplane and got Starling's baggage out of the backseat. In some confusion of hands he managed to give her the stuff and shake her hand.

And then, without meaning to, Brigham said, "Bless you, Starling." The words felt odd in his Marine mouth. He didn't know where they came from and his face felt hot.

"Thanks . . . thank you, Mr Brigham."

Crawford was in the copilot's seat, in shirtsleeves

78

and sunglasses. He turned to Starling when he heard the pilot slam the door.

She couldn't see his eyes behind the dark glasses, and she felt she didn't know him. Crawford looked pale and tough, like a root a bulldozer pushes up.

"Take a pew and read," is all he said.

A thick case file lay on the seat behind him. The cover said BUFFALO BILL. Starling hugged it tight as the Blue Canoe blatted and shuddered and began to roll.

THE EDGES of the runway blurred and fell away. To the
east, a flash of morning sun off the Chesapeake Bay as
the small plane turned out of traffic.

Clarice Starling could see the school down there,
and the surrounding Marine base at Quantico. On the
assault course, tiny figures of Marines scrambled and
ran.

This was how it looked from above.

Once, after a night-firing exercise, walking in the
dark along the deserted Hogan's Alley, walking to think,
she had heard airplanes roar over and then, in the new
silence, voices calling in the black sky above her—airborne troops in a night jump calling to each other as they
came down through the darkness. And she wondered
how it felt to wait for the jump light at the aircraft door,
how it felt to plunge into the bellowing dark.

Maybe it felt like this.

She opened the file.

He had done it five times that they knew of, had Bill.
At least five times, and probably more, over the past

ten months he had abducted a woman, killed her and skinned her. (Starling's eye raced down the autopsy protocols to the free-histamine tests to confirm that he killed them before he did the rest.)

He dumped each body in running water when he was through with it. Each was found in a different river, downstream from an interstate highway crossing, each in a different state. Everyone knew Buffalo Bill was a traveling man. That was all the law knew about him, absolutely all, except that he had at least one gun. It had six lands and grooves, left-hand twist—possibly a Colt revolver or a Colt clone. Skidmarks on recovered bullets indicated he preferred to fire .38 Specials in the longer chambers of a .357.

The rivers left no fingerprints, no trace evidence of hair or fiber.

He was almost certain to be a white male: white because serial murderers usually kill within their own ethnic group and all the victims were white; male because female serial murderers are almost unknown in our time.

Two big-city columnists had found a headline in e.e. cummings' deadly little poem, "Buffalo Bill": . . . *how do you like your blueeyed boy Mister Death.*

Someone, maybe Crawford, had pasted the quotation inside the cover of the file.

There was no clear correlation between where Bill abducted the young women and where he dumped them.

In the cases where the bodies were found soon enough for an accurate determination of time of death, police learned another thing the killer did: Bill kept them for a while, alive. These victims did not die until a week to ten days after they were abducted. That meant he had to have a place to keep them and a place to work in privacy. It meant he wasn't a drifter. He was more of a trapdoor spider. With his own digs. Somewhere.

That horrified the public more than anything—his holding them for a week or more, knowing he would kill them.

Two were hanged, three shot. There was no evidence of rape or physical abuse prior to death, and the autopsy protocols recorded no evidence of "specifically genital" disfigurement, though pathologists noted it would be almost impossible to determine these things in the more deteriorated bodies.

All were found naked. In two cases, articles of the victims' outer clothing were found beside the road near their homes, slit up the back like funeral suits.

Starling got through the photographs all right. Floaters are the worst kind of dead to deal with, physically. There is an absolute pathos about them too, as there often is about homicide victims out of doors. The indignities the victim suffers, the exposure to the elements and to casual eyes, anger you if your job permits you anger.

Often, at indoor homicides, evidences of a victim's unpleasant personal practices, and the victim's own victims—beaten spouses, abused children—crowd around to whisper that the dead one had it coming, and many times he did.

But nobody had this coming. Here they had not even their skins as they lay on littered riverbanks amid the outboard-oil bottles and sandwich bags that are our common squalor. The cold-weather ones largely retained their faces. Starling reminded herself that their teeth were not bared in pain, that turtles and fish in the course of feeding had created that expression. Bill peeled the torsos and mostly left the limbs alone.

They wouldn't have been so hard to look at, Starling thought, if this airplane cabin wasn't so warm and if the damned plane didn't have this crawly yaw as one prop caught the air better than the other, and if the God damned sun didn't splinter so on the scratched windows and jab like a headache.

It's possible to catch him. Starling squeezed on that thought to help herself sit in this ever-smaller airplane cabin with her lap full of awful information. She could help stop him cold. Then they could put this slightly sticky, smooth-covered file back in the drawer and turn the key on it.

She stared at the back of Crawford's head. If she wanted to stop Buffalo Bill, she was in the right crowd. Crawford had organized successful hunts for three serial murderers. But not without casualties. Will Graham, the keenest hound ever to run in Crawford's pack, was a legend at the Academy; he was also a drunk in Florida now with a face that was hard to look at, they said.

Maybe Crawford felt her staring at the back of his head. He climbed out of the copilot's seat. The pilot touched the trim wheel as Crawford came back to her and buckled in beside her. When he folded his sunglasses and put on his bifocals, she felt she knew him again.

When he looked from her face to the report and back again, something passed behind his face and was quickly gone. A more animated mug than Crawford's would have shown regret.

"I'm hot, are you hot?" he said. "Bobby, it's too damned hot in here," he called to the pilot. Bobby adjusted something and cold air came in. A few snowflakes formed in the moist cabin air and settled in Starling's hair.

Then it was Jack Crawford hunting, his eyes like a bright winter day.

He opened the file to a map of the Central and Eastern United States. Locations where bodies had been found were marked on the map—a scattering of dots as mute and crooked as Orion.

Crawford took a pen from his pocket and marked the newest location, their objective.

"Elk River, about six miles below US 79," he said. "We're lucky on this one. The body was snagged on a trotline—a fishing line set out in the river. They don't think she's been in the water all that long. They're bringing her to Potter, the county seat. I want to know who she is in a hurry so we can sweep for witnesses to the abduction. We'll send the prints back on a land line as soon as we get 'em." Crawford tilted his head to look at Starling through the bottoms of his glasses. "Jimmy Price says you can do a floater."

"Actually, I never had an entire floater," Starling said. "I fingerprinted the hands Mr Price got in his mail every day. A good many of them were from floaters, though."

Those who have never been under Jimmy Price's supervision believe him to be a lovable curmudgeon. Like most curmudgeons, he is really a mean old man.

Jimmy Price is a supervisor in Latent Prints at the Washington lab. Starling did time with him as a Forensic Fellow.

"That Jimmy," Crawford said fondly. "What is it they call that job . . ."

"The position is called 'lab wretch,' or some people prefer 'Igor'—that's what's printed on the rubber apron they give you."

"That's it."

"They tell you to pretend you're dissecting a frog."

"I see—"

"Then they bring you a package from UPS. They're all watching—some of them hurry back from coffee, hoping you'll barf. I can print a floater very well. In fact—"

"Good, now look at this. His first victim that we know of was found in the Blackwater River in Missouri, outside of Lone Jack, last June. The Bimmel girl, she'd been reported missing in Belvedere, Ohio, on April 15, two months before. We couldn't tell a lot about it—it took another three months just to get her identified. The next one he grabbed in Chicago the third week in April. She was found in the Wabash in downtown Lafayette, Indiana, just ten days after she was taken, so we could tell what had happened to her. Next we've got a white female, early twenties, dumped in the Rolling Fork near I-65, about thirty-eight miles south of Louisville, Kentucky. She's never been identified. And the Varner woman, grabbed in Evansville, Indiana, and dropped in the Embarras just below Interstate 70 in eastern Illinois.

"Then he moved south and dumped one in the

Conasauga below Damascus, Georgia, down from Interstate 75, that was this Kittridge girl from Pittsburgh—here's her graduation picture. His luck's ungodly—nobody's ever seen him make a snatch. Except for the dumps being near an Interstate, we haven't seen any pattern."

"If you trace heaviest-traffic routes backward from the dump sites, do they converge at all?"

"No."

"What if you . . . *postulate* . . . that he's making a dropoff and a new abduction on the same trip?" Starling asked, carefully avoiding the forbidden word *assume*. "He'd drop off the body first, wouldn't he, in case he got in trouble grabbing the next one? Then, if he was caught grabbing somebody, he might get off for assault, plead it down to zip if he didn't have a body in his car. So how about drawing vectors backward from each abduction site through the previous dump site? You've tried it."

"That's a good idea, but he had it too. If he *is* doing both things in one trip, he's zigging around. We've run computer simulations, first with him westbound on the Interstates, then eastbound, then various combinations with the best dates we can put on the dumps and abductions. You put it in the computer and smoke comes out. He lives in the East, it tells us. He's not in a moon cycle, it tells us. No convention dates in the cities correlate. Nothing but feathers. No, he's seen us coming, Starling."

"You think he's too careful to be a suicide."

Crawford nodded. "Definitely too careful. He's found out how to have a meaningful relationship now, and he wants to do it a lot. I'm not getting my hopes up for a suicide."

Crawford passed the pilot a cup of water from a thermos. He gave one to Starling and mixed himself an Alka-Seltzer.

Her stomach lifted as the airplane started down.

"Couple of things, Starling. I look for first-rate forensics from you, but I need more than that. You don't say much, and that's okay, neither do I. But don't ever feel you've got to have a new fact to tell me before you can bring something up. There aren't any silly questions. You'll see things that I won't, and I want to know what they are. Maybe you've got a knack for this. All of a sudden we've got this chance to see if you do."

Listening to him, her stomach lifting and her expression properly rapt, Starling wondered how long Crawford had known he'd use her on this case, how hungry for a chance he had wanted her to be. He was a leader, with a leader's frank-and-open bullshit, all right.

"You think about him enough, you see where he's been, you get a feel for him," Crawford went on. "You don't even dislike him all the time, hard as that is to believe. Then, if you're lucky, out of the stuff you know, part of it plucks at you, tries to get your attention. Always tell me when something plucks, Starling.

"Listen to me, a crime is confusing enough without the investigation mixing it up. Don't let a herd of policemen confuse you. Live right behind your eyes. Listen to yourself. Keep the crime separate from what's going on around you now. Don't try to impose any pattern or symmetry on this guy. Stay open and let him show you.

"One other thing: an investigation like this is a zoo. It's spread out over a lot of jurisdictions, and a few are run by losers. We have to get along with them so they won't hold out on us. We're going to Potter, West Virginia. I don't know about these people we're going to. They may be fine or they may think we're the revenuers."

The pilot lifted an earphone away from his head and spoke over his shoulder. "Final approach, Jack. You staying back there?"

"Yeah," Crawford said. "School's out, Starling."

NOW HERE is the Potter Funeral Home, the largest white frame house on Potter Street in Potter, West Virginia, serving as the morgue for Rankin County. The coroner is a family physician named Dr Akin. If he rules that a death is questionable, the body is sent on to Claxton Regional Medical Center in the neighboring county, where they have a trained pathologist.

Clarice Starling, riding into Potter from the airstrip in the back of a sheriff's department cruiser, had to lean up close to the prisoner screen to hear the deputy at the wheel as he explained these things to Jack Crawford.

A service was about to get under way at the mortuary. The mourners in their country Sunday best filed up the sidewalk between leggy boxwoods and bunched on the steps, waiting to get in. The freshly painted house and the steps had, each in its own direction, settled slightly out of plumb.

In the private parking lot behind the house, where the hearses waited, two young deputies and one old one stood with two state troopers under a bare elm. It was not cold enough for their breath to steam.

Starling looked at these men as the cruiser pulled into the lot, and at once she knew about them. She knew they came from houses that had chifforobes instead of closets and she knew pretty much what was in the chifforobes. She knew that these men had relatives who hung their clothes in suitbags on the walls of their trailers. She knew that the older deputy had grown up with a pump on the porch and had waded to the road in the muddy spring to catch the school bus with his shoes hanging around his neck by the laces, as her father had done. She knew they had carried their lunches to school in paper sacks with grease spots on them from being used over and over and that after lunch they folded the sacks and slipped them in the back pockets of their jeans.

She wondered how much Crawford knew about them.

There were no handles on the inside of the rear doors in the cruiser, as Starling discovered when the driver and Crawford got out and started toward the back of the funeral home. She had to bat on the glass until one of the deputies beneath the tree saw her, and the driver came back red-faced to let her out.

The deputies watched her sidelong as she passed. One said "ma'am." She gave them a nod and a smile of the correct dim wattage as she went to join Crawford on the back porch.

When she was far enough away, one of the younger deputies, a newlywed, scratched beneath his jaw and said, "She don't look half as good as she thinks she does."

"Well, if she just thinks she looks *pretty God damned good*, I'd have to agree with her, myself," the other young deputy said. "I'd put her on like a Mark Five gas mask."

"I'd just as soon have a big watermelon, if it was cold," the older deputy said, half to himself.

Crawford was already talking to the chief deputy, a small, taut man in steel-rimmed glasses and the kind of elastic-sided boots the catalogs call "Romeos."

They had moved into the funeral home's dim back corridor, where a Coke machine hummed and random odd objects stood against the wall—a treadle sewing machine, a tricycle, and a roll of artificial grass, a striped canvas awning wrapped around its poles. On the wall was a sepia print of Saint Cecilia at the keyboard. Her hair was braided around her head, and roses tumbled onto the keys out of thin air.

"I appreciate your letting us know so fast, Sheriff," Crawford said.

The chief deputy wasn't having any. "It was somebody from the district attorney's office called you," he said. "I know the sheriff didn't call you—Sheriff Perkins is on a guided tour of Hawaii at the present time with Mrs Perkins. I spoke to him on long distance this morning at eight o'clock, that's three A.M., Hawaii time. He'll get back to me later in the day, but he told me Job One is to find out if this is one of our local girls. It could be something that outside elements has just dumped on us. We'll tend to that before we do anything else. We've had 'em haul bodies here all the way from Phenix City, Alabama."

"That's where we can help you, Sheriff. If—"

"I've been on the phone with the field services commander of the state troopers in Charleston. He's sending some officers from the Criminal Investigation Section—what's known as the CIS. They'll give us all the backup we need." The corridor was filling with deputy sheriffs and troopers; the chief deputy had too much of an audience. "We'll get around to you just as soon as we can, and extend you ever courtesy, work with you ever *way* we can, but right now—"

"Sheriff, this kind of a sex crime has some aspects that I'd rather say to you just between us men, you understand what I mean?" Crawford said, indicating Starling's presence with a small movement of his head. He hustled the smaller man into a cluttered office off the hall and closed the door. Starling was left to mask her umbrage before the gaggle of deputies. Her teeth hard together, she gazed on Saint Cecilia and returned the saint's ethereal smile while eavesdropping through the door. She could hear raised voices, then scraps of a telephone conversation. They were back out in the hall in less than four minutes.

The chief deputy's mouth was tight. "Oscar, go out front and get Dr Akin. He's kind of obliged to attend those rites, but I don't think they've got started out there yet. Tell him we've got Claxton on the phone."

The coroner, Dr Akin, came to the little office and stood with his foot on a chair, tapping his front teeth with a Good Shepherd fan while he had a brief telephone conference with the pathologist in Claxton. Then he agreed to everything.

So, in an embalming room with cabbage roses in the wallpaper and a picture molding beneath its high

92

ceiling, in a white frame house of a type she understood, Clarice Starling met with her first direct evidence of Buffalo Bill.

The bright green body bag, tightly zipped, was the only modern object in the room. It lay on an old-fashioned porcelain embalming table, reflected many times in the glass panes of cabinets holding trocars and packages of Rock-Hard Cavity Fluid.

Crawford went to the car for the fingerprint transmitter while Starling unpacked her equipment on the drainboard of a large double sink against the wall.

Too many people were in the room. Several deputies, the chief deputy, all had wandered in with them and showed no inclination to leave. It wasn't right. *Why didn't Crawford come on and get rid of them?*

The wallpaper billowed in a draft, billowed inward as the doctor turned on the big, dusty vent fan.

Clarice Starling, standing at the sink, needed now a prototype of courage more apt and powerful than any Marine parachute jump. The image came to her, and helped her, but it pierced her too:

Her mother, standing at the sink, washing blood out of her father's hat, running cold water over the hat, saying, "We'll be all right, Clarice. Tell your brothers and sister to wash up and come to the table. We need to talk and then we'll fix our supper."

Starling took off her scarf and tied it over her hair like a mountain midwife. She took a pair of surgical gloves out of her kit. When she opened her mouth for the first time in Potter, her voice had more than its normal twang and the force of it brought Crawford to the door to listen. "Gentlemen. Gentlemen! You officers and gentlemen! Listen here a minute. Please. Now let me take care of her." She held her hands before their faces as she pulled on the gloves. "There's things we need to do for her. You brought her this far, and I know her folks would thank you if they could. Now please go on out and let me take care of her."

Crawford saw them suddenly go quiet and respectful and urge each other out in whispers: "Come on, Jess. Let's go out in the yard." And Crawford saw that the atmosphere had changed here in the presence of the dead: that wherever this victim came from, whoever she was, the river had carried her into the country, and, while she lay helpless in this room in the country, Clarice Starling had a special relationship to her. Crawford saw that in this place Starling was heir to the granny women, to the wise women, the herb healers, the stalwart country women who have always done the needful, who keep the watch and, when the watch is over, wash and dress the country dead.

Then there were only Crawford and Starling and the doctor in the room with the victim, Dr Akin and Starling looking at each other with a kind of recognition. Both of them were oddly pleased, oddly abashed.

Crawford took a jar of Vicks VapoRub out of his pocket and offered it around. Starling watched to see what to do, and when Crawford and the doctor rubbed it around the rims of their nostrils, she did too.

She dug her cameras out of the equipment bag on the drainboard, her back to the room. Behind her she heard the zipper of the body bag go down.

Starling blinked at the cabbage roses on the wall, took

a breath and let it out. She turned round and looked at the body on the table.

"They should have put paper bags on her hands," she said. "I'll bag them when we're through." Carefully, overriding the automatic camera to bracket her exposures, Starling photographed the body.

The victim was a heavy-hipped young woman sixty-seven inches long by Starling's tape. The water had leached her gray where the skin was gone, but it had been cold water and she clearly hadn't been in it more than a few days. The body was flayed neatly from a clean line just below the breasts to the knees, about the area that would be covered by a bullfighter's pants and sash.

Her breasts were small and between them, over the sternum, was the apparent cause of death, a ragged, star-shaped wound a hand's breadth across.

Her round head was peeled to the skull from just above the eyebrows and ears to the nape.

"Dr Lecter said he'd start scalping," Starling said.

Crawford stood with his arms folded while she took the pictures. "Get her ears with the Polaroid," was all he said.

He went so far as to purse his lips as he walked around the body. Starling peeled off her glove to trail her finger up the calf of the leg. A section of the trotline and treble fishhooks that had entangled and held the body in the moving river was still wrapped around the lower leg.

"What do you see, Starling?"

"Well, she's not a local—her ears are pierced three times each, and she wore glitter polish. Looks like town to me. She's got maybe two weeks' or so hair growth on her legs. And see how soft it's grown in? I think she got her legs waxed. Armpits too. Look how she bleached the fuzz on her upper lip. She was pretty careful about herself, but she hasn't been able to take care of it for a while."

"What about the wound?"

"I don't know," Starling said. "I would have said an exit gunshot wound, except that looks like part of an abrasion collar and a muzzle stamp at the top there."

"Good, Starling. It's a contact entrance wound over the sternum. The explosion gases expand between the bone and the skin and blow out the star around the hole."

On the other side of the wall a pipe organ wheezed as the service got under way in the front of the funeral home.

"Wrongful death," Dr Akins contributed, nodding his head. "I've got to get in there for at least part of this service. The family always expects me to go the last mile. Lamar will be in here to help you as soon as he finishes playing the musical offering. I take you at your word on preserving evidence for the pathologist at Claxton, Mr Crawford."

"She's got two nails broken off here on the left hand," Starling said when the doctor was gone. "They're broken back up in the quick and it looks like dirt or some hard particles driven up under some of the others. Can we take evidence?"

"Take samples of grit, take a couple of flakes of polish," Crawford said. "We'll tell 'em after we get the results."

Lamar, a lean funeral home assistant with a whiskey

bloom in the middle of his face, came in while she was doing it. "You must of been a manicurist one time," he said.

They were glad to see the young woman had no fingernail marks in her palms—an indication that, like the others, she had died before anything else was done to her.

"You want to print her facedown, Starling?" Crawford said.

"Be easier."

"Let's do teeth first, and then Lamar can help us turn her over."

"Just pictures, or a chart?" Starling attached the dental kit to the front of the fingerprint camera, privately relieved that all the parts were in the bag.

"Just pictures," Crawford said. "A chart can throw you off without X rays. We can eliminate a couple of missing women with the pictures."

Lamar was very gentle with his organist's hands, opening the young woman's mouth at Starling's direction and retracting her lips while Starling placed the one-to-one Polaroid against the face to get details of the front teeth. That part was easy, but she had to shoot the molars with a palatal reflector, watching from the side for the glow through the cheek to be sure the strobe around the lens was lighting the inside of the mouth. She had only seen it done in a forensics class.

Starling watched the first Polaroid print of the molars develop, adjusted the lightness control and tried again. This print was better. This one was very good.

"She's got something in her throat," Starling said.

Crawford looked at the picture. It showed a dark cylindrical object just behind the soft palate. "Give me the flashlight."

"When a body comes out of the water, a lot of times there's, like, leaves and things in the mouth," Lamar said, helping Crawford to look.

Starling took some forceps out of her bag. She looked at Crawford across the body. He nodded. It only took her a second to get it.

"What is it, some kind of seed pod?" Crawford said.

"Nawsir, that's a bug cocoon," Lamar said. He was right.

Starling put it in a jar.

"You might want the county agent to look at that," Lamar said.

Facedown, the body was easy to fingerprint. Starling had been prepared for the worst—but none of the tedious and delicate injection methods or finger stalls were necessary. She took the prints on thin card stock held in a device shaped like a shoehorn. She did a set of plantar prints as well, in case they had only baby footprints from a hospital for reference.

Two triangular pieces of skin were missing from high on the shoulders. Starling took pictures.

"Measure too," Crawford said. "He cut the girl from Akron when he slit her clothes off, not much more than a scratch, but it matched the cut up the back of her blouse when they found it beside the road. This is something new, though. I haven't seen this."

"Looks like a burn across the back of her calf," Starling said.

"Old people gets those a lot," Lamar said.

"What?" Crawford said.

"I SAID OLD PEOPLE GETS THOSE A LOT."

"I heard you fine, I want you to explain it. What about old people?"

"Old people pass away with a heating pad on them, and when they're dead it burns them, even when it's not all that hot. You burn under a heating pad when you're dead. No circulation under it."

"We'll ask the pathologist at Claxton to test it, and see if it's postmortem," Crawford said to Starling.

"Car muffler, most likely," Lamar said.

"What?"

"CAR MUFFL—car muffler. One time Billy Petrie got shot to death and they dumped him in the trunk of his car? His wife drove the car around two or three days looking for him. When they brought him in here, the muffler had got hot under the car trunk and burned him just like that, only across his hip," Lamar said. "I can't put groceries in the trunk of my car for it melting the ice cream."

"That's a good thought, Lamar, I wish you worked for me," Crawford said. "Do you know the fellows that found her in the river?"

"Jabbo Franklin and his brother, Bubba."

"What do they do?"

"Fight at the Moose, make fun of people that's not bothering them—someone just comes in the Moose after a simple drink, worn out from looking at the bereaved all day, and it's 'Set down there, Lamar, and play "Filipino Baby."' Make a person play 'Filipino Baby' over and over on that sticky old bar piano. That's what Jabbo likes. 'Well, make up some damn words if you don't know it,' he says, 'and make the damn thing rhyme this time.' He gets a check from the Veterans and goes to dry out at the VA around Christmas. I been looking for him on this table for fifteen years."

"We'll need serotonin tests on the fishhook punctures," Crawford said. "I'm sending the pathologist a note."

"Them hooks are too close together," Lamar said.

"What did you say?"

"The Franklins was running a trotline with the hooks too close together. It's a violation. That's prob'ly why they didn't call it in until this morning."

"The sheriff said they were duck hunters."

"I expect they did tell him that," Lamar said. "They'll tell you they wrestled Duke Keomuka in Honolulu one time too, tag team with Satellite Monroe. You can believe that too, if you feel like it. Grab a croaker sack and they'll take you on a snipe hunt too, if you favor snipe. Give you a glass of billiards with it."

"What do you think happened, Lamar?"

"The Franklins was running this trotline, it's their trotline with these unlawful hooks, and they was pulling it up to see if they had any fish."

"Why do you think so?"

"This lady's not near ready to float."

"No."

"Then if they hadna been pulling up on the trotline they never would have found her. They prob'ly went off scared and finally called in. I expect you'll want the game warden in on this."

"I expect so," Crawford said.

"Lots of times they've got a crank telephone behind

the seat in their Ramcharger, that's a big fine right there, if you don't have to go to the pen."

Crawford raised his eyebrows.

"To telephone fish with," Starling said. "Stun the fish with electric current when you hang the wires in the water and turn the crank. They come to the top and you just dip 'em out."

"Right," Lamar said, "are you from around here?"

"They do it lots of places," Starling said.

Starling felt the urge to say something before they zipped up the bag, to make a gesture or express some kind of commitment. In the end, she just shook her head and got busy packing the samples into her case.

It was different with the body and problem out of sight. In this slack moment, what she'd been doing came in on her. Starling stripped off her gloves and turned the water on in the sink. With her back to the room, she ran water over her wrists. The water in the pipes wasn't all that cool. Lamar, watching, disappeared into the hall. He came back from the Coke machine with an ice-cold can of soda, unopened, and offered it to her.

"No, thanks," Starling said. "I don't believe I'll have one."

"No, hold it under your neck there," Lamar said, "and on that little bump at the back of your head. Cold'll make you feel better. It does me."

By the time Starling had finished taping the memo to the pathologist across the zipper of the body bag, Crawford's fingerprint transmitter was clicking on the office desk.

Finding this victim so soon after the crime was a lucky break. Crawford was determined to identify her quickly and start a sweep around her home for witnesses to the abduction. His method was a lot of trouble to everyone, but it was fast.

Crawford carried a Litton Policefax fingerprint transmitter. Unlike federal-issue facsimile machines, the Policefax is compatible with most big-city police department systems. The fingerprint card Starling had assembled was barely dry.

"Load it, Starling, you've got the nimble fingers."

Don't smear it was what he meant, and Starling didn't. It was hard, wrapping the glued-together composite card around the little drum while six wire rooms waited around the country.

Crawford was on the telephone to the FBI switchboard and wire room in Washington. "Dorothy, is everybody on? Okay, gentlemen, we'll turn it down to one-twenty to keep it nice and sharp—check one-twenty, everybody? Atlanta, how about it? Okay, give me the picture wire . . . now."

Then it was spinning at slow speed for clarity, sending the dead woman's prints simultaneously to the FBI wire room and major police department wire rooms in the East. If Chicago, Detroit, Atlanta, or any of the others got a hit on the fingerprints, a sweep would begin in minutes.

Next, Crawford sent pictures of the victim's teeth and photos of her face, the head draped by Starling with a towel in the event the supermarket press got hold of the photographs.

Three officers of the West Virginia State Police Criminal Investigation Section arrived from Charleston as they were leaving. Crawford did a lot of handshaking, passing out cards with the National Crime Information Center hotline number. Starling was interested to see how fast he got them into a male-bonding mode. They sure would call up with anything they got, they sure would. You betcha and much oblige. Maybe it wasn't male bonding, she decided; it worked on her too.

Lamar waved with his fingers from the porch as Crawford and Starling rode away with the deputy toward the Elk River. The Coke was still pretty cold. Lamar took it into the storeroom and fixed a refreshing beverage for himself.

CHAPTER

13

"DROP ME at the lab, Jeff," Crawford told the driver. "Then I want you to wait for Officer Starling at the Smithsonian. She'll go on from there to Quantico."

"Yes, sir."

They were crossing the Potomac River against the after-dinner traffic, coming into downtown Washington from National Airport.

The young man at the wheel seemed in awe of Crawford and drove with excessive caution, Starling thought. She didn't blame him; it was an article of faith at the Academy that the last agent who'd committed a Full Fuck-Up in Crawford's command now investigated pilfering at DEW-line installations along the Arctic Circle.

Crawford was not in a good humor. Nine hours had passed since he transmitted the fingerprints and pictures of the victim, and she remained unidentified. Along with the West Virginia troopers, he and Starling had worked the bridge and the river bank until dark without result.

Starling had heard him on the phone from the airplane, arranging for an evening nurse at home.

The FBI plain-jane sedan seemed wonderfully quiet after the Blue Canoe, and talking was easier.

"I'll post the hotline and the Latent Descriptor Index when I take your prints up to ID," Crawford said. "You draft me an insert for the file. An insert, not a 302—do you know how to do it?"

"I know how."

"Say I'm the Index, tell me what's new."

It took her a second to get it together—she was glad Crawford seemed interested in the scaffolding on the Jefferson Memorial as they passed by.

The Latent Descriptor Index in the Identification Section's computer compares the characteristics of a crime under investigation to the known proclivities of criminals on file. When it finds pronounced similarities, it suggests suspects and produces their fingerprints. Then a human operator compares the file fingerprints with latent prints found at the scene. There were no prints yet on Buffalo Bill, but Crawford wanted to be ready.

The system requires brief, concise statements. Starling tried to come up with some.

"White female, late teens or early twenties, shot to death, lower torso and thighs flayed—"

"Starling, the Index already knows he kills young white women and skins their torsos—use 'skinned,' by the way, 'flayed' is an uncommon term another officer might not use, and you can't be sure the damned thing will read a synonym. It already knows he dumps them in rivers. It doesn't know what's *new* here. What's new here, Starling?"

"This is the sixth victim, the first one scalped, the first one with triangular patches taken from the back of the shoulders, the first one shot in the chest, the first one with a cocoon in her throat."

"You forgot broken fingernails."

"No, sir, she's the second one with broken fingernails."

"You're right. Listen, in your insert for the file, note that the cocoon is confidential. We'll use it to eliminate false confessions."

"I'm wondering if he's done that before—placed a cocoon or an insect," Starling said. "It would be easy to miss in an autopsy, especially with a floater. You know, the medical examiner sees an obvious cause of death, it's hot in there, and they want to get through . . . can we check back on that?"

"If we have to. You can count on the pathologists to say they didn't miss anything, naturally. The Cincinnati Jane Doe's still in the freezer out there. I'll ask them to look at her, but the other four are in the ground. Exhumation orders stir people up. We had to do it with four patients who passed away under Dr Lecter's care, just to make sure what killed them. Let me tell you, it's a lot of trouble and it upsets the relatives. I'll do it if I have to, but we'll see what you find out at the Smithsonian before I decide."

"Scalping . . . that's rare, isn't it?"

"Uncommon, yes," Crawford said.

"But Dr Lecter said Buffalo Bill would do it. How did he know that?"

"He didn't know it."

"He said it, though."

"It's not a big surprise, Starling. I wasn't surprised to see that. I should have said that it was rare until the Mengel case, remember that? Scalped the woman? There were two or three copycats after that. The papers, when they were playing around with the Buffalo Bill tag, they emphasized more than once that this killer doesn't take scalps. It's no surprise after that—he probably follows his press. Lecter was guessing. He didn't say *when* it would happen, so he could never be wrong. If we caught Bill and there was no scalping, Lecter could say we got him just *before* he did it."

"Dr Lecter also said Buffalo Bill lives in a two-story house. We never got into that. Why do you suppose he said it?"

"That's not a guess. He's very likely right, and he could have told you why, but he wanted to tease you with it. It's the only weakness I ever saw in him—he has to look smart, smarter than anybody. He's been doing it for years."

"You said ask if I don't know—well, I have to ask you to explain that."

"Okay, two of the victims were hanged, right? High ligature marks, cervical displacement, definite hanging. As Dr Lecter knows from personal experience, Starling, it's very hard for one person to hang another against his will. People hang *themselves* from doorknobs all the time. They hang themselves sitting down, it's easy. But it's hard to hang somebody else—even when they're bound up, they manage to get their feet under them, if there's any support to find with their feet. A ladder's threatening. Victims won't climb it blindfolded and they sure won't climb it if they can see the noose.

107

The way it's done is in a stairwell. Stairs are familiar. Tell them you're taking them up to use the bathroom, whatever, walk them up with a hood on, slip the noose on, and boot them off the top step with the rope fastened to the landing railing. It's the only good way in a house. Fellow in California popularized it. If Bill didn't have a stairwell, he'd kill them another way. Now give me those names, the senior deputy from Potter and the state police guy, the ranking officer."

Starling found them in her notepad, reading by a penlight held in her teeth.

"Good," Crawford said. "When you're posting a hotline, Starling, always credit the cops by name. They hear their own names, they get more friendly to the hotline. Fame helps them remember to call us if they get something. What does the burn on her leg say to you?"

"Depends if it's postmortem."

"If it is?"

"Then he's got a closed truck or a van or a station wagon, something long."

"Why?"

"Because the burn's across the back of her calf."

They were at Tenth and Pennsylvania, in front of the new FBI headquarters that nobody ever refers to as the J. Edgar Hoover Building.

"Jeff, you can let me out here," Crawford said. "Right here, don't go underneath. Stay in the car, Jeff, just pop the trunk. Come show me, Starling."

She got out with Crawford while he retrieved his datafax and briefcase from the luggage compartment.

"He hauled the body in something big enough for

the body to be stretched out on its back," Starling said. "That's the only way the back of her calf would rest on the floor over the exhaust pipe. In a car trunk like this, she'd be curled up on her side and—"

"Yeah, that's how I see it," Crawford said.

She realized then that he'd gotten her out of the car so he could speak with her privately.

"When I told that deputy he and I shouldn't talk in front of a woman, that burned you, didn't it?"

"Sure."

"It was just smoke. I wanted to get him by himself."

"I know that."

"Okay." Crawford slammed the trunk and turned away.

Starling couldn't let it go.

"It matters, Mr Crawford."

He was turning back to her, laden with his fax machine and briefcase, and she had his full attention.

"Those cops know who you are," she said. "They look at you to see how to act." She stood steady, shrugged her shoulders, opened her palms. There it was, it was true.

Crawford performed a measurement on his cold scales.

"Duly noted, Starling. Now get on with the bug."

"Yes, sir."

She watched him walk away, a middle-aged man laden with cases and rumpled from flying, his cuffs muddy from the riverbank, going home to what he did at home.

She would have killed for him then. That was one of Crawford's great talents.

THE SMITHSONIAN'S National Museum of Natural History had been closed for hours, but Crawford had called ahead and a guard waited to let Clarice Starling in the Constitution Avenue entrance.

The lights were dimmed in the closed museum and the air was still. Only the colossal figure of a South Seas chieftain facing the entrance stood tall enough for the weak ceiling light to shine on his face.

Starling's guide was a big black man in the neat turnout of the Smithsonian guards. She thought he resembled the chieftain as he raised his face to the elevator lights. There was a moment's relief in her idle fancy, like rubbing a cramp.

The second level above the great stuffed elephant, a vast floor closed to the public, is shared by the departments of Anthropology and Entomology. The anthropologists call it the fourth floor. The entomologists contend it is the third. A few scientists from Agriculture say they have proof that it is the sixth. Each faction has a case in the old building with its additions and subdivisions.

Starling followed the guard into a dim maze of corridors walled high with wooden cases of anthropological specimens. Only the small labels revealed their contents.

"Thousands of people in these boxes," the guard said. "Forty thousand specimens."

He found office numbers with his flashlight and trailed the light over the labels as they went along.

Dyak baby carriers and ceremonial skulls gave way to Aphids, and they left Man for the older and more orderly world of Insects. Now the corridor was walled with big metal boxes painted pale green.

"Thirty million insects—and the spiders on top of that. Don't lump the spiders in with the insects," the guard advised. "Spider people jump all over you about that. There, the office that's lit. Don't try to come out by yourself. If they don't say they'll bring you down, call me at this extension, it's the guard office. I'll come get you." He gave her a card and left her.

She was in the heart of Entomology, on a rotunda gallery high above the great stuffed elephant. There was the office with the lights on and the door open.

"Time, Pilch!" A man's voice, shrill with excitement. "Let's go here. Time!"

Starling stopped in the doorway. Two men sat at a laboratory table playing chess. Both were about thirty, one black-haired and lean, the other pudgy with wiry red hair. They appeared to be engrossed in the chessboard. If they noticed Starling, they gave no sign. If they noticed the enormous rhinoceros beetle slowly making its way across the board, weaving among the chessmen, they gave no sign of that either.

111

Then the beetle crossed the edge of the board.

"Time, Roden," the lean one said instantly.

The pudgy one moved his bishop and immediately turned the beetle around and started it trudging back the other way.

"If the beetle just cuts across the corner, is time up then?" Starling asked.

"Of course time's up then," the pudgy one said loudly, without looking up. "Of *course* it's up then. How do *you* play? Do you make him cross the whole board? Who do you play against, a sloth?"

"I have the specimen Special Agent Crawford called about."

"I can't imagine why we didn't hear your siren," the pudgy one said. "We're waiting all night here to identify a *bug* for the FBI. Bugs're all we do. Nobody said anything about Special Agent Crawford's *specimen*. He should show his *specimen* privately to his family doctor. Time, Pilch!"

"I'd love to catch your whole routine another time," Starling said, "but this is urgent, so let's do it now. Time, Pilch."

The black-haired one looked around at her, saw her leaning against the doorframe with her briefcase. He put the beetle on some rotten wood in a box and covered it with a lettuce leaf.

When he got up, he was tall.

"I'm Noble Pilcher," he said. "That's Albert Roden. You need an insect identified? We're happy to help you." Pilcher had a long friendly face, but his black eyes were a little witchy and too close together, and one of them had a slight cast that made it catch the light independently. He did not offer to shake hands. "You are . . . ?"

"Clarice Starling."

"Let's see what you've got."

Pilcher held the small jar to the light.

Roden came to look. "Where did you find it? Did you kill it with your *gun*? Did you see its *mommy*?"

It occurred to Starling how much Roden would benefit from an elbow smash in the hinge of his jaw.

"Shhh," Pilcher said. "Tell us where you found it. Was it attached to anything—a twig or a leaf—or was it in the soil?"

"I see," Starling said. "Nobody's talked to you."

"The Chairman asked us to stay late and identify a bug for the FBI," Pilcher said.

"*Told* us," Roden said. "*Told* us to stay late."

"We do it all the time for Customs and the Department of Agriculture," Pilcher said.

"But not in the middle of the night," Roden said.

"I need to tell you a couple of things involving a criminal case," Starling said. "I'm allowed to do that if you'll keep it in confidence until the case is resolved. It's important. It means some lives, and I'm not just saying that. Dr Roden, can you tell me seriously that you'll respect a confidence?"

"I'm not a doctor. Do I have to sign anything?"

"Not if your word's any good. You'll have to sign for the specimen if you need to keep it, that's all."

"Of course I'll help you. I'm not *uncaring*."

"Dr Pilcher?"

"That's true," Pilcher said. "He's not uncaring."

"Confidence?"

"I won't tell."

"Pilch isn't a doctor yet either," Roden said. "We're on an equal educational footing. But notice how he *allowed* you to call him that." Roden placed the tip of his forefinger against his chin, as though pointing to his judicious expression. "Give us all the details. What might seem irrelevant to *you* could be vital information to an expert."

"This insect was found lodged behind the soft palate of a murder victim. I don't know how it got there. Her body was in the Elk River in West Virginia, and she hadn't been dead more than a few days."

"It's Buffalo Bill, I heard it on the radio," Roden said.

"You didn't hear about the insect on the radio, did you?" Starling said.

"No, but they said Elk River—are you coming in from that today, is that why you're so late?"

"Yes," Starling said.

"You must be tired, do you want some coffee?" Roden said.

"No, thank you."

"Water?"

"No."

"A Coke?"

"I don't believe so. We want to know where this woman was held captive and where she was killed. We're hoping this bug has some specialized habitat, or it's limited in range, you know, or it only sleeps on some kind of tree—we want to know where this insect is from. I'm asking for your confidence because—if the perpetrator put the insect there deliberately—then only he would know that fact and we could use it to eliminate false confessions and save time. He's killed six at least. Time's eating us up."

"Do you think he's holding another woman right this minute, while we're looking at his bug?" Roden asked in her face. His eyes were wide and his mouth open. She could see into his mouth, and she flashed for a second on something else.

"*I don't know.*" A little shrill, that. "I don't know," she said again, to take the edge off it. "He'll do it again as soon as he can."

"So we'll do this as soon as we can," Pilcher said. "Don't worry, we're good at this. You couldn't be in better hands." He removed the brown object from the jar with a slender forceps and placed it on a sheet of white paper beneath the light. He swung a magnifying glass on a flexible arm over it.

The insect was long and it looked like a mummy. It was sheathed in a semitransparent cover that followed its general outlines like a sarcophagus. The appendages were bound so tightly against the body, they might have been carved in low relief. The little face looked wise.

"In the first place, it's not anything that would normally infest a body outdoors, and it wouldn't be in the water except by accident," Pilcher said. "I don't know how familiar you are with insects or how much you want to hear."

"Let's say I don't know diddly. I want you to tell me the whole thing."

"Okay, this is a pupa, an immature insect, in a chrysalis—that's the cocoon that holds it while it transforms itself from a larva into an adult," Pilcher said.

115

"Obtect pupa, Pilch?" Roden wrinkled his nose to hold his glasses up.

"Yeah, I think so. You want to pull down Chu on the immature insects? Okay, this is the pupal stage of a large insect. Most of the more advanced insects have a pupal stage. A lot of them spend the winter this way."

"Book or look, Pilch?" Roden said.

"I'll look." Pilcher moved the specimen to the stage of a microscope and hunched over it with a dental probe in his hand. "Here we go: No distinct respiratory organs on the dorsocephalic region, spiracles on the mesothorax and some abdominals, let's start with that."

"Ummhumm," Roden said, turning pages in a small manual. "Functional mandibles?"

"Nope."

"Paired galeae of maxillae on the ventro meson?"

"Yep, yep."

"Where are the antennae?"

"Adjacent to the mesal margin of the wings. Two pairs of wings, the inside pair are completely covered up. Only the bottom three abdominal segments are free. Little pointy cremaster—I'd say Lepidoptera."

"That's what it says here," Roden said.

"It's the family that includes the butterflies and moths. Covers a lot of territory," Pilcher said.

"It's gonna be tough if the wings are soaked. I'll pull the references," Roden said. "I guess there's no way I can keep you from talking about me while I'm gone."

"I guess not," Pilcher said. "Roden's all right," he told Starling as soon as Roden left the room.

"I'm sure he is."

"Are you now?" Pilcher seemed amused. "We were

116

undergraduates together, working and glomming any kind of fellowship we could. He got one where he had to sit down in a coal mine waiting for proton decay. He just stayed in the dark too long. He's all right. Just don't mention proton decay."

"I'll try to talk around it."

Pilcher turned away from the bright light. "It's a big family, Lepidoptera. Maybe thirty thousand butterflies and a hundred thirty thousand moths. I'd like to take it out of the chrysalis—I'll have to if we're going to narrow it down."

"Okay. Can you do it in one piece?"

"I think so. See, this one had started out on its own power before it died. It had started an irregular fracture in the chrysalis right here. This may take a little while."

Pilcher spread the natural split in the case and eased the insect out. The bunched wings were soaked. Spreading them was like working with a wet, wadded facial tissue. No pattern was visible.

Roden was back with the books.

"Ready?" Pilcher said. "Okay, the prothoracic femur is concealed."

"What about pilifers?"

"No pilifers," Pilcher said. "Would you turn out the light, Officer Starling?"

She waited by the wall switch until Pilcher's penlight came on. He stood back from the table and shined it on the specimen. The insect's eyes glowed in the dark, reflecting the narrow beam.

"Owlet," Roden said.

"Probably, but which one?" Pilcher said. "Give us

the lights, please. It's a Noctuid, Officer Starling—a night moth. How many Noctuids are there, Roden?"

"Twenty-six hundred and . . . about twenty-six hundred have been described."

"Not many this big, though. Okay, let's see you shine, my man."

Roden's wiry red head covered the microscope.

"We have to go to chaetaxy now—studying the skin of the insect to narrow it down to one species," Pilcher said. "Roden's the best at it."

Starling had the sense that a kindness had passed in the room.

Roden responded by starting a fierce argument with Pilcher over whether the specimen's larval warts were arranged in circles or not. It raged on through the arrangement of the hairs on the abdomen.

"*Erebus odora*," Roden said at last.

"Let's go look," Pilcher said.

They took the specimen with them, down in the elevator to the level just above the great stuffed elephant and back into an enormous quad filled with pale green boxes. What was formerly a great hall had been split into two levels with decks to provide more storage for the Smithsonian's insects. They were in Neo-tropical now, moving into Noctuids. Pilcher consulted his notepad and stopped at a box chest-high in the great wall stack.

"You have to be careful with these things," he said, sliding the heavy metal door off the box and setting it on the floor. "You drop one on your foot and you hop for weeks."

He ran his finger down the stacked drawers, selected one, and pulled it out.

In the tray Starling saw the tiny preserved eggs, the caterpillar in a tube of alcohol, a cocoon peeled away from a specimen very similar to hers, and the adult—a big brown-black moth with a wingspan of nearly six inches, a furry body, and slender antennae.

"*Erebus odora*," Pilcher said. "The Black Witch Moth."

Roden was already turning pages. "'A tropical species sometimes straying up to Canada in the fall,'" he read.

"'The larvae eat acacia, catclaw, and similar plants. Indigenous West Indies, Southern US, considered a pest in Hawaii.'"

Fuckola, Starling thought. "Nuts," she said aloud. "They're all over."

"But they're not all over all the time." Pilcher's head was down. He pulled at his chin. "Do they double-brood, Roden?"

"Wait a second . . . yeah, in extreme south Florida and south Texas."

"When?"

"May and August."

"I was just thinking," Pilcher said. "Your specimen's a little better developed than the one we have, and it's fresh. It had started fracturing its cocoon to come out. In the West Indies or Hawaii, maybe, I could understand it, but it's winter here. In this country it would wait three months to come out. Unless it happened accidentally in a greenhouse, or somebody raised it."

"Raised it how?"

"In a cage, in a warm place, with some acacia leaves for the larvae to eat until they're ready to button up in their cocoons. It's not hard to do."

119

"Is it a popular hobby? Outside professional study, do a lot of people do it?"

"No, primarily it's entomologists trying to get a perfect specimen, maybe a few collectors. There's the silk industry too, they raise moths, but not this kind."

"Entomologists must have periodicals, professional journals, people that sell equipment," Starling said.

"Sure, and most of the publications come here."

"Let me make you a bundle," Roden said. "A couple of people here subscribe privately to the smaller newsletters—keep 'em locked up and make you give them a quarter just to look at the stupid things. I'll have to get those in the morning."

"I'll see they're picked up, thank you, Mr Roden."

Pilcher photocopied the references on *Erebus odora* and gave them to her, along with the insect. "I'll take you down," he said.

They waited for the elevator. "Most people love butterflies and hate moths," he said. "But moths are more—interesting, engaging."

"They're destructive."

"Some are, a lot are, but they live in all kinds of ways. Just like we do." Silence for one floor. "There's a moth, more than one in fact, that lives only on tears," he offered. "That's all they eat or drink."

"What kind of tears? Whose tears?"

"The tears of large land mammals, about our size. The old definition of moth was 'anything that gradually, silently eats, consumes, or wastes any other thing.' It was a verb for destruction too . . . Is this what you do all the time—hunt Buffalo Bill?"

"I do it all I can."

Pilcher polished his teeth, his tongue moving behind his lips like a cat beneath the covers. "Do you ever go out for cheeseburgers and beer or the amusing house wine?"

"Not lately."

"Will you go for some with me now? It's not far."

"No, but I'll treat when this is over—and Mr Roden can go too, naturally."

"There's nothing natural about that," Pilcher said. And at the door, "I hope you're through with this soon, Officer Starling."

She hurried to the waiting car.

Ardelia Mapp had left Starling's mail and half a Mounds candy bar on her bed. Mapp was asleep.

Starling carried her portable typewriter down to the laundry room, put it on the clothes-folding shelf and cranked in a carbon set. She had organized her notes on *Erebus odora* in her head on the ride back to Quantico, and she covered that quickly.

Then she ate the Mounds and wrote a memo to Crawford suggesting they cross-check the entomology publications' computerized mailing lists against the FBI's known-offender files and the files in the cities closest to the abductions, plus felon and sex-offender files of Metro Dade, San Antonio, and Houston, the areas where the moths were most plentiful.

There was another thing, too, that she had to bring up for a second time: *Let's ask Dr Lecter why he thought the perpetrator would start taking scalps.*

She delivered the paper to the night duty officer and fell into her grateful bed, the voices of the day still whispering, softer than Mapp's breathing across the room. On the swarming dark she saw the moth's wise little face. Those glowing eyes had looked at Buffalo Bill.

Out of the cosmic hangover the Smithsonian leaves came her last thought and a coda for her day: *Over this odd world, this half of the world that's dark now, I have to hunt a thing that lives on tears.*

CHAPTER

15

IN EAST MEMPHIS, Tennessee, Catherine Baker Martin and her best boyfriend were watching a late movie on television in his apartment and having a few hits off a bong pipe loaded with hashish. The commercial breaks grew longer and more frequent.

"I've got the munchies, want some popcorn?" she said.

"I'll go get it, give me your keys."

"Sit still. I need to see if Mom called, anyway."

She got up from the couch, a tall young woman, big-boned and well fleshed, nearly heavy, with a handsome face and a lot of clean hair. She found her shoes under the coffee table and went outside.

The February evening was more raw than cold. A light fog off the Mississippi River hung breast-high over the big parking area. Directly overhead she could see the dying moon, pale and thin as a bone fishhook. Looking up made her a little dizzy. She started across the parking field, navigating steadily toward her own front door a hundred yards away.

The brown panel truck was parked near her apartment,

among some motor homes and boats on trailers. She noticed it because it resembled the parcel delivery trucks which often brought presents from her mother.

As she passed near the truck, a lamp came on in the fog. It was a floor lamp with a shade, standing on the asphalt behind the truck. Beneath the lamp was an overstuffed armchair in red-flowered chintz, the big red flowers blooming in the fog. The two items were like a furniture grouping in a showroom.

Catherine Baker Martin blinked several times and kept going. She thought the word *surreal* and blamed the bong. She was all right. Somebody was moving in or moving out. In. Out. Somebody was always moving at the Stonehinge Villas. The curtain stirred in her apartment and she saw her cat on the sill, arching and pressing his side against the glass.

She had her key ready, and before she used it she looked back. A man climbed out of the back of the truck. She could see by the lamplight that he had a cast on his hand and his arm was in a sling. She went inside and locked the door behind her.

Catherine Baker Martin peeped around the curtain and saw the man trying to put the chair into the back of the truck. He gripped it with his good hand and tried to boost it with his knee. The chair fell over. He righted it, licked his finger and rubbed at a spot of parking-lot grime on the chintz.

She went outside.

"Help you with that?" She got the tone just right—helpful and that's all.

"Would you? Thanks." An odd, strained voice. Not a local accent.

The floor lamp lit his face from below, distorting his features, but she could see his body plainly. He had on pressed khaki trousers and some kind of chamois shirt, unbuttoned over a freckled chest. His chin and cheeks were hairless, as smooth as a woman's, and his eyes only pinpoint gleams above his cheekbones in the shadows of the lamp.

He looked at her too, and she was sensitive to that. Men were often surprised at her size when she got close to them and some concealed it better than others.

"Good," he said.

There was an unpleasant odor about the man, and she noticed with distaste that his chamois shirt still had hairs on it, curly ones across the shoulders and beneath the arms.

It was easy lifting the chair onto the low floor of the truck.

"Let's slide it to the front, do you mind?" He climbed inside and moved some clutter, the big flat pans you can slide under a vehicle to drain the oil, and a small hand winch called a coffin hoist.

They pushed the chair forward until it was just behind the seats.

"Are you about a fourteen?" he said.

"What?"

"Would you hand me that rope? It's just at your feet."

When she bent to look, he brought the plaster cast down on the back of her head. She thought she'd bumped her head and she raised her hand to it as the cast came down again, smashing her fingers against her skull, and down again, this time behind her ear, a succession of blows, none of them too hard, as she slumped over the chair. She slid to the floor of the truck and lay on her side.

The man watched her for a second, then pulled off his cast and the arm sling. Quickly he brought the lamp into the truck and closed the rear doors.

He pulled her collar back and, with a flashlight, read the size tag on her blouse.

"Good," he said.

He slit the blouse up the back with a pair of bandage scissors, pulled the blouse off, and handcuffed her hands behind her. Spreading a mover's pad on the floor of the truck, he rolled her onto her back.

She was not wearing a brassiere. He prodded her big breasts with his fingers and felt their weight and resilience.

"Good," he said.

There was a pink suck mark on her left breast. He licked his finger to rub it as he had done the chintz and nodded when the lividity went away with light pressure. He rolled her onto her face and checked her scalp, parting her thick hair with his fingers. The padded cast hadn't cut her.

He checked her pulse with two fingers on the side of her neck and found it strong.

"Gooood," he said. He had a long way to drive to his two-story house and he'd rather not field-dress her here.

Catherine Baker Martin's cat watched out the window as the truck pulled away, the taillights getting closer and closer together.

Behind the cat the telephone was ringing. The machine

in the bedroom answered, its red light blinking in the dark.

The caller was Catherine's mother, the junior US Senator from Tennessee.

CHAPTER

16

IN THE 1980s, the Golden Age of Terrorism, procedures were in place to deal with a kidnapping affecting a member of Congress:

At 2:45 A.M. the special agent in charge of the Memphis FBI office reported to headquarters in Washington that Senator Ruth Martin's only daughter had disappeared.

At 3:00 A.M. two unmarked vans pulled out of the damp basement garage at the Washington field office, Buzzard's Point. One van went to the Senate Office Building, where technicians placed monitoring and recording equipment on the telephones in Senator Martin's office and put a Title 3 wiretap on the pay phones closest to the Senator's office. The Justice Department woke the most junior member of the Senate Select Intelligence Committee to provide the obligatory notice of the tap.

The other vehicle, an "eyeball van" with one-way glass and surveillance equipment, was parked on Virginia Avenue to cover the front of the Watergate West,

Senator Martin's Washington residence. Two of the van's occupants went inside to install monitoring equipment on the Senator's home telephones.

Bell Atlantic estimated the mean trace time at seventy seconds on any ransom call placed from a domestic digital switching system.

The Reactive Squad at Buzzard's Point went to double shifts in the event of a ransom drop in the Washington area. Their radio procedure changed to mandatory encryption to protect any possible ransom drop from intrusion by news helicoptors—that kind of irresponsibility on the part of the news business was rare, but it had happened.

The Hostage Rescue Team went to an alert status one level short of airborne.

Everyone hoped Catherine Baker Martin's disappearance was a professional kidnapping for ransom; that possibility offered the best chance for her survival.

Nobody mentioned the worst possibility of all.

Then, shortly before dawn in Memphis, a city patrolman investigating a prowler complaint on Winchester Avenue stopped an elderly man collecting aluminum cans and junk along the shoulder of the road. In his cart the patrolman found a woman's blouse, still buttoned in front. The blouse was slit up the back like a funeral suit. The laundry mark was Catherine Baker Martin's.

Jack Crawford was driving south from his home in Arlington at 6:30 A.M. when the telephone in his car beeped for the second time in two minutes.

"Nine twenty-two forty."

"Forty stand by for Alpha 4."

Crawford spotted a rest area, pulled in, and stopped to give his full attention to the telephone. Alpha 4 is the Director of the FBI

"Jack—you up on Catherine Martin?"

"The night duty officer called me just now."

"Then you know about the blouse. Talk to me."

"Buzzard's Point went to kidnap alert," Crawford said. "I'd prefer they didn't stand down yet. When they do stand down, I'd like to keep the phone surveillance. Slit blouse or not, we don't know for sure it's Bill. If it's a copycat, he might call for ransom. Who's doing taps and traces in Tennessee, us or them?"

"Them. The state police. They're pretty good. Phil Adler called from the White House to tell me about the President's 'intense interest.' We could use a win here, Jack."

"That had occurred to me. Where's the Senator?"

"En route to Memphis. She got me at home a minute ago. You can imagine."

"Yes." Crawford knew Senator Martin from budget hearings.

"She's coming down with all the weight she's got."

"I don't blame her."

"Neither do I," the Director said. "I've told her we're going flat-out, just as we've done all along. She is . . . she's aware of your personal situation and she's offered you a company Lear. Use it—come home at night if you can."

"Good. The Senator's tough, Tommy. If she tries to run it, we'll butt heads."

"I know. Do a set-pick off me if you have to. What have we got at the best—six or seven days, Jack?"

"I don't know. If he panics when he finds out who she is—he might just do her and dump her."

"Where are you?"

"Two miles from Quantico."

"Will the strip at Quantico take a Lear?"

"Yes."

"Twenty minutes."

"Yes, sir."

Crawford punched numbers into his phone and pulled back into the traffic.

SORE FROM a troubled sleep, Clarice Starling stood in her bathrobe and bunny slippers, towel over her shoulder, waiting to get in the bathroom she and Mapp shared with the students next door. The news from Memphis on the radio froze her for half a breath.

"Oh God," she said. "Oh boy. ALL RIGHT IN THERE! THIS BATHROOM IS SEIZED. COME OUT WITH YOUR PANTS UP. THIS IS NOT A DRILL!" She climbed into the shower with a startled nextdoor neighbor. "Ooch over, Gracie, and would you pass me that soap?"

Ear cocked to the telephone, she packed for overnight and set her forensic kit by the door. She made sure the switchboard knew she was in her room and gave up breakfast to stick by the phone. At ten minutes to class time, with no word, she hurried down to Behavioral Science with her equipment.

"Mr Crawford left for Memphis forty-five minutes ago," the secretary told her sweetly. "Burroughs went, and Stafford from the lab left from National."

"I put a report here for him last night. Did he leave any message for me? I'm Clarice Starling."

"Yes, I know who you are. I have three copies of your telephone number right here, and there are several more on his desk, I believe. No, he didn't leave a thing for you, Clarice." The woman looked at Starling's luggage. "Would you like me to tell him something when he calls in?"

"Did he leave a Memphis phone number on his three-card?"

"No, he'll call with it. Don't you have classes today, Clarice? You're still in school, aren't you?"

"Yes. Yes, I am."

Starling's entry, late, into the classroom was not eased by Gracie Pitman, the young woman she had displaced in the shower. Gracie Pitman sat directly behind Starling. It seemed a long way to her seat. Gracie Pitman's tongue had time to make two full revolutions in her downy cheek before Starling could submerge into the class.

With no breakfast she sat through two hours of "The Good-Faith Warrant Exception to the Exclusionary Rule in Search and Seizure" before she could get to the vending machine and chug a Coke.

She checked her box for a message at noon and there was nothing. It occurred to her then, as it had on a few other occasions in her life, that intense frustration tastes very much like the patent medicine called Fleet's that she'd had to take as a child.

Some days you wake up changed. This was one for Starling, she could tell. What she had seen yesterday at the Potter Funeral Home had caused in her a small tectonic shift.

Starling had studied psychology and criminology in a good school. In her life she had seen some of the hideously offhand ways in which the world breaks things. But she hadn't really *known* and now she knew: sometimes the family of man produces, behind a human face, a mind whose pleasure is what lay on the porcelain table at Potter, West Virginia, in the room with the cabbage roses. Starling's first apprehension of that mind was worse than anything she could see on the autopsy scales. The knowledge would lie against her skin forever, and she knew she had to form a callus or it would wear her through.

The school routine didn't help her. All day she had the feeling that things were going on just over the horizon. She seemed to hear a vast murmur of events, like the sound from a distant stadium. Suggestions of movement unsettled her, groups passing in the hallway, cloud shadows moving over, the sound of an airplane.

After class Starling ran too many laps and then she swam. She swam until she thought about the floaters and then she didn't want the water on her anymore.

She watched the seven o'clock news with Mapp and a dozen other students in the recreation room. The abduction of Senator Martin's daughter was not the lead item, but it was first after the Geneva arms talks.

There was film from Memphis, starting with the sign of the Stonehinge Villas, shot across the revolving light of a patrol car. The media was blitzing the story and, with little new to report, reporters interviewed each other in the parking lot at Stonehinge. Memphis and Shelby County authorities ducked their heads to unaccustomed banks of microphones. In a jostling, squealing hell of lens flare and audio feedback, they listed the things they didn't know. Still-photographers stooped and darted, back-pedaling into the TV minicams whenever investigators entered or left Catherine Baker Martin's apartment.

A brief, ironic cheer went up in the Academy recreation room when Crawford's face appeared briefly in the apartment window. Starling smiled on one side of her mouth.

She wondered if Buffalo Bill was watching. She wondered what he thought of Crawford's face or if he even knew who Crawford was.

Others seemed to think Bill might be watching too.

There was Senator Martin, on television live with Peter Jennings. She stood alone in her child's bedroom, a Southwestern University pennant and posters favoring Wile E. Coyote and the Equal Rights Amendment on the wall behind her.

She was a tall woman with a strong, plain face.

"I'm speaking now to the person who is holding my daughter," she said. She walked closer to the camera, causing an unscheduled refocus, and spoke as she never would have spoken to a terrorist.

"You have the power to let my daughter go unharmed. Her name is Catherine. She's very gentle and understanding. Please let my daughter go, please release her unharmed. You have control of this situation. You have the power. You are in charge. I know you can feel love and compassion. You can protect her against anything that might want to harm her. You now have a wonderful chance to show the whole world that you are capable of great kindness, that you are big enough to treat others better than the world has treated you. Her name is Catherine."

Senator Martin's eyes cut away from the camera as the picture switched to a home movie of a toddler helping herself walk by hanging onto the mane of a large collie.

The Senator's voice went on: "The film you're seeing now is Catherine as a little child. Release Catherine. Release her unharmed anywhere in this country and you'll have my help and my friendship."

Now a series of still photographs—Catherine Martin at eight, holding the tiller of a sailboat. The boat was up on blocks and her father was painting the hull. Two recent photographs of the young woman, a full shot and a close-up of her face.

Now back to the Senator in close-up: "I promise you in front of this entire country, you'll have my unstinting aid whenever you need it. I'm well equipped to help you. I am a United States Senator. I serve on the Armed Services Committee. I am deeply involved in the Strategic Defense Initiative, the space weapons systems which everyone calls 'Star Wars.' If you have enemies, I will fight them. If anyone interferes with you, I can stop them. You can call me at any time, day or night. Catherine is my daughter's name. Please, show us your strength," Senator Martin said in closing, "release Catherine unharmed."

"Boy, is that smart," Starling said. She was trembling like a terrier. "Jesus, that's smart."

"What, the Star Wars?" Mapp said. "If the aliens are trying to control Buffalo Bill's thoughts from another planet, Senator Martin can protect him—is that the pitch?"

Starling nodded. "A lot of paranoid schizophrenics have that specific hallucination—alien control. If that's the way Bill's wired, maybe this approach could bring him out. It's a damn good shot, though, and she stood up there and fired it, didn't she? At the least it might buy Catherine a few more days. They may have time to work on Bill a little. Or they may not; Crawford thinks his period may be getting shorter. They can *try* this, they can try other things."

"Nothing I *wouldn't* try if he had one of mine. Why did she keep saying 'Catherine,' why the name all the time?"

"She's trying to make Buffalo Bill see Catherine as a person. They're thinking he'll have to depersonalize her, he'll have to see her as an object before he can tear her up. Serial murderers talk about that in prison interviews, some of them. They say it's like working on a doll."

"Do you see Crawford behind Senator Martin's statement?"

"Maybe, or maybe Dr Bloom—there he is," Starling said. On the screen was an interview taped several weeks earlier with Dr Alan Bloom of the University of Chicago on the subject of serial murder.

Dr Bloom refused to compare Buffalo Bill with Francis Dolarhyde or Garrett Hobbs, or any of the others in his experience. He refused to use the term "Buffalo Bill." In fact he didn't say much at all, but he was known to be an expert, probably *the* expert on the subject, and the network wanted to show his face.

They used his final statement for the snapper at the end of the report: "There's nothing we can threaten him with that's more terrible than what he faces every day. What we *can* do is ask him to come to us. We can promise him kind treatment and relief, and we can mean it absolutely and sincerely."

"Couldn't we all use some relief," Mapp said. "Damn if I couldn't use some relief myself. Slick obfuscation and facile bullshit, I love it. He didn't tell them anything, but then he probably didn't stir Bill up much either."

"I can stop thinking about that kid in West Virginia for a while," Starling said, "it goes away for, say, a half an hour at a time, and then it pokes me in the throat. Glitter polish on her nails—let me not get into it."

Mapp, rummaging among her many enthusiasms, lightened Starling's gloom at dinner and fascinated eavesdroppers by comparing slant-rhymes in the works of Stevie Wonder and Emily Dickinson.

On the way back to the room, Starling snatched a message out of her box and read this: *Please call Albert Roden*, and a telephone number.

"That just proves my theory," she told Mapp as they flopped on their beds with their books.

"What's that?"

"You meet two guys, right? The wrong one'll call you every God damned time."

"I *been* knowing that."

The telephone rang.

Mapp touched the end of her nose with her pencil. "If that's Hot Bobby Lowrance, would you tell him

I'm in the library?" Mapp said. "I'll call him tomorrow, tell him."

It was Crawford calling from an airplane, his voice scratchy on the phone. "Starling, pack for two nights and meet me in an hour."

She thought he was gone, there was only a hollow humming on the telephone, then the voice came back abruptly "—won't need the kit, just clothes."

"Meet you where?"

"The Smithsonian." He started talking to someone else before he punched off.

"Jack Crawford," Starling said, flipping her bag on the bed.

Mapp appeared over the top of her *Federal Code of Criminal Procedure*. She watched Starling pack, an eyelid dropping over one of her great dark eyes.

"I don't want to put anything on your mind," she said.

"Yes, you do," Starling said. She knew what was coming.

Mapp had made the Law Review at the University of Maryland while working at night. Her academic standing at the Academy was number two in the class, her attitude toward the books was pure banzai.

"You're supposed to take the Criminal Code exam tomorrow and the PE test in two days. You make sure Supremo Crawford knows you could get recycled if he's not careful. Soon as he says, 'Good work, Trainee Starling,' don't you say, 'The pleasure was mine.' You get right in his old Easter Island face and say, 'I'm counting on you to see to it *yourself* that I'm not recycled for missing school.' Understand what I'm saying?"

139

"I can get a makeup on the Code," Starling said, opening a barrette with her teeth.

"Right, and, you fail it with no time to study, you think they won't recycle you? Are you kidding me? Girl, they'll sail you off the back steps like a dead Easter chick. Gratitude's got a short half-life, Clarice. Make him say *no recycle.* You've got good grades—make him say it. I never would find another roommate that can iron as fast as you can at one minute to class."

Starling had her old Pinto moving up the four-lane at a steady lope, one mile an hour below the speed where the shimmy sets in. The smells of hot oil and mildew, the rattles underneath, the transmission's whine resonated faintly with memories of her father's pickup truck, her memories of riding beside him with her squirming brothers and sister.

She was doing the driving now, driving at night, the white dashes passing under blip blip blip. She had time to think. Her fears breathed on her from close behind her neck; other, recent memories squirmed beside her.

Starling was very much afraid Catherine Baker Martin's body had been found. When Buffalo Bill found out who she was, he might have panicked. He might have killed her and dumped her body with a bug in the throat.

Maybe Crawford was bringing the bug to be identified. Why else would he want her at the Smithsonian? But any agent could carry a bug into the Smithsonian, an FBI messenger could do it for that matter. And he told her to pack for two days.

She could understand Crawford not explaining it to her over an unsecured radio link, but it was maddening to wonder.

She found an all-news station on the radio and waited through the weather report. When the news came, it was no help. The story from Memphis was a rehash of the seven o'clock news. Senator Martin's daughter was missing. Her blouse had been found slit up the back in the style of Buffalo Bill. No witnesses. The victim found in West Virginia remained unidentified.

West Virginia. Among Clarice Starling's memories of the Potter Funeral Home was something hard and valuable. Something durable, shining apart from the dark revelations. Something to keep. She deliberately recalled it now and found that she could squeeze it like a talisman. In the Potter Funeral Home, standing at the sink, she had found strength from a source that surprised and pleased her—the memory of her mother. Starling was a seasoned survivor on hand-me-down grace from her late father through her brothers; she was surprised and moved by this bounty she had found.

She parked the Pinto beneath FBI headquarters at Tenth and Pennsylvania. Two television crews were set up on the sidewalk, reporters looking over-groomed in the lights. They were intoning standup reports with the J. Edgar Hoover Building in the background. Starling skirted the lights and walked the two blocks to the Smithsonian's National Museum of Natural History.

She could see a few lighted windows high in the old building. A Baltimore County Police van was parked in the semicircular drive. Crawford's driver, Jeff, waited at the wheel of a new surveillance van behind it. When he saw Starling coming, he spoke into a hand-held radio.

THE GUARD took Clarice Starling to the second level above the Smithsonian's great stuffed elephant. The elevator door opened onto that vast dim floor and Crawford was waiting there alone, his hands in the pockets of his raincoat.

"Evening, Starling."

"Hello," she said.

Crawford spoke over her shoulder to the guard. "We can make it from here by ourselves, Officer, thank you."

Crawford and Starling walked side by side along a corridor in the stacked trays and cases of anthropological specimens. A few ceiling lights were on, not many. As she fell with him into the hunched, reflective attitude of a campus stroll, Starling became aware that Crawford wanted to put his hand on her shoulder, that he would have done it if it were possible for him to touch her.

She waited for him to say something. Finally, she stopped, put her hands in her pockets too, and they faced each other across the passage in the silence of the bones.

Crawford leaned his head back against the cases and took a deep breath through his nose. "Catherine Martin's probably still alive," he said.

Starling nodded, kept her head down after the last nod. Maybe he would find it easier to talk if she didn't look at him. He was steady, but something had hold of him. Starling wondered for a second if his wife had died. Or maybe spending all day with Catherine's grieving mother had done it.

"Memphis was pretty much of a wipe," he said. "He got her on the parking lot, I think. Nobody saw it. She went in her apartment and then she came back out for some reason. She didn't mean to stay out long—she left the door ajar and flipped the deadbolt so it wouldn't lock behind her. Her keys were on top of the TV. Nothing disturbed inside. I don't think she was in the apartment long. She never got as far as her answering machine in the bedroom. The message light was still blinking when her yo-yo boyfriend finally called the Police." Crawford idly let his hand fall into a tray of bones, and quickly took it out again.

"So now he's got her, Starling. The networks agreed not to do a countdown on the evening news—Dr Bloom thinks it eggs him on. A couple of the tabloids'll do it anyway."

In one previous abduction, clothing slit up the back had been found soon enough to identify a Buffalo Bill victim while she was still being held alive. Starling remembered the black-bordered countdown on the front pages of the trash papers. It reached eighteen days before the body floated.

"So Catherine Baker Martin's waiting in Bill's green

room, Starling, and we have maybe a week. That's at the outside—Bloom thinks his period's getting shorter."

This seemed like a lot of talk for Crawford. The theatrical "green room" reference smacked of bullshit. Starling waited for him to get to the point, and then he did.

"But this time, Starling, *this* time we may have a little break."

She looked up at him beneath her brows, hopeful and watchful too.

"We've got another insect. Your fellows, Pilcher and that . . . other one."

"Roden."

"They're working on it."

"Where was it—Cincinnati?—the girl in the freezer?"

"No. Come on and I'll show you. Let's see what you think about it."

"Entomology's the other way, Mr Crawford."

"I know," he said.

They rounded the corner to the door of Anthropology. Light and voices came through the frosted glass. She went in.

Three men in laboratory coats worked at a table in the center of the room beneath a brilliant light. Starling couldn't see what they were doing. Jerry Burroughs from Behavioral Science was looking over their shoulders taking notes on a clipboard. There was a familiar odor in the room.

Then one of the men in white moved to put something in the sink and she could see all right.

In a stainless-steel tray on the workbench was "Klaus," the head she had found in the Split City Mini-Storage.

"Klaus had the bug in his throat," Crawford said. "Hold on a minute, Starling. Jerry, are you talking to the wire room?"

Burroughs was reading from his clipboard into the telephone. He put his hand over the mouthpiece. "Yeah, Jack, they're drying the art on Klaus."

Crawford took the receiver from him. "Bobby, don't wait for the Interpol split. Get a picture wire and transmit the photographs now, along with the medical. Scandinavian countries, West Germany, the Netherlands. Be sure to say Klaus could be a merchant sailor that jumped ship. Mention that their National Health may have a claim for the cheekbone fracture. Call it the what, the zygomatic arch. Make sure you move both dental charts, the universal and the Fédération Dentaire. They're coming with an age, but emphasize that it's a rough estimate—you can't depend on skull sutures for that." He gave the phone back to Burroughs. "Where's your gear, Starling?"

"The guard office downstairs."

"Johns Hopkins found the insect," Crawford said as they waited for the elevator. "They were doing the head for the Baltimore County Police. It was in the throat, just like the girl in West Virginia."

"Just like West Virginia."

"You clucked. Johns Hopkins found it about seven tonight. The Baltimore district attorney called me on the plane. They sent the whole thing over, Klaus and all, so we could see it *in situ*. They also wanted an opinion from Dr Angel on Klaus's age and how old he was when he fractured his cheekbone. They consult the Smithsonian just like we do."

146

"I have to deal with this a second. You're saying maybe Buffalo Bill killed *Klaus?* Years ago?"

"Does it seem farfetched, too much of a coincidence?"

"Right this second it does."

"Let it cook a minute."

"Dr Lecter told me where to find Klaus," Starling said.

"Yes, he did."

"Dr Lecter told me his patient, Benjamin Raspail, claimed to have killed Klaus. But Lecter said he believed it was probably accidental erotic asphyxia."

"That's what he said."

"You think maybe Dr Lecter knows exactly how Klaus died, and it wasn't Raspail, and it wasn't erotic asphyxia?"

"Klaus had a bug in his throat, the girl in West Virginia had a bug in her throat. I never saw that anywhere else. Never read about it, never heard of it. What do you think?"

"I think you told me to pack for two days. You want me to ask Dr Lecter, don't you?"

"You're the one he talks to, Starling." Crawford looked so sad when he said, "I figure you're game."

She nodded.

"We'll talk on the way to the asylum," he said.

"DR LECTER had a big psychiatric practice for years before we caught him for the murders," Crawford said. "He did a slew of psychiatric evaluations for the Maryland and Virginia courts and some others up and down the East Coast. He's seen a lot of the criminally insane. Who knows what he turned loose, just for fun? That's one way he could know. Also, he knew Raspail socially and Raspail told him things in therapy. Maybe Raspail told him who killed Klaus."

Crawford and Starling faced each other in swivel chairs in the back of the surveillance van, whizzing north on US 95 toward Baltimore, thirty-seven miles away. Jeff, in the driver's compartment, clearly had orders to step on it.

"Lecter offered to help, and I had no part of him. I've had his help before. He gave us nothing useful and he helped Will Graham get a knife jammed through his face last time. For fun.

"But a bug in Klaus's throat, a bug in the girl's throat in West Virginia, I can't ignore that. Alan Bloom's never heard of that specific act before, and neither have I. Have you ever run across it before, Starling? You've read the literature since I have."

"Never. Inserting other objects, yes, but never an insect."

"Two things to begin with. First, we go on the premise that Dr Lecter really knows something concrete. Second, we remember that Lecter looks only for the fun. Never forget fun. He has to want Buffalo Bill caught while Catherine Martin's still alive. All the fun and benefits have to lie in that direction. We've got nothing to threaten him with—he's lost his commode seat and his books already. That cleans him out."

"What would happen if we just told him the situation and offered him something—a cell with a view? That's what he asked for when he offered to help."

"He offered to *help*, Starling. He didn't offer to snitch. Snitching wouldn't give him enough of a chance to show off. You're doubtful. You favor the truth. Listen, Lecter's in no hurry. He's followed this like it was baseball. We ask him to snitch, he'll wait. He won't do it right away."

"Even for a reward? Something he won't get if Catherine Martin dies?"

"Say we tell him we *know* he's got information and we want him to snitch. He'd have the most fun by waiting and acting like he's trying to remember week after week, getting Senator Martin's hopes up and letting Catherine die, and then tormenting the next mother and the next, getting their hopes up, always just about to remember—that would be better than

149

having a view. It's the kind of thing he lives on. It's his nourishment.

"I'm not sure you get wiser as you get older, Starling, but you do learn to dodge a certain amount of hell. We can dodge some right there."

"So Dr Lecter has to think we're coming to him strictly for theory and insight," Starling said.

"Correct."

"Why did you tell me? Why didn't you just send me in to ask him that way?"

"I level with you. You'll do the same when you have a command. Nothing else works for long."

"So there's no mention of the insect in Klaus's throat, no connection between Klaus and Buffalo Bill."

"No. You came back to him because you were so impressed that he could predict Buffalo Bill would start scalping. I'm on the record dismissing him and so is Alan Bloom. But I'm letting you fool with it. You have an offer for some privileges—stuff that only somebody as powerful as Senator Martin could get for him. He has to believe he should hurry because the offer ends if Catherine dies. The Senator totally loses interest in him if that happens. And if he fails, it's because he's not smart and knowledgeable enough to do what he said he could do—it's not because he's holding out to spite us."

"*Will* the Senator lose interest?"

"Better you should be able to say under oath that you never knew the answer to that question."

"I see." So Senator Martin hadn't been told. That took some nerve. Clearly, Crawford was afraid of interference, afraid the Senator might make the mistake of appealing to Dr Lecter.

"*Do* you see?"

"Yes. How can he be specific enough to steer us to Buffalo Bill without showing he's got special knowledge? How can he do that with just theory and insight?"

"I don't know, Starling. He's had a long time to think about it. He's waited through six victims."

The scrambler phone in the van buzzed and blinked with the first of a series of calls Crawford had placed with the FBI switchboard.

Over the next twenty minutes he talked to officers he knew in the Dutch State Police and Royal Marechausee, an *Overstelojtnant* in the Swedish Technical Police who had studied at Quantico, a personal acquaintance who was assistant to the *Rigspolitichef* of the Danish governmental police, and he surprised Starling by breaking into French with the night command desk of the Belgian Police Criminelle. Always he stressed the need for speed in identifying Klaus and his associates. Each jurisdiction would already have the request on its Interpol telex but, with the old-boy network buzzing, the request wouldn't hang from the machine for hours.

Starling could see that Crawford had chosen the van for its communications—it had the new Voice Privacy system—but the job would have been easier from his office. Here he had to juggle his notebooks on the tiny desk in marginal light, and they bounced each time the tires hit a tar strip. Starling's field experience was small, but she knew how unusual it was for a section chief to be booming along in a van on an errand like this. He could have briefed her over the radio telephone. She was glad he had not.

Starling had the feeling that the quiet and calm in

this van, the time allowed for this mission to proceed in an orderly way, had been purchased at a high price. Listening to Crawford on the phone confirmed it.

He was speaking with the Director at home now. "No, sir. Did they roll over for it? . . . How long? No, sir. No. No wire. Tommy, that's my recommendation, I stand on it. I *do not* want her to wear a wire. Dr Bloom says the same thing. He's fogged in at O'Hare. He'll come as soon as it clears. Right."

Then Crawford had a cryptic telephone conversation with the night nurse at his house. When he had finished, he looked out the one-way window of the van for perhaps a minute, his glasses held on his knee in the crook of his finger, his face looking naked as the oncoming lights crawled across it. Then he put the glasses on and turned back to Starling.

"We have Lecter for three days. If we don't get any results, Baltimore sweats him until the court pulls them off."

"Sweating him didn't work last time. Dr Lecter doesn't sweat much."

"What did he give them after all that, a paper chicken?"

"A chicken, yes." The crumpled origami chicken was still in Starling's purse. She smoothed it out on the little desk and made it peck.

"I don't blame the Baltimore cops. He's their prisoner. If Catherine floats, they have to be able to tell Senator Martin they tried it all."

"How is Senator Martin?"

"Game but hurting. She's a smart, tough woman with a lot of sense, Starling. You'd probably like her."

"Will Johns Hopkins and Baltimore County Homicide keep quiet about the bug in Klaus's throat? Can we keep it out of the papers?"

"For three days at least."

"That took some doing."

"We can't trust Frederick Chilton, or anybody else at the hospital," Crawford said. "If Chilton knows, the world knows. Chilton has to know you're there, but it's simply a favor you're doing Baltimore Homicide, trying to close the Klaus case—it has nothing to do with Buffalo Bill."

"And I'm doing this late at night?"

"That's the only time I'd give you. I should tell you, the business about the bug in West Virginia will be in the morning papers. The Cincinnati coroner's office spilled it, so that's no secret anymore. It's an inside detail that Lecter can get from you, and it doesn't matter, really, as long as he doesn't know we found one in Klaus too."

"What have we got to trade him?"

"I'm working on it," Crawford said, and turned back to his telephones.

A BIG BATHROOM, all white tile and skylights and sleek
Italian fixtures standing against exposed old brick.
An elaborate vanity flanked by tall plants and loaded
with cosmetics, the mirror beaded by the steam the
shower made. From the shower came humming in a
key too high for the unearthly voice. The song was Fats
Waller's "Cash for Your Trash," from the musical *Ain't
Misbehavin'*. Sometimes the voice broke into the words:

"Save up all your old newsPA-PERS.
Save and pile 'em like a high skySCRAPER
DAH DAHDAHDAH DAH DAH DAHDAH
DAH DAH . . ."

Whenever there were words, a small dog scratched at
the bathroom door.

In the shower was Jame Gumb, white male, thirty-
four, six feet one inch, 205 pounds, brown and blue,
no distinguishing marks. He pronounces his first name
like *James* without the *s*, Jame. He insists on it.

After his first rinse, Gumb applied Friction des Bains, rubbing it over his chest and buttocks with his hands and using a dishmop on the parts he did not like to touch. His legs and feet were a little stubbly, but he decided they would do.

Gumb toweled himself pink and applied a good skin emollient. His full-length mirror had a shower curtain on a bar in front of it.

Gumb used the dishmop to tuck his penis and testicles back between his legs. He whipped the shower curtain aside and stood before the mirror, hitting a hipshot pose despite the grinding it caused in his private parts.

"Do something *for* me, honey. Do something for me SOON." He used the upper range of his naturally deep voice, and he believed he was getting better at it. The hormones he'd taken—Premarin for a while and then diethylstilbestrol, orally—couldn't do anything for his voice, but they had thinned the hair a little across his slightly budding breasts. A lot of electrolysis had removed Gumb's beard and shaped his hairline into a widow's peak, but he did not look like a woman. He looked like a man inclined to fight with his nails as well as his fists and feet.

Whether his behavior was an earnest, inept attempt to swish or a hateful mocking would be hard to say on short acquaintance, and short acquaintances were the only kind he had.

"Whatcha gonna do for meeee?"

The dog scratched on the door at the sound of his voice. Gumb put on his robe and let the dog in. He picked up the little champagne-colored poodle and kissed her plump back.

"Ye-e-e-e-s. Are you *famished*, Precious? I am too."

He switched the little dog from one arm to the other to open the bedroom door. She squirmed to get down.

"Just a mo', sweetheart." With his free hand he picked up a Mini-14 carbine from the floor beside the bed and laid it across the pillows. "*Now*. Now, then. We'll have our supper in a minute." He put the little dog on the floor while he found his nightclothes. She trailed him eagerly downstairs to the kitchen.

Jame Gumb took three TV dinners from his microwave oven. There were two Hungry Man dinners for himself and one Lean Cuisine for the poodle.

The poodle greedily ate her entrée and the dessert, leaving the vegetable. Jame Gumb left only the bones on his two trays.

He let the little dog out the back door and, clutching his robe closed against the chill, he watched her squat in the narrow strip of light from the doorway.

"You haven't done Number Two-ooo. All right, I won't watch." But he took a sly peek between his fingers. "Oh, *super*, you little baggage, aren't you a perfect lady? Come on, let's go to bed."

Mr Gumb liked to go to bed. He did it several times a night. He liked to get up too, and sit in one or another of his many rooms without turning on the light, or work for a little while in the night, when he was hot with something creative.

He started to turn out the kitchen light, but paused, his lips in a judicious pout as he considered the litter of supper. He gathered up the three TV trays and wiped off the table.

A switch at the head of the stairs turned on the lights

in the basement. Jame Gumb started down, carrying the trays. The little dog cried in the kitchen and nosed open the door behind him.

"All right, Silly Billy." He scooped up the poodle and carried her down. She wriggled and nosed at the trays in his other hand. "No you don't, you've had enough." He put her down and she followed close beside him through the rambling, multilevel basement.

In a basement room directly beneath the kitchen was a well, long dry. Its stone rim, reinforced with modern well rings and cement, rose two feet above the sandy floor. The original wooden safety cover, too heavy for a child to lift, was still in place. There was a trap in the lid big enough to lower a bucket through. The trap was open and Jame Gumb scraped his trays and the dog's tray into it.

The bones and bits of vegetable winked out of sight into the absolute blackness of the well. The little dog sat up and begged.

"No, no, all gone," Gumb said. "You're too fat as it is."

He climbed the basement stairs, whispering "Fatty Bread, Fatty Bread" to his little dog. He gave no sign if he heard the cry, still fairly strong and sane, that echoed up from the black hole:

"PLEEASE."

CLARICE STARLING entered the Baltimore State Hospital for the Criminally Insane at a little after 10:00 P.M. She was alone. Starling had hoped Dr Frederick Chilton wouldn't be there, but he was waiting for her in his office.

Chilton wore an English-cut sportscoat in windowpane check. The double vent and skirts gave it a peplum effect, Starling thought. She hoped to God he hadn't dressed for her.

The room was bare in front of his desk, except for a straight chair screwed to the floor. Starling stood beside it while her greeting hung in the air. She could smell the cold, rank pipes in the rack beside Chilton's humidor.

Dr Chilton finished examining his collection of Franklin Mint locomotives and turned to her.

"Would you like a cup of decaf?"

"No, thanks. I'm sorry to interrupt your evening."

"You're still trying to find out something about that head business," Dr Chilton said.

"Yes. The Baltimore district attorney's office told

158

me they'd made the arrangements with you, Doctor."

"Oh yes. I work *very* closely with the authorities here, Miss Starling. Are you doing an article or a thesis, by the way?"

"No."

"Have you ever been published in any of the professional journals?"

"No, I never have. This is just an errand the US Attorney's office asked me to do for Baltimore County Homicide. We left them with an open case and we're just helping them tidy up the loose ends." Starling found her distaste for Chilton made the lying easier.

"Are you wired, Miss Starling?"

"Am I—"

"Are you wearing a microphone device to record what Dr Lecter says? The police term is 'wired,' I'm sure you've heard it."

"No."

Dr Chilton took a small Pearlcorder from his desk and popped a cassette into it. "Then put this in your purse. I'll have it transcribed and forward you a copy. You can use it to augment your notes."

"No, I can't do that, Dr Chilton."

"Why on earth not? The Baltimore authorities have asked me all along for my analysis of anything Lecter says about this Klaus business."

Get around Chilton if you can, Crawford told her. *We can step on him in a minute with a court order, but Lecter will smell it. He can see through Chilton like a CAT scan.*

"The US Attorney thought we'd try an informal approach first. If I recorded Dr Lecter without his

159

knowledge, and he found out, it would really, it would be the end of any kind of working atmosphere we had. I'm sure you'd agree with that."

"How would he find out?"

He'd read it in the newspaper with everything else you know, you fucking jerk. She didn't answer. "If this should go anywhere and he has to depose, you'd be the first one to see the material and I'm sure you'd be invited to serve as expert witness. We're just trying to get a lead out of him now."

"Do you know why he talks to you, Miss Starling?"

"No, Dr Chilton."

He looked at each item in the claque of certificates and diplomas on the walls behind his desk as though he were conducting a poll. Now a slow turn to Starling. "Do you *really* feel you know what you're doing?"

"Sure I do." *Lot of "do's" there.* Starling's legs were shaky from too much exercise. She didn't want to fight with Chilton. She had to have something left when she got to Lecter.

"What you're doing is coming into my hospital to conduct an interview and refusing to share information with me."

"I'm acting on my instructions, Dr Chilton. I have the US Attorney's night number here. Now, please, either discuss it with him or let me do my job."

"I'm not a turnkey here, Miss Starling. I don't come running down here at night just to let people in and out. I had a ticket to *Holiday on Ice*."

He realized he'd said *a* ticket. In that instant Starling saw his life, and he knew it.

She saw his bleak refrigerator, the crumbs on the

TV tray where he ate alone, the still piles his things stayed in for months until he moved them—she felt the ache of his whole yellow-smiling Sen-Sen lonesome life—and switchblade-quick she knew not to spare him, not to talk on or look away. She stared into his face, and with the smallest tilt of her head, she gave him her good looks and bored her knowledge in, speared him with it, knowing he couldn't stand for the conversation to go on.

He sent her with an orderly named Alonzo.

DESCENDING THROUGH the asylum with Alonzo toward
the final keep, Starling managed to shut out much of
the slammings and the screaming, though she felt them
shiver the air against her skin. Pressure built on her as
though she sank through water, down and down.

The proximity of madmen—the thought of Catherine
Martin bound and alone, with one of them snuffling
her, patting his pockets for his tools—braced Starling for her job. But she needed more than resolution.
She needed to be calm, to be still, to be the keenest
instrument. She had to use patience in the face of the
awful need to hurry. If Dr Lecter knew the answer,
she'd have to find it down among the tendrils of his
thought.

Starling found she thought of Catherine Baker Martin as the child she'd seen in the film on the news, the
little girl in the sailboat.

Alonzo pushed the buzzer at the last heavy door.

"Teach us to care and not to care, teach us to be
still."

"Pardon me?" Alonzo said, and Starling realized she had spoken aloud.

He left her with the big orderly who opened the door. As Alonzo turned away, she saw him cross himself.

"Welcome back," the orderly said, and shot the bolts home behind her.

"Hello, Barney."

A paperback book was wrapped around Barney's massive index finger as he held his place. It was Jane Austen's *Sense and Sensibility*; Starling was set to notice everything.

"How do you want the lights?" he said.

The corridor between the cells was dim. Near the far end she could see bright light from the last cell shining on the corridor floor.

"Dr Lecter's awake."

"At night, always—even when his lights are off."

"Let's leave them like they are."

"Stay in the middle going down, don't touch the bars, right?"

"I want to shut that TV off." The television had been moved. It was at the far end, facing up the center of the corridor. Some inmates could see it by leaning their heads against the bars.

"Sure, turn the sound off, but leave the picture if you don't mind. Some of 'em like to look at it. The chair's right there if you want it."

Starling went down the dim corridor alone. She did not look into the cells on either side. Her footfalls seemed loud to her. The only other sounds were wet snoring from one cell, maybe two, and a low chuckle from another.

The late Miggs's cell had a new occupant. She could see long legs outstretched on the floor, the top of a head resting against the bars. She looked as she passed. A man sat on the cell floor in a litter of shredded construction paper. His face was vacant. The television was reflected in his eyes and a shiny thread of spit connected the corner of his mouth and his shoulder.

She didn't want to look into Dr Lecter's cell until she was sure he had seen her. She passed it, feeling itchy between the shoulders, went to the television and turned off the sound.

Dr Lecter wore the white asylum pajamas in his white cell. The only colors in the cell were his hair and eyes and his red mouth, in a face so long out of the sun it leached into the surrounding whiteness; his features seemed suspended above the collar of his shirt. He sat at his table behind the nylon net that kept him back from the bars. He was sketching on butcher paper, using his hand for a model. As she watched, he turned his hand over and, flexing his fingers to great tension, drew the inside of the forearm. He used his little finger as a shading stump to modify a charcoal line.

She came a little closer to the bars, and he looked up. For Starling every shadow in the cell flew into his eyes and widow's peak.

"Good evening, Dr Lecter."

The tip of his tongue appeared, with his lips equally red. It touched his upper lip in the exact center and went back in again.

"Clarice."

She heard the slight metallic rasp beneath his voice

and wondered how long it had been since last he spoke. Beats of silence . . .

"You're up late for a school night," he said.

"This is night school," she said, wishing her voice were stronger. "Yesterday I was in West Virginia—"

"Did you hurt yourself?"

"No, I—"

"You have on a fresh Band-Aid, Clarice."

Then she remembered. "I got a scrape on the side of the pool, swimming today." The Band-Aid was out of sight, on her calf beneath her trousers. He must smell it. "I was in West Virginia yesterday. They found a body over there, Buffalo Bill's latest."

"Not quite his *latest*, Clarice."

"His next-to-latest."

"Yes."

"She was scalped. Just as you said she would be."

"Do you mind if I go on sketching while we talk?"

"No, please."

"You viewed the remains?"

"Yes."

"Had you seen his earlier efforts?"

"No. Only pictures."

"How did you feel?"

"Apprehensive. Then I was busy."

"And after?"

"Shaken."

"Could you function all right?" Dr Lecter rubbed his charcoal on the edge of his butcher paper to refine the point.

"Very well. I functioned very well."

"For Jack Crawford? Or does he still make house calls?"

"He was there."

"Indulge me a moment, Clarice. Would you let your head hang forward, just let it hang forward as though you were asleep. A second more. Thank you, I've got it now. Have a seat, if you like. You had told Jack Crawford what I said before they found her?"

"Yes. He pretty much pooh-poohed it."

"And after he saw the body in West Virginia?"

"He talked to his main authority, from the University of—"

"Alan Bloom."

"That's right. Dr Bloom said Buffalo Bill was fulfilling a persona the newspapers created, the Buffalo Bill scalp-taking business the tabloids were playing with. Dr Bloom said anybody could see that was coming."

"Dr Bloom saw that coming?"

"He said he did."

"He saw it coming, but he kept it to himself. I see. What do you think, Clarice?"

"I'm not sure."

"You have some psychology, some forensics. Where the two flow together you fish, don't you? Catching anything, Clarice?"

"It's pretty slow so far."

"What do your two disciplines tell you about Buffalo Bill?"

"By the book, he's a sadist."

"Life's too slippery for books, Clarice; anger appears as lust, lupus presents as hives." Dr Lecter finished sketching his left hand with his right, switched the charcoal and began to sketch his right with his left, and just as well. "Do you mean Dr Bloom's book?"

"Yes."

"You looked me up in it, didn't you?"

"Yes."

"How did he describe me?"

"A pure sociopath."

"Would you say Dr Bloom is always right?"

"I'm still waiting for the shallowness of affect."

Dr Lecter's smile revealed his small white teeth. "We have experts at every hand, Clarice. Dr Chilton says Sammie, behind you there, is a hebephrenic schizoid and irretrievably lost. He put Sammie in Miggs' old cell, because he thinks Sammie's said bye-bye. Do you know how hebephrenics usually go? Don't worry, he won't hear you."

"They're the hardest to treat," she said. "Usually they go into terminal withdrawal and personality disintegration."

Dr Lecter took something from between his sheets of butcher paper and put it in the sliding food carrier. Starling pulled it through.

"Only yesterday Sammie sent that across with my supper," he said.

It was a scrap of construction paper with writing in crayon.

Starling read:

I WAN TOO GO TO JESA
I WAN TOO GO WIV CRIEZ
I CAN GO WIV JESA
EF I AC RELL NIZE

SAMMIE

Starling looked back over her right shoulder. Sammie sat vacant-faced against the wall of his cell, his head leaning against the bars.

"Would you read it aloud? He won't hear you."

Starling began. "'I want to go to Jesus, I want to go with Christ, I can go with Jesus if I act real nice.'"

"No, no. Get a more assertive 'Pease porridge hot' quality into it. The meter varies but the intensity is the same." Lecter clapped time softly, "Pease porridge *in* the pot *nine days old*. Intensely, you see. Fervently. 'I *wan* to go to Jesa, I *wan* to go wiv Criez.'"

"I see," Starling said, putting the paper back in the carrier.

"No, you don't see anything at all." Dr Lecter bounded to his feet, his lithe body suddenly grotesque, bent in a gnomish squat, and he was bouncing, clapping time, his voice ringing like sonar, "I *wan* to go to Jesa—"

Sammie's voice boomed behind her sudden as a leopard's cough, louder than a howler monkey, Sammie up and mashing his face into the bars, livid and straining, the cords standing out in his neck:

"I *WAN* TOO GO TO JESA
I *WAN* TOO GO WIV *CRIEZ*

I CAN *GO* WIV JESA *EF I AC RELL NIIIZE*."

Silence. Starling found that she was standing and her folding chair was over backwards. Her papers had spilled from her lap.

"Please," Dr Lecter said, erect and graceful as a dancer once again, inviting her to sit. He dropped easily into his seat and rested his chin on his hand. "You don't see at all," he said again. "Sammie is intensely religious. He's simply disappointed because Jesus is so late. May I tell Clarice why you're here, Sammie?"

Sammie grabbed the lower part of his face and halted its movement.

"Please?" Dr Lecter said.

"Eaaah," Sammie said between his fingers.

"Sammie put his mother's head in the collection plate at the Highway Baptist Church in Trune. They were singing 'Give of Your Best to the Master' and it was the nicest thing he had." Lecter spoke over her shoulder. "Thank you, Sammie. It's perfectly all right. Watch television."

The tall man subsided to the floor with his head against the bars, just as before, the images from the television worming on his pupils, three streaks of silver on his face now, spit and tears.

"Now. See if you can apply yourself to his problem and perhaps I'll apply myself to yours. Quid pro quo. He's not listening."

Starling had to bear down hard. "The verse changes from 'go to Jesus' to 'go with Christ,'" she said. "That's a reasoned sequence: going to, arriving at, going with."

"Yes. It's a linear progression. I'm particularly pleased that he knows 'Jesa' and 'Criez' are the same. That's progress. The idea of a single Godhead also being a Trinity is hard to reconcile, particularly for Sammie, who's not positive how many people he is himself.

Eldridge Cleaver gives us the parable of the 3-in-One Oil, and we find that useful."

"He sees a causal relationship between his behavior and his aims, that's structured thinking," Starling said. "So is the management of a rhyme. He's not blunted—he's crying. You believe he's a catatonic schizoid?"

"Yes. Can you smell his sweat? That peculiar goatish odor is trans-3-methyl-2 hexenoic acid. Remember it, it's the smell of schizophrenia."

"And you believe he's treatable?"

"Particularly now, when he's coming out of a stuporous phase. How his cheeks shine!"

"Dr Lecter, why do you say Buffalo Bill's not a sadist?"

"Because the newspapers have reported the bodies had ligature marks on the wrists, but not the ankles. Did you see any on the person's ankles in West Virginia?"

"No."

"Clarice, recreational flayings are always conducted with the victim inverted, so that blood pressure is maintained longer in the head and chest and the subject remains conscious. Didn't you know that?"

"No."

"When you're back in Washington, go to the National Gallery and look at Titian's *Flaying of Marsyas* before they send it back to Czechoslovakia. Wonderful for details, Titian—look at helpful Pan, bringing the bucket of water."

"Dr Lecter, we have some extraordinary circumstances here and some unusual opportunities."

"For whom?"

"For you, if we save this one. Did you see Senator Martin on television?"

"Yes, I saw the news."

"What did you think of the statement?"

"Misguided but harmless. She's badly advised."

"She's very powerful, Senator Martin. And determined."

"Let's have it."

"I think you have extraordinary insight. Senator Martin has indicated that if you help us get Catherine Baker Martin back alive and unharmed, she'll help you get transferred to a federal institution, and, if there's a view available, you'll get it. You may also be asked to review written psychiatric evaluations of incoming patients—a job, in other words. No relaxing of security restrictions."

"I don't believe that, Clarice."

"You should."

"Oh, I believe *you*. But there are more things you don't know about human behavior than how a proper flaying is conducted. Would you say that for a United States Senator, you're an odd choice of messenger?"

"I was *your* choice, Dr Lecter. You chose to speak to me. Would you prefer someone else now? Or maybe you don't think you could help."

"That is both impudent and untrue, Clarice. I don't believe Jack Crawford would allow any compensation ever to reach me . . . Possibly I'll tell you one thing you can tell the Senator, but I operate strictly COD. Maybe I'll trade for a piece of information about you. Yes or no?"

"Let's hear the question."

171

"Yes or no? Catherine's waiting, isn't she? Listening to the whetstone? What do you think she'd ask you to do?"

"Let's hear the question."

"What's your worst memory of childhood?"

Starling took a deep breath.

"Quicker than that," Dr Lecter said. "I'm not interested in your worst *invention*."

"The death of my father," Starling said.

"Tell me."

"He was a town marshal. One night he surprised two burglars, addicts, coming out of the back of the drugstore. As he was getting out of his pickup he short-shucked a pump shotgun and they shot him."

"Short-shucked?"

"He didn't work the slide fully. It was an old pump gun, a Remington 870, and the shell hung up in the shell carrier. When it happens, the gun won't shoot and you have to take it down to clear it. I think he must have hit the slide on the door getting out."

"Was he killed outright?"

"No. He was strong. He lasted a month."

"Did you see him in the hospital?"

"Dr Lecter—yes."

"Tell me a detail you remember from the hospital."

Starling closed her eyes. "A neighbor came, an older woman, a single lady, and she recited the end of 'Thanatopsis' to him. I guess that was all she knew to say. That's it. We've traded."

"Yes, we have. You've been very frank, Clarice. I always know. I think it would be quite something to know you in private life."

"Quid pro quo."

"In life, was the girl in West Virginia very attractive physically, do you think?"

"She was well-groomed."

"Don't waste my time with loyalty."

"She was heavy."

"Large?"

"Yes."

"Shot in the chest."

"Yes."

"Flat-chested, I expect."

"For her size, yes."

"But big through the hips. Roomy."

"She was, yes."

"What else?"

"She had an insect deliberately inserted in her throat—that hasn't been made public."

"Was it a butterfly?"

Her breath stopped for a moment. She hoped he didn't hear it. "It was a moth," she said. "Please tell me how you anticipated that."

"Clarice, I'm going to tell you what Buffalo Bill wants Catherine Baker Martin for, and then good night. This is my last word under the current terms. You can tell the Senator what he wants with Catherine and she can come up with a more interesting offer for me . . . or she can wait until Catherine bobs to the surface and see that I was right."

"What does he want her for, Dr Lecter?"

"He wants a vest with tits on it," Dr Lecter said.

CHAPTER

23

CATHERINE BAKER MARTIN lay seventeen feet below the cellar floor. The darkness was loud with her breathing, loud with her heart. Sometimes the fear stood on her chest the way a trapper kills a fox. Sometimes she could think: she knew she was kidnapped, but she didn't know by whom. She knew she wasn't dreaming; in the absolute dark she could hear the tiny clicks her eyes made when she blinked.

She was better now than when she first regained consciousness. Much of the awful vertigo was gone, and she knew there was enough air. She could tell *down* from *up* and she had some sense of her body's position.

Her shoulder, hip, and knee hurt from being pressed against the cement floor where she lay. That side was *down. Up* was the rough futon she had crawled beneath during the last interval of blazing, blinding light. The throbbing in her head had subsided now and her only real pain was in the fingers of her left hand. The ring finger was broken, she knew.

174

She wore a quilted jumpsuit that was strange to her. It was clean and smelled of fabric softener. The floor was clean too, except for the chicken bones and bits of vegetable her captor had raked into the hole. The only other objects with her were the futon and a plastic sanitation bucket with a thin string tied to the handle. It felt like cotton kitchen string and it led up into the darkness as far as she could reach.

Catherine Martin was free to move around, but there was no place to go. The floor she lay on was oval, about eight by ten feet, with a small drain in the center. It was the bottom of a deep covered pit. The smooth cement walls sloped gently inward as they rose.

Sounds from above now or was it her heart? Sounds from above. Sounds came clearly to her from overhead. The oubliette that held her was in the part of the basement directly beneath the kitchen. Footsteps now across the kitchen floor, and running water. The scratching of dog claws on linoleum. Nothing then until a weak disc of yellow light through the open trap above as the basement lights came on. Then blazing light in the pit, and this time she sat up into the light, the futon across her legs, determined to look around, trying to peer through her fingers as her eyes adjusted, her shadow swaying around her as a flood-lamp lowered into the pit swung on its cord high above.

She flinched as her toilet bucket moved, lifted, swayed upward on its flimsy string, twisting slowly as it rose toward the light. She tried to swallow down her fear, got too much air with it, but managed to speak.

"My family will pay," she said. "Cash. My mother will pay it now, no questions asked. This is her private—

oh!" a flapping shadow down on her, only a towel. "This is her private number. It's 202—"

"Wash yourself."

It was the same unearthly voice she'd heard talking to the dog.

Another bucket coming down on a thin cord. She smelled hot, soapy water.

"Take it off and wash yourself all over, or you'll get the hose." And an aside to the dog as the voice faded, "Yes, it will get the hose, won't it, Darlingheart, yes it *will*!"

Catherine Martin heard the footsteps and the claws on the floor above the basement. The double vision she'd had the first time the lights went on was gone now. She could see. How high was the top, was the floodlight on a strong cord? Could she snag it with the jumpsuit, catch something with the towel? Do *something*, hell. The walls were so smooth, a smooth tube upward.

A crack in the cement a foot above her reach, the only blemish she could see. She rolled the futon as tightly as she could and tied the roll with the towel. Standing on it, wobbly, reaching for the crack, she got her fingernails in it for balance and peered up into the light. Squinting into the glare. It's a floodlight with a shade, hanging just a foot down into the pit, almost ten feet above her upstretched hand, it might as well be the moon, and he was coming, the futon was wobbling, she scrabbling at the crack in the wall for balance, hopping down, something, a flake falling past her face.

Something coming down past the light, a hose. A single spatter of icy water, a threat.

"Wash yourself. All over."

There was a washcloth in the bucket and floating in the water was a plastic bottle of an expensive foreign skin emollient.

She did it, goosebumps on her arms and thighs, nipples sore and shriveled in the cool air, she squatted beside the bucket of warm water as close to the wall as she could get and washed.

"Now dry off and rub the cream all over. Rub it all over."

The cream was warm from the bath water. Its moisture made the jumpsuit stick to her skin.

"Now pick up your litter and wash the floor."

She did that too, gathering the chicken bones and picking up the English peas. She put them in the bucket, and dabbed the little spots of grease on the cement. Something else here, near the wall. The flake that had fluttered down from the crack above. It was a human fingernail, covered with glitter polish and torn off far back in the quick.

The bucket was pulled aloft.

"My mother will pay," Catherine Martin said. "No questions asked. She'll pay enough for you all to be rich. If it's a cause, Iran or Palestine, or Black Liberation, she'll give the money for that. All you have to do—"

The lights went out. Sudden and total darkness.

She flinched and went "Uhhhhhh!" when her sanitation bucket settled beside her on its string. She sat on the futon, her mind racing. She believed now that her captor was alone, that he was a white American. She'd tried to give the impression she had no idea what he was, what color or how many, that her memory of the parking lot was wiped out by the blows on her head.

She hoped that he believed he could safely let her go. Her mind was working, working, and at last it worked too well:

The fingernail, someone else was here. A woman, a girl was here. Where was she now? What did he do to her?

Except for shock and disorientation, it would not have been so long in coming to her. As it was, the skin emollient did it. Skin. She knew who had her then. The knowledge fell on her like every scalding awful thing on earth and she was screaming, screaming, under the futon, up and climbing, clawing at the wall, screaming until she was coughing something warm and salty in her mouth, hands to her face, drying sticky on the backs of her hands and she lay rigid on the futon, arching off the floor from head to heels, her hands clenched in her hair.

CLARICE STARLING'S quarter bonged down through the telephone in the shabby orderlies' lounge. She dialed the van.

"Crawford."

"I'm at a pay phone outside the maximum-security ward," Starling said. "Dr Lecter asked me if the insect in West Virginia was a butterfly. He wouldn't elaborate. He said Buffalo Bill needs Catherine Martin because, I'm quoting, 'He wants a vest with tits on it.' Dr Lecter wants to trade. He wants a 'more interesting' offer from the Senator."

"Did he break it off?"

"Yes."

"How soon do you think he'll talk again?"

"I think he'd like to do this over the next few days, but I'd rather hit him again now, if I can have some kind of urgent offer from the Senator."

"Urgent is right. We got an ID on the girl in West Virginia, Starling. A missing-person fingerprint card from Detroit rang the cherries in ID section

179

about a half hour ago. Kimberly Jane Emberg, twenty-two, missing from Detroit since February seventh. We're canvassing her neighborhood for witnesses. The Charlottesville medical examiner says she died not later than February eleventh, and possibly the day before, the tenth."

"He only kept her alive three days," Starling said.

"His period's getting shorter. I don't think anybody's surprised." Crawford's voice was even. "He's had Catherine Martin about twenty-six hours. I think if Lecter can deliver he'd better do it in your next conversation. I'm set up in the Baltimore field office, the van patched you through. I have a room for you in the HoJo two blocks from the hospital if you need a catnap later on."

"He's leery, Mr Crawford, he's not sure you'd let him have anything good. What he said about Buffalo Bill, he traded for personal information about me. I don't think there's any textual correlation between his questions and the case . . . Do you want to know the questions?"

"No."

"That's why you didn't make me wear a wire, isn't it? You thought it'd be easier for me, I'd be more likely to tell him stuff and please him if nobody else could hear."

"Here's another possibility for you: What if I trusted your judgment, Starling? What if I thought you were my best shot, and I wanted to keep a lot of second-guessers off your back? Would I have you wear a wire then?"

"No, sir." *You're famous for handling agents, aren't you, Mr Crawfish?* "What can we offer Dr Lecter?"

180

"A couple of things I'm sending over. It'll be there in five minutes, unless you want to rest a little first."

"I'd rather do it now," Starling said. "Tell them to ask for Alonzo. Tell Alonzo I'll meet him in the corridor outside Section 8."

"Five minutes," Crawford said.

Starling walked up and down the linoleum of the shabby lounge far underground. She was the only brightness in the room.

We rarely get to prepare ourselves in meadows or on graveled walks; we do it on short notice in places without windows, hospital corridors, rooms like this lounge with its cracked plastic sofa and Cinzano ashtrays, where the café curtains cover blank concrete. In rooms like this, with so little time, we prepare our gestures, get them by heart so we can do them when we're frightened in the face of Doom. Starling was old enough to know that; she didn't let the room affect her.

Starling walked up and down. She gestured to the air. "Hold on, girl," she said aloud. She said it to Catherine Martin and she said it to herself. "We're better than this room. We're better than this fucking place," she said aloud. "We're better than wherever he's got you. Help me. Help me. Help me." She thought for an instant of her late parents. She wondered if they would be ashamed of her now—just that question, not its pertinence, no qualifications—the way we always ask it. The answer was no, they would not be ashamed of her.

She washed her face and went out into the hall.

The orderly Alonzo was in the corridor with a sealed

package from Crawford. It contained a map and instructions. She read them quickly by the corridor light and pushed the button for Barney to let her in.

25

Dr Lecter was at his table, examining his correspondence. Starling found it easier to approach the cage when he wasn't looking at her.

"Doctor."

He held up a finger for silence. When he had finished reading his letter, he sat musing, the thumb of his six-fingered hand beneath his chin, his index finger beside his nose. "What do you make of this?" he said, putting the document into the food carrier.

It was a letter from the US Patent Office.

"This is about my crucifixion watch," Dr Lecter said. "They won't give me a patent, but they advise me to copyright the face. Look here." He put a drawing the size of a dinner napkin in the carrier and Starling pulled it through. "You may have noticed that in most crucifixions the hands point to, say, a quarter to three, or ten till two at the earliest, while the feet are at six. On this watch face, Jesus is on the cross, as you see there, and the arms revolve to indicate the time, just like the arms on the popular Disney watches. The feet remain

183

at six and at the top a small second hand revolves in the halo. What do you think?"

The quality of the anatomical sketching was very good. The head was hers.

"You'll lose a lot of detail when it's reduced to watch size," Starling said.

"True, unfortunately, but think of the clocks. Do you think this is safe without a patent?"

"You'd be buying quartz watch movements—wouldn't you?—and they're already under patent. I'm not sure, but I think patents only apply to unique mechanical devices and copyright applies to design."

"But you're not a lawyer, are you? They don't require that in the FBI anymore."

"I have a proposal for you," Starling said, opening her briefcase.

Barney was coming. She closed the briefcase again. She envied Barney's enormous calm. His eyes read negative for dope and there was considerable intelligence behind them.

"Excuse me," Barney said. "If you've got a lot of papers to wrestle, there's a one-armed desk, a school desk, in the closet here that the shrinks use. Want it?"

School image. Yes or no?

"May we talk now, Dr Lecter?"

The doctor held up an open palm.

"Yes, Barney. Thank you."

Seated now and Barney safely away.

"Dr Lecter, the Senator has a remarkable offer."

"I'll decide that. You spoke to her so soon?"

"Yes. She's not holding anything back. This is all she's got, so it's not a matter for bargaining. This is it, everything, one offer." She glanced up from her briefcase.

Dr Lecter, murderer of nine, had his fingers steepled beneath his nose and he was watching her. Behind his eyes was endless night.

"If you help us find Buffalo Bill in time to save Catherine Martin unharmed, you get the following: transfer to the Veterans' Administration hospital at Oneida Park, New York, to a cell with a view of the woods around the hospital. Maximum security measures still apply. You'll be asked to help evaluate written psychological tests on some federal inmates, though not necessarily those sharing your own institution. You'll do the evaluations blind. No identities. You'll have reasonable access to books." She glanced up.

Silence can mock.

"The best thing, the remarkable thing: one week a year, you will leave the hospital and go here." She put a map in the food carrier. Dr Lecter did not pull it through.

"Plum Island," she continued. "Every afternoon of that week you can walk on the beach or swim in the ocean with no surveillance closer than seventy-five yards, but it'll be SWAT surveillance. That's it."

"If I decline?"

"Maybe you could hang some café curtains in there. It might help. We don't have anything to threaten you with, Dr Lecter. What I've got is a way for you to see the daylight."

She didn't look at him. She didn't want to match stares now. This was not a confrontation.

"Will Catherine Martin come and talk to me—only about her captor—if I decide to publish? Talk *exclusively* to me?"

"Yes. You can take that as a given."

"How do you know? *Given* by whom?"

"I'll bring her myself."

"If she'll come."

"We'll have to ask her first, won't we?"

He pulled the carrier through. "Plum Island."

"Look off the tip of Long Island, the north finger there."

"Plum Island. 'The Plum Island Animal Disease Center. (Federal, hoof and mouth disease research),' it says. Sounds charming."

"That's just part of the island. It has a nice beach and good quarters. The terns nest there in the spring."

"Terns." Dr Lecter sighed. He cocked his head slightly and touched the center of his red lip with his red tongue. "If we talk about this, Clarice, I have to have something on account. Quid pro quo. I tell you things, and you tell me."

"Go," Starling said.

She had to wait a full minute before he said, "A caterpillar becomes a pupa in a chrysalis. Then it emerges, comes out of its secret changing room as the beautiful imago. Do you know what an imago is, Clarice?"

"An adult winged insect."

"But what else?"

She shook her head.

"It's a term from the dead religion of psychoanalysis. An imago is an image of the parent buried in the unconscious from infancy and bound with infantile affect. The word comes from the wax portrait busts of their ancestors the ancient Romans carried in funeral processions . . . Even the phlegmatic Crawford must see some significance in the insect chrysalis."

"Nothing to jump on except checking the entomology journals' subscription lists against known sex offenders in the descriptor index."

"First, let's drop Buffalo Bill. It's a misleading term and has nothing to do with the person you want. For convenience we'll call him Billy. I'll give you a précis of what I think. Ready?"

"Ready."

"The significance of the chrysalis is change. Worm into butterfly, or moth. Billy thinks he wants to change. He's making himself a girl suit out of real girls. Hence the large victims—he has to have things that fit. The number of victims suggests he may see it as a series of molts. He's doing this in a two-story house, did you find out why two stories?"

"For a while he was hanging them on the stairs."

"Correct."

"Dr Lecter, there's no correlation that I ever saw between transsexualism and violence—transsexuals are passive types, usually."

"That's true, Clarice. Sometimes you see a tendency to surgical addiction—cosmetically, transsexuals are hard to satisfy—but that's about all. Billy's not a real transsexual. You're very close, Clarice, to the way you're going to catch him, do you realize that?"

"No, Dr Lecter."

"Good. Then you won't mind telling me what happened to you after your father's death."

Starling looked at the scarred top of the school desk.

"I don't imagine the answer's in your papers, Clarice."

"My mother kept us together for more than two years."

"Doing what?"

"Working as a motel maid in the daytime, cooking at a café at night."

"And then?"

"I went to my mother's cousin and her husband in Montana."

"Just you?"

"I was the oldest."

"The town did nothing for your family?"

"A check for five hundred dollars."

"Curious there was no insurance. Clarice, you said your father hit the shotgun slide on the door of his pickup."

"Yes."

"He didn't have a patrol car?"

"No."

"It happened at night?"

"Yes."

"Didn't he have a pistol?"

"No."

"Clarice, he was working at night, in a pickup truck, armed only with a shotgun . . . Tell me, did he wear a time clock on his belt, by any chance? One of those things where they have keys screwed to posts all over town and you have to drive to them and stick them in your clock? So the town fathers know you weren't asleep. Tell me if he wore one, Clarice."

"Yes."

"He was a night watchman, wasn't he, Clarice, he wasn't a marshal at all. I'll know if you lie."

"The job description said night marshal."

"What happened to it?"

"What happened to what?"

"The time clock. What happened to it after your father was shot?"

"I don't remember."

"If you do remember, will you tell me?"

"Yes. Wait—the mayor came to the hospital and asked my mother for the clock and the badge." She hadn't known she knew that. The mayor in his leisure suit and Navy-surplus shoes. The cocksucker. "Quid pro quo, Dr Lecter."

"Did you think for a second you'd made that up? No, if you'd made it up, it wouldn't sting. We were talking about transsexuals. You said violence and destructive aberrant behavior are not statistical correlatives of transsexualism. True. Do you remember what we said about anger expressed as lust, and lupus presenting as hives? Billy's not a transsexual, Clarice, but he thinks he is, he tries to be. He's tried to be a lot of things, I expect."

"You said that was close to the way we'd catch him."

"There are three major centers for transsexual surgery: Johns Hopkins, the University of Minnesota, and Columbus Medical Center. I wouldn't be surprised if he's applied for sex reassignment at one or all of them and been denied."

"On what basis would they reject him, what would show up?"

"You're very quick, Clarice. The first reason would be criminal record. That disqualifies an applicant, unless the crime is relatively harmless and related to the gender-identity problem. Cross-dressing in public, something like that. If he lied successfully about a serious criminal record, then the personality inventories would get him."

"How?"

"You have to know how in order to sieve them, don't you?"

"Yes."

"Why don't you ask Dr Bloom?"

"I'd rather ask you."

"What will you get out of this, Clarice, a promotion and a raise? What are you, a G-9? What do little G-9s get nowadays?"

"A key to the front door, for one thing. How would he show up on the diagnostics?"

"How did you like Montana, Clarice?"

"Montana's fine."

"How did you like your mother's cousin's husband?"

"We were different."

"How were they?"

"Worn out from work."

"Were there other children?"

"No."

"Where did you live?"

"On a ranch."

"A sheep ranch?"

"Sheep and horses."

"How long were you there?"

"Seven months."

"How old were you?"

"Ten."

"Where did you go from there?"

"The Lutheran Home in Bozeman."

"Tell me the truth."

"I am telling you the truth."

"You're hopping around the truth. If you're tired, we could talk toward the end of the week. I'm rather bored myself. Or had you rather talk now?"

"Now, Dr Lecter."

"All right. A child is sent away from her mother to a ranch in Montana. A sheep and horse ranch. Missing the mother, excited by the animals . . ." Dr Lecter invited Starling with his open hands.

"It was great. I had my own room with an Indian rug on the floor. They let me ride a horse—they led me around on this horse—she couldn't see very well. There was something wrong with all the horses. Lame or sick. Some of them had been raised with children and they would, you know, nicker at me in the mornings when I went out to the school bus."

"But then?"

"I found something strange in the barn. They had a little tack room out there. I thought this thing was some kind of old helmet. When I got it down, it was stamped 'W. W. Greener's Humane Horse Killer.' It was sort of a bell-shaped metal cap and it had a place in the top to chamber a cartridge. Looked like about a .32."

"Did they feed out slaughter horses on this ranch, Clarice?"

"Yes, they did."

"Did they kill them at the ranch?"

"The glue and fertilizer ones they did. You can stack six in a truck if they're dead. The ones for dog food they hauled away alive."

"The one you rode around the yard?"

"We ran away together."

"How far did you get?"

"I got about as far as I'm going until you break down the diagnostics for me."

"Do you know the procedure for testing male applicants for transsexual surgery?"

"No."

"It may help if you bring me a copy of the regimen from any of the centers, but to begin: the battery of tests usually includes Wechsler Adult Intelligence Scale, House-Tree-Person, Rorschach, Drawing of Self-Concept, Thematic Apperception, MMPI, of course, and a couple of others—the Jenkins, I think, that NYU developed. You need something you can see quickly, don't you? Don't you, Clarice?"

"That would be the best, something quick."

"Let's see . . . our hypothesis is we're looking for a male who will test differently from the way a true transsexual would test. All right—on House-Tree-Person, look for someone who didn't draw the female figure first. Male transsexuals almost always draw the female first and, typically, they pay a lot of attention to adornments on the females they draw. Their male figures are simple stereotypes—there are some notable exceptions where they draw Mr America—but not much in between.

"Look for a house drawing without the rosy-future

embellishments—no baby carriage outside, no curtains, no flowers in the yard.

"You get two kinds of trees with real transsexuals—flowing, copious willows and castration themes. The trees that are cut off by the edge of the drawing or the edge of the paper, the castration images, are full of life in the drawings of true transsexuals. Flowering and fruitful stumps. That's an important distinction. They're very unlike the frightened, dead, mutilated trees you see in drawings by people with mental disturbances. That's a good one—Billy's tree will be frightful. Am I going too fast?"

"No, Dr Lecter."

"On his drawing of himself, a transsexual will almost never draw himself naked. Don't be misled by a certain amount of paranoid ideation in the TAT cards—that's fairly common among transsexual subjects who cross-dress a lot; oftentimes they've had bad experiences with the authorities. Shall I summarize?"

"Yes, I'd like a summary."

"You should try to obtain a list of people rejected from all three gender-reassignment centers. Check first the ones rejected for criminal record—and among those look hard at the burglars. Among those who tried to conceal criminal records, look for severe childhood disturbances associated with violence. Possibly internment in childhood. Then go to the tests. You're looking for a white male, probably under thirty-five and sizable. He's not a transsexual, Clarice. He just thinks he is, and he's puzzled and angry because they won't help him. That's all I want to say, I think, until I've read the case. You *will* leave it with me?"

193

"Yes."

"And the pictures?"

"They're included."

"Then you'd better run with what you have, Clarice, and we'll see how you do."

"I need to know how you—"

"No. Don't be grabby or we'll discuss it next week. Come back when you've made some progress. Or not. And, Clarice?"

"Yes."

"Next time you'll tell me two things. What happened with the horse is one. The other thing I wonder is . . . how do you manage your rage?"

Alonzo came for her. She held her notes against her chest, walking head bent, trying to hold it all in her mind. Eager for the outside air, she didn't even glance toward Chilton's office as she hurried out of the hospital.

Dr Chilton's light was on. You could see it under the door.

FAR BENEATH the rusty Baltimore dawn, stirrings in the maximum-security ward. Down where it is never dark, the tormented sense beginning day as oysters in a barrel open to their lost tide. God's creatures who cried themselves to sleep stirred to cry again and the ravers cleared their throats.

Dr Hannibal Lecter stood stiffly upright at the end of the corridor, his face a foot from the wall. Heavy canvas webbing bound him tightly to a mover's tall hand truck as though he were a grandfather clock. Beneath the webbing he wore a straitjacket and leg restraints. A hockey mask over his face precluded biting; it was as effective as a mouthpiece, and not so wet for the orderlies to handle.

Behind Dr Lecter, a small, round-shouldered orderly mopped Lecter's cage. Barney supervised the thrice-weekly cleaning and searched for contraband at the same time. Moppers tended to hurry, finding it spooky in Dr Lecter's quarters. Barney checked behind them. He checked everything and he neglected nothing.

Only Barney supervised the handling of Dr Lecter, because Barney never forgot what he was dealing with. His two assistants watched taped hockey highlights on television.

Dr Lecter amused himself—he has extensive internal resources and can entertain himself for years at a time. His thoughts were no more bound by fear or kindness than Milton's were by physics. He was free in his head.

His inner world has intense colors and smells, and not much sound. In fact, he had to strain a bit to hear the voice of the late Benjamin Raspail. Dr Lecter was musing on how he would give Jame Gumb to Clarice Starling, and it was useful to remember Raspail. Here was the fat flutist on the last day of his life, lying on Lecter's therapy couch, telling him about Jame Gumb:

"Jame had the most atrocious room imaginable in this San Francisco flophouse, sort of aubergine walls with smears of psychedelic Day-Glo here and there from the hippie years, terribly battered everything.

"Jame—you know, it's actually spelled that way on his birth certificate, that's where he got it and you have to pronounce it 'Jame,' like 'name,' or he gets livid, even though it was a mistake at the hospital—they were hiring cheap help even then that couldn't even get a name right. It's even worse today, it's worth your life to go in a hospital. Anyway, here was Jame sitting on his bed with his head in his hands in that awful room, and he'd been fired from the curio store and he'd done the bad thing again.

"*I'd told him I simply couldn't put up with his behavior, and Klaus had just come into my life, of course. Jame is not really gay, you know, it's just something he picked up in jail. He's not anything, really, just a sort of total lack that he wants to fill, and so angry. You always felt the room was a little emptier when he came in. I mean, he* killed *his grandparents when he was twelve, you'd think a person that volatile would have some presence, wouldn't you?*

"*And here he was, no job, he'd done the bad thing again to some luckless bag person.* I *was gone. He'd gone by the post office and picked up his former employer's mail, hoping there was something he could sell. And there was a package from Malaysia, or somewhere over there. He eagerly opened it up and it was a suitcase full of dead butterflies, just in there loose.*

"*His boss sent money to postmasters on all those islands and they sent him boxes and boxes of dead butterflies. He set them in Lucite and made the tackiest ornaments imaginable—and he had the gall to call them* objets. *The butterflies were useless to Jame and he dug his hands in them, thinking there might be jewellery underneath—sometimes they got bracelets from Bali— and he got butterfly powder on his fingers. Nothing. He sat on the bed with his head in his hands, butterfly colors on his hands and face and he was at the bottom, just as we've all been, and he was crying. He heard a little noise and it was a butterfly in the open suitcase. It was struggling out of a cocoon that had been thrown in with the butterflies and it climbed out. There was dust in the air from the butterflies and dust in the sun from the window—you know how terribly* vivid *it all is when somebody's describing it to you stoned. He watched it pump up its wings. It was a big one, he said. Green. And he opened the window and it flew away and he felt so light, he said, and he knew what to do.*

"Jame found the little beach house Klaus and I were using, and when I came home from rehearsal, there he was. But I didn't see Klaus. Klaus wasn't there. I said where's Klaus and he said swimming. I knew that was a lie, Klaus never swam, the Pacific's much too crashy-bangy. And when I opened the refrigerator, well, you know what I found. Klaus's head looking out from behind the orange juice. Jame had made himself an apron too, you know, from Klaus, and he put it on and asked me how I liked him now. I know you must be appalled that I'd ever have anything else to do with Jame—he was even more unstable when you met him, I think he was just astounded that you weren't afraid of him."

And then, the last words Raspail ever said: "I wonder why my parents didn't kill me before I was old enough to fool them."

The slender handle of the stiletto wiggled as Raspail's spiked heart tried to keep beating, and Dr Lecter said, "Looks like a straw down a doodlebug hole, doesn't it?" but it was too late for Raspail to answer.

Dr Lecter could remember every word, and much more too. Pleasant thoughts to pass the time while they cleaned his cell.

Clarice Starling was astute, the doctor mused. She might get Jame Gumb with what he had told her, but it was a long shot. To get him in time, she would need more specifics. Dr Lecter felt sure that, when he read the details of the crimes, hints would suggest themselves—possibly having to do with Gumb's job training in the juvenile correction facility after he killed his grandparents. He'd give her Jame Gumb tomorrow, and make it clear enough so that even Jack Crawford couldn't miss it. Tomorrow should see it done.

Behind him, Dr Lecter heard footsteps and the television was turned off. He felt the hand truck tilt back. Now would begin the long, tedious process of freeing him within the cell. It was always done the same way. First Barney and his helpers laid him gently on his cot, face down. Then Barney tied his ankles to the bar at the foot of the cot with towels, removed the leg restraints, and, covered by his two helpers armed with Mace and riot batons, undid the buckles on the back of the straitjacket and backed out of the cell, locking the net and the barred door in place, and leaving Dr Lecter to work his way out of his bonds. Then the doctor traded the equipment for his breakfast. The procedure had been in effect ever since Dr Lecter savaged the nurse, and it worked out nicely for everyone.

Today the process was interrupted.

A SLIGHT BUMP as the hand truck carrying Dr Lecter rolled over the threshold of the cage. And here was Dr Chilton, sitting on the cot, looking through Dr Lecter's private correspondence. Chilton had his tie and coat off. Dr Lecter could see some kind of medal hanging from his neck.

"Stand him up beside the toilet, Barney," Dr Chilton said without looking up. "You and the others wait at your station."

Dr Chilton finished reading Dr Lecter's most recent exchange with the General Archives of Psychiatry. He tossed the letters on the cot and went outside the cell. A glint from behind the hockey mask as Dr Lecter's eyes tracked him, but Lecter's head didn't move.

Chilton went to the school desk in the hall and, bending stiffly, removed a small listening device from beneath the seat.

He waggled it in front of the eye holes in Dr Lecter's mask and resumed his seat on the cot.

"I thought she might be looking for a civil rights

violation in Miggs' death, so I listened," Chilton said. "I hadn't heard your voice in years—I suppose the last time was when you gave me all the misleading answers in my interviews and then ridiculed me in your *Journal* articles. It's hard to believe an inmate's opinions could count for anything in the professional community, isn't it? But I'm still here. And so are you."

Dr Lecter said nothing.

"Years of silence, and then Jack Crawford sends down his girl and you just went to jelly, didn't you? What was it that got you, Hannibal? Was it those good, hard ankles? The way her hair shines? She's glorious, isn't she? Remote and glorious. A winter sunset of a girl, that's the way I think of her. I know it's been some time since you've seen a winter sunset, but take my word for it.

"You only get one more day with her. Then Baltimore Homicide takes over the interrogation. They're screwing a chair to the floor for you in the electroshock therapy room. The chair has a commode seat for your convenience, and for their convenience when they attach the wires. I won't know a thing.

"Do you get it yet? They *know*, Hannibal. They know that you know exactly who Buffalo Bill is. They think you probably treated him. When I heard Miss Starling ask about Buffalo Bill, I was puzzled. I called a friend at Baltimore Homicide. They found an insect in Klaus's throat, Hannibal. They know Buffalo Bill killed him. Crawford's letting you think you're smart. I don't think you know how much Crawford hates you for cutting up his protégé. He's got you now. Do you feel *smart* now?"

Dr Lecter watched Chilton's eyes moving over the straps that held on the mask. Clearly, Chilton wanted to remove it so he could watch Lecter's face. Lecter wondered if Chilton would do it the safe way, from behind. If he did it from the front, he'd have to reach around Dr Lecter's head, with the blue-veined insides of his forearms close to Lecter's face. Come, Doctor. Come close. No, he's decided against it.

"Do you still think you're going someplace with a window? Do you think you'll walk on the beach and see the birds? I don't think so. I called Senator Ruth Martin and she never heard of any deal with you. I had to remind her who you were. She never heard of Clarice Starling, either. It's a scam. We have to expect *small* dishonesties in a woman, but that's a shocker, wouldn't you say?

"When they get through milking you, Hannibal, Crawford's charging you with misprision of a felony. You'll duck it on *M'Naghten*, of course, but the judge won't like it. You sat through six deaths. The judge won't take such interest in your welfare anymore.

"No window, Hannibal. You'll spend the rest of your life sitting on the floor in a state institution watching the diaper cart go by. Your teeth will go and your strength and nobody will be afraid of you anymore and you'll be out in the ward at someplace like Flendauer. The young ones will just push you around and use you for sex when they feel like it. All you'll get to read is what you write on the wall. You think the court will care? You've seen the old ones. They cry when they don't like the stewed apricots.

"Jack Crawford and his fluff. They'll get together openly after his wife dies. He'll dress younger and take

202

up some sport they can enjoy together. They've been intimate ever since Bella Crawford got sick, they're certainly not fooling anybody about that. They'll get their promotions and they won't think about you once a year. Crawford probably wants to come personally at the end to tell you what *you're* getting. Up the booty. I'm sure he has a speech all prepared.

"Hannibal, he doesn't know you as well as I do. He thought if he asked you for the information you'd just torment the mother with it."

Quite right, too, Dr Lecter reflected. *How wise of Jack—that obtuse Scotch-Irish mien is misleading. His face is all scars if you know how to look. Well, possibly there's room for a few more.*

"I know what you're afraid of. It's not pain, or solitude. It's *indignity* you can't stand, Hannibal, you're like a cat that way. I'm on my honor to look after you, Hannibal, and I do it. No personal considerations have ever entered into our relationship, from my end. And I'm looking after you now.

"There never was a deal for you with Senator Martin, but there is now. Or there could be. I've been on the phone for hours on your behalf and for the sake of that girl. I'm going to tell you the first condition: you speak only through me. I alone publish a professional account of this, my successful interview with you. You publish nothing. I have exclusive access to any material from Catherine Martin, if she should be saved.

"That condition is non-negotiable. You'll answer me now. Do you accept that condition?"

Dr Lecter smiled to himself.

"You'd better answer me now or you can answer

Baltimore Homicide. This is what you get: If you identify Buffalo Bill and the girl is found in time, Senator Martin—and she'll confirm this by telephone—Senator Martin will have you installed in Brushy Mountain State Prison in Tennessee, out of the reach of the Maryland authorities. You'll be in her bailiwick, away from Jack Crawford. You'll be in a maximum-security cell with a view of the woods. You get books. Any outdoor exercise, the details will have to be worked out, but she's amenable. Name him and you can go at once. The Tennessee State Police will take custody of you at the airport, the Governor has agreed."

At last Dr Chilton has said something interesting, and he doesn't even know what it is. Dr Lecter pursed his red lips behind the mask. *The custody of police. Police are not as wise as Barney. Police are accustomed to handling criminals. They're inclined to use leg irons and handcuffs. Handcuffs and leg irons open with a handcuff key. Like mine.*

"His first name is Billy," Dr Lecter said. "I'll tell the rest to the Senator. In Tennessee."

28

JACK CRAWFORD declined Dr Danielson's coffee, but took the cup to mix himself an Alka-Seltzer at the stainless-steel sink behind the nursing station. Everything was stainless steel, the cup dispenser, the counter, the waste bin, the rims of Dr Danielson's spectacles. The bright metal suggested the wink of instruments and gave Crawford a distinct twinge in the area of his inguinal ring.

He and the doctor were alone in the little gallery.

"Not without a court order, you don't," Dr Danielson said again. He was brusque this time, to counter the hospitality he'd shown with the coffee.

Danielson was head of the Gender Identity Clinic at Johns Hopkins and he had agreed to meet Crawford at first light, long before morning rounds. "You'll have to show me a separate court order for each specific case and we'll fight every one. What did Columbus and Minnesota tell you—same thing, am I right?"

"The Justice Department's asking them right now. We have to do this fast, Doctor. If the girl's not dead already, he'll kill her soon—tonight or tomorrow. Then he'll pick the next one," Crawford said.

"To even mention Buffalo Bill in the same breath with the problems we treat here is ignorant and unfair and dangerous, Mr Crawford. It makes my hair stand on end. It's taken years—we're not through yet—showing the public that transsexuals aren't crazy, they aren't perverts, they aren't *queers*, whatever that is—"

"I agree with you—"

"Hold on. The incidence of violence among transsexuals is a lot lower than in the general population. These are decent people with a real problem—a famously intransigent problem. They deserve help and we can give it. I'm not having a witch hunt here. We've never violated a patient's confidence, and we never will. Better start from there, Mr Crawford."

For months now in his private life, Crawford had been cultivating his wife's doctors and nurses, trying to weasel every minute advantage for her. He was pretty sick of doctors. But this was not his private life. This was Baltimore and it was business. Be nice now.

"Then I haven't made myself clear, Doctor. My fault—it's early, I'm not a morning person. The whole idea is, the man we want is *not your patient*. It would be someone you *refused* because you recognized that he was *not a transsexual*. We're not flying blind here—I'll show you some specific ways he'd deviate from typical transsexual patterns in your personality inventories. Here's a short list of things your staff could look for among your rejects."

Dr Danielson rubbed the side of his nose with his finger as he read. He handed the paper back. "That's original, Mr Crawford. In fact it's extremely bizarre, and that's a word I don't use very often. May I ask who provided you with that piece of . . . conjecture?"

I don't think you'd like to know that, Dr Danielson.
"The Behavioral Science staff," Crawford said, "in consultation with Dr Alan Bloom at the University of Chicago."

"*Alan Bloom* endorsed that?"

"And we don't just depend on the tests. There's another way Buffalo Bill's likely to stand out in your records—he probably tried to conceal a record of criminal violence, or falsified other background material. Show me the ones you turned away, Doctor."

Danielson was shaking his head the whole time. "Examination and interview materials are confidential."

"Dr Danielson, how can fraud and misrepresentation be confidential? How does a criminal's real name and real background fall under the doctor-patient relationship when he never told it to you, you had to find it out for yourself? I know how thorough Johns Hopkins is. You've got cases like that, I'm sure of it. Surgical addicts apply every place surgery's performed. It's no reflection on the institution or the legitimate patients. You think nuts don't apply to the FBI? We get 'em all the time. A man in a Moe hairpiece applied in St Louis last week. He had a bazooka, two rockets, and a bearskin shako in his golf bag."

"Did you hire him?"

"Help me, Dr Danielson. Time's eating us up. While we're standing here, Buffalo Bill may be turning Catherine Martin into one of these." Crawford put a photograph on the gleaming counter.

"Don't even do that," Dr Danielson said. "That's a childish, bullying thing to do. I was a battle surgeon, Mr Crawford. Put your picture back in your pocket."

"Sure, a surgeon can stand to look at a mutilated body," Crawford said, crumpling his cup and stepping on the pedal of the covered wastebasket. "But I don't think a doctor can stand to see a life wasted." He dropped in his cup and the lid of the wastebasket came down with a satisfactory clang. "Here's my best offer: I won't ask you for patient information, only application information selected by you, with reference to these guidelines. You and your psychiatric review board can handle your rejected applications a lot faster than I can. If we find Buffalo Bill through your information, I'll suppress that fact. I'll find another way we could have done it and we'll walk through it that way, for the record."

"Could Johns Hopkins be a protected witness, Mr Crawford? Could we have a new identity? Move us to Bob Jones College, say? I doubt very much that the FBI or any other government agency can keep a secret very long."

"You'd be surprised."

"I doubt it. Trying to crawl out from under an inept bureaucratic lie would be more damaging than just telling the truth. Please don't ever protect us that way, thank you very much."

"Thank *you*, Dr Danielson, for your humorous remarks. They're very helpful to me—I'll show you how in a minute. You like the truth—try this. He kidnaps young women and rips their skins off. He puts on these skins and capers around in them. We

208

don't want him to do that anymore. If you don't help me as fast as you can, this is what I'll do to you: this morning the Justice Department will ask publicly for a court order, saying you've refused to help. We'll ask twice a day, in plenty of time for the A.M. and P.M. news cycles. Every news release from Justice about this case will say how we're coming along with Dr Danielson at Johns Hopkins, trying to get him to pitch in. Every time there's news in the Buffalo Bill case—when Catherine Martin floats, when the next one floats, and the next one floats—we'll issue a news release right away about how we're doing with Dr Danielson at Johns Hopkins, complete with your humorous comments about Bob Jones College. One more thing, Doctor. You know, Health and Human Services is right here in Baltimore. My thoughts are running to the Office of Eligibility Policy, and I expect *your* thoughts got there first, didn't they? What if Senator Martin, sometime after her daughter's funeral, asked the fellows over at Eligibility this question: Should the sex-change operations you perform here be considered cosmetic surgery? Maybe they'll scratch their heads and decide, 'Why, you know, Senator Martin's *right*. Yes. We think it's cosmetic surgery,' then this program won't qualify for federal assistance any more than a nose-job clinic."

"That's insulting."

"No, it's just the truth."

"You don't frighten me, you don't intimidate me—"

"Good. I don't want to do either one, Doctor. I just want you to know I'm serious. Help me, Doctor. Please."

"You said you're working with Alan Bloom?"

"Yes. The University of Chicago—"

"I know Alan Bloom, and I'd rather discuss this on a professional level. Tell him I'll be in touch with him this morning. I'll tell you what I've decided before noon. I do care about the young woman, Mr Crawford. And the others. But there's a lot at stake here, and I don't think it's as important to you as it ought to be . . . Mr Crawford, have you had your blood pressure checked recently?"

"I do it myself."

"And do you prescribe for yourself?"

"That's against the law, Dr Danielson."

"But you have a doctor?"

"Yes."

"Share your findings with him, Mr Crawford. What a loss to us all if you dropped dead. You'll hear from me later in the morning."

"How much later, Doctor? How about an hour?"

"An hour."

Crawford's beeper sounded as he got off the elevator at the ground floor. His driver, Jeff, was beckoning as Crawford trotted to the van. *She's dead and they found her*, Crawford thought as he grabbed the phone. It was the Director calling. The news wasn't as bad as it could get, but it was bad enough: Chilton had butted into the case and now Senator Martin was stepping in. The Attorney General of the state of Maryland, on instructions from the Governor, had authorized the extradition to Tennessee of Dr Hannibal Lecter. It would take all the muscle of the Federal Court, District of Maryland, to prevent or delay the move. The

Director wanted a judgment call from Crawford and he wanted it now.

"Hold on," Crawford said. He held the receiver on his thigh and looked out the van window. There wasn't much color in February for the first light to find. All gray. So bleak.

Jeff started to say something and Crawford hushed him with a motion of his hand.

Lecter's monster ego. Chilton's ambition. Senator Martin's terror for her child. Catherine Martin's life. Call it.

"Let them go," he said into the phone.

DR CHILTON and three well-pressed Tennessee state troopers stood close together on the windy tarmac at sunrise, raising their voices over a wash of radio traffic from the open door of the Grumman Gulfstream and from the ambulance idling beside the airplane.

The trooper captain in charge handed Dr Chilton a pen. The papers blew over the end of the clipboard and the policeman had to smooth them down.

"Can't we do this in the air?" Chilton asked.

"Sir, we have to do the documentation at the moment of physical transfer. That's my instructions."

The copilot finished clamping the ramp over the airplane steps. "Okay," he called.

The troopers gathered with Dr Chilton at the back of the ambulance. When he opened the back doors, they tensed as though they expected something to jump out.

Dr Hannibal Lecter stood upright on his hand truck, wrapped in canvas webbing and wearing his hockey mask. He was relieving his bladder while Barney held the urinal.

One of the troopers snorted. The other two looked away.

"Sorry," Barney said to Dr Lecter, and closed the doors again.

"That's all right, Barney," Dr Lecter said. "I'm quite finished, thank you."

Barney rearranged Lecter's clothing and rolled him to the back of the ambulance.

"Barney?"

"Yes, Dr Lecter?"

"You've been decent to me for a long time. Thank you."

"You're welcome."

"Next time Sammie's at himself, would you say good-bye for me?"

"Sure."

"Good-bye, Barney."

The big orderly pushed open the doors and called to the troopers. "You want to catch the bottom there, fellows? Take it on both sides. We'll set him on the ground. Easy."

Barney rolled Dr Lecter up the ramp and into the airplane. Three seats had been removed on the craft's right side. The copilot lashed the hand truck to the seat brackets in the floor.

"He's gonna fly laying down?" one trooper asked. "Has he got rubber britches on?"

"You'll just have to hold your water to Memphis, buddy ruff," the other trooper said.

"Dr Chilton, could I speak to you?" Barney said.

They stood outside the airplane while the wind made little twisters of dust and trash around them.

"These fellows don't know anything," Barney said.

"I'll have some help on the other end—experienced psychiatric orderlies. He's their responsibility now."

"You think they'll treat him all right? You know how he is—you have to threaten him with boredom. That's all he's afraid of. Slapping him around's no good."

"I'd never allow that, Barney."

"You'll be there when they question him?"

"Yes." *And you won't*, Chilton added privately.

"I could get him settled on the other end and be back here just a couple of hours behind my shift," Barney said.

"He's not your job anymore, Barney. I'll be there. I'll show them how to manage him, every step."

"They better pay attention," Barney said. "*He* will."

CLARICE STARLING sat on the side of her motel bed and stared at the black telephone for almost a minute after Crawford hung up. Her hair was tousled and she had twisted her FBI Academy nightgown about her, tossing in her short sleep. She felt like she had been kicked in the stomach.

It had only been three hours since she left Dr Lecter, and two hours since she and Crawford finished working out the sheet of characteristics to check against applications at the medical centers. In that short time, while she slept, Dr Frederick Chilton had managed to screw it up.

Crawford was coming for her. She needed to get ready, had to think about getting ready.

God dammit. God DAMMIT. GOD DAMMIT. You've killed her, Dr Chilton. You've killed her, Dr Fuck Face. Lecter knew some more and I could have gotten it. All gone, all gone, now. All for nothing. When Catherine Martin floats, I'll see that you have to look at her, I swear I will. You took it away from me. I really

*have to have something useful to do. Right now. What can
I do right now, what can I do this minute? Get clean.*

In the bathroom, a little basket of paper-wrapped
soaps, tubes of shampoo and lotion, a little sewing kit,
the favors you get at a good motel.

Stepping into the shower, Starling saw in a flash
herself at eight, bringing in the towels and the shampoo and paper-wrapped soap to her mother when her
mother cleaned motel rooms. When she was eight,
there was a crow, one of a flock on the gritty wind
of that sour town, and this crow liked to steal from the
motel cleaning carts. It took anything bright. The crow
would wait for its chance, and then rummage among
the many housekeeping items on the cart. Sometimes,
in an emergency takeoff, it crapped on the clean linens.
One of the other cleaning women threw bleach at it, to
no effect except to mottle its feathers with snow-white
patches. The black-and-white crow was always watching for Clarice to leave the cart, to take things to her
mother, who was scrubbing bathrooms. Her mother
was standing in the door of a motel bathroom when
she told Starling she would have to go away, to live
in Montana. Her mother put down the towels she was
holding and sat down on the side of the motel bed and
held her. Starling still dreamed about the crow, saw it
now with no time to think why. Her hand came up in a
shooing motion and then, as though it needed to excuse
the gesture, her hand continued to her forehead to slick
back the wet hair.

She dressed quickly. Slacks, blouse, and a light sweater
vest, the snub-nosed revolver tucked tight against her
ribs in the pancake holster, the speedloader straddling

her belt on the other side. Her blazer needed a little work. A seam in the lining was fraying over the speedloader. She was determined to be busy, be busy, until she cooled off. She got the motel's little paper sewing kit and tacked the lining down. Some agents sewed washers into the tail of the jacket so it would swing away cleanly, she'd have to do that . . .

Crawford was knocking on the door.

CHAPTER

31

IN CRAWFORD'S experience, anger made women look tacky. Rage made their hair stick out behind and played hell with their color and they forgot to zip. Any unattractive feature was magnified. Starling looked herself when she opened the door of her motel room, but she was mad all right.

Crawford knew he might learn a large new truth about her now.

Fragrance of soap and steamy air puffed at him as she stood in the doorway. The covers on the bed behind her had been pulled up over the pillow.

"What do you *say*, Starling?"

"I say God dammit, Mr Crawford, what do *you* say?"

He beckoned with his head. "Drugstore's open on the corner already. We'll get some coffee."

It was a mild morning for February. The sun, still low in the east, shone red on the front of the asylum as they walked past. Jeff trailed them slowly in the van, the radios crackling. Once he handed a phone out the window to Crawford for a brief conversation.

"Can I file obstruction of justice on Chilton?"

Starling was walking slightly ahead. Crawford could see her jaw muscles bunch after she asked.

"No, it wouldn't stick."

"What if he's wasted her, what if Catherine dies because of him? I really want to get in his face . . . Let me stay with this, Mr Crawford. Don't send me back to school."

"Two things. If I keep you, it won't be to get in Chilton's face, that comes later. Second, if I keep you much longer, you'll be recycled. Cost you some months. The Academy cuts nobody any slack. I can guarantee you get back in, but that's all—there'll be a place for you, I can tell you that."

She leaned her head far back, then put it down again, walking. "Maybe this isn't a polite question to ask the boss, but are you in the glue? Can Senator Martin do anything to you?"

"Starling, I have to retire in two years. If I find Jimmy Hoffa and the Tylenol killer I still have to hang it up. It's not a consideration."

Crawford, ever wary of desire, knew how badly he wanted to be wise. He knew that a middle-aged man can be so desperate for wisdom he may try to make some up, and how deadly that can be to a youngster who believes him. So he spoke carefully, and only of things he knew.

What Crawford told her on that mean street in Baltimore he had learned in a succession of freezing dawns in Korea, in a war before she was born. He left the Korea part out, since he didn't need it for authority.

"This is the hardest time, Starling. Use this time and it'll temper you. Now's the hardest test—not letting rage and frustration keep you from thinking. It's the core of whether you can command or not. Waste and stupidity get you the worst. Chilton's a God damned fool and he may have cost Catherine Martin her life. But maybe not. We're her chance. Starling, how cold is liquid nitrogen in the lab?"

"What? Ah, liquid nitrogen . . . minus two hundred degrees Centigrade, about. It boils at a little more than that."

"Did you ever freeze stuff with it?"

"Sure."

"I want you to freeze something now. Freeze the business with Chilton. Keep the information you got from Lecter and freeze the feelings. I want you to keep your eyes on the prize, Starling. That's all that matters. You worked for some information, paid for it, got it, now we'll use it. It's just as good—or as worthless—as it was before Chilton messed in this. We just won't get any more from Lecter, probably. Take the knowledge of Buffalo Bill you got from Lecter and keep fit. Freeze the rest. The waste, the loss, your anger, Chilton. Freeze it. When we have time, we'll kick Chilton's butt up between his shoulder blades. Freeze it now and slide it aside. So you can see past it to the prize, Starling. Catherine Martin's life. And Buffalo Bill's hide on the barn door. Keep your eyes on the prize. If you can do that, I need you."

"To work with the medical records?"

They were in front of the drugstore now.

"Not unless the clinics stonewall us and we have to

take the records. I want you in Memphis. We have to hope Lecter tells Senator Martin something useful. But I want you to be close by, just in case—if he gets tired of toying with her, maybe he'll talk to you. In the meantime, I want you to try to get a feel for Catherine, how Bill might have spotted her. You're not a lot older than Catherine, and her friends might tell you things they wouldn't tell somebody that looks more like a cop.

"We've still got the other things going. Interpol's working on identifying Klaus. With an ID on Klaus, we can take a look at his associates in Europe and in California where he had his romance with Benjamin Raspail. I'm going to the University of Minnesota— we got off on the wrong foot up there—and I'll be in Washington tonight. I'll get the coffee now. Whistle up Jeff and the van. You're on a plane in forty minutes."

The red sun had reached three-quarters of the way down the telephone poles. The sidewalks were still violet. Starling could reach up into the light as she waved for Jeff.

She felt lighter, better. Crawford really was very good. She knew that his little nitrogen question was a nod to her forensic background, meant to please her and to trigger ingrained habits of disciplined thinking. She wondered if men actually regard that kind of manipulation as subtle. Curious how things can work on you even when you recognize them. Curious how the gift of leadership is often a coarse gift.

Across the street, a figure coming down the steps of the Baltimore State Hospital for the Criminally Insane.

It was Barney, looking even larger in his lumber jacket. He was carrying his lunchpail.

Starling mouthed "Five minutes" to Jeff waiting in the van. She caught Barney as he was unlocking his old Studebaker.

"Barney."

He turned to face her, expressionless. His eyes may have been a bit wider than usual. He had his weight on both feet.

"Did Dr Chilton tell you you'd be all right from this?"

"What else would he tell me?"

"You believe it?"

The corner of his mouth turned down. He didn't say yes or no.

"I want you to do something for me. I want you to do it now, with no questions. I'll ask you nicely—we'll start with that. What's left in Lecter's cell?"

"A couple of books—*Joy of Cooking*, medical journals. They took his court papers."

"The stuff on the walls, the drawings?"

"It's still there."

"I want it all and I'm in a hell of a hurry."

He considered her for a second. "Hold on," he said and trotted back up the steps, lightly for such a big man.

Crawford was waiting for her in the van when Barney came back out with rolled drawings and the papers and books in a shopping bag.

"You sure I knew the bug was in that desk I brought you?" Barney said as he handed her the stuff.

"I have to give that some thought. Here's a pen, write

your phone numbers on the bag. Barney, you think they can *handle* Dr Lecter?"

"I got my doubts and I said so to Dr Chilton. Remember I told you that, in case it slips his mind. You're all right, Officer Starling. Listen, when you get Buffalo Bill?"

"Yeah?"

"Don't bring him to me just because I got a vacancy, all right?" He smiled. Barney had little baby teeth.

Starling grinned at him in spite of herself. She flapped a wave back over her shoulder as she ran to the van.

Crawford was pleased.

THE GRUMMAN GULFSTREAM carrying Dr Hannibal Lecter touched down in Memphis with two puffs of blue tire smoke. Following directions from the tower, it taxied fast toward the Air National Guard hangars, away from the passenger terminal. An Emergency Service ambulance and a limousine waited inside the first hangar.

Senator Ruth Martin watched through the smoked glass of the limousine as the state troopers rolled Dr Lecter out of the airplane. She wanted to run up to the bound and masked figure and tear the information out of him, but she was smarter than that.

Senator Martin's telephone beeped. Her assistant, Brian Gossage, reached it from the jump seat.

"It's the FBI—Jack Crawford," Gossage said.

Senator Martin held out her hand for the phone without taking her eyes off Dr Lecter.

"Why didn't you tell me about Dr Lecter, Mr Crawford?"

"I was afraid you'd do just what you're doing, Senator."

"I'm not fighting you, Mr Crawford. If you fight me, you'll be sorry."

"Where's Lecter now?"

"I'm looking at him."

"Can he hear you?"

"No."

"Senator Martin, listen to me. You want to make personal guarantees to Lecter—all right, fine. But do this for me. Let Dr Alan Bloom brief you before you go up against Lecter. Bloom can help you, believe me."

"I've got professional advice."

"Better than Chilton, I hope."

Dr Chilton was pecking on the window of the limousine. Senator Martin sent Brian Gossage out to take care of him.

"Infighting wastes time, Mr Crawford. You sent a green recruit to Lecter with a phony offer. I can do better than that. Dr Chilton says Lecter's capable of responding to a straight offer and I'm giving him one— no red tape, no personalities, no questions of credit. If we get Catherine back safe, everybody smells like a rose, you included. If she . . . dies, I don't give a God damn about excuses."

"*Use* us, then, Senator Martin."

She heard no anger in his voice, only a professional, cut-your-losses cool that she recognized. She responded to it. "Go on."

"If you get something, let us act on it. Make sure we have everything. Make sure the local police share. Don't let them think they'll please you by cutting us out."

"Paul Krendler from Justice is coming. He'll see to it."

225

"Who's your ranking officer there now?"

"Major Bachman from the Tennessee Bureau of Investigation."

"Good. If it's not too late, try for a media black-out. You better threaten Chilton about that—he likes attention. We don't want Buffalo Bill to know anything. When we find him, we want to use the Hostage Rescue Team. We want to hit him fast and avoid a standoff. You mean to question Lecter yourself?"

"Yes."

"Will you talk to Clarice Starling first? She's on the way."

"To what purpose? Dr Chilton's summarized that material for me. We've fooled around enough."

Chilton was pecking on the window again, mouthing words through the glass. Brian Gossage put a hand on his wrist and shook his head.

"I want access to Lecter after you've talked to him," Crawford said.

"Mr Crawford, he's promised he'll name Buffalo Bill in exchange for privileges—amenities, really. If he doesn't do that, you can have him forever."

"Senator Martin, I know this is sensitive, but I have to say it to you: whatever you do, don't beg him."

"Right, Mr Crawford. I really can't talk right now." She hung up the phone. "If I'm wrong, she won't be any deader than the last six you handled," she said under her breath, and waved Gossage and Chilton into the car.

Dr Chilton had requested an office setting in Memphis for Senator Martin's interview with Hannibal Lecter. To save time, an Air National Guard briefing room in the hangar had been rearranged hastily for the meeting.

226

Senator Martin had to wait out in the hangar while Dr Chilton got Lecter settled in the office. She couldn't stand to stay in the car. She paced in a small circle beneath the great roof of the hangar, looking up at the high, latticed rafters and down again at the painted stripes on the floor. Once she stopped beside an old Phantom F-4 and rested her head against its cold side where the stencil said NO STEP. *This airplane must be older than Catherine. Sweet Jesus, come on.*

"Senator Martin." Major Bachman was calling her. Chilton beckoned from the door.

There was a desk for Chilton in the room, and chairs for Senator Martin and her assistant and for Major Bachman. A video cameraman was ready to record the meeting. Chilton claimed it was one of Lecter's requirements.

Senator Martin went in looking good. Her navy suit breathed power. She had put some starch in Gossage too.

Dr Hannibal Lecter sat alone in the middle of the room in a stout oak armchair bolted to the floor. A blanket covered his straitjacket and leg restraints and concealed the fact that he was chained to the chair. But he still wore the hockey mask that kept him from biting.

Why? the Senator wondered—the idea had been to permit Dr Lecter some dignity in an office setting. Senator Martin gave Chilton a look and turned to Gossage for papers.

Chilton went behind Dr Lecter and, with a glance at the camera, undid the straps and removed the mask with a flourish.

227

"Senator Martin, meet Dr Hannibal Lecter."

Seeing what Dr Chilton had done for showmanship frightened Senator Martin as much as anything that had happened since her daughter disappeared. Any confidence she might have had in Chilton's judgment was replaced with the cold fear that he was a fool.

She'd have to wing it.

A lock of Dr Lecter's hair fell between his maroon eyes. He was as pale as the mask. Senator Martin and Hannibal Lecter considered each other, one extremely bright and the other not measurable by any means known to man.

Dr Chilton returned to his desk, looked around at everyone, and began:

"Dr Lecter has indicated to me, Senator, that he wants to contribute to the investigation some special knowledge, in return for considerations regarding the conditions of his confinement."

Senator Martin held up a document. "Dr Lecter, this is an affidavit which I'll now sign. It says I'll help you. Want to read it?"

She thought he wasn't going to reply and turned to the desk to sign, when he said:

"I won't waste your time and Catherine's time bargaining for petty privileges. Career climbers have wasted enough already. Let me help you now, and I'll trust you to help me when it's over."

"You can count on it. Brian?"

Gossage raised his pad.

"Buffalo Bill's name is William Rubin. He goes by Billy Rubin. He was referred to me in April or May 1975, by my patient Benjamin Raspail. He said he lived in Philadelphia, I can't remember an address, but he was staying with Raspail in Baltimore."

"Where are your records?" Major Bachman broke in.

"My records were destroyed by court order shortly after—"

"What did he look like?" Major Bachman said.

"Do you *mind*, Major? Senator Martin, the only—"

"Give me an age and a physical description, anything else you can remember," Major Bachman said.

Dr Lecter simply went away. He thought about something else—Géricault's anatomical studies for *The Raft of the Medusa*—and, if he heard the questions that followed, he didn't show it.

When Senator Martin regained his attention, they were alone in the room. She had Gossage's pad.

Dr Lecter's eyes focused on her. "That flag smells like cigars," he said. "Did you nurse Catherine?"

"Pardon me? Did I . . ."

"Did you breast-feed her?"

"Yes."

"Thirsty work, isn't it . . . ?"

When her pupils darkened, Dr Lecter took a single sip of her pain and found it exquisite. That was enough for today. He went on: "William Rubin is about six feet one, and would be thirty-five years old now. He's strongly built—about one hundred ninety pounds when I knew him and he's gained since then, I expect. He has brown hair and pale blue eyes. Give them that much, and then we'll go on."

"Yes, I'll do that," Senator Martin said. She passed her notes out the door.

"I only saw him once. He made another appointment, but he never came again."

"Why do you think he's Buffalo Bill?"

"He was murdering people then, and doing some similar things with them, anatomically. He said he wanted some help to stop, but actually he just wanted to schmooze about it. To *rap*."

"And you didn't—he was sure you wouldn't turn him in?"

"He didn't think I would, and he likes to take chances. I had honored the confidences of his friend Raspail."

"*Raspail* knew he was doing this?"

"Raspail's appetites ran to the louche—he was covered with scars.

"Billy Rubin told me he had a criminal record, but no details. I took a brief medical history. It was unexceptional, except for one thing: Rubin told me he once suffered from elephant ivory anthrax. That's all I remember, Senator Martin, and I expect you're anxious to go. If anything else occurs to me, I'll send you word."

"Did Billy Rubin kill the person whose head was in the car?"

"I believe so."

"Do you know who that is?"

"No. Raspail called him Klaus."

"Were the other things you told the FBI true?"

"At least as true as what the FBI told *me*, Senator Martin."

"I've made some temporary arrangements for you here in Memphis. We'll talk about your situation and

230

you'll go on to Brushy Mountain when this is . . . when we've got it settled."

"Thank you. I'd like a telephone, if I think of something . . ."

"You'll have it."

"And music. Glenn Gould, the *Goldberg Variations*? Would that be too much?"

"Fine."

"Senator Martin, don't entrust any lead solely to the FBI. Jack Crawford never plays fair with the other agencies. It's such a game with those people. He's determined to have the arrest himself. A 'collar,' they call it."

"Thank you, Dr Lecter."

"Love your suit," he said as she went out the door.

ROOM INTO room, Jame Gumb's basement rambles like the maze that thwarts us in dreams. When he was still shy, lives and lives ago, Mr Gumb took his pleasure in the rooms most hidden, far from the stairs. There are rooms in the farthest corners, rooms from other lives, that Gumb hasn't opened in years. Some of them are still occupied, so to speak, though the sounds from behind the doors peaked and trailed off to silence long ago.

The levels of the floors vary from room to room by as much as a foot. There are thresholds to step over, lintels to duck. Loads are impossible to roll and difficult to drag. To march something ahead of you— it stumbling and crying, begging, banging its dazed head—is difficult, dangerous even.

As he grew in wisdom and in confidence, Mr Gumb no longer felt he had to meet his needs in the hidden parts of the basement. He now uses a suite of basement rooms around the stairs, large rooms with running water and electricity.

The basement is in total darkness now.

Beneath the sand-floored room, in the oubliette, Catherine Martin is quiet.

Mr Gumb is here in the basement, but he is not in this chamber.

The room beyond the stairs is black to human vision, but it is full of small sounds. Water trickles here and small pumps hum. In little echoes the room sounds large. The air is moist and cool. Smell the greenery. A flutter of wings against the cheek, a few clicks across the air. A low nasal sound of pleasure, a human sound.

The room has none of the wavelengths of light the human eye can use, but Mr Gumb is here and he can see very well, though he sees everything in shades and intensities of green. He's wearing an excellent pair of infrared goggles (Israeli military surplus, less than four hundred dollars) and he directs the beam of an infrared flashlight on the wire cage in front of him. He is sitting on the edge of a straight chair, rapt, watching an insect climb a plant in the screen cage. The young imago has just emerged from a split chrysalis in the moist earth of the cage floor. She climbs carefully on a stalk of night-shade, seeking space to unfurl the damp new wings still wadded on her back. She selects a horizontal twig.

Mr Gumb must tilt his head to see. Little by little the wings are pumped full of blood and air. They are still stuck together over the insect's back.

Two hours pass. Mr Gumb has hardly moved. He turns the infrared flashlight on and off to surprise himself with the progress the insect has made. To pass the time he plays the light over the rest of the room—over his big aquariums full of vegetable tanning solution. On forms and stretchers in the tanks, his recent acquisitions stand like broken classic statuary green beneath the sea. His light moves over the big galvanized worktable with its metal pillow block and backsplash and drains, touches the hoist above it. Against the wall, his long industrial sinks. All in the green images of filtered infrared. Flutters, streaks of phosphorescence cross his vision, little comet trails of moths free in the room.

He switches back to the cage just in time. The big insect's wings are held above her back, hiding and distorting her markings. Now she brings down her wings to cloak her body and the famous design is clear. A human skull, wonderfully executed in the furlike scales, stares from the back of the moth. Under the shaded dome of the skull are the black eye holes and prominent cheekbones. Beneath them darkness lies like a gag across the face above the jaw. The skull rests on a marking flared like the top of a pelvis.

A skull stacked upon a pelvis, all drawn on the back of a moth by an accident of nature.

Mr Gumb feels so good and light inside. He leans forward, puffs soft air across the moth. She raises her sharp proboscis and squeaks angrily.

He walks quietly with his light into the oubliette room. He opens his mouth to quiet his breathing. He doesn't want to spoil his mood with a lot of noise from the pit. The lenses of his goggles on their small protruding barrels look like crab eyes on stalks. Mr Gumb knows the goggles aren't the least bit attractive, but he has had some great times with them in the black basement, playing basement games.

He leans over and shines his invisible light down the shaft.

The material is lying on her side, curled like a shrimp. She seems to be asleep. Her waste bucket stands beside her. She has not foolishly broken the string again, trying to pull herself up the sheer walls. In her sleep, she clutches the corner of the futon against her face and sucks her thumb.

Watching Catherine, playing the infrared flashlight up and down her, Mr Gumb prepares himself for the very real problems ahead.

The human skin is fiendishly difficult to deal with if your standards are as high as Mr Gumb's. There are fundamental structural decisions to make, and the first one is where to put the zipper.

He moves the beam down Catherine's back. Normally he would put the closure in the back, but then how could he do it alone? It won't be the sort of thing he can ask someone to help him with, exciting as that prospect might be. He knows of places, circles, where his efforts would be much admired—there are certain yachts where he could preen—but that will have to wait. He must have things he can use alone. To split the center front would be sacrilege—he puts that right out of his mind.

Mr Gumb can tell nothing of Catherine's color by infrared, but she looks thinner. He believes she may have been dieting when he took her.

Experience has taught him to wait from four days to a week before harvesting the hide. Sudden weight loss makes the hide looser and easier to remove. In addition, starvation takes much of his subjects' strength and makes them more manageable. More docile. A stuporous resignation comes over some of them. At the same time, it's necessary to provide a few rations to prevent despair and destructive tantrums that might damage the skin.

It definitely has lost weight. This one is so special, so central to what he is doing, he can't stand to wait long, and he doesn't have to. Tomorrow afternoon, he can do it, or tomorrow night. The next day at the latest. Soon.

CLARICE STARLING recognized the Stonehinge Villas sign from television news. The East Memphis housing complex, a mix of flats and town houses, formed a large U around a parking field.

Starling parked her rented Chevrolet Celebrity in the middle of the big lot. Well-paid blue-collar workers and bottom-echelon executives lived here—the Trans-Ams and IROC-Z Camaros told her that. Motor homes for the weekends and ski boats bright with glitter paint were parked in their own section of the lot.

Stonehinge Villas—the spelling grated on Starling every time she looked at it. Probably the apartments were full of white wicker and peach shag. Snapshots under the glass of the coffee table. The *Dinner for Two Cookbook* and *Fondue on the Menu*. Starling, whose only residence was a dormitory room at the FBI Academy, was a severe critic of these things.

She needed to know Catherine Baker Martin, and this seemed an odd place for a senator's daughter to live. Starling had read the brief biographical material the

FBI had gathered, and it showed Catherine Martin to be a bright underachiever. She'd failed at Farmington and had two unhappy years at Middlebury. Now she was a student at Southwestern and a practice teacher.

Starling could easily have pictured her as a self-absorbed, blunted, boarding-school kid, one of those people who never listen. Starling knew she had to be careful here because she had her own prejudices and resentments. Starling had done her time in boarding schools, living on scholarships, her grades much better than her clothes. She had seen a lot of kids from rich, troubled families, with too much boarding-school time. She didn't give a damn about some of them, but she had grown to learn that inattention can be a stratagem to avoid pain, and that it is often misread as shallowness and indifference.

Better to think of Catherine as a child sailing with her father, as she was in the film they showed with Senator Martin's plea on television. She wondered if Catherine tried to please her father when she was little. She wondered what Catherine was doing when they came and told her that her father was dead, of a heart attack at forty-two. Starling was positive Catherine missed him. Missing your father, the common wound, made Starling feel close to this young woman.

Starling found it essential to like Catherine Martin, because it helped her to bear down.

Starling could see where Catherine's apartment was located—two Tennessee Highway Patrol cruisers were parked in front of it. There were spots of white powder on the parking lot in the area closest to the apartment. The Tennessee Bureau of Investigation must have been lifting oil stains with pumice or some other inert powder. Crawford said the TBI was pretty good.

Starling walked over to the recreational vehicles and boats parked in the special section of the lot in front of the apartment. This is where Buffalo Bill got her. Close enough to her door so that she left it unlocked when she came out. Something tempted her out. It must have been a harmless-looking setup.

Starling knew the Memphis police had done exhaustive door-to-door interviews and nobody had seen anything, so maybe it happened among the tall motor homes. He must have watched from here. Sitting in some kind of vehicle, had to be. But Buffalo Bill *knew* Catherine was here. He must have spotted her somewhere and stalked her, waiting for his chance. Girls the size of Catherine aren't common. He didn't just sit around at random locations until a woman of the right size came by. He could sit for days and not see one.

All the victims were big. All of them were big. Some were fat, but all were big. "So he can get something that will fit." Remembering Dr Lecter's words, Starling shuddered. Dr Lecter, the new Memphian.

Starling took a deep breath, puffed up her cheeks and let the air out slowly. *Let's see what we can tell about Catherine.*

A Tennessee state trooper wearing his Smokey the Bear hat answered the door of Catherine Martin's apartment. When Starling showed him her credentials, he motioned her inside.

"Officer, I need to look over the premises here." *Premises* seemed a good word to use to a man who had his hat on in the house.

He nodded. "If the phone rings, leave it alone. I'll answer it."

On the counter in the open kitchen Starling could see a tape recorder attached to the telephone. Beside it were two new telephones. One had no dial—a direct line to Southern Bell security, the mid-South tracing facility.

"Can I help you any way?" the young officer asked.

"Are the police through in here?"

"The apartment's been released to the family. I'm just here for the telephone. You can touch stuff, if that's what you want to know."

"Good, I'll look around, then."

"Okay." The young policeman retrieved the newspaper he had stuffed beneath the couch and resumed his seat.

Starling wanted to concentrate. She wished she were alone in the apartment, but she knew she was lucky the place wasn't full of cops.

She started in the kitchen. It was not equipped by a serious cook. Catherine had come for popcorn, the boyfriend had told police. Starling opened the freezer. There were two boxes of microwave popcorn. You couldn't see the parking lot from the kitchen.

"Where you from?"

Starling didn't register the question the first time.

"Where you from?"

The trooper on the couch was watching her over his newspaper.

"Washington," she said.

Under the sink—yep, scratches on the pipe joint, they'd taken the trap out and examined it. Good for the TBI. The knives were not sharp. The dishwasher had been run, but not emptied. The refrigerator was devoted to cottage cheese and deli fruit salad. Catherine Martin shopped for fast-food groceries, probably had a regular place, a drive-in she used close by. Maybe somebody cruised the store. That's worth checking.

"You with the Attorney General?"

"No, the FBI"

"The Attorney General's coming. That's what I heard at turnout. How long you been in the FBI?"

Starling looked at the young policeman.

"Officer, tell you what. I'll probably need to ask you a couple of things after I've finished looking around here. Maybe you could help me out then."

"Sure. If I can—"

"Good, okay. Let's wait and talk then. I have to think about this right now."

"No problem, there."

The bedroom was bright, with a sunny, drowsy quality Starling liked. It was done with better fabrics and better furnishings than most young women could afford. There were a Coromandel screen, two pieces of cloisonné on the shelves, and a good secretary in burled walnut. Twin beds. Starling lifted the edge of the coverlets. Rollers were locked on the left bed, but not on the right-hand one. *Catherine must push them together when it suits her. May have a lover the boyfriend doesn't know about. Or maybe they stay over here sometimes. There's no remote beeper on her answering machine. She may need to be here when her mom calls.*

The answering machine was like her own, the basic Phone-Mate. She opened the top panel. Both incoming

241

and outgoing tapes were gone. In their place was a note, TAPES TBI PROPERTY #6.

The room was reasonably neat but it had the ruffled appearance left by searchers with big hands, men who try to put things back exactly, but miss just a little bit. Starling would have known the place had been searched even without the traces of fingerprint powder on all the smooth surfaces.

Starling didn't believe that any part of the crime had happened in the bedroom. Crawford probably was right: Catherine had been grabbed in the parking lot. But Starling wanted to know her, and this is where she lived. *Lives*, Starling corrected herself. She *lives* here.

In the cabinet of the nightstand were a telephone book, Kleenex, a box of grooming items and, behind the box, a Polaroid SX-70 camera with a cable release and a short tripod folded beside it. Ummmm. Intent as a lizard, Starling looked at the camera. She blinked as a lizard blinks and didn't touch it.

The closet interested Starling most. Catherine Baker Martin, laundry mark C-B-M, had a lot of clothes and some of them were very good. Starling recognized many of the labels, including Garfinkel's and Britches in Washington. *Presents from Mommy*, Starling said to herself. Catherine had fine, classic clothes in two sizes, made to fit her at about 145 and 165 pounds, Starling guessed, and there were a few pairs of crisis fat pants and pullovers from the Statuesque Shop. In a hanging rack were twenty-three pairs of shoes. Seven pairs were Ferragamos in 10C, and there were some Reeboks and run-over loafers. A light backpack and a tennis racket were on the top shelf.

The belongings of a privileged kid, a student and practice teacher who lived better than most.

Lots of letters in the secretary. Loopy backhand notes from former classmates in the East. Stamps, mailing labels. Gift wrapping paper in the bottom drawer, a sheaf in various colors and patterns. Starling's fingers walked through it. She was thinking about questioning the clerks at the local drive-in market when her fingers found a sheet in the stack of gift wrap that was too thick and stiff. Her fingers went past it, walked back to it. She was trained to register anomalies and she had it half pulled out when she looked at it. The sheet was blue, of a material similar to a lightweight blotter, and the pattern printed on it was a crude imitation of the cartoon dog Pluto. The little rows of dogs all looked like Pluto, they were the proper yellow, but they weren't exactly right in their proportions.

"Catherine, Catherine," Starling said. She took some tweezers from her bag and used them to slide the sheet of colored paper into a plastic envelope. She placed it on the bed for the time being.

The jewelry box on the dresser was a stamped-leather affair, the kind you see in every girl's dormitory room. The two drawers in front and the tiered lid contained costume jewelry, no valuable pieces. Starling wondered if the best things had been in the rubber cabbage in the refrigerator, and, if so, who took them.

She hooked her finger under the side of the lid and released the secret drawer in the back of the jewelry box. The secret drawer was empty. She wondered whom these drawers were a secret from—certainly not burglars. She was reaching behind the jewelry box, pushing the drawer back in, when her fingers touched the envelope taped to the underside of the secret drawer.

Starling pulled on a pair of cotton gloves and turned the jewelry box around. She took out the empty drawer and inverted it. A brown envelope was taped to the bottom of the drawer with masking tape. The flap was just tucked in, not sealed. She held the paper close to her nose. The envelope had not been fumed for fingerprints. Starling used the tweezers to open it and extract the contents. There were five Polaroid pictures in the envelope and she took them out one by one. The pictures were of a man and a woman coupling. No heads or faces appeared. Two of the pictures were taken by the woman, two by the man, and one appeared to have been shot from the tripod set up on the nightstand.

It was hard to judge scale in a photograph, but with that spectacular 145 pounds on a long frame, the woman had to be Catherine Martin. The man wore what appeared to be a carved ivory ring on his penis. The resolution of the photograph was not sharp enough to reveal the details of it. The man had had his appendix out. Starling bagged the photographs, each in a sandwich bag, and put them in her own brown envelope. She returned the drawer to the jewelry box.

"I have the good stuff in my pocketbook," said a voice behind her. "I don't think anything was taken."

Starling looked in the mirror. Senator Ruth Martin stood in the bedroom door. She looked drained.

Starling turned around. "Hello, Senator Martin. Would you like to lie down? I'm almost finished."

Even exhausted, Senator Martin had a lot of presence. Under her careful finish, Starling saw a scrapper.

"Who are you, please? I thought the police were through in here."

"I'm Clarice Starling, FBI. Did you talk to Dr Lecter, Senator?"

"He gave me a name." Senator Martin lit a cigarette and looked Starling up and down. "We'll see what it's worth. And what did you find in the jewelry box, Officer Starling? What's *it* worth?"

"Some documentation we can check out in just a few minutes," was the best Starling could do.

"In my daughter's jewelry box? Let's see it."

Starling heard voices in the next room and hoped for an interruption. "Is Mr Copley with you, the Memphis special agent in—"

"No, he's not, and that's not an answer. No offense, Officer, but I'll see what you got out of my daughter's jewelry box." She turned her head and called over her shoulder. "Paul. Paul, would you come in here? Officer Starling, you may know Mr Krendler from the Department of Justice. Paul, this is the girl Jack Crawford sent in to Lecter."

Krendler's bald spot was tanned and he looked fit at forty.

"Mr Krendler, I know who you are. Hello," Starling said. *DeeJay Criminal Division congressional liaison, troubleshooter, at least an Assistant Deputy Attorney General, Jesus God, save my bod.*

"Officer Starling found something in my daughter's jewelry box and she put it in her brown envelope. I think we'd better see what it is, don't you?"

"Officer," Krendler said.

"May I speak to you, Mr Krendler?"

"Of course you can. Later." He held out his hand.

Starling's face was hot. She knew Senator Martin was not herself, but she would never forgive Krendler for the doubt in his face. Never.

"You got it," Starling said. She handed him the envelope.

Krendler looked in at the first picture and had closed the flap again when Senator Martin took the envelope out of his hands.

It was painful to watch her examine the pictures. When she finished, she went to the window and stood with her face turned up to the overcast sky, her eyes closed. She looked old in the daylight and her hand trembled when she tried to smoke.

"Senator, I—" Krendler began.

"The police searched this room," Senator Martin said. "I'm sure they found those pictures and had sense enough to put them back and keep their mouths shut."

"No they did *not*," Starling said. The woman was wounded but, hell. "Mrs Martin, we need to know who this man is, you can see that. If it's the boyfriend, fine. I can find that out in five minutes. Nobody else needs to see the pictures and Catherine never needs to know."

"I'll tend to it." Senator Martin put the envelope in her purse, and Krendler let her do it.

"Senator, did you take the jewelry out of the rubber cabbage in the kitchen?" Starling asked.

Senator Martin's aide, Brian Gossage, stuck his head in the door. "Excuse me, Senator, they've got the terminal set up. We can watch them search the William Rubin name at the FBI."

"Go ahead, Senator Martin," Krendler said. "I'll be out in a second."

Ruth Martin left the room without answering Starling's question.

Starling had a chance to look Krendler over as he was closing the bedroom door. His suit was a triumph of single-needle tailoring and he was not armed. The shine was buffed off the bottom half-inch of his heels from walking on much deep carpet, and the edges of the heels were sharp.

He stood for a moment with his hand on the doorknob, his head down.

"That was a good search," he said when he turned around.

Starling couldn't be had that cheap. She looked back at him.

"They turn out good rummagers at Quantico," Krendler said.

"They don't turn out thieves."

"I know that," he said.

"Hard to tell."

"Drop it."

"We'll follow up on the pictures and the rubber cabbage, right?" she said.

"Yes."

"What's the 'William Rubin' name, Mr Krendler?"

"Lecter says that's Buffalo Bill's name. Here's our transmission to ID Section and NCIC. Look at this."
He gave her a transcript of the Lecter interview with Senator Martin, blurry copy from a dot-matrix printer.

"Any thoughts?" he said when she finished reading.

"There's nothing here he'll ever have to eat," Starling

said. "He says it's a white male named Billy Rubin who had elephant ivory anthrax. You couldn't catch him in a lie here, no matter what happens. At the worst he'd just be mistaken. I hope this is true. But he could be having fun with her. Mr Krendler, he's perfectly capable of that. Have you ever . . . met him?"

Krendler shook his head and snorted air from his nose.

"Dr Lecter killed nine people we know of. He's not walking, no matter—he could raise the dead and they wouldn't let him out. So all that's left for him is *fun*. That's why we were playing him—"

"I know how you were playing him. I heard Chilton's tape. I'm not saying it was wrong—I'm saying it's over. Behavioral Science can follow up what you got—the transsexual angle—for what it's worth. And you'll be back in school at Quantico tomorrow."

Oh boy. "I found something else."

The sheet of colored paper had lain on the bed unnoticed. She gave it to him.

"What is it?"

"Looks like a sheet of Plutos." She made him ask the rest.

He beckoned for the information with his hand.

"I'm pretty sure it's blotter acid. LSD. From maybe the middle seventies or before. It's a curiosity now. It's worth finding out where she got it. We should test it to be sure."

"You can take it back to Washington and give it to the lab. You'll be going in a few minutes."

"If you don't want to wait, we can do it now with a field kit. If the police've got a standard Narcotics

Identification Kit, it's test J, take two seconds, we can—"

"Back to Washington, back to school," he said, opening the door.

"Mr Crawford instructed me—"

"Your *instructions* are what I'm telling you. You're not under Jack Crawford's direction now. You're back under the same supervision as any other trainee forthwith, and your business is at Quantico, do you understand me? There's a plane at two-ten. Be on it."

"Mr Krendler, Dr Lecter talked to me after he refused to talk to the Baltimore police. He might do that again. Mr Crawford thought—"

Krendler closed the door again, harder than he had to. "Officer Starling, I don't have to explain myself to you, but listen to me. Behavioral Science's brief is advisory, always has been. It's going back to that. Jack Crawford should be on compassionate leave anyway. I'm surprised he's been able to perform as well as he has. He took a foolish chance with this, keeping it from Senator Martin, and he got his butt sawed off. With his record, this close to retirement, even *she* can't hurt him that much. So I wouldn't worry about his pension, if I were you."

Starling lost it a little. "You've got somebody else who's caught three serial murderers? You know anybody else who's caught one? You shouldn't let her run this, Mr Krendler."

"You must be a bright kid, or Crawford wouldn't bother with you, so I'll tell you one time: do something about that mouth or it'll put you in the typing pool. Don't you understand—the only reason you were ever sent to Lecter in the first place was to get some news for your Director to use on Capitol Hill. Harmless stuff on major crimes, the 'inside scoop' on Dr Lecter, he hands that stuff out like pocket candy while he's trying to get the budget through. Congressmen eat it up, they dine out on it. You're out of line, Officer Starling, and you're out of this case. I know you got supplementary ID. Let's have it."

"I need the ID to fly with the gun. The gun belongs at Quantico."

"Gun. *Jesus*. Turn in the ID as soon as you get back."

Senator Martin, Gossage, a technician, and several policemen were gathered around a video display terminal with a modem connected to the telephone. The National Crime Information Center's hotline kept a running account of progress as Dr Lecter's information was processed in Washington. Here was news from the National Center for Disease Control in Atlanta: Elephant ivory anthrax is contracted by breathing dust from grinding African ivory, usually for decorative handles. In the United States it is a disease of knife-makers.

At the word "knifemakers," Senator Martin closed her eyes. They were hot and dry. She squeezed the Kleenex in her hand.

The young trooper who had let Starling into the apartment was bringing the Senator a cup of coffee. He still had on his hat.

Starling was damned if she'd slink out. She stopped before the woman and said, "Good luck, Senator. I hope Catherine's all right."

Senator Martin nodded without looking at her. Krendler urged Starling out.

"I didn't know she wasn't s'posed to be in here," the young trooper said as she left the room.

Krendler stepped outside with her. "I have nothing but respect for Jack Crawford," he said. "Please tell him how sorry we all are about . . . Bella's problem, all that. Now let's get back to school and get busy, all right?"

"Good-bye, Mr Krendler."

Then she was alone on the parking lot, with the unsteady feeling that she understood nothing at all in this world.

She watched a pigeon walk around beneath the motor homes and boats. It picked up a peanut hull and put it back down. The damp wind ruffled its feathers.

Starling wished she could talk to Crawford. *Waste and stupidity get you the worst*, that's what he said. *Use this time and it'll temper you. Now's the hardest test— not letting rage and frustration keep you from thinking. It's the core of whether you can command or not.*

She didn't give a damn about commanding. She found she didn't give a damn, or a shit for that matter, about being Special Agent Starling. Not if you play this way.

She thought about the poor, fat, sad, dead girl she saw on the table in the funeral home at Potter, West Virginia. *Painted her nails with glitter just like these God damned redneck ski boats.*

What was her name? Kimberly.

Damn if these assholes are gonna see me cry.

Jesus, everybody was named Kimberly, four in her class. Three guys named Sean. Kimberly with her

251

soap-opera name tried to fix herself, punched all those holes in her ears trying to look pretty, trying to decorate herself. And Buffalo Bill looked at her sad flat tits and stuck the muzzle of a gun between them and blew a starfish on her chest.

Kimberly, her sad, fat sister who waxed her legs. No wonder—judging from her face and her arms and legs, her skin was her best feature. *Kimberly, are you angry somewhere?* No senators looking out for her. No jets to carry crazy men around. *Crazy* was a word she wasn't supposed to use. Lot of stuff she wasn't supposed to do. *Crazy men.*

Starling looked at her watch. She had an hour and a half before the plane, and there was one small thing she could do. She wanted to look in Dr Lecter's face when he said "Billy Rubin." If she could stand to meet those strange maroon eyes for long enough, if she looked deeply where the dark sucks in the sparks, she might see something useful. She thought she might see glee.

Thank God I've still got the ID.

She laid twelve feet of rubber pulling out of the parking lot.

CLARICE STARLING driving in a hurry through the perilous Memphis traffic, two tears of anger dried stiff on her cheeks. She felt oddly floaty and free now. An unnatural clarity in her vision warned her that she was inclined to fight, so she was careful of herself.

She had passed the old courthouse earlier on her way from the airport, and she found it again without trouble.

The Tennessee authorities were taking no chances with Hannibal Lecter. They were determined to hold him securely without exposing him to the dangers of the city jail.

Their answer was the former courthouse and jail, a massive Gothic-style structure built of granite back when labor was free. It was a city office building now, somewhat over-restored in this prosperous, history-conscious town.

Today it looked like a medieval stronghold surrounded by police.

A mix of law-enforcement cruisers—highway patrol,

Shelby County Sheriff's Department, Tennessee Bureau of Investigation, and Department of Corrections— crowded the parking lot. There was a police post to pass before Starling even could get in to park her rented car.

Dr Lecter presented an additional security problem from outside. Threatening calls had been coming in ever since the mid-morning newscasts reported his whereabouts; his victims had many friends and relatives who would love to see him dead.

Starling hoped the resident FBI agent, Copley, wasn't here. She didn't want to get him in trouble.

She saw the back of Chilton's head in a knot of reporters on the grass beside the main steps. There were two television minicams in the crowd. Starling wished her head were covered. She turned her face away as she approached the entrance to the tower.

A state trooper stationed in front of the door examined her ID card before she could go into the foyer. The foyer of the tower looked like a guardroom now. A city policeman was stationed at the single tower elevator, and another at the stairs. State troopers, the relief for the patrol units stationed around the building, read the *Commercial Appeal* on the couches where the public could not see them.

A sergeant manned the desk opposite the elevator. His name tag said TATE, C.L.

"No press," Sergeant Tate said when he saw Starling.

"No," she said.

"You with the Attorney General's people?" he said when he looked at her card.

254

"Deputy Assistant Attorney General Krendler," she said. "I just left him."

He nodded. "We've had every kind of cop in West Tennessee in here wanting to look at Dr Lecter. Don't see something like that very often, thank God. You'll need to talk to Dr Chilton before you go up."

"I saw him outside," Starling said. "We were working on this in Baltimore earlier today. Is this where I log in, Sergeant Tate?"

The sergeant briefly checked a molar with his tongue. "Right there," he said. "Detention rules, miss. Visitors check weapons, cops or not."

Starling nodded. She dumped the cartridges from her revolver, the sergeant glad to watch her hands move on the gun. She gave it to him butt first, and he locked it in his drawer.

"Vernon, take her up." He dialed three digits and spoke her name into the phone.

The elevator, an addition from the 1920s, creaked up to the top floor. It opened onto a stair landing and a short corridor.

"Right straight across, ma'am," the trooper said.

Painted on the frosted glass of the door was SHELBY COUNTY HISTORICAL SOCIETY.

Almost all the top floor of the tower was one octagonal room painted white, with a floor and moldings of polished oak. It smelled of wax and library paste. With its few furnishings, the room had a spare, Congregational feeling. It looked better now than it ever had as a bailiff's office.

Two men in the uniform of the Tennessee Department of Corrections were on duty. The small one stood up at his desk when Starling came in. The bigger one sat in a folding chair at the far end of the room, facing the door of a cell. He was the suicide watch.

"You're authorized to talk with the prisoner, ma'am?" the officer at the desk said. His nameplate read PEMBRY, T.W. and his desk set included a telephone, two riot batons, and Chemical Mace. A long pinion stood in the corner behind him.

"Yes, I am," Starling said. "I've questioned him before."

"You know the rules? Don't pass the barrier."

"Absolutely."

The only color in the room was the police traffic barrier, a brightly striped sawhorse in orange and yellow mounted with round yellow flashers, now turned off. It stood on the polished floor five feet in front of the cell door. On a coat tree nearby hung the doctor's things—the hockey mask and something Starling had never seen before, a Kansas gallows vest. Made of heavy leather, with double-locking wrist shackles at the waist and buckles in the back, it may be the most infallible restraint garment in the world. The mask and the black vest suspended by its nape from the coat tree made a disturbing composition against the white wall.

Starling could see Dr Lecter as she approached the cell. He was reading at a small table bolted to the floor. His back was to the door. He had a number of books and the copy of the running file on Buffalo Bill she had given him in Baltimore. A small cassette player was chained to the table leg. How strange to see him outside the asylum.

Starling had seen cells like this before, as a child.

256

They were prefabricated by a St Louis company around the turn of the century, and no one has ever built them better—a tempered steel modular cage that turns any room into a cell. The floor was sheet steel laid over bars, and the walls and ceiling of cold-forged bars completely lined the room. There was no window. The cell was spotlessly white and brightly lit. A flimsy paper screen stood in front of the toilet.

These white bars ribbed the walls. Dr Lecter had a sleek dark head.

He's a cemetery mink. He lives down in a ribcage in the dry leaves of a heart.

She blinked it away.

"Good morning, Clarice," he said without turning around. He finished his page, marked his place and spun in his chair to face her, his forearms on the chair back, his chin resting on them. "Dumas tells us that the addition of a crow to bouillon in the fall, when the crow has fattened on juniper berries, greatly improves the color and flavor of stock. How do *you* like it in the soup, Clarice?"

"I thought you might want your drawings, the stuff from your cell, just until you get your view."

"How thoughtful. Dr Chilton's euphoric about you and Jack Crawford being put off the case. Or did they send you in for one last wheedle?"

The officer on suicide watch had strolled back to talk to Officer Pembry at the desk. Starling hoped they couldn't hear.

"They didn't send me. I just came."

"People will say we're in love. Don't you want to ask about Billy Rubin, Clarice?"

"Dr Lecter, without in any way . . . impugning what

257

you've told Senator Martin, would you advise me to go
on with your idea about—"

"*Impugning*—I love it. I wouldn't advise you at all.
You tried to fool me, Clarice. Do you think I'm playing
with these people?"

"I think you were telling me the truth."

"Pity you tried to fool me, isn't it?" Dr Lecter's face
sank behind his arms until only his eyes were visible.
"Pity Catherine Martin won't ever see the sun again.
The sun's a mattress fire her God died in, Clarice."

"Pity you have to pander now and lick a few tears
when you can," Starling said. "It's a pity we didn't get
to finish what we were talking about. Your idea of the
imago, the structure of it, had a kind of . . . elegance
that's hard to get away from. Now it's like a ruin, half
an arch standing there."

"Half an arch won't stand. Speaking of arches, will
they still let you pound a beat, Clarice? Did they take
your badge?"

"No."

"What's that under your jacket, a watchman's clock
just like Dad's?"

"No, that's a speedloader."

"So you go around armed?"

"Yes."

"Then you should let your jacket out. Do you sew
at all?"

"Yes."

"Did you make that costume?"

"No. Dr Lecter, you find out everything. You couldn't
have talked intimately with this 'Billy Rubin' and come
out knowing so little about him."

"You think not?"

"If you met him, you know *everything*. But today you happened to remember just one detail. He'd had elephant ivory anthrax. You should have seen them jump when Atlanta said it's a disease of knifemakers. They ate it up, just like you knew they would. You should have gotten a suite at the Peabody for that. Dr Lecter, if you met him, you know about him. I think maybe you didn't meet him and Raspail told you about him. Secondhand stuff wouldn't sell as well to Senator Martin, would it?"

Starling took a quick look over her shoulder. One of the officers was showing the other something in *Guns & Ammo* magazine. "You had more to tell me in Baltimore, Dr Lecter. I believe that stuff was valid. Tell me the rest."

"I've read the cases, Clarice, have you? Everything you need to know to find him is right there, if you're paying attention. Even Inspector Emeritus Crawford should have figured it out. Incidentally, did you read Crawford's *stupefying* speech last year to the National Police Academy? Spouting Marcus Aurelius on duty and honor and fortitude—we'll see what kind of a Stoic Crawford is when Bella bites the big one. He copies his philosophy out of *Bartlett's Familiar*, I think. If he understood Marcus Aurelius, he might solve his case."

"Tell me how."

"When you show the odd flash of contextual intelligence, I forget your generation can't read, Clarice. The Emperor counsels simplicity. First principles. Of each particular thing, ask: What is it in itself, in its own constitution? What is its causal nature?"

"That doesn't mean anything to me."

"What does he do, the man you want?"

"He kills—"

"Ah—" he said sharply, averting his face for a moment from her wrongheadedness. "That's incidental. What is the first and principal thing he does, what need does he serve by killing?"

"Anger, social resentment, sexual frus—"

"No."

"What, then?"

"He covets. In fact, he covets being the very thing you are. It's his nature to covet. How do we begin to covet, Clarice? Do we seek out things to covet? Make an effort at an answer."

"No. We just—"

"No. Precisely so. We begin by coveting what we see every day. Don't you feel eyes moving over you every day, Clarice, in chance encounters? I hardly see how you could not. And don't your eyes move over things?"

"All right, then tell me how—"

"It's your turn to tell *me*, Clarice. You don't have any beach vacations at the Hoof and Mouth Disease Station to offer me anymore. It's strictly quid pro quo from here on out. I have to be careful doing business with you. Tell me, Clarice."

"Tell you what?"

"The two things you owe me from before. What happened to you and the horse, and what you do with your anger."

"Dr Lecter, when there's time I'll—"

"We don't reckon time the same way, Clarice. This is all the time you'll ever have."

"Later, listen, I'll—"

"I'll *listen now*. Two years after your father's death, your mother sent you to live with her cousin and her husband on a ranch in Montana. You were ten years old. You discovered they fed out slaughter horses. You ran away with a horse that couldn't see very well. And?"

"—It was summer and we could sleep out. We got as far as Bozeman by a back road."

"Did the horse have a name?"

"Probably, but they don't—you don't find that out when you're feeding out slaughter horses. I called her Hannah, that seemed like a good name."

"Were you leading her or riding?"

"Some of both. I had to lead her up beside a fence to climb on."

"You rode and walked to Bozeman."

"There was a livery stable, dude ranch, riding academy sort of thing just outside of town. I tried to see about them keeping her. It was twenty dollars a week in the corral. More for a stall. They could tell right off she couldn't see. I said okay, I'll lead her around. Little kids can sit on her and I'll lead her around while their parents are, you know, regular riding. I can stay right here and muck out stalls. One of them, the man, agreed to everything I said while his wife called the sheriff."

"The sheriff was a policeman, like your father."

"That didn't keep me from being scared of him, at first. He had a big red face. The sheriff finally put up twenty dollars for a week's board while he 'straightened things out.' He said there was no use going for the stall in warm weather. The papers picked it up. There was a flap. My mother's cousin agreed to let me go. I wound up going to the Lutheran Home in Bozeman."

"It's an orphanage?"

"Yes."

"And Hannah?"

"She went too. A big Lutheran rancher put up the hay. They already had a barn at the orphanage. We plowed the garden with her. You had to watch where she was going, though. She'd walk through the butterbean trellises and step on any kind of plant that was too short for her to feel it against her legs. And we led her around pulling kids in a cart."

"She died though."

"Well, yes."

"Tell me about that."

"It was last year, they wrote me at school. They think she was about twenty-two. Pulled a cart full of kids the last day she lived, and died in her sleep."

Dr Lecter seemed disappointed. "How heartwarming," he said. "Did your foster father in Montana fuck you, Clarice?"

"No."

"Did he try?"

"No."

"What made you run away with the horse?"

"They were going to kill her."

"Did you know when?"

"Not exactly. I worried about it all the time. She was getting pretty fat."

"What triggered you then? What set you off on that particular day?"

"I don't know."

"I think you do."

"I had worried about it all the time."

"What set you off, Clarice? You started what time?"

"Early. Still dark."

"Then something woke you. What woke you up? Did you dream? What was it?"

"I woke up and heard the lambs screaming. I woke up in the dark and the lambs were screaming."

"They were slaughtering the spring lambs?"

"Yes."

"What did you do?"

"I couldn't do anything for them. I was just a—"

"What did you do with the *horse*?"

"I got dressed without turning on the light and went outside. She was scared. All the horses in the pen were scared and milling around. I blew in her nose and she knew it was me. Finally, she'd put her nose in my hand. The lights were on in the barn and in the shed by the sheep pen. Bare bulbs, big shadows. The refrigerator truck had come and it was idling, roaring. I led her away."

"Did you saddle her?"

"No. I didn't take their saddle. Just a rope hackamore was all."

"As you went off in the dark, could you hear the lambs back where the lights were?"

"Not long. There weren't but twelve."

"You still wake up sometimes, don't you? Wake up in the iron dark with the lambs screaming?"

"Sometimes."

"Do you think, if you caught Buffalo Bill yourself and if you made Catherine all right, you could make the lambs stop screaming, do you think they'd be all right too and you wouldn't wake up again in the dark and hear the lambs screaming? Clarice?"

"Yes. I don't know. Maybe."

"Thank you, Clarice." Dr Lecter seemed oddly at peace.

"Tell me his name, Dr Lecter," Starling said.

"Dr Chilton," Lecter said, "I believe you know each other."

For an instant, Starling didn't realize Chilton was behind her. Then he took her elbow.

She took it back. Officer Pembry and his big partner were with Chilton.

"In the elevator," Chilton said. His face was mottled red.

"Did you know Dr Chilton has no medical degree?" Dr Lecter said. "Please bear that in mind later on."

"Let's go," Chilton said.

"You're not in charge here, Dr Chilton," Starling said.

Officer Pembry came around Chilton. "No, ma'am, but I am. He called my boss and your boss both. I'm sorry, but I've got orders to see you out. Come on with me, now."

"Good-bye, Clarice. Will you let me know if ever the lambs stop screaming?"

"Yes."

Pembry was taking her arm. It was go or fight him.

"Yes," she said. "I'll tell you."

"Do you promise?"

"Yes."

"Then why not finish the arch? Take your case file

with you, Clarice, I won't need it anymore." He held it at arm's length through the bars, his forefinger along the spine. She reached across the barrier and took it. For an instant the tip of her forefinger touched Dr Lecter's. The touch crackled in his eyes.

"Thank you, Clarice."

"Thank you, Dr Lecter."

And that is how he remained in Starling's mind. Caught in the instant when he did not mock. Standing in his white cell, arched like a dancer, his hands clasped in front of him and his head slightly to the side.

She went over a speed bump at the airport fast enough to bang her head on the roof of the car, and had to run for the airplane Krendler had ordered her to catch.

OFFICERS PEMBRY and Boyle were experienced men brought especially from Brushy Mountain State Prison to be Dr Lecter's warders. They were calm and careful and did not feel they needed their job explained to them by Dr Chilton.

They had arrived in Memphis ahead of Lecter and examined the cell minutely. When Dr Lecter was brought to the old courthouse, they examined him as well. He was subjected to an internal body search by a male nurse while he was still in restraints. His clothing was searched thoroughly and a metal detector run over the seams.

Boyle and Pembry came to an understanding with him, speaking in low, civil tones close to his ears as he was examined.

"Dr Lecter, we can get along just fine. We'll treat you just as good as you treat us. Act like a gentleman and you get the Eskimo Pie. But we're not pussyfooting around with you, buddy. Try to bite, and we'll leave you smooth-mouthed. Looks like you got something good going here. You don't want to fuck it up, do you?"

Dr Lecter crinkled his eyes at them in a friendly fashion. If he had been inclined to reply, he would have been prevented by the wooden peg between his molars as the nurse shone a flashlight in his mouth and ran a gloved finger into his cheeks.

The metal detector beeped at his cheeks.

"What's that?" the nurse asked.

"Fillings," Pembry said. "Pull his lip back there. You've put some miles on them back ones, haven't you, Doc?"

"Strikes me he's pretty much of a broke-dick," Boyle confided to Pembry after they had Dr Lecter secure in his cell. "He won't be no trouble if he don't flip out."

The cell, while secure and strong, lacked a rolling food carrier. At lunchtime, in the unpleasant atmosphere that followed Starling's visit, Dr Chilton inconvenienced everyone, making Boyle and Pembry go through the long process of securing the compliant Dr Lecter in the straitjacket and leg restraints as he stood with his back to the bars, Chilton poised with the Mace, before they opened the door to carry in his tray.

Chilton refused to use Boyle's and Pembry's names, though they wore nameplates, and addressed them indiscriminately as "you, there."

For their part, after the warders heard Chilton was not a real MD, Boyle observed to Pembry that he was just "some kind of a God damned schoolteacher."

Pembry tried once to explain to Chilton that Starling's visit had been approved not by them but by the desk downstairs, and saw that in Chilton's anger it didn't matter.

Dr Chilton was absent at supper and, with Dr Lecter's bemused cooperation, Boyle and Pembry used their own method to take in his tray. It worked very well.

"Dr Lecter, you not gonna be needing your dinner jacket tonight," Pembry said. "I'll ask you to sit on the floor and scoot backwards till you can just stick your hands out through the bars, arms extended backward. There you go. Scoot up a little and straighten 'em out more behind you, elbows straight." Pembry handcuffed Dr Lecter tightly outside the bars, with a bar between his arms, and a low crossbar above them. "That hurts just a little bit, don't it? I know it does and they won't be on there but a minute, save us both a lot of trouble."

Dr Lecter could not rise, even to a squat, and with his legs straight in front of him on the floor, he couldn't kick.

Only when Dr Lecter was pinioned did Pembry return to the desk for the key to the cell door. Pembry slid his riot baton in the ring at his wrist, put a canister of Mace in his pocket, and returned to the cell. He opened the door while Boyle took in the tray. When the door was secured, Pembry took the key back to the desk before he took the cuffs off Dr Lecter. At no time was he near the bars with the key while the doctor was free in the cell.

"Now that was pretty easy, wasn't it?" Pembry said.

"It was very convenient, thank you, Officer," Dr Lecter said. "You know, I'm just trying to get by."

"We all are, brother," Pembry said.

Dr Lecter toyed with his food while he wrote and

drew and doodled on his pad with a felt-tipped pen. He flipped over the cassette in the tape player chained to the table leg and punched the play button. Glenn Gould playing Bach's *Goldberg Variations* on the piano. The music, beautiful beyond plight and time, filled the bright cage and the room where the warders sat.

For Dr Lecter, sitting still at the table, time slowed and spread as it does in action. For him the notes of music moved apart without losing tempo. Even Bach's silver pounces were discrete notes glittering off the steel around him. Dr Lecter rose, his expression abstracted, and watched his paper napkin slide off his thighs to the floor. The napkin was in the air a long time, brushed the table leg, flared, sideslipped, stalled and turned over before it came to rest on the steel floor. He made no effort to pick it up, but took a stroll across his cell, went behind the paper screen and sat on the lid of his toilet, his only private place. Listening to the music, he leaned sideways on the sink, his chin in his hand, his strange maroon eyes half-closed. The *Goldberg Variations* interested him structurally. Here it came again, the bass progression from the saraband repeated, repeated. He nodded along, his tongue moving over the edges of his teeth. All the way around on top, all the way around on the bottom. It was a long and interesting trip for his tongue, like a good walk in the Alps.

He did his gums now, sliding his tongue high in the crevice between his cheek and gum and moving it slowly around as some men do when ruminating. His gums were cooler than his tongue. It was cool up in the crevice. When his tongue got to the little metal tube, it stopped.

269

Over the music, he heard the elevator clank and whir as it started up. Many notes of music later, the elevator door opened and a voice he did not know said, "I'm s'posed to get the tray."

Dr Lector heard the smaller one coming, Pembry. He could see through the crack between the panels in his screen. Pembry was at the bars.

"Dr Lecter. Come sit on the floor with your back to the bars like we did before."

"Officer Pembry, would you mind if I just finish up here? I'm afraid my trip's gotten my digestion a little out of sorts." It took a very long time to say.

"All right." Pembry calling down the room, "We'll call down when we got it."

"Can I look at him?"

"We'll call you."

The elevator again and then only the music.

Dr Lecter took the tube from his mouth and dried it on a piece of toilet tissue. His hands were steady, his palms perfectly dry.

In his years of detention, with his unending curiosity, Dr Lecter had learned many of the secret prison crafts. In all the years after he savaged the nurse in the Baltimore asylum, there had been only two lapses in the security around him, both on Barney's days off. Once a psychiatric researcher loaned him a ballpoint pen and then forgot it. Before the man was out of the ward, Dr Lecter had broken up the plastic barrel of the pen and flushed it down his toilet. The metal ink tube went in the rolled seam edging his mattress.

The only sharp edge in his cell at the asylum was a burr on the head of a bolt holding his cot to the wall. It was enough. In two months of rubbing, Dr Lecter cut the required two incisions, parallel and a quarter-inch long, running along the tube from its open end. Then he cut the ink tube in two pieces one inch from the open end and flushed the long piece with the point down the toilet. Barney did not spot the calluses on his fingers from the nights of rubbing.

Six months later, an orderly left a heavy-duty paper clip on some documents sent to Dr Lecter by his attorney. One inch of the steel clip went inside the tube and the rest went down the toilet. The little tube, smooth and short, was easy to conceal in seams of clothing, between the cheek and gum, in the rectum.

Now, behind his paper screen, Dr Lecter tapped the little metal tube on his thumbnail until the wire inside it slipped out. The wire was a tool and this was the difficult part. Dr Lecter stuck the wire halfway into the little tube and with infinite care used it as a lever to bend down the strip of metal between the two incisions. Sometimes they break. Carefully, with his powerful hands, he bent the metal and it was coming. Now. The minute strip of metal was at right angles to the tube. Now he had a handcuff key.

Dr Lecter put his hands behind him and passed the key back and forth between them fifteen times. He put the key back in his mouth while he washed his hands and meticulously dried them. Then, with his tongue, he hid the key between the fingers of his right hand, knowing Pembry would stare at his strange left hand when it was behind his back.

"I'm ready when you are, Officer Pembry," Dr Lecter said. He sat on the floor of the cell and stretched his arms behind him, his hands and wrists through the bars. "Thank you for waiting." It seemed a long speech, but it was leavened by the music.

He heard Pembry behind him now. Pembry felt his wrist to see if he had soaped it. Pembry felt his other wrist to see if he had soaped it. Pembry put the cuffs on tight. He went back to the desk for the key to the cell. Over the piano, Dr Lecter heard the clink of the key ring as Pembry took it from the desk drawer. Now he was coming back, walking through the notes, parting the air that swarmed with crystal notes. This time Boyle came back with him. Dr Lecter could hear the holes they made in the echoes of the music.

Pembry checked the cuffs again. Dr Lecter could smell Pembry's breath behind him. Now Pembry unlocked the cell and swung the door open. Boyle came in. Dr Lecter turned his head, the cell moving by his vision at a rate that seemed slow to him, the details wonderfully sharp—Boyle at the table gathering the scattered supper things onto the tray with a clatter of annoyance at the mess. The tape player with its reels turning, the napkin on the floor beside the bolted-down leg of the table. Through the bars, Dr Lecter saw in the corner of his eye the back of Pembry's knee, the tip of the baton hanging from his belt as he stood outside the cell holding the door.

Dr Lecter found the keyhole in his left cuff, inserted the key and turned it. He felt the cuff spring loose on his wrist. He passed the key to his left hand, found the keyhole, put in the key and turned it.

Boyle bent for the napkin on the floor. Fast as a snapping turtle, the handcuff closed on Boyle's wrist and as he turned his rolling eye to Lecter the other cuff locked around the fixed leg of the table. Dr Lecter's legs under him now, driving to the door, Pembry trying to come from behind it and Lecter's shoulder drove the iron door into him, Pembry going for the Mace in his belt, his arm mashed to his body by the door. Lecter grabbed the long end of the baton and lifted. With the leverage twisting Pembry's belt tight around him, he hit Pembry in the throat with his elbow and sank his teeth into Pembry's face. Pembry trying to claw at Lecter, his nose and upper lip caught between the tearing teeth. Lecter shook his head like a rat-killing dog and pulled the riot baton from Pembry's belt. In the cell Boyle bellowing now, sitting on the floor, digging desperately in his pocket for his handcuff key, fumbling, dropping it, finding it again. Lecter drove the end of the baton into Pembry's stomach and throat and he went to his knees. Boyle got the key in a lock of the handcuffs, he was bellowing, Lecter coming to him now. Lecter shut Boyle up with a shot of the Mace and, as he wheezed, cracked his upstretched arm with two blows of the baton. Boyle tried to get under the table, but blinded by the Mace he crawled the wrong way and it was easy, with five judicious blows, to beat him to death.

Pembry had managed to sit up and he was crying. Dr Lecter looked down at him with his red smile. "I'm ready if you are, Officer Pembry," he said.

The baton, whistling in a flat arc, caught Pembry *pock* on the back of the head and he shivered out straight like a clubbed fish.

Dr Lecter's pulse was elevated to more than one

hundred by the exercise, but quickly slowed to normal. He turned off the music and listened.

He went to the stairs and listened again. He turned out Pembry's pockets, got the desk key and opened all its drawers. In the bottom drawer were Boyle's and Pembry's duty weapons, a pair of .38 Special revolvers. Even better, in Boyle's pocket he found a pocket knife.

THE LOBBY was full of policemen. It was 6:30 P.M. and the police at the outside guard posts had just been relieved at their regular two-hour interval. The men coming into the lobby from the raw evening warmed their hands at several electric heaters. Some of them had money down on the Memphis State basketball game in progress and were anxious to know how it was going.

Sergeant Tate would not allow a radio to be played aloud in the lobby, but one officer had a Walkman plugged in his ear. He reported the score often, but not often enough to suit the bettors.

In all there were fifteen armed policemen in the lobby plus two Corrections officers to relieve Pembry and Boyle at 7:00 P.M. Sergeant Tate himself was looking forward to going off duty with the eleven-to-seven shift.

All posts reported quiet. None of the nut calls threatening Lecter had come to anything.

At 6:45, Tate heard the elevator start up. He saw the

bronze arrow above the door begin to crawl around the dial. It stopped at five.

Tate looked around the lobby. "Did Sweeney go up for the tray?"

"Naw, I'm here, Sarge. You mind calling, see if they're through? I need to get going."

Sergeant Tate dialed three digits and listened. "Phone's busy," he said. "Go ahead up and see." He turned back to the log he was completing for the eleven-to-seven shift.

Patrolman Sweeney pushed the elevator button. It didn't come.

"Had to have *lamb chops* tonight, rare," Sweeney said. "What you reckon he'll want for breakfast, some fucking thing from the zoo? And who'll have to catch it for him? Sweeney."

The bronze arrow above the door stayed on five.

Sweeney waited another minute. "What *is* this shit?" he said.

The .38 boomed somewhere above them, the reports echoing down the stone stairs, two fast shots and then a third.

Sergeant Tate, on his feet at the third one, microphone in his hand. "CP, shots fired upstairs at the tower. Outside posts, look sharp. We're going up."

Yelling, milling in the lobby.

Tate saw the bronze arrow of the elevator moving then. It was already down to four. Tate roared over the racket, "Hold it! Guard mount, double up at your outside posts, first squad stays with me. Berry and Howard cover that fucking elevator if it comes—" The needle stopped at three.

"First squad, here we go. Don't pass a door without checking it. Bobby, outside—get a shotgun and the vests and bring 'em up."

Tate's mind was racing on the first flight of stairs. Caution fought with the terrible need to help the officers upstairs. *God, don't let him be out. Nobody wearing vests, shit. Fucking Corrections screws.*

The offices on two, three and four were supposed to be empty and locked. You could get from the tower to the main building on those floors, if you went through the offices. You couldn't on five.

Tate had been to the excellent Tennessee SWAT school and he knew how to do it. He went first and took the young ones in hand. Fast and careful they took the stairs, covering each other from landing to landing.

"You turn your back on a door before you check it, I'll ream your ass."

The doors off the second-floor landing were dark and locked.

Up to three now, the little corridor dim. One rectangle of light on the floor from the open elevator car. Tate moved down the wall opposite the open elevator, no mirrors in the car to help him. With two pounds' pressure on a nine-pound trigger, he looked inside the car. Empty.

Tate yelled up the stairs, *"Boyle! Pembry!* Shit." He posted a man on three and moved up.

Four was flooded with the music of the piano coming from above. The door into the offices opened at a push. Beyond the offices, the beam of the long flashlight shone on a door open wide into the great dark building beyond.

"*Boyle! Pembry!*" He left two on the landing. "Cover the door. Vests are coming. Don't show your ass in that doorway."

Tate climbed the stone stairs into the music. At the top of the tower now, the fifth-floor landing, light dim in the short corridor. Bright light through the frosted glass that said SHELBY COUNTY HISTORICAL SOCIETY.

Tate moved low beneath the door glass to the side opposite the hinges. He nodded to Jacobs on the other side, turned the knob and shoved hard, the door swinging all the way back hard enough for the glass to shatter, Tate inside fast and out of the doorframe, covering the room over the wide sights of his revolver.

Tate had seen many things. He had seen accidents beyond reckoning, fights, murders. He had seen six dead policemen in his time. But he thought that what lay at his feet was the worst thing he had ever seen happen to an officer. The meat above the uniform collar no longer resembled a face. The front and top of the head were a slick of blood peaked with torn flesh and a single eye was stuck beside the nostrils, the sockets full of blood.

Jacobs passed Tate, slipping on the bloody floor as he went into the cell. He bent over Boyle, still handcuffed to the table leg. Boyle, partly eviscerated, his face hacked to pieces, seemed to have exploded blood in the cell, the walls and the stripped cot covered with gouts and splashes.

Jacobs put his fingers on the neck. "This one's dead," he called over the music. "Sarge?"

Tate, back at himself, ashamed of a second's lapse, and he was talking into his radio. "Command post, two

278

officers down. Repeat, two officers down. Prisoner is missing. Lecter is missing. Outside posts, watch the windows, subject has stripped the bed, he may be making a rope. Confirm ambulances en route."

"Pembry dead, Sarge?" Jacobs shut the music off.

Tate knelt and, as he reached for the neck to feel, the awful thing on the floor groaned and blew a bloody bubble.

"Pembry's alive." Tate didn't want to put his mouth in the bloody mess, knew he would if he had to to help Pembry breathe, knew he wouldn't make one of the patrolmen do it. Better if Pembry died, but he would help him breathe. But there was a heartbeat, he found it, there was breathing. It was ragged and gurgling but it was breathing. The ruin was breathing on its own.

Tate's radio crackled. A patrol lieutenant set up on the lot outside took command and wanted news. Tate had to talk.

"Come here, Murray," Tate called to a young patrol-man. "Get down here with Pembry and take ahold of him where he can feel your hands on him. Talk to him."

"What's his name, Sarge?" Murray was green.

"It's Pembry, now talk to him, God dammit." Tate on the radio. "Two officers down, Boyle's dead and Pembry's bad hurt. Lecter's missing and armed—he took their guns. Belts and holsters are on the desk."

The lieutenant's voice was scratchy through the thick walls. "Can you confirm the stairway clear for stretchers?"

"Yes, sir. Call up to four before they pass. I have men on every landing."

"Roger, Sergeant. Post Eight out here thought he saw some movement behind the windows in the main building on four. We've got the exits covered, he's not getting out. Hold your positions on the landings. SWAT's rolling. We're gonna let SWAT flush him out. Confirm."

"I understand. SWAT's play."

"What's he got?"

"Two pistols and a knife, Lieutenant—Jacobs, see if there's any ammo in the gunbelts."

"Dump pouches," the patrolman said. "Pembry's still full, Boyle's too. Dumb shit didn't take the extra rounds."

"What are they?"

"Thirty-eight + Ps JHP."

Tate was back on the radio. "Lieutenant, it looks like he's got two six-shot .38s. We heard three rounds fired and the dump pouches on the gunbelts are still full, so he may just have nine left. Advise SWAT its + Ps jacketed hollowpoints. This guy favors the face."

Plus Ps were hot rounds, but they would not penetrate SWAT's body armor. A hit in the face would very likely be fatal, a hit on a limb would maim.

"Stretchers coming up, Tate."

The ambulances were there amazingly fast, but it did not seem fast enough to Tate, listening to the pitiful thing at his feet. Young Murray was trying to hold the groaning, jerking body, trying to talk reassuringly and not look at him, and he was saying, "You're just fine, Pembry, looking good," over and over in the same sick tone.

As soon as he saw the ambulance attendants on the landing, Tate yelled, "Corpsman!" as he had in war.

He got Murray by the shoulder and moved him out of the way. The ambulance attendants worked fast, expertly securing the clenched, blood-slick fists under the belt, getting an airway in and peeling a nonstick surgical bandage to get some pressure on the bloody face and head. One of them popped an intravenous plasma pack, but the other, taking blood pressure and pulse, shook his head and said, "Downstairs."

Orders on the radio now. "Tate, I want you to clear the offices in the tower and seal it off. Secure the doors from the main building. Then cover from the landings. I'm sending up vests and shotguns. We'll get him alive if he wants to come, but we take no special risks to preserve his life. Understand me?"

"I got it, Lieutenant."

"I want SWAT and nobody but SWAT in the main building. Let me have that back."

Tate repeated the order.

Tate was a good sergeant and he showed it now as he and Jacobs shrugged into their heavy armored vests and followed the gurney as the orderlies carried it down the stairs to the ambulance. A second crew followed with Boyle. The men on the landings were angry, seeing the gurneys pass, and Tate had a word of wisdom for them: "Don't let your temper get your ass shot off."

As the sirens wailed outside, Tate, backed by the veteran Jacobs, carefully cleared the offices and sealed off the tower.

A cool draft blew down the hall on four. Beyond the door, in the vast dark spaces of the main building, the telephones were ringing. In dark offices all over the building, buttons on telephones were winking like fire-flies, the bells sounding over and over.

The word was out that Dr Lecter was "barricaded" in the building, and radio and television reporters were calling, dialing fast with their modems, trying to get live interviews with the monster. To avoid this, SWAT usually has the telephones shut off, except for one that the negotiator uses. This building was too big, the offices too many.

Tate closed and locked the door on the rooms of blinking telephones. His chest and back were wet and itching under the hardshell vest.

He took his radio off his belt. "CP, this is Tate, the tower's clear, over."

"Roger, Tate. Captain wants you at the CP."

"Ten-four. Tower lobby, you there?"

"Here, Sarge."

"It's me on the elevator, I'm bringing it down."

"Gotcha, Sarge."

Jacobs and Tate were in the elevator riding down to the lobby when a drop of blood fell on Tate's shoulder. Another hit his shoe.

He looked at the ceiling of the car, touched Jacobs, motioning for silence.

Blood was dripping from the crack around the service hatch in the top of the car. It seemed a long ride down to the lobby. Tate and Jacobs stepped off backwards, guns pointed at the ceiling of the elevator. Tate reached back in and locked the car.

"Shhhh," Tate said in the lobby. Quietly, "Berry, Howard, he's on the roof of the elevator. Keep it covered."

Tate went outside. The black SWAT van was on the lot. SWAT always had a variety of elevator keys.

They were set up in moments, two SWAT officers in black body armor and headsets climbing the stairs to the third-floor landing. With Tate in the lobby were two more, their assault rifles pointed at the elevator ceiling.

Like the big ants that fight, Tate thought.

The SWAT commander was talking into his headset. "Okay, Johnny."

On the third floor, high above the elevator, Officer Johnny Peterson turned his key in the lock and the elevator door slid open. The shaft was dark. Lying on his back in the corridor, he took a stun grenade from his tactical vest and put it on the floor beside him. "Okay, I'll take a look now."

He took out his mirror with its long handle and stuck it over the edge while his partner shined a powerful flashlight down the shaft.

"I see him. He's on top of the elevator. I see a weapon beside him. He's not moving."

The question in Peterson's earphone, "Can you see his hands?"

"I see one hand, the other one's under him. He's got the sheets around him."

"Tell him."

"PUT YOUR HANDS ON TOP OF YOUR HEAD AND FREEZE," Peterson yelled down the shaft. "He didn't move, Lieutenant . . . Right.

"IF YOU DON'T PUT YOUR HANDS ON TOP OF YOUR HEAD, I'LL DROP A STUN GRENADE ON YOU. I'LL GIVE YOU THREE SECONDS," Peterson called. He took from his vest one of the door-stops every SWAT officer carries. "OKAY, GUYS, WATCH OUT DOWN THERE—HERE COMES THE GRENADE." He dropped the doorstop over the edge, saw it bounce on the figure. "He didn't move, Lieutenant."

"Okay, Johnny, we're gonna push the hatch up with a pole from outside the car. Can you get the drop?"

Peterson rolled over. His 10 mm Colt, cocked and locked, pointed straight down at the figure. "Got the drop," he said.

Looking down the elevator shaft, Peterson could see the crack of light appear below as the officers in the foyer pushed up on the hatch with a SWAT boathook. The still figure was partly over the hatch and one of the arms moved as the officers pushed from below.

Peterson's thumb pressed a shade harder on the safety of the Colt. "His arm moved, Lieutenant, but I think it's just the hatch moving it."

"Roger. Heave."

The hatch banged backward and lay against the wall of the elevator shaft. It was hard for Peterson to look down into the light. "He hasn't moved. His hand's *not* on the weapon."

The calm voice in his ear, "Okay, Johnny, hold up. We're coming into the car, so watch with the mirror for movement. Any fire will come from us. Affirm?"

"Got it."

In the lobby, Tate watched them go into the car. A rifleman loaded with armor-piercing aimed his weapon at the ceiling of the elevator. A second officer climbed on a ladder. He was armed with a large automatic pistol with a flashlight clamped beneath it. A mirror and the pistol-light went up through the hatch. Then the officer's head and shoulders. He handed down a .38 revolver. "He's dead," the officer called down.

Tate wondered if the death of Dr Lecter meant Catherine Martin would die too, all the information lost when the lights went out in that monster mind.

The officers were pulling him down now, the body coming upside down through the elevator hatch, eased down into many arms, an odd deposition in a lighted box. The lobby was filling up, policemen crowding up to see.

A corrections officer pushed forward, looked at the body's outflung tattooed arms.

"That's Pembry," he said.

In the back of the howling ambulance, the young attendant braced himself against the sway and turned to his radio to report to his emergency room supervisor, talking loud above the siren.

"He's comatose but the vital signs are good. He's got good pressure. One-thirty over ninety. Yeah, ninety. Pulse eighty-five. He's got severe facial cuts with elevated flaps, one eye enucleated. I've got pressure on the face and an airway in place. Possible gunshot in the head, I can't tell."

Behind him on the stretcher, the balled and bloody fists relax inside the waistband. The right hand slides out, finds the buckle on the strap across the chest.

"I'm scared to put much pressure on the head—he showed some convulsive movement before we put him on the gurney. Yeah, got him in the Fowler position."

Behind the young man, the hand gripped the surgical bandage and wiped out the eyes.

The attendant heard the airway hiss close behind him, turned and saw the bloody face in his, did not see the pistol descending and it caught him hard over the ear.

The ambulance slowing to a stop in traffic on the six-lane freeway, drivers behind it confused and honking, hesitant to pull around an emergency vehicle. Two small pops like backfires in the traffic and the ambulance started up again, weaving, straightening out, moving to the right lane.

The airport exit coming up. The ambulance piddled along in the right lane, various emergency lights going on and off on the outside of it, wipers on and off, then the siren wailing down, starting up, wailing down to silence and the flashing lights going off. The ambulance proceeding quietly, taking the exit to Memphis International Airport, the beautiful building floodlit in the winter evening. It took the curving drive as far as the automated gates to the vast underground parking field. A bloody hand came out to take a ticket. And the ambulance disappeared down the tunnel to the parking field beneath the ground.

39

NORMALLY, CLARICE STARLING would have been curious to see Crawford's house in Arlington, but the bulletin on the car radio about Dr Lecter's escape knocked all that out of her.

Lips numb and scalp prickling, she drove by rote, saw the neat 1950s ranch house without looking at it, and only wondered dimly if the lit, curtained windows on the left were where Bella was lying. The doorbell seemed too loud.

Crawford opened the door on the second ring. He wore a baggy cardigan and he was talking on a wireless phone. "Copley in Memphis," he said. Motioning for her to follow, he led her through the house, grunting into the telephone as he went.

In the kitchen, a nurse took a tiny bottle from the refrigerator and held it to the light. When Crawford raised his eyebrows to the nurse, she shook her head, she didn't need him.

He took Starling to his study, down three steps into what was clearly a converted double garage. There was good space here, a sofa and chairs, and on the cluttered desk a computer terminal glowed green beside an antique astrolabe. The rug felt as though it was laid on concrete. Crawford waved her to a seat.

He put his hand over the receiver. "Starling, this is baloney, but did you hand Lecter anything at all in Memphis?"

"No."

"No object?"

"Nothing."

"You took him the drawings and stuff from his cell."

"I never gave it to him. The stuff's still in my bag. He gave *me* the file. That's all that passed between us."

Crawford tucked the phone under his jowl. "Copley, that's unmitigated bullshit. I want you to step on that bastard and do it now. Straight to the chief, straight to the TBI. See the hotline's posted with the rest. Burroughs is on it. Yes." He turned off the phone and stuffed it in his pocket.

"Want some coffee, Starling? Coke?"

"What was that about handing things to Dr Lecter?"

"Chilton's saying you must have given Lecter something he used to slip the ratchet on the cuffs. You didn't do it on purpose, he says—it was just ignorance." Sometimes Crawford had angry little turtle-eyes. He watched how she took it. "Did Chilton try to snap your garters, Starling? Is that what's the matter with him?"

"Maybe. I'll take black with sugar, please."

While he was in the kitchen, she took deep breaths and looked around the room. If you live in a dormitory or a barracks, it's comforting to be in a home. Even with the ground shaking under Starling, her sense of the Crawfords' lives in this house helped her.

Crawford was coming, careful down the steps in his bifocals, carrying the cups. He was half an inch shorter in his moccasins. When Starling stood to take her coffee, their eyes were almost level. He smelled like soap, and his hair looked fluffy and gray.

"Copley said they haven't found the ambulance yet. Police barracks are turning out all over the South."

She shook her head. "I don't know any details. The radio just had the bulletin—Dr Lecter killed two policemen and got away."

"Two corrections officers." Crawford punched up the crawling text on his computer screen. "Names were Boyle and Pembry. You deal with them?"

She nodded. "They . . . put me out of the lockup. They were okay about it." *Pembry coming around Chilton, uncomfortable, determined, but country-courteous. Come on with me, now, he said. He had liver spots on his hands and forehead. Dead now, pale beneath his spots.*

Suddenly, Starling had to put her coffee down. She filled her lungs deep and looked at the ceiling for a moment. "How'd he do it?"

"He got away in an ambulance, Copley said. We'll go into it. How did you make out with the blotter acid?"

Starling had spent the late afternoon and early evening walking the sheet of Plutos through Scientific Analysis on Krendler's orders. "Nothing. They're trying the DEA files for a batch-match, but the stuff's ten years old. Documents may do better with the printing than DEA can do with the dope."

"But it *was* blotter acid."

"Yes. How'd he do it, Mr Crawford?"

"Want to know?"

She nodded.

"Then I'll tell you. They loaded Lecter into an ambulance by mistake. They thought he was Pembry, badly injured."

"Did he have on Pembry's uniform? They were about the same size."

"He put on Pembry's uniform and part of Pembry's face. And about a pound off Boyle too. He wrapped Pembry's body in the waterproof mattress cover and the sheets from his cell to keep it from dripping and stuffed it on top of the elevator. He put on the uniform, got himself fixed up, laid on the floor and fired shots into the ceiling to start the stampede. I don't know what he did with the gun, stuffed it down the back of his pants, maybe. The ambulance comes, cops everywhere with their guns out. The ambulance crew came in fast and did what they're trained to do under fire—they stuffed in an airway, slapped a bandage over the worst of it, pressure to stop bleeding, and hauled out of there. They did their job. The ambulance never made it to the hospital. The police are still looking for it. I don't feel good about those medics. Copley said they're playing the dispatcher's tapes. The ambulances were called a couple of times. They think Lecter called the ambulances himself before he fired the shots, so he wouldn't have to lie around too long. *Dr Lecter likes his fun.*"

Starling had never heard the bitter snarl in Crawford's voice before. Because she associated bitter with weak, it frightened her.

"This escape doesn't mean Dr Lecter was lying," Starling said. "Sure, he was lying to somebody—us or Senator Martin—but maybe he wasn't lying to both of us. He told Senator Martin it was Billy Rubin and claimed that's all he knew. He told me it was somebody with delusions of being a transsexual. About the last thing he said to me was, 'Why not finish the arch?' He was talking about following the sex-change theory that—"

"I know, I saw your summary. There's nowhere to go with that until we get names from the clinics. Alan Bloom's gone personally to the department heads. They say they're looking. I have to believe it."

"Mr Crawford, are you in the glue?"

"I'm directed to take compassionate leave," Crawford said. "There's a new task force of FBI, DEA, and 'additional elements' from the Attorney General's office —meaning Krendler."

"Who's boss?"

"Officially, FBI Assistant Director John Golby. Let's say he and I are in close consultation. John's a good man. What about you, are *you* in the glue?"

"Krendler told me to turn in my ID and the roscoe and report back to school."

"That was all he did *before* your visit to Lecter. Starling, he sent a rocket this afternoon to the Office of Professional Responsibility. It was a request 'without prejudice' that the Academy suspend you pending a reevaluation of your fitness for the service. It's a chicken-shit backshot. The Chief Gunny, John Brigham, saw it in the faculty meeting at Quantico a little while ago. He gave 'em an earful and got on the horn to me."

"How bad is that?"

"You're entitled to a hearing. I'll vouch for your fitness and that'll be enough. But if you spend any more time away, you'll definitely be recycled, regardless of any finding at a hearing. Do you know what happens when you're recycled?"

"Sure, you're sent back to the regional office that recruited you. You get to file reports and make coffee until you get another spot in a class."

"I can promise you a place in a later class, but I can't keep them from recycling you if you miss the time."

"So I go back to school and stop working on this, or . . ."

"Yeah."

"What do you want me to do?"

"Your job was Lecter. You did it. I'm not asking you to take a recycle. It could cost you, maybe half a year, maybe more."

"What about Catherine Martin?"

"He's had her almost forty-eight hours—be forty-eight hours at midnight. If we don't catch him, he'll probably do her tomorrow or the next day, if it's like last time."

"Lecter's not all we had."

"They got six William Rubins so far, all with priors of one kind or another. None of 'em look like much. No Billy Rubins on the bug journal subscription lists. The Knifemakers Guild knows about five cases of ivory anthrax in the last ten years. We've got a couple of those left to check. What else? Klaus hasn't been identified— yet. Interpol reports a fugitive warrant outstanding in Marseilles for a Norwegian merchant seaman, a 'Klaus

Bjetland,' however you say it. Norway's looking for his dental records to send. If we get anything from the clinics, and you've got the time, you can help with it. Starling?"

"Yes, Mr Crawford?"

"Go back to school."

"If you didn't want me to chase him, you shouldn't have taken me in that funeral home, Mr Crawford."

"No," Crawford said. "I suppose I shouldn't. But then we wouldn't have the insect. You don't turn in your roscoe. Quantico's safe enough, but you'll be armed any time you're off the base at Quantico until Lecter's caught or dead."

"What about you? He hates you. I mean, he's given this some thought."

"Lot of people have, Starling, in a lot of jails. One of these days he might get around to it, but he's way too busy now. It's sweet to be out and he's not ready to waste it that way. And this place is safer than it looks."

The phone in Crawford's pocket buzzed. The one on the desk purred and blinked. He listened for a few moments, said "Okay," and hung up.

"They found the ambulance in the underground garage at the Memphis airport." He shook his head. "No good. Crew was in the back. Dead, both of them." Crawford took off his glasses, rummaged for his handkerchief to polish them.

"Starling, the Smithsonian called Burroughs asking for you. The Pilcher fellow. They're pretty close to finishing up on the bug. I want you to write a 302 on that and sign it for the permanent file. You found the bug and followed up on it and I want the record to say so. You up to it?"

Starling was as tired as she had ever been. "Sure," she said.

"Leave your car at the garage, and Jeff'll drive you back to Quantico when you're through."

On the steps she turned her face toward the lighted, curtained windows where the nurse kept watch, and then looked back at Crawford.

"I'm thinking about you both, Mr Crawford."

"Thank you, Starling," he said.

"OFFICER STARLING, Dr Pilcher said he'd meet you in the Insect Zoo. I'll take you over there," the guard said.

To reach the Insect Zoo from the Constitution Avenue side of the museum, you must take the elevator one level above the great stuffed elephant and cross a vast floor devoted to the study of man.

Tiers of skulls were first, rising and spreading, representing the explosion of human population since the time of Christ.

Starling and the guard moved in a dim landscape peopled with figures illustrating human origin and variation. Here were displays of ritual—tattoos, bound feet, tooth modification, Peruvian surgery, mummification.

"Did you ever see Wilhelm von Ellenbogen?" the guard asked, shining his light into a case.

"I don't believe I have," Starling said without slowing her pace.

"You should come sometime when the lights are up and take a look at him. Buried him in Philadelphia in the eighteenth century? Turned right to soap when the ground water hit him."

The Insect Zoo is a large room, dim now and loud with chirps and whirs. Cages and cases of live insects fill it. Children particularly like the zoo and troop through it all day. At night, left to themselves, the insects are busy. A few of the cases were lit with red, and the fire exit signs burned fiercely red in the dim room.

"Dr Pilcher?" the guard called from the door.

"Here," Pilcher said, holding a penlight up as a beacon.

"Will you bring this lady out?"

"Yes, thank you, Officer."

Starling took her own small flashlight out of her purse and found the switch already on, the batteries dead. The flash of anger she felt reminded her that she was tired and she had to bear down.

"Hello, Officer Starling."

"Dr Pilcher."

"How about 'Professor Pilcher'?"

"*Are* you a professor?"

"No, but I'm not a doctor either. What I *am* is glad to see you. Want to look at some bugs?"

"Sure. Where's Dr Roden?"

"He made most of the progress over the last two nights with chaetaxy and finally he had to crash. Did you see the bug before we started on it?"

"No."

"It was just mush, really."

"But you got it, you figured it out."

"Yep. Just now." He stopped at a mesh cage. "First let me show you a moth like the one you brought in

297

Monday. This is not exactly the same as yours, but the same family, an owlet." The beam of his flashlight found the large sheeny blue moth sitting on a small branch, its wings folded. Pilcher blew air at it and instantly the fierce face of an owl appeared as the moth flared the undersides of its wings at them, the eye-spots on the wings glaring like the last sight a rat ever sees. "This one's *Caligo beltrao*—fairly common. But with this Klaus specimen, you're talking some heavy moths. Come on."

At the end of the room was a case set back in a niche with a rail in front of it. The case was beyond the reach of children and it was covered with a cloth. A small humidifier hummed beside it.

"We keep it behind glass to protect people's fingers— it can fight. It likes the damp too, and glass keeps the humidity in." Pilcher lifted the cage carefully by its handles and moved it to the front of the niche. He lifted off the cover and turned on a small light above the cage.

"This is the Death's-head Moth," he said. "That's nightshade she's sitting on—we're hoping she'll lay."

The moth was wonderful and terrible to see, its large brown-black wings tented like a cloak, and on its wide furry back the signature device that has struck fear in men for as long as men have come upon it suddenly in their happy gardens. The domed skull, a skull that is both skull and face, watching from its dark eyes, the cheekbones, the zygomatic arch traced exquisitely beside the eyes.

"*Acherontia styx*," Pilcher said. "It's named for two rivers in Hell. Your man, he drops the bodies in a river every time—did I read that?"

"Yes," Starling said. "Is it rare?"

"In this part of the world it is. There aren't any at all in nature."

"Where's it from?" Starling leaned her face close to the mesh roof of the case. Her breath stirred the fur on the moth's back. She jerked back when it squeaked and fiercely flapped its wings. She could feel the tiny breeze it made.

"Malaysia. There's a European type too, called *atropos*, but this one and the one in Klaus's mouth are Malaysian."

"So somebody raised it."

Pilcher nodded. "Yes," he said when she didn't look at him. "It had to be shipped from Malaysia as an egg or more likely as a pupa. Nobody's ever been able to get them to lay eggs in captivity. They mate, but no eggs. The hard part is finding the caterpillar in the jungle. After that, they're not hard to raise."

"You said they can fight."

"The proboscis is sharp and stout, and they'll jam it in your finger if you fool with them. It's an unusual weapon and alcohol doesn't affect it in preserved specimens. That helped us narrow the field so we could identify it so fast." Pilcher seemed suddenly embarrassed, as though he had boasted. "They're tough too," he hurried on to say. "They go in beehives and Bogart honey. One time we were collecting in Sabah, Borneo, and they'd come to the light behind the youth hostel. It was weird to hear them, we'd be—"

"Where did this one come from?"

"A swap with the Malaysian government. I don't know what we traded. It was funny, there we were in the dark, waiting with this cyanide bucket, when—"

"What kind of customs declaration came with this one? Do you have records of that? Do they have to be cleared out of Malaysia? Who would have that?"

"You're in a hurry. Look, I've written down all the stuff we have and the places to put ads if you want to do that kind of thing. Come on, I'll take you out."

They crossed the vast floor in silence. In the light of the elevator, Starling could see that Pilcher was as tired as she was.

"You stayed up with this," she said. "That was a good thing to do. I didn't mean to be abrupt before, I just—"

"I hope they get him. I hope you're through with this soon," he said. "I put down a couple of chemicals he might be buying if he's putting up soft specimens ... Officer Starling, I'd like to get to know you."

"Maybe I should call you when I can."

"You definitely should, absolutely, I'd like that," Pilcher said.

The elevator closed and Pilcher and Starling were gone. The floor devoted to man was still and no human figure moved, not the tattooed, not the mummified; the bound feet didn't stir.

The fire lights glowed red in the Insect Zoo, reflected in ten thousand active eyes of the older phylum. The humidifier hummed and hissed. Beneath the cover, in the black cage, the Death's-head Moth climbed down the nightshade. She moved across the floor, her wings trailing like a cape, and found the bit of honeycomb in her dish. Grasping the honeycomb in her powerful front legs, she uncoiled her sharp proboscis and plunged it through the wax cap of a honey cell. Now she sat sucking quietly while all around her in the dark the chirps and whirs resumed, and with them the tiny tillings and killings.

CHAPTER

41

CATHERINE BAKER MARTIN down in the hateful dark. Dark swarmed behind her eyelids and, in jerky seconds of sleep, she dreamed the dark came into her. Dark came insidious, up her nose and into her ears, damp fingers of dark proposed themselves to each of her body openings. She put her hand over her mouth and nose, put her other hand over her vagina, clenched her buttocks, turned one ear to the mattress and sacrificed the other ear to the intrusion of the dark. With the dark came a sound, and she jerked awake. A familiar busy sound, a sewing machine. Variable speed. Slow, now fast.

Up in the basement the lights were on—she could see a feeble disc of yellow high above her where the small hatch in the well lid stood open. The poodle barked a couple of times and the unearthly voice was talking to it, muffled.

Sewing. Sewing was so wrong down here. Sewing belongs to the light. The sunny sewing room of Catherine's childhood flashed so welcome in her mind

. . . the housekeeper, dear Bea Love, at the machine . . . her little cat batted at the blowing curtain.

The voice blew it all away, fussing at the poodle.

"Precious, put that *down*. You'll stick yourself with a pin and *then* where will we be? I'm almost done. Yes, Darlingheart. You get a Chew-wy *when we get through-y*, you get a Chew-wy *doody doody doo*."

Catherine did not know how long she had been captive. She knew that she had washed twice—the last time she had stood up in the light, wanting him to see her body, not sure if he was looking down from behind the blinding light. Catherine Baker Martin naked was a show-stopper, a girl and a half in all directions, and she knew it. She wanted him to see. She wanted out of the pit. Close enough to fuck is close enough to fight—she said it silently to herself over and over as she washed. She was getting very little to eat and she knew she'd better do it while she had her strength. She knew she would fight him. She knew she could fight. Would it be better to fuck him first, fuck him as many times as he could do it and wear him out? She knew if she could ever get her legs around his neck she could send him home to Jesus in about a second and a half. *Can I stand to do that? You're damned right I can. Balls and eyes, balls and eyes, balls and eyes.* But there had been no sound from above as she finished washing and put on the fresh jumpsuit. There was no reply to her offers as the bath bucket swayed up on its flimsy string and was replaced by her toilet bucket.

She waited now, hours later, listening to the sewing machine. She did not call out to him. In time, maybe a thousand breaths, she heard him going up the stairs, talking to the dog, saying something, "—breakfast when I get back." He left the basement light on. Sometimes he did that.

Toenails and footsteps on the kitchen floor above. The dog whining. She believed her captor was leaving. Sometimes he went away for a long time.

Breaths went by. The little dog walked around in the kitchen above, whining, rattling something along the floor, bonging something along the floor, maybe its bowl. Scratching, scratching above. And barking again, short sharp barks, this time not as clear as the sounds had been when the dog was above her in the kitchen. Because the little dog was not in the kitchen. It had nosed the door open and it was down in the basement chasing mice, as it had done before when he was out.

Down in the dark, Catherine Martin felt beneath her mattress. She found the piece of chicken bone and sniffed it. It was hard not to eat the little shreds of meat and gristle on it. She put it in her mouth to get it warm. She stood up now, swaying a little in the dizzy dark. With her in the sheer pit was nothing but her futon, the jumpsuit she was wearing, the plastic toilet bucket and its flimsy cotton string stretching upward toward the pale yellow light.

She had thought about it in every interval when she could think. Catherine stretched as high as she could and grasped the string. Better to jerk or to pull? She had thought about it through thousands of breaths. Better to pull steadily.

The cotton string stretched more than she expected. She got a new grip as high as she could and pulled, swinging her arm from side to side, hoping the string was fraying where it passed over the wooden lip of the opening above her. She frayed until her shoulder ached. She pulled, the string stretching, now not stretching, no more stretch. Please break high. Pop, and it fell, hanks of it across her face.

Squatting on the floor, the string lying on her head and shoulder, not enough light from the hole far above to see the string piled on her. She didn't know how much she had. Must not tangle. Carefully, she laid the string out on the floor in bights, measuring them on her forearm. She counted fourteen forearms. The string had broken at the lip of the well.

She tied the chicken bone with its shredded morsels of flesh securely into the line where it attached to the bucket handle.

Now the harder part.

Work carefully. She was in her heavy-weather mindset. It was like taking care of yourself in a small boat in heavy weather.

She tied the broken end of the string to her wrist, tightening the knot with her teeth.

She stood as clear of the string as possible. Holding the bucket by the handle, she swung it in a big circle and threw it straight upward at the faint disc of light above her. The plastic bucket missed the open hatch, hit the underside of the lid and fell back, hitting her in the face and shoulder. The little dog barked louder.

She took the time to lay out the line and threw again, and again. On the third throw, the bucket hit her broken finger when it fell and she had to lean against the in-sloping wall and breathe until the nausea went away. Throw four banged down on her, but five did not.

It was out. The bucket was somewhere on the wooden cover of the well beside the open trap. How far from the hole? Get steady. Gently she pulled. She twitched the string to hear the bucket handle rattle against the wood above her.

The little dog barked louder.

She mustn't pull the bucket over the edge of the hole, but she must pull it close. She pulled it close.

The little dog among the mirrors and the mannequins in a nearby basement room. Sniffing at the threads and shreds beneath the sewing machine. Nosing around the great black armoire. Looking toward the end of the basement where the sounds were coming from. Dashing toward the gloomy section to bark and dash back again.

Now a voice, echoing faintly through the basement. "Preeeee-cious."

The little dog barked and jumped in place. Its fat little body quivered with the barks.

Now a wet kissing sound.

The dog looked up at the kitchen floor above, but that wasn't where the sound came from.

A smack-smack sound like eating. "Come on, Precious. Come on, Sweetheart."

On its tiptoes, ears up, the dog went into the gloom.

Slurp-slurp. "Come on, Sweetums, come on, Precious."

The poodle could smell the chicken bone tied to the bucket handle. It scratched at the side of the well and whined.

Smack-smack-smack.

The small poodle jumped up onto the wooden cover of the well. The smell was over here, between the

306

bucket and the hole. The little dog barked at the bucket, whined in indecision. The chicken bone twitched ever so slightly.

The poodle crouched with its nose between its front paws, behind in the air, wagging furiously. It barked twice and pounced on the chicken bone, gripping it with its teeth. The bucket seemed to be trying to nose the little dog away from the chicken. The poodle growled at the bucket and held on, straddling the handle, teeth firmly clamped on the bone. Suddenly, the bucket bumped the poodle over, off its feet, pushed it, it struggled to get up, bumped again, it struggled with the bucket, a back foot and haunch went off in the hole, its claws scrabbled frantically at the wood, the bucket sliding, wedging in the hole with the dog's hindquarters and the little dog pulled free, the bucket slipping over the edge and plunging, the bucket escaping down the hole with the chicken bone. The poodle barked angrily down the hole, barks ringing down in the well. Then it stopped barking and cocked its head at a sound only it could hear. It scrambled off the top of the well and went up the stairs yipping as a door slammed somewhere upstairs.

Catherine Baker Martin's tears spread hot on her cheeks and fell, plucking at the front of her jumpsuit, soaking through, warm on her breasts, and she believed that she would surely die.

CRAWFORD STOOD alone in the center of his study with his hands jammed deep in his pockets. He stood there from 12:30 A.M. to 12:33, demanding an idea. Then he telexed the California Department of Motor Vehicles requesting a trace on the motor home Dr Lecter said Raspail had bought in California, the one Raspail used in his romance with Klaus. Crawford asked the DMV to check for traffic tickets issued to any driver other than Benjamin Raspail.

Then he sat on the sofa with a clipboard and worked out a proactive personal ad to run in the major papers:

Junoesque creamy passion flower, 21, model, seeks man who appreciates quality AND quantity. Hand and cosmetic model, you've seen me in the magazine ads, now I'd like to see you. Send pix first letter.

Crawford considered for a moment, scratched out "Junoesque," and substituted "full-figured."

His head dipped and he dozed. The green screen

of the computer terminal made tiny squares in the lenses of his glasses. Movement on the screen now, the lines crawling upward, moving on Crawford's lenses. In his sleep he shook his head as though the image tickled him.

The message was:

MEMPHIS POX RECOVERED 2 ITEMS IN SEARCH OF LECTER'S CELL.

(1) IMPROVISED HANDCUFF KEY MADE FROM BALL-POINT TUBE. INCISIONS BY ABRASION, BALTIMORE REQUESTED TO CHECK HOSPITAL CELL FOR TRACES OF MANUFACTURE, AUTH COPLEY, SAC MEMPHIS.

(2) SHEET OF NOTEPAPER LEFT FLOATING IN TOILET BY FUGITIVE. ORIGINAL EN ROUTE TO WX DOCUMENT SECTION / LAB. GRAPHIC OF WRITING FOLLOWS. GRAPHIC SPLIT TO LANGLEY, ATTN: BENSON— CRYPTOGRAPHY.

When the graphic appeared, rising like something peeping over the bottom edge of the screen, it was this:

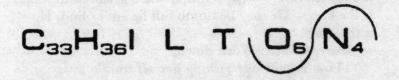

The soft double beep of the computer terminal did not wake Crawford, but three minutes later the telephone did. It was Jerry Burroughs at the National Crime Information Center hotline.

"See your screen, Jack?"

"Just a second," Crawford said. "Yeah, okay."

"The lab's got it already, Jack. The drawing Lecter left in the john. The numbers between the letters in Chilton's name, it's biochemistry—$C_{33}H_{36}N_4O_6$—it's the formula for a pigment in human bile called bilirubin. Lab advises it's a chief coloring agent in shit."

"Balls."

"You were right about Lecter, Jack. He was just jerking them around. Too bad for Senator Martin. Lab says bilirubin's just about exactly the color of Chilton's hair. Asylum humor, they call it. Did you see Chilton on the six o'clock news?"

"No."

"Marilyn Sutter saw it upstairs. Chilton was blowing off about 'The Search for Billy Rubin.' Then he went to dinner with a television reporter. That's where he was when Lecter took a walk. What a pluperfect asshole."

"Lecter told Starling to 'bear in mind' that Chilton didn't have a medical degree," Crawford said.

"Yeah, I saw it in the summary. I think Chilton tried to fuck Starling's what I think, and she sawed him off at the knees. He may be dumb but he ain't blind. How is the kid?"

"Okay, I think. Worn down."

"Think Lecter was jerking her off too?"

"Maybe. We'll stay with it, though. I don't know what the clinics are doing, I keep thinking I should've gone after the records in court. I hate to have to depend on them. Midmorning, if we haven't heard anything, we'll go the court route."

"Say, Jack . . . you got some people outside that know what Lecter looks like, right?"

"Sure."

"Don't you know he's laughing somewhere."

"Maybe not for long," Crawford said.

43

DR HANNIBAL LECTER stood at the registration desk of the elegant Marcus Hotel in St Louis. He wore a brown hat and a raincoat buttoned to the neck. A neat surgical bandage covered his nose and cheeks.

He signed the register "Lloyd Wyman," a signature he had practiced in Wyman's car.

"How will you be paying, Mr Wyman?" the clerk said.

"American Express." Dr Lecter handed the man Lloyd Wyman's credit card.

Soft piano music came from the lounge. At the bar, Dr Lecter could see two people with bandages across their noses. A middle-aged couple crossed to the elevators, humming a Cole Porter tune. The woman wore a gauze patch over her eye.

The clerk finished making the credit-card impression. "You do know, Mr Wyman, you're entitled to use the hospital garage?"

"Yes, thank you," Dr Lecter said. He had already parked Wyman's car in the garage, with Wyman in the trunk.

The bellman who carried Wyman's bags to the small suite got one of Wyman's five-dollar bills in compensation.

Dr Lecter ordered a drink and a sandwich and relaxed with a long shower.

The suite seemed enormous to Dr Lecter after his long confinement. He enjoyed going to and fro in his suite and walking up and down in it.

From his windows he could see across the street the Myron and Sadie Fleischer Pavilion of St Louis City Hospital, housing one of the world's foremost centers for craniofacial surgery.

Dr Lecter's visage was too well known for him to be able to take advantage of the plastic surgeons here, but it was one place in the world where he could walk around with a bandage on his face without exciting interest.

He had stayed here once before, years ago, when he was doing psychiatric research in the superb Robert J. Brockman Memorial Library.

Heady to have a window, several windows. He stood at his windows in the dark, watching the car lights move across the MacArthur Bridge and savoring his drink. He was pleasantly fatigued by the five-hour drive from Memphis.

The only real rush of the evening had been in the underground garage at Memphis International Airport. Cleaning up with cotton pads and alcohol and distilled water in the back of the parked ambulance was not at all convenient. Once he was in the attendant's whites, it was just a matter of catching a single traveler in a deserted aisle of long-term parking in the great garage. The man obligingly leaned into the trunk of his car for his sample case, and never saw Dr Lecter come up behind him.

Dr Lecter wondered if the police believed he was fool enough to fly from the airport.

The only problem on the drive to St Louis was finding the lights, the dimmers, and the wipers in the foreign car, as Dr Lecter was unfamiliar with stalk controls beside the steering wheel.

Tomorrow he would shop for things he needed, hair bleach, barbering supplies, a sunlamp, and there were other, prescription, items that he would obtain to make some immediate changes in his appearance. When it was convenient, he would move on.

There was no reason to hurry.

ARDELIA MAPP was in her usual position, propped up in bed with a book. She was listening to all-news radio. She turned it off when Clarice Starling trudged in. Looking into Starling's drawn face, blessedly she didn't ask anything except, "Want some tea?"

When she was studying, Mapp drank a beverage she brewed of mixed loose leaves her grandmother sent her, which she called "Smart People's Tea."

Of the two brightest people Starling knew, one was also the steadiest person she knew and the other was the most frightening. Starling hoped that gave her some balance in her acquaintance.

"You were lucky to miss today," Mapp said. "That damn Kim Won ran us right into the *ground*. I'm not lying. I believe they must have more gravity in Korea than we do. Then they come over here and get *light*, see, get jobs teaching PE because it's not any work for them . . . John Brigham came by."

"When?"

"Tonight, a little while ago. Wanted to know if you

315

were back yet. He had his hair slicked down. Shifted
around like a freshman in the lobby. We had a little talk.
He said if you're behind and we need to jam instead of
shoot during the range period the next couple of days,
he'll open up the range this weekend and let us make
it up. I said I'd let him know. He's a nice man."

"Yeah, he is."

"Did you know he wants you to shoot against the
DEA and Customs in the interservice match?"

"Nope."

"Not the Women's. The Open. Next question: Do
you know the Fourth Amendment stuff for Friday?"

"A lot of it I do."

"Okay, what's *Chimel versus California?*"

"Searches in secondary schools."

"What *about* school searches?"

"I don't know."

"It's the 'immediate reach' concept. Who was *Schneck-loth?*"

"Hell, I don't know."

"Schneckloth versus Bustamonte."

"Is it the reasonable expectation of privacy?"

"Boo to you. Expectation of privacy is the *Katz*
principle. *Sckneckloth* is consent to search. I can see
we've got to jam on the books, my girl. I've got the
notes."

"Not tonight."

"No. But tomorrow you'll wake up with your mind
fertile and ignorant, and then we'll begin to plant the
harvest for Friday. Starling, Brigham said—he's not
supposed to tell, so I promised—he said you'll beat
the hearing. He thinks that signifying son of a bitch

Krendler won't remember you two days from now. Your grades are good, we'll knock this stuff out easy." Mapp studied Starling's tired face. "You did the best anybody could for that poor soul, Starling. You stuck your neck out for her and you got your butt kicked for her and you moved things along. You deserve a chance yourself. Why don't you go ahead and crash? I'm fixing to shut this down myself."

"Ardelia. Thanks."

And after the lights were out.

"Starling?"

"Yeah?"

"Who do you think's prettiest, Brigham or Hot Bobby Lowrance?"

"That's a hard one."

"Brigham's got a tattoo on his shoulder, I could see it through his shirt. What does it say?"

"I wouldn't have any idea."

"Will you let me know soon as you find out?"

"Probably not."

"I told you about Hot Bobby's python briefs."

"You just saw 'em through the window when he was lifting weights."

"Did Gracie tell you that? That girl's mouth is gonna—"

Starling was asleep.

SHORTLY BEFORE 3:00 A.M., Crawford, dozing beside his wife, came awake. There was a catch in Bella's breathing and she had stirred on her bed. He sat up and took her hand.

"Bella?"

She took a deep breath and let it out. Her eyes were open for the first time in days. Crawford put his face close before hers, but he didn't think she could see him.

"Bella, I love you, kid," he said in case she could hear.

Fear brushed the walls of his chest, circling inside him like a bat in a house. Then he got hold of it.

He wanted to get something for her, anything, but he did not want her to feel him let go of her hand.

He put his ear to her chest. He heard a soft beat, a flutter, and then her heart stopped. There was nothing to hear, there was only a curious cool rushing. He didn't know if the sound was in her chest or only in his ears.

"God bless you and keep you with Him . . . and

with your folks," Crawford said, words he wanted to be true.

He gathered her to him on the bed, sitting against the headboard, held her to his chest while her brain died. His chin pushed back the scarf from the remnants of her hair. He did not cry. He had done all that.

Crawford changed her into her favorite, her best bed gown and sat for a while beside the high bed, holding her hand against his cheek. It was a square, clever hand, marked with a lifetime of gardening, marked by IV needles now.

When she came in from the garden, her hands smelled like thyme.

("Think about it like egg white on your fingers," the girls at school had counseled Bella about sex. She and Crawford had joked about it in bed, years ago, years later, last year. Don't think about that, think about the good stuff, the pure stuff. That *was* the pure stuff. She wore a round hat and white gloves and going up in the elevator the first time he whistled a dramatic arrangement of "Begin the Beguine." In the room she teased him that he had the cluttered pockets of a boy.)

Crawford tried going into the next room—he still could turn when he wanted to and see her through the open door, composed in the warm light of the bedside lamp. He was waiting for her body to become a ceremonial object apart from him, separate from the person he had held upon the bed and separate from the life's companion he held now in his mind. So he could call them to come for her.

His empty hands hanging palms forward at his sides, he stood at the window looking to the empty east. He did not look for dawn; east was only the way the window faced.

CHAPTER
46

"READY, PRECIOUS?"

Jame Gumb was propped against the headboard of his bed and very comfortable, the little dog curled up warm on his tummy.

Mr Gumb had just washed his hair and he had a towel wrapped around his head. He rummaged in the sheets, found the remote control for his VCR, and pushed the play button.

He had composed his program from two pieces of videotape copied onto one cassette. He watched it every day when he was making vital preparations, and he always watched it just before he harvested a hide.

The first tape was from scratchy film of *Movietone News*, a black-and-white newsreel from 1948. It was the quarter-finals of the Miss Sacramento contest, a preliminary event on the long road to the Miss America pageant in Atlantic City.

This was the swimsuit competition, and all the girls carried flowers as they came in a file to the stairs and mounted to the stage.

Mr Gumb's poodle had been through this many times and she squinted her eyes when she heard the music, knowing she'd be squeezed.

The beauty contestants looked very World War II. They wore Rose Marie Reid swimsuits, and some of the faces were lovely. Their legs were nicely shaped too, some of them, but they lacked muscle tone and seemed to lap a little at the knee.

Gumb squeezed the poodle.

"Precious, here she comes, hereshecomes hereshecomes!"

And here she came, approaching the stairs in her white swimsuit, with a radiant smile for the young man who assisted at the stairs, then quick on her high heels away, the camera following the backs of her thighs: Mom. There was Mom.

Mr Gumb didn't have to touch his remote control, he'd done it all when he dubbed this copy. In reverse, here she came backward, backward down the stairs, took back her smile from the young man, backed up the aisle, now forward again, and back and forward, forward and back.

When she smiled at the young man, Gumb smiled too.

There was one more shot of her in a group, but it always blurred in freeze-frame. Better just to run it at speed and get the glimpse. Mom was with the other girls, congratulating the winners.

The next item he'd taped off cable television in a motel in Chicago—he'd had to rush out and buy a VCR and stay an extra night to get it. This was the loop film they run on seedy cable channels late at night as background for the sex ads that crawl up the screen in print. The loops are made of junk film, fairly innocuous naughty movies from the forties and fifties, and there was nudist camp volleyball and the less explicit parts of thirties sex movies where the male actors wore false noses and still had their socks on. The sound was any music at all. Right now it was "The Look of Love," totally out of sync with the sprightly action.

There was nothing Mr Gumb could do about the ads crawling up the screen. He just had to put up with them.

Here it is, an outdoor pool—in California, judging from the foliage. Good pool furniture, everything very fifties. Naked swimming, some graceful girls. A few of them might have appeared in a couple of B-pictures. Sprightly and bouncing, they climbed out of the pool and ran, much faster than the music, to the ladder of a water slide, climbed up—down they came, Wheeee! Breasts lifting as they plunged down the slide, laughing, legs out straight, Splash!

Here came Mom. Here she came, climbing out of the pool behind the girl with the curly hair. Her face was partly covered by a crawl ad from Sinderella, a sex boutique, but here you saw her going away, and there she went up the ladder all shiny and wet, wonderfully buxom and supple, with a small Cesarean scar, and down the slide, Wheeee! So beautiful, and, even if he couldn't see her face, Mr Gumb knew in his heart it was Mom, filmed after the last time in his life that he ever got to really see her. Except in his mind, of course.

The scene switched to a filmed ad for a marital aid and abruptly ended.

The poodle squinted her eyes two seconds before Mr Gumb hugged her tight.

"Oh, Precious. Come here to Mommy. Mommy's gonna be *so* beautiful."

Much to do, much to do, much to do to get ready for tomorrow.

He could never hear it from the kitchen even at the top of its voice, thank goodness, but he could hear it on the stairs as he went down to the basement. He had hoped it would be quiet and asleep. The poodle, riding beneath his arm, growled back at the sounds from the pit.

"*You've* been raised better than that," he said into the fur on the back of her head.

The oubliette room is through a door to the left at the bottom of the stairs. He didn't spare it a glance, nor did he listen to the words from the pit—as far as he was concerned, they bore not the slightest resemblance to English.

Mr Gumb turned right into the workroom, put the poodle down and turned on the lights. A few moths fluttered and lit harmlessly on the wire mesh covering the ceiling lights.

Mr Gumb was meticulous in the workroom. He always mixed his fresh solutions in stainless steel, never in aluminum.

He had learned to do everything well ahead of time. As he worked, he admonished himself:

You have to be orderly, you have to be precise, you have to be expeditious, because the problems are formidable.

The human skin is heavy—sixteen to eighteen percent of body weight—and slippery. An entire hide is hard to handle and easy to drop when it's still wet. Time is important too; skin begins to shrink immediately after it has been harvested, most notably from young adults, whose skin is tightest to begin with.

Add to that the fact that the skin is not perfectly elastic, even in the young. If you stretch it, it never regains its original proportions. Stitch something perfectly smooth, then pull it too hard over a tailor's ham, and it bulges and puckers. Sitting at the machine and crying your eyes out won't remove one pucker. Then there are the cleavage lines, and you'd better know where they are. Skin doesn't stretch the same amount in all directions before the collagen bundles deform and the fibers tear; pull the wrong way, and you get a stretch mark.

Green material is simply impossible to work with. Much experimentation went into this, along with much heartbreak, before Mr Gumb got it right.

In the end he found the old ways were best. His procedures were these: First he soaked his items in the aquariums, in vegetable extracts developed by the Native Americans—all-natural substances that contain no mineral salts whatsoever. Then he used the method that produced the matchless butter-soft buckskin of the New World—classic brain tanning. The Native Americans believed that each animal has just enough brains to tan its own hide. Mr Gumb knew that this was not true and long ago had quit trying it, even with the largest-brained primate. He had a freezer full of beef brains now, so he never ran short.

The problems of processing the material he could manage; practice had made him near perfect.

Difficult structural problems remained, but he was especially well qualified to solve them too.

The workroom opened into a basement corridor leading to a disused bath where Mr Gumb stored his hoisting tackle and his timepiece, and on to the studio and the vast black warren beyond.

He opened his studio door to brilliant light—floodlights and incandescent tubes, color-corrected to daylight, were fastened to ceiling beams. Mannequins posed on a raised floor of pickled oak. All were partly clad, some in leather and some in muslin patterns for leather garments. Eight mannequins were doubled in the two mirrored walls—good plate mirror too, not tiles. A makeup table held cosmetics, several wig forms, and wigs. This was the brightest of studios, all white and blond oak.

The mannequins wore commercial work in progress, dramatic Armani knockoffs mostly, in fine black cabretta leather, all roll-pleats and pointed shoulders and breastplates.

The third wall was taken up by a large worktable, two commercial sewing machines, two dressmaker's forms, and a tailor's form cast from the very torso of Jame Gumb.

Against the fourth wall, dominating this bright room, was a great black armoire in Chinese lacquer that rose almost to the eight-foot ceiling. It was old and the designs on it had faded; a few gold scales remained where a dragon was, his white eye still clear and staring, and here was the red tongue of another dragon whose body had faded away. The lacquer beneath them remained intact, though it was crackled.

The armoire, immense and deep, had nothing to do with commercial work. It contained on forms and hangers the Special Things, and its doors were closed.

The little dog lapped from her water bowl in the corner and lay down between the feet of a mannequin, her eyes on Mr Gumb.

He had been working on a leather jacket. He needed to finish it—he'd meant to get everything out of the way, but he was in a creative fever now and his own muslin fitting garment didn't satisfy him yet.

Mr Gumb had progressed in tailoring far beyond what the California Department of Corrections had taught him in his youth, but this was a true challenge. Even working delicate cabretta leather does not prepare you for really fine work.

Here he had two muslin fitting garments, like white waistcoats, one his exact size and one he had made from measurements he took while Catherine Baker Martin was still unconscious. When he put the smaller one on his tailor's form, the problems were apparent. She was a big girl, and wonderfully proportioned, but she wasn't as big as Mr Gumb, and not nearly so broad across the back.

His ideal was a seamless garment. This was not possible. He was determined, though, that the bodice front be absolutely seamless and without blemish. This meant all figure corrections had to be made on the back. Very difficult. He'd already discarded one fitting muslin and started over. With judicious stretching, he could get by with two underarm darts—not French darts, but vertical inset darts, apexes down. Two waist darts also in the back, just inside his kidneys. He was used to working with only a tiny seam allowance.

His considerations went beyond the visual aspects to the tactile; it was not inconceivable that an attractive person might be hugged.

Mr Gumb sprinkled talc lightly on his hands and embraced the tailor's form of his body in a natural, comfortable hug.

"Give me a kiss," he said playfully to the empty air where the head should be. "Not *you*, silly," he told the little dog, when she raised her ears.

Gumb caressed the back of the form at the natural reach of his arms. Then he walked behind it to consider the powder marks. Nobody wanted to feel a seam. In an embrace, though, the hands lap over the center of the back. Also, he reasoned, we are accustomed to the center line of a spine. It is not as jarring as an asymmetry in our bodies. Shoulder seams were definitely out, then. A center dart at the top was the answer, apex a little above the center of the shoulder blades. He could use the same seam to anchor the stout yoke built into the lining to provide support. Lycra panels beneath plackets on both sides—he must remember to get the Lycra—and a Velcro closure beneath the placket on the right. He thought about those marvelous Charles James gowns where the seams were staggered to lie perfectly flat.

The dart in back would be covered by his hair, or rather the hair he would have soon.

Mr Gumb slipped the muslin off the dressmaker's form and started to work.

The sewing machine was old and finely made, an

ornate foot-treadle machine that had been converted to electricity perhaps forty years ago. On the arm of the machine was painted in gold-leaf scroll "I Never Tire, I Serve." The foot treadle remained operative, and Gumb started the machine with it for each series of stitches. For fine stitching, he preferred to work barefoot, rocking the treadle delicately with his meaty foot, gripping the front edge of it with his painted toes to prevent overruns. For a while there were only the sounds of the machine, and the little dog snoring, and the hiss of the steam pipes in the warm basement.

When he had finished inserting the darts in the muslin pattern garment, he tried it on in front of the mirrors. The little dog watched from the corner, her head cocked.

He needed to ease it a little under the arm holes. There were a few remaining problems with facings and interfacings. Otherwise, it was so nice. It was supple, pliant, bouncy. He could see himself just running up the ladder of a water slide as fast as you please.

Mr Gumb played with the lights and his wigs for some dramatic effects, and he tried a wonderful choker necklace of shells over the collar line. It would be stunning when he wore a décolleté gown or hostess pajamas over his new thorax.

It was so tempting to just go on with it now, to really get busy, but his eyes were tired. He wanted his hands to be absolutely steady too, and he just wasn't up for the noise. Patiently, he picked out the stitches and laid out the pieces. A perfect pattern to cut by.

"Tomorrow, Precious," he told the little dog as he set the beef brains out to thaw. "We'll do it first thing tomooooooorooow. Mommy's gonna be so *beautiful*!"

STARLING SLEPT hard for five hours and woke in the pit of the night, driven awake by fear of the dream. She bit the corner of the sheet and pressed her palms over her ears, waiting to find out if she was truly awake and away from it. Silence and no lambs screaming. When she knew she was awake, her heart slowed, but her feet would not stay still beneath the covers. In a moment her mind would race, she knew it.

It was a relief when a flush of hot anger rather than fear shot through her.

"Nuts," she said, and put a foot out in the air.

In all the long day, when she had been disrupted by Chilton, insulted by Senator Martin, abandoned, and rebuked by Krendler, taunted by Dr Lecter and sickened by his bloody escape, and put off the job by Jack Crawford, there was one thing that stung the worst: being called a thief.

Senator Martin was a mother under extreme duress, and she was sick of policemen pawing her daughter's things. She hadn't meant it.

Still, the accusation stuck in Starling like a hot needle.

As a small child, Starling had been taught that thieving is the cheapest, most despicable act short of rape and murder for money. Some kinds of manslaughter were preferable to theft.

As a child in institutions where there were few prizes and many hungers, she had learned to hate a thief.

Lying in the dark, she faced another reason Senator Martin's implication bothered her so.

Starling knew what the malicious Dr Lecter would say, and it was true: she was afraid there was something tacky that Senator Martin saw in her, something cheap, something thieflike that Senator Martin reacted to. That Vanderbilt bitch.

Dr Lecter would relish pointing out that class resentment, the buried anger that comes with mother's milk, was a factor too. Starling gave away nothing to any Martin in education, intelligence, drive, and certainly physical appearance, but still it was there and she knew it.

Starling was an isolated member of a fierce tribe with no formal genealogy but the honors list and the penal register. Dispossessed in Scotland, starved out of Ireland, a lot of them were inclined to the dangerous trades. Many generic Starlings had been used up this way, had thumped on the bottom of narrow holes or slid off planks with a shot at their feet, or were commended to glory with a cracked "Taps" in the cold when everyone wanted to go home. A few may have been recalled tearily by the officers on regimental mess nights, the way a man in drink remembers a good bird dog. Faded names in a Bible.

None of them had been very smart, as far as Starling could tell, except for a great-aunt who wrote wonderfully in her diary until she got "brain fever."

They didn't steal, though.

School was the thing in America, don't you know, and the Starlings caught on to that. One of Starling's uncles had his junior college degree cut on his tombstone.

Starling had lived by schools, her weapon the competitive exam, for all the years when there was no place else for her to go.

She knew she could pull out of this. She could be what she had always been, ever since she'd learned how it works: she could be near the top of her class, approved, included, chosen, and not sent away.

It was a matter of working hard and being careful. Her grades would be good. The Korean couldn't kill her in PE. Her name would be engraved on the big plaque in the lobby, the "Possible Board," for extraordinary performance on the range.

In four weeks she would be a special agent of the Federal Bureau of Investigation.

Would she have to watch out for that fucking Krendler for the rest of her life?

In the presence of the Senator, he had wanted to wash his hands of her. Every time Starling thought about it, it stung. He wasn't positive that he would find evidence in the envelope. That was shocking. Picturing Krendler now in her mind, she saw him wearing Navy oxfords on his feet like the mayor, her father's boss, coming to collect the watchman's clock.

Worse, Jack Crawford in her mind seemed diminished. The man was under more strain than anyone should have to bear. He had sent her in to check out Raspail's car with no support or evidence of authority. Okay, she had asked to go under those terms—the trouble was a fluke. But Crawford had to know there'd be trouble when Senator Martin saw her in Memphis; there would have been trouble even if she hadn't found the fuck pictures.

Catherine Baker Martin lay in this same darkness that held her now. Starling had forgotten it for a moment while she thought about her own best interests.

Pictures of the past few days punished Starling for the lapse, flashed on her in sudden color, too much color, shocking color, the color that leaps out of black when lightning strikes at night.

It was Kimberly that haunted her now. Fat dead Kimberly who had her ears pierced trying to look pretty and saved to have her legs waxed. Kimberly with her hair gone. Kimberly her sister. Starling did not think Catherine Baker Martin would have much time for Kimberly. Now they were sisters under the skin. Kimberly lying in a funeral home full of state trooper buckaroos.

Starling couldn't look at it anymore. She tried to turn her face away as a swimmer turns to breathe.

All of Buffalo Bill's victims were women, his obsession was women, he lived to hunt women. Not one woman was hunting him full time. Not one woman investigator had looked at every one of his crimes.

Starling wondered if Crawford would have the nerve to use her as a technician when he had to go look at Catherine Martin. Bill would "do her tomorrow," Crawford predicted. *Do her. Do her. Do her.*

"*Fuck* this," Starling said aloud and put her feet on the floor.

"You're over there corrupting a moron, aren't you, Starling?" Ardelia Mapp said. "Sneaked him in here while I was asleep and now you're giving him instructions—don't think I don't hear you."

"Sorry, Ardelia, I didn't—"

"You've got to be a lot more specific with 'em than that, Starling. You can't just say what *you* said. Corrupting morons is just like journalism, you've got to tell 'em *What*, *When*, *Where*, and *How*. I think *Why* gets self-explanatory as you go along."

"Have you got any laundry?"

"I thought you said did I have any laundry."

"Yep, I think I'll run a load. Whatcha got?"

"Just those sweats on the back of the door."

"Okay. Shut your eyes, I'm gonna turn on the light for just a second."

It was not the Fourth Amendment notes for her upcoming exam that she piled on top of the clothes basket and lugged down the hall to the laundry room.

She took the Buffalo Bill file, a four-inch-thick pile of hell and pain in a buff cover printed with ink the color of blood. With it was a hotline printout of her report on the Death's-head Moth.

She'd have to give the file back tomorrow and, if she wanted this copy to be complete, sooner or later she had to insert her report. In the warm laundry room, in the washing machine's comforting chug, she took off the rubber bands that held the file together. She laid out the papers on the clothes-folding shelf and tried to do the insert without seeing any of the pictures, without thinking of what pictures might be added soon. The map was on top, that was fine. But there was handwriting on the map.

Dr Lecter's elegant script ran across the Great Lakes, and it said:

Clarice, does this *random* scattering of sites seem overdone to you? Doesn't it seem *desperately* random? Random past all possible convenience? Does it suggest to you the elaborations of a bad liar?

Ta,

Hannibal Lecter

P.S. Don't bother to flip through, there isn't anything else.

It took twenty minutes of page-turning to be sure there wasn't anything else.

Starling called the hotline from the pay phone in the hall and read the message to Burroughs. She wondered when Burroughs slept.

"I have to tell you, Starling, the market in Lecter information is way down," Burroughs said. "Did Jack call you about Billy Rubin?"

"No."

She leaned against the wall with her eyes closed while he described Dr Lecter's joke.

"I don't know," he said at last. "Jack says they'll go on with the sex-change clinics, but how hard? If you look at the information in the computer, the way the field entries are styled, you can see that all the Lecter information, yours and the stuff from Memphis, has special prefixes. All the Baltimore stuff or all the Memphis stuff or both can be knocked out of consideration with one button. I think Justice wants to push the button on all of it. I got a memo here suggesting the bug in Klaus's throat was, let's see, 'flotsam.'"

"You'll punch this up for Mr Crawford, though," Starling said.

"Sure, I'll put it on his screen, but we're not calling him right now. You shouldn't either. Bella died a little while ago."

"Oh," Starling said.

"Listen, on the bright side, our guys in Baltimore took a look at Lecter's cell in the asylum. That orderly, Barney, helped out. They got brass grindings off a bolt head in Lecter's cot where he made his handcuff key. Hang in there, kid. You're gonna come out smelling like a rose."

"Thank you, Mr Burroughs. Good night."

Smelling like a rose. Putting Vicks VapoRub under her nostrils.

Daylight coming on the last day of Catherine Martin's life.

What could Dr Lecter mean?

There was no knowing what Dr Lecter knew. When she first gave him the file, she expected him to enjoy the pictures and use the file as a prop while he told her what he already knew about Buffalo Bill.

Maybe he was always lying to her, just as he lied to Senator Martin. Maybe he didn't know or understand anything about Buffalo Bill.

He sees very clearly—he damn sure sees through me. It's hard to accept that someone can understand you

337

without wishing you well. At Starling's age it hadn't happened to her much.

Desperately random, Dr Lecter said.

Starling and Crawford and everyone else had stared at the map with its dots marking the abductions and body dumps. It had looked to Starling like a black constellation with a date beside each star, and she knew Behavioral Science had once tried imposing zodiac signs on the map without result.

If Dr Lecter was reading for recreation, why would he fool with the map? She could see him flipping through the report, making fun of the prose style of some of the contributors.

There was no pattern in the abductions and body dumps, no relationships of convenience, no coordination in time with any known business conventions, any spate of burglaries or clothes-line thefts or other fetish-oriented crimes.

Back in the laundry room, with the dryer spinning, Starling walked her fingers over the map. Here an abduction, there the dump. Here the second abduction, there the dump. Here the third and—But are these dates backward or, no, the second body was discovered first.

That fact was recorded, unremarked, in smudged ink beside the location on the map. The body of the second woman abducted was found first, floating in the Wabash River in downtown Lafayette, Indiana, just below Interstate 65.

The first young woman reported missing was taken from Belvedere, Ohio, near Columbus, and found much later in the Blackwater River in Missouri, outside of

Lone Jack. The body was weighted. No others were weighted.

The body of the first victim was sunk in water in a remote area. The second was dumped in a river upstream from a city, where quick discovery was certain.

Why?

The one he started with was well hidden, the second one, not.

Why?

What does "desperately random" mean?

The first, first. What did Dr Lecter say about "first"? What did anything mean that Dr Lecter said?

Starling looked at the notes she had scribbled on the airplane from Memphis.

Dr Lecter said there was enough in the file to locate the killer. "Simplicity," he said. What about "first," where was first? Here—"First principles" were important. "First Principles" sounded like pretentious bullshit when he said it.

What does he do, Clarice? What is the first and principal thing he does, what need does he serve by killing? He covets. How do we begin to covet? We begin by coveting what we see every day.

It was easier to think about Dr Lecter's statements when she wasn't feeling his eyes on her skin. It was easier here in the safe heart of Quantico.

If we begin to covet by coveting what we see every day, did Buffalo Bill surprise himself when he killed the first one? Did he do someone close around him? Is that why he hid the first body well, and the second one poorly? Did he abduct the second one far from home and dump her where she'd be found quickly because he wanted to establish early the belief that the abduction sites were random?

When Starling thought of the victims, Kimberly Emberg came first to mind because she had seen Kimberly dead and, in a sense, had taken Kimberly's part.

Here was the first one. Fredrica Bimmel, twenty-two, Belvedere, Ohio. There were two photos. In her yearbook picture she looked large and plain, with good thick hair and a good complexion. In the second photo, taken at the Kansas City morgue, she looked like nothing human.

Starling called Burroughs again. He was sounding a little hoarse by now, but he listened.

"So what are you saying, Starling?"

"Maybe he lives in Belvedere, Ohio, where the first victim lived. Maybe he saw her every day, and he killed her sort of spontaneously. Maybe he just meant to . . . give her a 7-Up and talk about the choir. So he did a good job of hiding the body and then he grabbed another one far from home. He didn't hide that one very well, so it would be found first and the attention would be directed away from him. You know how much attention a missing-person report gets, it gets zip until the body's found."

"Starling, the return's better where the trail is fresh, people remember better, witnesses—"

"That's what I'm saying. He *knows* that."

"For instance, you won't be able to sneeze today without spraying a cop in that last one's hometown— Kimberly Emberg from Detroit. Lot of interest in

Kimberly Emberg all of a sudden since little Martin disappeared. All of a sudden they're working the hell out of it. You never heard me say that."

"Will you put it up for Mr Crawford, about the first town?"

"Sure. Hell, I'll put it on the hotline for everybody. I'm not saying it's bad thinking, Starling, but the town was picked over pretty good as soon as the woman—what's her name, Bimmel, is it?—as soon as Bimmel was identified. The Columbus office worked Belvedere, and so did a lot of locals. You've got it all there. You're not gonna raise much interest in Belvedere or any other theory of Dr Lecter's this morning."

"All he—"

"Starling, we're sending a gift to UNICEF for Bella. You want in, I'll put your name on the card."

"Sure, thanks, Mr Burroughs."

Starling got the clothes out of the dryer. The warm laundry felt good and smelled good. She hugged the warm laundry close to her chest.

Her mother with an armload of sheets.

Today is the last day of Catherine's life.

The black-and-white crow stole from the cart. She couldn't be outside to shoo it and in the room too.

Today is the last day of Catherine's life.

Her father used an arm signal instead of the blinkers when he turned his pickup into the driveway. Playing in the yard, she thought with his big arm he showed the pickup where to turn, grandly directed it to turn.

When Starling decided what she would do, a few tears came. She put her face in the warm laundry.

CRAWFORD CAME out of the funeral home and looked up and down the street for Jeff with the car. Instead he saw Clarice Starling waiting under the awning, dressed in a dark suit, looking real in the light.

"Send me," she said.

Crawford had just picked out his wife's coffin and he carried in a paper sack a pair of her shoes he had mistakenly brought. He collected himself.

"Forgive me," Starling said. "I wouldn't come now if there were any other time. Send me."

Crawford jammed his hands in his pockets, turned his neck in his collar until it popped. His eyes were bright, maybe dangerous. "Send you where?"

"You sent me to get a feel for Catherine Martin— let me go to the others. All we've got left is to find out how he hunts. How he finds them, how he picks them. I'm as good as anybody you've got at the cop stuff, better at some things. The victims are all women and there aren't any women working this. I can walk in a woman's room and know three times as much about

342

her as a man would know, and *you* know that's a fact. Send me."

"You ready to accept a recycle?"

"Yes."

"Six months of your life, probably."

She didn't say anything.

Crawford stubbed at the grass with his toe. He looked up at her, at the prairie distance in her eyes. She had backbone, like Bella. "Who would you start with?"

"The first one, Fredrica Bimmel, Belvedere, Ohio."

"Not Kimberly Emberg, the one you saw?"

"*He* didn't start with her." *Mention Lecter? No. He'd see it on the hotline.*

"Emberg would be the *emotional* choice, wouldn't she, Starling? Travel's by reimbursement. Got any money?" The banks wouldn't open for an hour.

"I've got some left on my Visa."

Crawford dug in his pockets. He gave her three hundred dollars cash and a personal check.

"Go, Starling. Just to the first one. Post the hotline. Call me."

She raised her hand to him. She didn't touch his face or his hand, there didn't seem to be any place to touch, and she turned and ran for the Pinto.

Crawford patted his pockets as she drove away. He had given her the last cent he had with him.

"Baby needs a new pair of shoes," he said. "My baby doesn't need any shoes." He was crying in the middle of the sidewalk, sheets of tears on his face, a Section Chief of the FBI, silly now.

Jeff from the car saw his cheeks shine and backed into an alley where Crawford couldn't see him. Jeff got out

of the car. He lit a cigarette and smoked furiously. As
his gift to Crawford he would dawdle until Crawford
was dried off and pissed off and justified in chewing
him out.

CHAPTER

49

ON THE morning of the fourth day, Mr Gumb was ready to harvest the hide.

He came in from shopping with the last things he needed, and it was hard to keep from running down the basement stairs. In the studio he unpacked his shopping bags, new bias seam-binding, panels of stretchy Lycra to go under the plackets, a box of kosher salt. He had forgotten nothing.

In the workroom, he laid out his knives on a clean towel beside the long sinks. The knives were four: a sway-backed skinning-knife, a delicate drop-point caper that perfectly followed the curve of the index finger in close places, a scalpel for the closest work, and a World War I-era bayonet. The rolled edge of the bayonet is the finest tool for fleshing a hide without tearing it.

In addition he had a Strycker autopsy saw, which he hardly ever used and regretted buying.

Now he greased the head of a wig stand, packed coarse salt over the grease and set the stand in a shallow drip pan. Playfully, he tweaked the nose on the face of the wig stand and blew it a kiss.

It was hard to behave in a responsible manner—he wanted to fly about the room like Danny Kaye. He laughed and blew a moth away from his face with a gentle puff of air.

Time to start the aquarium pumps in his fresh tanks of solution. Oh, was there a nice chrysalis buried in the humus in the cage? He poked with his finger. Yes, there was.

The pistol, now.

The problem of killing this one had perplexed Mr Gumb for days. Hanging her was out because he didn't want the pectoral mottling, and, besides, he couldn't risk the knot tearing her behind the ear.

Mr Gumb had learned from each of his previous efforts, sometimes painfully. He was determined to avoid some of the nightmares he'd gone through before. One cardinal principle: no matter how weak from hunger or faint with fright, they always fought you when they saw the apparatus.

He had in the past hunted young women through the blacked-out basement using his infrared goggles and light, and it was wonderful to do, watching them feel their way around, seeing them try to scrunch into corners. He liked to hunt them with the pistol. He liked to use the pistol. Always they became disoriented, lost their balance, ran into things. He could stand in absolute darkness with his goggles on, wait until they took their hands down from their faces, and shoot them right in the head. Or in the legs first, below the knee so they could still crawl.

That was childish and a waste. They were useless afterward and he had quit doing it altogether.

In his current project, he had offered showers upstairs to the first three, before he booted them down the staircase with a noose around their necks—no problem. But the fourth had been a disaster. He'd had to use the pistol in the bathroom and it had taken an hour to clean up. He thought about the girl, wet, goosebumps on her, and how she shivered when he cocked the pistol. He liked to cock it, snick snick, one big bang and no more racket.

He liked his pistol, and well he should, because it was a very handsome piece, a stainless steel Colt Python with a six-inch barrel. All Python actions are tuned at the Colt custom shop, and this one was a pleasure to feel. He cocked it now and squeezed it off, catching the hammer with his thumb. He loaded the Python and put it on the workroom counter.

Mr Gumb wanted very much to offer this one a shampoo, because he wanted to watch it comb out the hair. He could learn much for his own grooming about how the hair lay on the head. But this one was tall and probably strong. This one was too rare to risk having to waste the whole thing with gunshot wounds.

No, he'd get his hoisting tackle from the bathroom, offer her a bath, and when she had put herself securely in the hoisting sling he'd bring her halfway up the shaft of the oubliette and shoot her several times low in the spine. When she lost consciousness, he could do the rest with chloroform.

That's it. He'd go upstairs now and get out of his clothes. He'd wake up Precious and watch his video with her and then go to work, naked in the warm basement, naked as the day he was born.

He felt almost giddy going up the stairs. Quickly out of his clothes and into his robe. He plugged in his videocassette.

"Precious, come on, Precious. Busybusy day. Come on, Sweetheart." He'd have to shut her up here in the upstairs bedroom while he got through with the noisy part in the basement—she hated the noise and got terribly upset. To keep her occupied, he'd gotten her a whole box of Cheweez while he was out shopping.

"Precious." When she didn't come, he called in the hall, "Precious!" and then in the kitchen, and in the basement, "Precious!" When he called at the door of the oubliette room, he got an answer:

"She's down here, you son of a bitch," Catherine Martin said.

Mr Gumb sickened all over in a plunge of fear for Precious. Then rage tightened him again and, fists against the sides of his head, he pressed his forehead into the doorframe and tried to get hold of himself. One sound between a retch and a groan escaped him and the little dog answered with a yip.

He went to the workroom and got his pistol.

The string to the sanitation bucket was broken. He still wasn't sure how she'd done it. Last time the string was broken, he'd assumed she'd broken it in an absurd attempt to climb. They had tried to climb it before— they had done every fool thing imaginable.

He leaned over the opening, his voice carefully controlled.

"Precious, are you all right? Answer me."

Catherine pinched the dog's plump behind. It yipped and paid her back with a nip on the arm.

"How's that?" Catherine said.

It seemed very unnatural to Mr Gumb to speak to Catherine in this way, but he overcame his distaste.

"I'll lower a basket. You'll put her in it."

"You'll lower a telephone or I'll have to break her neck. I don't want to hurt you, I don't want to hurt this little dog. Just give me the telephone."

Mr Gumb brought the pistol up. Catherine saw the muzzle extending past the light. She crouched, holding the dog above her, weaving it between her and the gun. She heard him cock the pistol.

"You shoot, motherfucker, you better kill me quick or I'll break her fucking neck. I swear to God."

She put the dog under her arm, put her hand around its muzzle, raised its head. "Back off, you son of a bitch." The little dog whined. The gun withdrew.

Catherine brushed the hair back from her wet forehead with her free hand. "I didn't mean to insult you," she said. "Just lower me a phone. I want a live phone. You can go away. I don't care about you. I never saw you. I'll take good care of Precious."

"No."

"I'll see she has everything. Think about her welfare, not just yourself. You shoot in here, she'll be deaf whatever happens. All I want's a live telephone. Get a long extension, get five or six and clip them together— they come with the connections on the ends—and lower it down here. I'd air-freight you the dog anywhere. My family has dogs. My mother loves dogs. You can run, I don't care what you do."

"You won't get any more water, you've had your last water."

"She won't get any either, and I won't give her any from my water bottle. I'm sorry to tell you, I think her leg's broken." This was a lie—the little dog, along with the baited bucket, had fallen onto Catherine and it was Catherine who suffered a scratched cheek from the dog's scrabbling claws. She couldn't put it down or he'd see it didn't limp. "She's in pain. Her leg's all crooked and she's trying to lick it. It just makes me sick," Catherine lied. "I've got to get her to a vet."

Mr Gumb's groan of rage and anguish made the little dog cry. "You think *she's* in pain," Mr Gumb said. "You don't know what pain is. You hurt her and I'll scald you."

When she heard him pounding up the stairs, Catherine Martin sat down, shaken by gross jerks in her arms and legs. She couldn't hold the dog, she couldn't hold her water, she couldn't hold anything.

When the little dog climbed into her lap, she hugged it, grateful for the warmth.

FEATHERS RODE on the thick brown water, curled feathers blown from the coops, carried on breaths of air that shivered the skin of the river. The houses on Fell Street, Fredrica Bimmel's street, were termed waterfront on the weathered realtors' signs because their backyards ended at a slough, a backwater of the Licking River in Belvedere, Ohio, a Rust Belt town of 112,000, east of Columbus.

It was a shabby neighborhood of big, old houses. A few of them had been bought cheap by young couples and renovated with Sears Best enamel, making the rest of the houses look worse. The Bimmel house had not been renovated.

Clarice Starling stood for a moment in Fredrica's backyard looking at the feathers on the water, her hands deep in the pockets of her trenchcoat. There was some rotten snow in the reeds, blue beneath the blue sky on this mild winter day.

Behind her Starling could hear Fredrica's father hammering in the city of pigeon coops, the Orvieto of pigeon coops rising from the water's edge and reaching almost to the house. She hadn't seen Mr Bimmel yet. The neighbors said he was there. Their faces were closed when they said it.

Starling was having some trouble with herself. At that moment in the night when she knew she had to leave the Academy to hunt Buffalo Bill, a lot of extraneous noises had stopped. She felt a pure new silence in the center of her mind, and a calm there. In a different place, down the front of her, she felt in flashes that she was a truant and a fool.

The petty annoyances of the morning hadn't touched her—not the gymnasium stink of the airplane to Columbus, not the confusion and ineptitude at the rental-car counter. She'd snapped at the car clerk to make him move, but she hadn't felt anything.

Starling had paid a high price for this time and she meant to use it as she thought best. Her time could be up at any moment, if Crawford was overruled and they pulled her credentials.

She should hurry, but to think about why, to dwell on Catherine's plight on this final day, would be to waste the day entirely. To think of her in real time, being processed at this moment as Kimberly Emberg and Fredrica Bimmel had been processed, would jam all other thought.

The breeze fell off, the water still as death. Near her feet a curled feather spun on the surface tension. Hang on, Catherine.

Starling caught her lip between her teeth. If he shot her, she hoped he'd do a competent job of it.

Teach us to care and not to care.

Teach us to be still.

She turned to the leaning stack of coops and followed a path of boards laid on the mud between them, toward the sound of hammering. The hundreds of pigeons were of all sizes and colors; there were tall knock-kneed ones and pouters with their chests stuck out. Eyes bright, heads jerking as they paced, the birds spread their wings in the pale sun and made pleasant sounds as she passed.

Fredrica's father, Gustav Bimmel, was a tall man, flat and wide-hipped with red-rimmed eyes of watery blue. A knit cap was pulled down to his eyebrows. He was building another coop on sawhorses in front of his work shed. Starling smelled vodka on his breath as he squinted at her identification.

"I don't know nothing new to tell you," he said. "The policemen come back here night before last. They went back over my statement with me again. Read it back to me. 'Is that right? Is that right?' I told him, I said hell yes, if that wasn't right I wouldn't have told you in the first place."

"I'm trying to get an idea where the—get an idea where the kidnapper might have seen Fredrica, Mr Bimmel. Where he might have spotted her and decided to take her away."

"She went into Columbus on the bus to see about a job at that store there. The police said she got to the interview all right. She never came home. We don't know where else she went that day. The FBI got her Master Charge slips, but there wasn't nothing for that day. You know all that, don't you?"

"About the credit card, yes, sir, I do. Mr Bimmel, do you have Fredrica's things, are they here?"

"Her room's in the top of the house."

"May I see?"

It took him a moment to decide where to lay down his hammer. "All right," he said, "come along."

JACK CRAWFORD'S office in the FBI's Washington headquarters was painted an oppressive gray, but it had big windows.

Crawford stood at these windows with his clipboard held to the light, peering at a list off a Goddamned fuzzy dot-matrix printer that he'd told them to get rid of.

He'd come here from the funeral home and worked all morning, tweaking the Norwegians to hurry with their dental records on the missing seaman named Klaus, jerking San Diego's chain to check Benjamin Raspail's familiars at the Conservatory where he had taught, and stirring up Customs, which was supposed to be checking for import violations involving living insects.

Within five minutes of Crawford's arrival, FBI Assistant Director John Golby, head of the new inter-service task force, stuck his head in the office for a moment to say "Jack, we're all thinking about you. Everybody appreciates you coming in. Has the service been set yet?"

"The wake's tomorrow evening. Service is Saturday at eleven o'clock."

Golby nodded. "There's a UNICEF memorial, Jack, a fund. You want it to read Phyllis or Bella, we'll do it any way you like."

"Bella, John. Let's make it Bella."

"Can I do anything for you, Jack?"

Crawford shook his head. "I'm just working. I'm just gonna work now."

"Right," Golby said. He waited the decent interval. "Frederick Chilton asked for federal protective custody."

"Grand. John, is somebody in Baltimore talking to Everett Yow, Raspail's lawyer? I mentioned him to you. He might know something about Raspail's friends."

"Yeah, they're on it this morning. I just sent Burroughs my memo on it. The Director's putting Lecter on the Most Wanted. Jack, if you need anything . . ." Golby raised his eyebrows and his hand and backed out of sight.

If you need anything.

Crawford turned to the windows. He had a fine view from his office. There was the handsome old Post Office building where he'd done some of his training. To the left was the old FBI headquarters. At graduation, he'd filed through J. Edgar Hoover's office with the others. Hoover stood on a little box and shook their hands in turn. That was the only time Crawford ever met the man. The next day he married Bella.

They had met in Livorno, Italy. He was Army, she NATO staff, and she was Phyllis then. They walked on the quays and a boatman called "Bella" across the glittering water and she was always Bella to him after that. She was only Phyllis when they disagreed.

Bella's dead. That should change the view from these windows. It wasn't right this view stayed the same. Had to fucking *die* on me. Jesus, kid. I knew it was coming but it *smarts*.

What do they say about forced retirement at fifty-five? You fall in love with the Bureau, but it doesn't fall in love with you. He'd seen it.

Thank God, Bella had saved him from that. He hoped she was somewhere today and that she was comfortable at last. He hoped she could see in his heart.

The phone was buzzing its intraoffice buzz.

"Mr Crawford, a Dr Danielson from—"

"Right." Punch. "Jack Crawford, Doctor."

"Is this line secure, Mr Crawford?"

"Yes. On this end it is."

"You're not taping, are you?"

"No, Dr Danielson. Tell me what's on your mind."

"I want to make it clear this has nothing to do with anybody who was ever a patient at Johns Hopkins."

"Understood."

"If anything comes of it, I want you to make it clear to the public he's not a transsexual, he had nothing to do with this institution."

"Fine. You got it. Absolutely." *Come on, you stuffy bastard*. Crawford would have said anything.

"He shoved Dr Purvis down."

"Who, Dr Danielson?"

"He applied to the program three years ago as John Grant of Harrisburg, Pennsylvania."

"Description?"

"Caucasian male, he was thirty-one. Six feet one, a hundred and ninety pounds. He came to be tested and did very well on the Wechsler Intelligence Scale—bright normal—but the psychological testing and the interviews were another story. In fact, his House-Tree-Person and his TAT were spot-on with the sheet you gave me. You let me think Alan Bloom authored that little theory, but it was Hannibal Lecter, wasn't it?"

"Go on with Grant, Doctor."

"The board would have turned him down anyway, but, by the time we met to discuss it, the question was moot because the background checks got him."

"Got him how?"

"We routinely check with the police in an applicant's hometown. The Harrisburg police were after him for two assaults on homosexual men. The last one nearly died. He'd given us an address that turned out to be a boarding house he stayed in from time to time. The police got his fingerprints there and a credit-card gas receipt with his license number on it. His name wasn't John Grant at all, he'd just told us that. About a week later he waited outside the building here and shoved Dr Purvis down, just for spite."

"What was his name, Dr Danielson?"

"I'd better spell it for you, it's J-A-M-E G-U-M-B."

CHAPTER

52

FREDRICA BIMMEL'S house was three stories tall and gaunt, covered with asphalt shingles stained rusty where the gutters had spilled over. Volunteer maples growing in the gutters had stood up to the winter pretty well. The windows on the north side were covered with sheet plastic.

In a small parlor, very warm from a space heater, a middle-aged woman sat on a rug, playing with an infant.

"My wife," Bimmel said as they passed through the room. "We just got married Christmas."

"Hello," Starling said. The woman smiled vaguely in her direction.

Cold in the hall again and everywhere boxes stacked waist-high filling the rooms, passageways among them, cardboard cartons filled with lampshades and canning lids, picnic hampers, back numbers of the *Reader's Digest* and *National Geographic*, thick old tennis rackets, bed linens, a case of dartboards, fiber car-seat covers in a fifties plaid with the intense smell of mouse pee.

359

"We're moving pretty soon," Mr Bimmel said.

The stuff near the windows was bleached by the sun, the boxes stacked for years and bellied with age, the random rugs worn bare in the paths through the rooms.

Sunlight dappled the bannister as Starling climbed the stairs behind Fredrica's father. His clothes smelled stale in the cold air. She could see sunlight coming through the sagging ceiling at the top of the stairwell. The cartons stacked on the landing were covered with plastic.

Fredrica's room was small, under the eaves on the third floor.

"You want me anymore?"

"Later, I'd like to talk to you, Mr Bimmel. What about Fredrica's mother?" The file said "deceased," it didn't say when.

"What do you mean, what about her? She died when Fredrica was twelve."

"I see."

"Did you think that was Fredrica's mother downstairs? After I told you we just been married since Christmas? That what you thought, is it? I guess the law's used to handling a different class of people, missy. She never knew Fredrica at all."

"Mr Bimmel, is the room pretty much like Fredrica left it?"

The anger wandered somewhere else in him.

"Yah," he said softly. "We just left it alone. Nobody much could wear her stuff. Plug in the heater if you want it. Remember and unplug it before you come down."

He didn't want to see the room. He left her on the landing.

Starling stood for a moment with her hand on the cold porcelain knob. She needed to organize a little, before her head was full of Fredrica's things.

Okay, the premise is Buffalo Bill did Fredrica first, weighted her and hid her well, in a river far from home. He hid her better than the others—she was the only one weighted—because he wanted the later ones found first. He wanted the idea of random selection of victims in widely scattered towns well established before Fredrica, of Belvedere, was found. It was important to take attention away from Belvedere. Because he lives here, or maybe in Columbus.

He started with Fredrica because he coveted her hide. We don't begin to covet with imagined things. Coveting is a very literal sin—we begin to covet with tangibles, we begin with what we see every day. He saw Fredrica in the course of his daily life. He saw her in the course of her daily life.

What was the course of Fredrica's daily life? All right . . .

Starling pushed the door open. Here it was, this still room smelling of mildew in the cold. On the wall, last year's calendar was forever turned to April. Fredrica had been dead ten months.

Cat food, hard and black, was in a saucer in the corner.

Starling, veteran yard-sale decorator, stood in the center of the room and turned slowly around. Fredrica had done a pretty good job with what she had. There were curtains of flowered chintz. Judging from the piped edges, she had recycled some slipcovers to make the curtains.

There was a bulletin board with a sash pinned to it.

BHS BAND was printed on the sash in glitter. A poster of the performer Madonna was on the wall, and another of Deborah Harry and Blondie. On a shelf above the desk, Starling could see a roll of the bright self-adhesive wallpaper Fredrica had used to cover her walls. It was not a great job of papering, but better than her own first effort, Starling thought.

In an average home, Fredrica's room would have been cheerful. In this bleak house, it was shrill; there was an echo of desperation in it.

Fredrica did not display photographs of herself in the room.

Starling found one in the school yearbook on the small bookcase. Glee Club, Home-Ec Club, Sew 'n' Sew, Band, 4-H Club—maybe the pigeons served as her 4-H project.

Fredrica's school annual had some signatures. "To a great pal," and a "great gal" and "my chemistry buddy," and "Remember the bake sale?!!"

Could Fredrica bring her friends up here? Did she have a friend good enough to bring up those stairs beneath the drip? There was an umbrella beside the door.

Look at this picture of Fredrica, here she's in the front row of the band. Fredrica is wide and fat, but her uniform fits better than the others. She's big and she has beautiful skin. Her irregular features combine to make a pleasant face, but she is not attractive looking by conventional standards.

Kimberly Emberg wasn't what you would call fetching either, not to the mindless gape of high school, and neither were a couple of the others.

Catherine Martin, though, would be attractive to anybody, a big, good-looking young woman who would have to fight the fat when she was thirty.

Remember, he doesn't look at women as a man looks at them. Conventionally attractive doesn't count. They just have to be smooth and roomy.

Starling wondered if he thought of women as "skins," the way some cretins call them "cunts."

She became aware of her own hand tracing the line of credits beneath the yearbook picture, became aware of her entire body, the space she filled, her figure and her face, their effect, the power in them, her breasts above the book, her hard belly against it, her legs below it. What of her experience applied?

Starling saw herself in the full-length mirror on the end wall and was glad to be different from Fredrica. But she knew the difference was a matrix in her thinking. What might it keep her from seeing?

How did Fredrica want to appear? What was she hungry for, where did she seek it? What did she try to do about herself?

Here were a couple of diet plans, the Fruit Juice Diet, the Rice Diet, and a crackpot plan where you don't eat and drink at the same sitting.

Organized diet groups—did Buffalo Bill watch them to find big girls? Hard to check. Starling knew from the file that two of the victims had belonged to diet groups and that the membership rosters had been compared. An agent from the Kansas City office, the FBI's traditional Fat Boys' Bureau, and some overweight police were sent around to work out at Slenderella, and Diet Center, and join Weight Watchers and other diet denominations in the victims' towns. She didn't know if Catherine Martin belonged to a diet group. Money would have been a problem for Fredrica in organized dieting.

Fredrica had several issues of *Big Beautiful Girl*, a magazine for large women. Here she was advised to "come to New York City, where you can meet newcomers from parts of the world where your size is considered a prized asset." Right. Alternatively, "you could travel to Italy or Germany, where you won't be alone after the first day." You bet. Here's what to do if your toes hang out over the ends of your shoes. Jesus! All Fredrica needed was to meet Buffalo Bill, who considered her size a "prized asset."

How did Fredrica manage? She had some makeup, a lot of skin stuff. Good for you, *use* that asset. Starling found herself rooting for Fredrica as though it mattered anymore.

She had some junk jewelry in a White Owl cigar box. Here was a gold-filled circle pin that most likely had belonged to her late mother. She'd tried to cut the fingers off some old gloves of machine lace, to wear them Madonna-style, but they'd raveled on her.

She had some music, a single-shot Decca record player from the fifties with a jackknife attached to the tone arm with rubber bands for weight. Yard-sale records. Love themes by Zamfir, Master of the Pan Flute.

When she pulled the string to light the closet, Starling was surprised at Fredrica's wardrobe. She had nice clothes, not a great many, but plenty for school, enough to get along in a fairly formal office or even a dressy retail job. A quick look inside them, and Starling saw the reason. Fredrica made her own, and made them well; the seams were bound with a serger, the facings carefully fitted. Stacks of patterns were on a shelf at the back of the closet. Most of them were Simplicity, but there were a couple of Vogues that looked hard.

She probably wore her best thing to the job interview. What had she worn? Starling flipped through her file. Here: last seen wearing a green outfit. Come on, Officer, what the hell is a "green outfit"?

Fredrica suffered from the Achilles' heel of the budget wardrobe—she was short on shoes—and at her weight she was hard on the shoes she had. Her loafers were strained into ovals. She wore Odor-Eaters in her sandals. The eyelets were stretched in her running shoes.

Maybe Fredrica exercised a little—she had some outsized warmups.

They were made by Juno.

Catherine Martin also had some fat pants made by Juno.

Starling backed out of the closet. She sat on the foot of the bed with her arms folded and stared into the lighted closet.

Juno was a common brand, sold in a lot of places that handle outsizes, but it raised the question of clothing. Every town of any size has at least one store specializing in clothes for fat people.

Did Buffalo Bill watch fat stores, select a customer and follow her?

Did he go into oversize shops in drag and look around? Every oversize shop in a city gets both transvestites and drag queens as customers.

The idea of Buffalo Bill trying to cross over sexually had just been applied to the investigation very recently, since Dr Lecter gave Starling his theory. What about his clothes?

All of the victims must have shopped in fat stores— Catherine Martin would wear a twelve, but the others couldn't, and Catherine must have shopped in an over-size store to buy the big Juno sweats.

Catherine Martin could wear a twelve. She was the smallest of the victims. Fredrica, the first victim, was largest. How was Buffalo Bill managing to down-size with the choice of Catherine Martin? Catherine was plenty buxom, but she wasn't that big around. Had he lost weight himself? Might he have joined a diet group lately? Kimberly Emberg was sort of in-between, big, but with a good waist indention . . .

Starling had specifically avoided thinking about Kimberly Emberg, but now the memory swamped her for a second. Starling saw Kimberly on the slab in Potter. Buffalo Bill hadn't cared about her waxed legs, her carefully glittered fingernails: he looked at Kimberly's flat bosom and it wasn't good enough and he took his pistol and blew a starfish in her chest.

The door to the room pushed open a few inches. Starling felt the movement in her heart before she knew what it was. A cat came in, a large tortoise-shell cat with one eye gold, the other blue. It hopped up on the bed and rubbed against her. Looking for Fredrica.

Loneliness. Big lonesome girls trying to satisfy some-body.

The police had eliminated lonely-hearts clubs early.

Did Buffalo Bill have another way to take advantage of loneliness? Nothing makes us more vulnerable than loneliness, except greed.

Loneliness might have permitted Buffalo Bill an opening with Fredrica, but not with Catherine. Catherine wasn't lonesome.

Kimberly was lonesome. *Don't start this*. Kimberly, obedient and limp, past rigor mortis, being rolled over on the mortician's table so Starling could fingerprint her. *Stop it. Can't stop it*. Kimberly lonesome, anxious to please; had Kimberly ever rolled over obediently for someone, just to feel his heart beat against her back? She wondered if Kimberly had felt whiskers grating between her shoulder blades.

Staring into the lighted closet, Starling remembered Kimberly's plump back, the triangular patches of skin missing from her shoulders.

Staring into the lighted closet, Starling saw the triangles on Kimberly's shoulders outlined in the blue dashes of a dressmaking pattern. The idea swam away and circled and came again, came close enough for her to grab it this time and she did with a fierce pulse of joy: THEY'RE DARTS—HE TOOK THOSE TRIANGLES TO MAKE DARTS SO HE COULD LET OUT HER WAIST. MOTHERFUCKER CAN SEW. BUFFALO BILL'S TRAINED TO SERIOUSLY SEW—HE'S NOT JUST PICKING OUT READY-TO-WEAR.

What did Dr Lecter say? "He's making himself a girl suit out of real girls." What did he say to me? "Do you sew, Clarice?" Damn straight I do.

Starling put her head back, closed her eyes for one

second. Problem-solving is hunting; it is savage pleasure and we are born to it.

She'd seen a telephone in the parlor. She started downstairs to use it, but Mrs Bimmel's reedy voice was calling up to her already, calling her to the phone.

MRS BIMMEL gave Starling the telephone and picked up the fretting baby. She didn't leave the parlor.

"Clarice Starling."

"Jerry Burroughs, Starling—"

"Good, Jerry, listen. I think Buffalo Bill can sew. He cut the triangles—just a sec—Mrs Bimmel, could I ask you to take the baby in the kitchen? I need to talk here. Thank you . . . Jerry, he can sew. He took—"

"Starling—"

"He took those triangles off of Kimberly Emberg to make darts, dressmaking darts, do you know what I'm saying? He's skilled, he's not just making caveman stuff. ID Section can search Known Offenders for tailors, sailmakers, drapers, upholsterers—run a scan on the Distinguishing Marks field for a tailor's notch in his teeth—"

"Right, right, right, I'm punching up a line now to ID. Now listen up—I may have to get off the phone here. Jack wanted me to brief you. We got a name and a place that looks not bad. The Hostage Rescue Team's airborne from Andrews. Jack's briefing them on the scrambler."

"Going where?"

"Calumet City, edge of Chicago. Subject's Jame, like 'Name' with a *J*, last name Gumb, a.k.a. John Grant, WM, thirty-four, one-ninety, brown and blue. Jack got a beep from Johns Hopkins. Your thing— your profile on how he'd be different from a trans-sexual—it rang the cherries at Johns Hopkins. Guy applied for sex reassignment three years ago. Roughed up a doctor after they turned him down. Hopkins had the Grant alias and a flop address in Harrisburg, Pennsylvania. The cops had a gas receipt with his tag number and we went from there. Big jacket in California as a juvenile—he killed his grandparents when he was twelve and did six years in Tulare Psychiatric. The state let him out sixteen years ago when they shut down the asylum. He disappeared a long time. He's a fag-basher. Had a couple of scrapes in Harrisburg and faded out again."

"Chicago, you said. How do you know Chicago?"

"Customs. They had some paper on the John Grant alias. Customs stopped a suitcase at LAX a couple of years ago shipped from Surinam with live 'pupae'— is that how you say it?—insects anyway, moths, in it. The addressee was John Grant, care of a business in Calumet called—get this—called 'Mr Hide.' Leather goods. Maybe the sewing fits with that. I'm relaying the sewing to Chicago and Calumet. No home address yet on Grant, or Gumb—the business is closed, but we're close."

"Any pictures?"

"Just the juveniles from Sacramento PD so far. They're not much use—he was twelve. Looked like Beaver Cleaver. The wire room's faxing them around anyway."

"Can I go?"

"No. Jack said you'd ask. They've got two female marshals from Chicago and a nurse to take charge of Martin if they get her. You'd never be in time anyway, Starling."

"What if he's barricaded? It could take—"

"There won't be any standoff. They find him, they fall on him—Crawford's authorized an explosive entry. Special problems with this guy, Starling, he's been in a hostage situation before. His juvenile homicides, they got him in a barricade situation in Sacramento with his grandmother as hostage—he'd already killed his grandfather—and it came out gruesome, let me tell you. He walked her out in front of the cops, they had this preacher talking to him. He's a kid, nobody took the shot. He was behind her and he did her kidneys. Medical attention no avail. At twelve, he did this. So this time no negotiations, no warning. Martin's probably dead already, but say we're lucky. Say he had a lot on his mind, one thing and another he didn't get around to it yet. If he sees us coming, he'll do her right in our faces for spite. Costs him nothing, right? So they find him and—Boom!—the door's down."

The room was too damned hot and it smelled of baby ammonia.

Burroughs was still talking. "We're looking for both names on the entomology magazine subscription lists,

371

Knifemakers Guild, Known Offenders, the works—nobody stands down until it's over. You're doing Bimmel's acquaintances, right?"

"Right."

"Justice says it's a tricky case to make if we don't catch him dirty. We need him with Martin or with something identifiable—something with teeth or fingers, frankly. Goes without saying, if he's dumped Martin already, we need witnesses to put him with a victim before the fact. We can use your stuff from Bimmel regardless . . . Starling, I wish to God this had happened yesterday for more reasons than the Martin kid. They throw the switch on you at Quantico?"

"I think so. They put in somebody else that was waiting out a recycle—that's what they tell me."

"If we get him in Chicago, you made a lot of contribution here. They're hardasses at Quantico like they're supposed to be, but they have to see *that*. Wait a minute."

Starling could hear Burroughs barking, away from the phone. Then he was back again.

"Nothing—they can deploy in Calumet City in forty to fifty-five, depends on the winds aloft. Chicago SWAT's deputized in case they find him sooner. Calumet Power and Light's come up with four possible addresses. Starling, watch for anything they can use up there to narrow it down. You see anything about Chicago or Calumet, get to me fast."

"Righto."

"Now listen—this and I gotta go. If it happens, if we get him in Calumet City, you fall in at Quantico 0800 *mañana* with your Mary Janes shined. Jack's going before the board with you. So is the chief gunny, Brigham. It don't hurt to ask."

"Jerry, one other thing: Fredrica Bimmel had some warmups made by Juno, it's a brand of fat clothes. Catherine Martin had some too, for what it's worth. He might watch fat stores to find large victims. We could ask Memphis, Akron, the other places."

"Got it. Keep smiling."

Starling walked out in the junky yard in Belvedere, Ohio, 380 long miles from the action in Chicago. The cold air felt good on her face. She threw a small punch in the air, rooting hard for the Hostage Rescue Team. At the same time, she felt a little trembly in her chin and cheeks. What the hell was this? What the hell would she have done if she'd found anything? She'd have called the cavalry, the Cleveland field office, and Columbus SWAT, the Belvedere PD too.

Saving the young woman, saving the daughter of Senator Fuck-You Martin and the ones that might come after—truly, that was what mattered. If they did it, everybody was right.

If they weren't in time, if they found something awful, please God they got Buffa—got Jame Gumb or Mr Hide or whatever they wanted to call the damned thing.

Still, to be so close, to get a hand on the rump of it, to have a good idea a day late and wind up far from the arrest, busted out of school, it all smacked of losing. Starling had long suspected, guiltily, that the Starlings' luck had been sour for a couple of hundred years now— that all the Starlings had been wandering around pissed off and confused back through the mists of time. That if you could find the tracks of the first Starling, they would lead in a circle. This was classic loser thinking, and she was damned if she'd entertain it.

If they caught him because of the profile she'd gotten from Dr Lecter, it had to help her with the Department of Justice. Starling had to think about that a little; her career hopes were twitching like a phantom limb.

Whatever happened, having the flash on the dressmaking pattern had felt nearly as good as anything ever had. There was stuff to keep here. She'd found courage in the memory of her mother as well as her father. She'd earned and kept Crawford's confidence. These were things to keep in her own White Owl cigar box.

Her job, her duty, was to think about Fredrica and how Gumb might have gotten her. A criminal prosecution of Buffalo Bill would require all the facts.

Think about Fredrica, stuck here all her young life. Where would she look for the exit? Did her longings resonate with Buffalo Bill's? Did that draw them together? Awful thought, that he might have understood her out of his own experience, empathized even, and still helped himself to her skin.

Starling stood at the edge of the water.

Almost every place has a moment of the day, an angle and intensity of light, in which it looks its best. When you're stuck someplace, you learn that time and you look forward to it. This, midafternoon, was probably the time for the Licking River behind Fell Street. Was this the Bimmel girl's time to dream? The pale sun raised enough vapor off the water to blur the old refrigerators and ranges dumped in the brush on the far side of the backwater. The northeast wind, opposite the light, pushed the cattails toward the sun.

A piece of white PVC pipe led from Mr Bimmel's shed toward the river. It gurgled and a brief rush of bloody water came out, staining the old snow. Bimmel came out into the sun. The front of his trousers was flecked with blood and he carried some pink and gray lumps in a plastic food bag.

"Squab," he said, when he saw Starling looking. "Ever eat squab?"

"No," Starling said, turning back to the water, "I've eaten doves."

"Never have to worry about biting on a shot in these."

"Mr Bimmel, did Fredrica know anybody from Calumet City or the Chicago area?"

He shrugged and shook his head.

"Had she ever been to Chicago, to your knowledge?"

"What do you mean, 'to my knowledge'? You think a girl of mine's going off to Chicago and I don't know it? She didn't go to *Columbus* I didn't know it."

"Did she know any men that sew, tailors or sailmakers?"

"She sewed for everybody. She could sew like her mother. I don't know of any men. She sewed for stores, for ladies, I don't know who."

"Who was her best friend, Mr Bimmel? Who did she hang out with?" *Didn't mean to say "hang." Good, it didn't stick him—he's just pissed off.*

"She didn't hang out like the good-for-nothings. She always had some work. God didn't make her pretty, he made her busy."

"Who would you say was her best friend?"

"Stacy Hubka, I guess, since they were little. Fredrica's mother used to say Stacy went around with Fredrica just to have somebody to wait on her, I don't know."

"Do you know where I could get in touch with her?"

"Stacy worked at the insurance, I guess she still does. The Franklin Insurance."

Starling walked to her car across the rutted yard, her head down, hands deep in her pockets. Fredrica's cat watched her from the high window.

FBI CREDENTIALS get a snappier response the farther west you go. Starling's ID, which might have raised one bored eyebrow on a Washington functionary, got the undivided attention of Stacy Hubka's boss at the Franklin Insurance Agency in Belvedere, Ohio. He relieved Stacy Hubka at the counter and the telephones himself, and offered Starling the privacy of his cubicle for the interview.

Stacy Hubka had a round, downy face and stood five-four in heels. She wore her hair in frosted wings and used a Cher Bono move to brush them back from her face. She looked Starling up and down whenever Starling wasn't facing her.

"Stacy—may I call you Stacy?"

"Sure."

"I'd like you to tell me, Stacy, how you think this might have happened to Fredrica Bimmel—where this man might have spotted Fredrica."

"Freaked me *out*. Get your *skin* peeled off, is that a bummer? Did you see her? They said she was just like

377

rags, like somebody let the air out of—"

"Stacy, did she ever mention anybody from Chicago or Calumet City?"

Calumet City. The clock above Stacy Hubka's head worried Starling. If the Hostage Rescue Team makes it in forty minutes, they're just ten minutes from touchdown. Did they have a hard address? Tend to your business.

"Chicago?" Stacy said. "No, we marched at Chicago one time in the Thanksgiving parade."

"When?"

"Eighth grade, that would be what?—nine years ago. The band just went there and back on the bus."

"What did you think last spring when she first disappeared?"

"I just didn't know."

"Remember where you were when you first found it out? When you got the news? What did you think then?"

"That first night she was gone, Skip and me went to the show and then we went to Mr Toad's for a drink and Pam and them, Pam Malavesi, came in and said Fredrica had disappeared, and Skip goes, *Houdini* couldn't make Fredrica disappear. And then he's got to tell everybody who Houdini was, he's always showing off how much he knows, and we just sort of blew it off. I thought she was just mad at her dad. Did you *see* her house? Is *that* the pits? I mean, wherever she is, I know she's embarrassed you saw it. Wouldn't *you* run away?"

"Did you think maybe she'd run away *with* somebody, did anybody pop into your mind—even if it was wrong?"

"Skip said maybe she'd found her a chubby-chaser. But, no, she never had anybody like that. She had one boyfriend, but that's, like, ancient history. He was in the band in the tenth grade. I say 'boyfriend,' but they just talked and giggled like a couple of girls and did homework. He was a big sissy though, wore one of these little Greek fisherman's caps? Skip thought he was a, you know, a queer. She got kidded about going out with a queer. Him and his sister got killed in a car wreck though, and she never got anybody else."

"What did you think when she didn't come back?"

"Pam thought maybe it was some Moonies got her. I didn't know, I was scared every time I thought about it. I wouldn't any more go out at night without Skip. I told him, I said uh-uh, buddy, when the sun goes down, *we* go out."

"Did you ever hear her mention anybody named Jame Gumb? Or John Grant?"

"Ummmm . . . no."

"Do you think she could have had a friend you didn't know about? Were there gaps in time, days when you didn't see her?"

"No. She had a guy, I'd of known, believe me. She never had a guy."

"Do you think it might be just possible, let's say, she could have had a friend and didn't say anything about it?"

"Why wouldn't she?"

"Scared she'd get kidded, maybe?"

"Kidded by us? What are you saying, because of the other time? The sissy kid in high school?" Stacy reddened. "No. No way we would hurt her. I just mentioned that together. She didn't . . . everybody was, like, *kind* to her after he died."

"Did you work with Fredrica, Stacy?"

"Me and her and Pam Malavesi and Jaronda Askew all worked down at the Bargain Center summers in high school. Then Pam and me went to Richards' to see could we get on, it's real nice clothes, and they hired me and then Pam, so Pam says to Fredrica come on they need another girl and she came, but Mrs Burdine—the merchandizing manager?—she goes, 'Well, Fred*rica*, we need somebody that, you know, people can relate to, that they come in and say I want to look like *her*, and you can give them advice how they look in this and stuff. And if you get yourself together and lose your weight, I want you to come right back here and see me,' she says. 'But, right now, if you want to take over some of our alterations I'll try you at that, I'll put in a word with Mrs Lippman.' Mrs Burdine talked in this sweety voice but she turned out to be a bitch really, but I didn't know it right at first."

"So Fredrica did alterations for Richards', the store where you worked?"

"It hurt her feelings, but sure. Old Mrs Lippman did everybody's alterations. She had the business and she had more than she could do, and Fredrica worked for her. She did them for old Mrs Lippman. Mrs Lippman sewed for everybody, made dresses. After Mrs Lippman retired, her kid or whatever didn't want to do it and Fredrica got it all and just kept sewing for everybody. That's all she did. She'd meet me and Pam, we'd go to Pam's house on lunch and watch *The Young and the Restless* and she'd bring something and be working in her lap the whole time."

"Did Fredrica ever work at the store, taking measurements? Did she meet customers or the wholesale people?"

"Sometimes, not much. I didn't work every day."

"Did Mrs Burdine work every day, would she know?"

"Yeah, I guess."

"Did Fredrica ever mention sewing for a company called Mr Hide in Chicago or Calumet City, maybe lining leather goods?"

"I don't know, Mrs Lippman might have."

"Did you ever see the Mr Hide brand? Did Richards' ever carry it, or one of the boutiques?"

"No."

"Do you know where Mrs Lippman is? I'd like to talk to her."

"She died. She went to Florida to retire and she died down there, Fredrica said. I never did know her, me and Skip just picked up Fredrica over there sometimes when she had a bunch of clothes. You might talk to her family or something. I'll write it down for you."

This was extremely tedious, when what Starling wanted was news from Calumet City. Forty minutes was up. The Hostage Rescue Team ought to be on the ground. She shifted so she didn't have to look at the clock, and pressed on.

"Stacy, where did Fredrica buy clothes, where did she get those oversize Juno workout clothes, the sweats?"

"She made just about everything. I expect she got the sweats at Richards', you know, when everybody started wearing them real big, so they came down over tights like that? A lot of places carried them then.

She got a discount at Richards' because she sewed for them."

"Did she ever shop at an oversize store?"

"We went in every place to look, you know how you do. We'd go in Personality Plus and she'd look for ideas, you know, flattering patterns for big sizes."

"Did anybody ever come up and bug you around an oversize store, or did Fredrica ever feel somebody had his eye on her?"

Stacy looked at the ceiling for a second and shook her head.

"Stacy, did transvestites ever come into Richards', or men buying large dresses, did you ever run into that?"

"No. Me and Skip saw some at a bar in Columbus one time."

"Was Fredrica with you?"

"Not *hardly*. We'd gone, like, for the weekend."

"Would you write down the oversize places you went with Fredrica, do you think you could remember all of them?"

"Just here, or here and Columbus?"

"Here and Columbus. And Richards' too, I want to talk to Mrs Burdine."

"Okay. Is it a pretty good job, being a FBI agent?"

"I think it is."

"You get to travel around and stuff? I mean places better than this."

"Sometimes you do."

"Got to look good every day, right?"

"Well, yeah. You have to try to look businesslike."

"How do you get into that, being a FBI agent?"

"You have to go to college first, Stacy."

"That's tough to pay for."

"Yeah, it is. Sometimes there are grants and fellowships that help out, though. Would you like me to send you some stuff?"

"Yeah. I was just thinking, Fredrica was so *happy* for me when I got this job. She really got her rocks off—she never had a real office job—she thought this was getting somewhere. *This*—cardboard files and Barry Manilow on the speakers all day—she thought it was hot shit. What did she know, big dummy." Tears stood in Stacy Hubka's eyes. She opened them wide and held her head back to keep from having to do her eyes over.

"How about my list now?"

"I better do it at my desk, I got my word processor and I need my phone book and stuff." She went out with her head back, navigating by the ceiling.

It was the telephone that was tantalizing Starling. The moment Stacy Hubka was out of the cubicle, Starling called Washington collect to get the news.

AT THAT moment, over the southern tip of Lake
Michigan, a twenty-four-passenger business jet with
civilian markings came off maximum cruise and began
the long curve down to Calumet City, Illinois.

The twelve men of the Hostage Rescue Team felt
the lift in their stomachs. There were a few elaborately
casual tension yawns up and down the aisle.

Team commander Joel Randall, at the front of the
passenger compartment, took off the headset and glanced
over his notes before he got up to talk. He believed he
had the best-trained SWAT team in the world, and he
may have been right. Several of them had never been
shot at, but as far as simulations and tests could tell,
these were the best of the best.

Randall had spent a lot of time in airplane aisles, and
kept his balance easily in the bumpy descent.

"Gentlemen, our ground transportation's courtesy
of DEA undercover. They've got a florist's truck and
a plumbing van. So, Vernon, Eddie, into your long
handles and your civvies. If we go in behind stun

grenades, remember you've got no flash protection on your faces."

Vernon muttered to Eddie, "Make sure you cover up your cheeks."

"Did he say don't moon? I thought he said don't flash," Eddie murmured back.

Vernon and Eddie, who would make the initial approach to the door, had to wear thin ballistic armor beneath civilian clothes. The rest could go in hardshell armor, proof against rifle fire.

"Bobby, make sure and put one of your handsets in each van for the driver, so we don't get fucked up talking to those DEA guys," Randall said.

The Drug Enforcement Administration uses UHF radios in raids, while the FBI has VHF. There had been problems in the past.

They were equipped for most eventualities, day or night: for walls they had basic rappelling equipment, to listen they had Wolf's Ears and a VanSleek Farfoon, to see they had night-vision devices. The weapons with night scopes looked like band instruments in their bulging cases.

This was to be a precise surgical operation and the weapons reflected it—there was nothing that fired from an open bolt.

The team shrugged into their web gear as the flaps went down.

Randall got news from Calumet on his headset. He covered the microphone and spoke to the team again. "Guys, they got it down to two addresses. We take the best one and Chicago SWAT's on the other."

The field was Lansing Municipal, the closest to

Calumet on the southeast side of Chicago. The plane was cleared straight in. The pilot brought it to a stop in a stink of brakes beside two vehicles idling at the end of the field farthest from the terminal.

There were quick greetings beside the florist's truck. The DEA commander handed Randall what looked like a tall flower arrangement. It was a twelve-pound door-buster sledgehammer, the head wrapped in colored foil like a flowerpot, foliage attached to the handle.

"You might want to deliver this," he said. "Welcome to Chicago."

Mr Gumb went ahead with it in the late afternoon.

With dangerous steady tears standing in his eyes, he'd watched his video again and again and again. On the small screen, Mom climbed the waterslide and whee down into the pool, whee down into the pool. Tears blurred Jame Gumb's vision as though he were in the pool himself.

On his middle a hot-water bottle gurgled, as the little dog's stomach had gurgled when she lay on him.

He couldn't stand it any longer—what he had in the basement holding Precious prisoner, threatening her. Precious was in pain, he knew she was. He wasn't sure he could kill it before it fatally injured Precious, but he had to try. Right now.

He took off his clothes and put on the robe—he always finished a harvest naked and bloody as a newborn.

From his vast medicine cabinet he took the salve he had used on Precious when the cat scratched her. He got out some little Band-Aids and Q-tips and the plastic "Elizabethan collar" the vet gave him to keep

387

her from worrying a sore place with her teeth. He had tongue depressors in the basement to use for splints on her little broken leg, and a tube of Sting-Eez to take the hurt away if the stupid thing scratched her thrashing around before it died.

A careful head shot, and he'd just sacrifice the hair. Precious was worth more to him than the hair. The hair was a sacrifice, an offering for her safety.

Quietly down the stairs now, to the kitchen. Out of his slippers and down the dark basement stairs, staying close to the wall to keep the stairs from creaking.

He didn't turn on the light. At the bottom of the stairs, he took a right into the workroom, moving by touch in the familiar dark, feeling the floor change under his feet.

His sleeve brushed the cage and he heard the soft angry chirp of a brood moth. Here was the cabinet. He found his infrared light and slipped the goggles on his head. Now the world glowed green. He stood for a moment in the comforting burble of the tanks, in the warm hiss of the steam pipes. Master of the dark, queen of the dark.

Moths free in the air left green trails of fluorescence across his vision, faint breaths across his face as their downy wings brushed the darkness.

He checked the Python. It was loaded with .38 Special lead wad-cutters. They would slam into the skull and expand for an instant kill. If it was standing when he shot, if he shot down into the top of the head, the bullet was less likely than a Magnum load to exit the lower jaw and tear the bosom.

Quiet, quiet he crept, knees bent, painted toes gripping the old boards. Silent on the sand floor of the oubliette room. Quiet but not too slow. He didn't want his scent to have time to reach the little dog in the bottom of the well.

The top of the oubliette glowed green, the stones and mortar distinct, the grain of the wooden cover sharp in his vision. Hold the light and lean over. There they were. It was on its side like a giant shrimp. Perhaps asleep. Precious was curled up close against its body, surely sleeping, oh please not dead.

The head was exposed. A neck shot was tempting—save the hair. Too risky.

Mr Gumb leaned over the hole, the stalk-eyes of his goggles peering down. The Python has a good, muzzle-heavy feel, wonderfully pointable it is. Have to hold it in the beam of infrared. He lined up the sights on the side of its head, just where the hair was damp against the temple.

Noise or smell, he never knew—but Precious up and yipping, jumping straight up in the dark, Catherine Baker Martin doubling around the little dog and pulling the futon over them. Just lumps moving under the futon, he couldn't tell what was dog and what was Catherine. Looking down in infrared, his depth perception was impaired. He couldn't tell which lumps were Catherine.

But he had seen Precious jump. He knew her leg was all right, and at once he knew something more: Catherine Baker Martin wouldn't hurt the dog, any more than he would. Oh, sweet relief. Because of their shared feeling, he could shoot her in the God damned legs, and, when she clutched her legs, blow her fucking head off. No caution necessary.

He turned on the lights, all the damned lights in the basement, and got the floodlight from the storeroom. He had control of himself, he was reasoning well— on his way through the workroom he remembered to run a little water in the sinks so nothing would clot in the traps.

As he hurried past the stairs, ready to go, carrying the floodlight, the doorbell rang.

The doorbell grating, rasping, he had to stop and think about what it was. He hadn't heard it in years, hadn't even known whether it worked. Mounted in the stairway so it could be heard upstairs and down, clanging now, black metal tit covered with dust. As he looked at it, it rang again, kept ringing, dust flying off it. Someone was at the front, pushing the old button marked SUPERINTENDENT.

They would go away.

He rigged the floodlight.

They didn't go away.

Down in the well, it said something he paid no attention to. The bell was clanging, grating, they were just leaning on the button.

Better go upstairs and peek out the front. The long-barreled Python wouldn't go in the pocket of his robe. He put it on the workroom counter.

He was halfway up the stairs when the bell stopped ringing. He waited a few moments halfway up. Silence. He decided to look anyway. As he went through the kitchen, a heavy knock on the back door made him jump. In the pantry near the back door was a pump shotgun. He knew it was loaded.

With the door closed to the basement stairs, nobody

could hear it yelling down there, even at the top of its voice, he was sure of that.

Banging again. He opened the door a crack on the chain.

"I tried the front but nobody came," Clarice Starling said. "I'm looking for Mrs Lippman's family, could you help me?"

"They don't live here," Mr Gumb said, and closed the door. He had started for the stairs again when the banging resumed, louder this time.

He opened the door on the chain.

The young woman held an ID close to the crack. It said Federal Bureau of Investigation. "Excuse me, but I need to talk to you. I want to find the family of Mrs Lippman. I know she lived here. I want you to help me, please."

"Mrs Lippman's been dead for ages. She didn't have any relatives that I know of."

"What about a lawyer, or an accountant? Somebody who'd have her business records? Did you know Mrs Lippman?"

"Just briefly. What's the problem?"

"I'm investigating the death of Fredrica Bimmel. Who are you, please?"

"Jack Gordon."

"Did you know Fredrica Bimmel when she worked for Mrs Lippman?"

"No. Was she a great, fat person? I may have seen her, I'm not sure. I didn't mean to be rude—I was sleeping . . . Mrs Lippman had a lawyer, I may have his card somewhere. I'll see if I can find it. Do you mind stepping in? I'm freezing and my cat will *streak* through here in a second. She'll be outside like a shot before I can catch her."

He went to a rolltop desk in the far corner of the kitchen, raised the top and looked in a couple of pigeon-holes. Starling stepped inside the door and took her notebook out of her purse.

"That horrible business," he said, rummaging the desk. "I shiver every time I think about it. Are they close to catching somebody, do you think?"

"Not yet, but we're working. Mr Gordon, did you take over this place after Mrs Lippman died?"

"Yes." Gumb bent over the desk, his back to Starling. He opened a drawer and poked around in it.

"Were there any records left here? Business records?"

"No, nothing at all. Does the FBI have any ideas? The police here don't seem to know the first thing. Do they have a description, or fingerprints?"

Out of the folds in the back of Mr Gumb's robe crawled a Death's-head Moth. It stopped in the center of his back, about where his heart would be, and adjusted its wings.

Starling dropped her notebook into the bag.

Mister Gumb. Thank God my coat's open. Talk out of here, go to a phone. No. He knows I'm FBI. I let him out of my sight, he'll kill her. Do her kidneys. They find him, they fall on him. His phone. Don't see it. Not in here, ask for his phone. Get the connection, then throw down on him. Make him lie facedown, wait for the cops. That's it, do it. He's turning around.

"Here's the number," he said. He had a business card.

Take it? No.

"Good, thank you. Mr Gordon, do you have a telephone I could use?"

As he put the card on the table, the moth flew. It came from behind him, past his head and lit between them, on a cabinet above the sink.

He looked at it. When she didn't look at it, when her eyes never left his face, he knew.

Their eyes met and they knew each other.

Mr Gumb tilted his head a little to the side. He smiled. "I have a cordless phone in the pantry, I'll get it for you."

No! Do it. She went for the gun, one smooth move she'd done four thousand times and it was right where it was supposed to be, good two-hand hold, her world the front sight and the center of his chest. "Freeze."

He pursed his lips.

"Now. Slowly. Put up your hands."

Move him outside, keep the table between us. Walk him to the front. Facedown in the middle of the street and hold up the badge.

"Mr Gub—Mr Gumb, you're under arrest. I want you to walk slowly outside for me."

Instead, he walked out of the room. If he had reached for his pocket, reached behind him, if she'd seen a weapon, she could have fired. He just walked out of the room.

She heard him go down the basement stairs fast, she around the table and to the door at the top of the stairwell. He was gone, the stairwell brightly lit and empty. *Trap.* Be a sitting duck on the stairs.

From the basement then a thin paper cut of a scream.

She didn't like the stairs, didn't like the stairs, Clarice Starling in the quick where you give it or you don't.

Catherine Martin screamed again, he's killing her and Starling went down them anyway, one hand on the bannister, gun arm out, the gun just under her line of vision, floor below bounding over the gunsight, gun arm swinging with her head as she tried to cover the two facing doors open at the bottom of the staircase.

Lights blazing in the basement, she couldn't go through one door without turning her back on the other, do it quick then, to the left toward the scream. Into the sand-floored oubliette room, clearing the doorframe fast, eyes wider than they had ever been. Only place to hide was behind the well, she sliding sideways around the wall, both hands on the gun, arms out straight, a little pressure on the trigger, on around the well and nobody behind it.

A small scream rising from the well like thin smoke. Yipping now, a dog. She approached the well, eyes on the door, got to the rim, looked over the edge. Saw the girl, looked up again, down again, said what she was trained to say, calm the hostage:

"FBI, you're safe."

"Safe SHIT, he's got a gun. Getmeout. GETMEOUT."

"Catherine, you'll be all right. Shut up. Do you know where he is?"

"GETMEOUT, I DON'T GIVE A SHIT WHERE HE IS, GETMEOUT."

"I'll get you out. Be quiet. Help me. Be quiet so I can hear. Try and shut that dog up."

Braced behind the well, covering the door, her heart

pounded and her breath blew dust off the stone. She could not leave Catherine Martin to get help when she didn't know where Gumb was. She moved up to the door and took cover behind the frame. She could see across the foot of the stairs and into part of the workroom beyond.

Either she found Gumb, or she made sure he'd fled, or she took Catherine out with her, those were the only choices.

A quick look over her shoulder, around the oubliette room.

"Catherine. Catherine. Is there is a ladder?"

"I don't know, I woke up down here. He let the bucket down on strings."

Bolted to a wall beam was a small hand winch. There was no line on the drum of the winch.

"Catherine, I have to find something to get you out with. Can you walk?"

"Yes. Don't leave me."

"I have to leave the room for just a minute."

"You fucking bitch, don't you leave me down here, my mother will tear your goddamn shit brains out—"

"Catherine, shut up. I want you to be quiet so I can hear. To *save* yourself, be quiet, do you understand?" Then, louder, "The other officers will be here any minute, now shut up. We won't leave you down there."

He had to have a rope. Where was it? Go see.

Starling moved across the stairwell in one rush, to the door of the workroom, door's the worst place, in fast, back and forth along the near wall until she had seen all the room, familiar shapes swimming in the glass tanks, she too alert to be startled. Quickly through the room, past the tanks, the sinks, past the cage, a few big moths flying. She ignored them.

Approaching the corridor beyond, it blazing with light. The refrigerator turned on behind her and she spun in a crouch, hammer lifting off the frame of the Magnum, eased the pressure off. On to the corridor. She wasn't taught to peek. Head and gun at once, but low. The corridor empty. The studio blazing with light at the end of it. Fast along it, gambling past the closed door, on to the studio door. The room all white and blond oak. Hell to clear from the doorway. Make sure every mannequin is a mannequin, every reflection is a mannequin. Only movement in the mirror's *your* movement.

The great armoire stood open and empty. The far door open onto darkness, the basement beyond. No rope, no ladder anywhere. No lights beyond the studio. She closed the door into the dark part of the basement, pushed a chair under the knob, and pushed a sewing machine against it. If she could be positive he wasn't in this part of the basement, she'd risk going upstairs for a moment to find a phone.

Back down the corridor, one door she'd passed. Get on the side opposite the hinges. All the way open in one move. The door slammed back, nobody behind it. An old bathroom. In it, rope, hooks, a sling. Get Catherine or go for the phone? In the bottom of the well, Catherine wouldn't get shot by accident. But if Starling got killed, Catherine was dead too. Take Catherine with her to the phone.

Starling didn't want to stay in the bathroom long.

396

He could come to the door and hose her. She looked both ways and ducked inside for the rope. There was a big bathtub in the room. The tub was almost filled with hard red-purple plaster. A hand and wrist stuck up from the plaster, the hand turned dark and shriveled, the fingernails painted pink. On the wrist was a dainty watch. Starling was seeing everything at once, the rope, the tub, the hand, the watch.

The tiny insect-crawl of the second-hand was the last thing she saw before the lights went out.

Her heart knocked hard enough to shake her chest and arms. *Dizzy dark, need to touch something, the edge of the tub. The bathroom. Get out of the bathroom. If he can find the door, he can hose this room, nothing to get behind. Oh dear Jesus, go out. Go out down low and out in the hall. Every light out? Every light. He must have done it at the fuse box, pulled the lever, where would it be? Where would the fuse box be? Near the stairs. Lot of times near the stairs. If it is, he'll come from that way. But he's between me and Catherine.*

Catherine Martin was keening again.

Wait here? Wait forever? Maybe he's gone. He can't be sure no backup's coming. Yes, he can. But soon I'll be missed. Tonight. The stairs are in the direction of the screams. Solve it now.

She moved, quietly, her shoulder barely brushing the wall, brushing it too lightly for sound, one hand extended ahead, the gun at waist level, close to her in the confined hallway. Out into the workroom now. Feel the space opening up. Open room. In the crouch in the open room, arms out, both hands on the gun. You know exactly where the gun is, it's just below eye level. Stop, listen. Head and body and arms turning together like a turret. Stop, listen.

In absolute black the hiss of steam pipes, trickle of water.

Heavy in her nostrils the smell of the goat.

Catherine keening.

Against the wall stood Mr Gumb with his goggles on. There was no danger she'd bump into him—there was an equipment table between them. He played his infrared light up and down her. She was too slender to be of great utility to him. He remembered her hair though, from the kitchen, and it was glorious, and that would only take a minute. He could slip it right off. Put it on himself. He could lean over the well wearing it and tell that thing "Surprise!"

It was fun to watch her trying to sneak along. She had her hip against the sinks now, creeping toward the screams with her gun stuck out. It would have been fun to hunt her for a long time—he'd never hunted one armed before. He would have *thoroughly* enjoyed it. No time for that. Pity.

A shot in the face would be fine and easy at eight feet. Now.

He cocked the Python as he brought it up snick snick and the figure blurred, bloomed, bloomed green in his vision and his gun bucked in his hand and the floor hit him hard in the back and his light was on and he saw the ceiling. Starling on the floor, flash-blind, ears ringing, deafened by the blast of the guns. She worked in the dark while neither could hear, dump the empties, tip it, feel to see they're all out, in with the speedloader, feel it, tip it down, twist, drop it, close the cylinder. She'd fired four. Two shots and two shots. He'd fired once. She found the two good cartridges she'd dumped. Put them where? In the speedloader pouch. She lay still. Move before he can hear?

The sound of a revolver being cocked is like no other. She'd fired at the sound, seen nothing past the great muzzle flashes of the guns. She hoped he'd fire now in the wrong direction, give her the muzzle flash to shoot at. Her hearing was coming back, her ears still rang, but she could hear.

What was that sound? Whistling? Like a teakettle, but interrupted. What was it? Like breathing. Is it me? No. Her breath blew warm off the floor, back in her face. Careful, don't get dust, don't sneeze. It's breathing. It's a sucking chest wound. He's hit in the chest. They'd taught her how to seal one, to put something over it, a rain slicker, a plastic bag, something airtight, strap it tight. Reinflate the lung. She'd hit him in the chest, then. What to do? Wait. Let him stiffen up and bleed. Wait.

Starling's cheek stung. She didn't touch it, if it was bleeding she didn't want her hands slick.

The moaning from the well came again, Catherine talking, crying. Starling had to wait. She couldn't answer Catherine. She couldn't say anything or move.

Mr Gumb's invisible light played on the ceiling. He tried to move it and he couldn't, any more than he could move his head. A great Malaysian Luna Moth passing close beneath the ceiling picked up the infrared and came down, circled, lit on the light. The pulsing shadows of its wings, enormous on the ceiling, were visible only to Mr Gumb.

Over the sucking in the dark, Starling heard Mr Gumb's ghastly voice, choking: "How . . . does . . . it feel . . . to be . . . so beautiful?"

And then another sound. A gurgle, a rattle and the whistling stopped.

Starling knew that sound too. She'd heard it once before, at the hospital when her father died.

She felt for the edge of the table and got to her feet. Feeling her way along, going toward the sound of Catherine, she found the stairwell and climbed the stairs in the dark.

It seemed to take a long time. There was a candle in the kitchen drawer. With it she found the fuse box beside the stairs, jumped when the lights came on. To get to the fuse box and shut off the lights, he must have left the basement another way and come down again behind her.

Starling had to be positive he was dead. She waited until her eyes were well adjusted to the light before she went back in the workroom, and then she was careful. She could see his naked feet and legs sticking out from under the worktable. She kept her eyes on the hand beside the gun until she kicked the gun away. His eyes were open. He was dead, shot through the right side of the chest, thick blood under him. He had put on some of his things from the armoire and she couldn't look at him long.

She went to the sink, put the Magnum on the drain-board and ran cold water on her wrists, wiped her face with her wet hand. No blood. Moths batted at the mesh around the lights. She had to step around the body to retrieve the Python.

At the well she said, "Catherine, he's dead. He can't hurt you. I'm going upstairs and call—"

"No! GET ME OUT. GET ME OUT. GET ME OUT."

"Look here. He's dead. This is his gun. Remember it? I'm going to call the police and the fire department. I'm afraid to hoist you out myself, you might fall. Soon as I call them, I'll come back down and wait with you. Okay? Okay. Try to shut that dog up. Okay? Okay."

The local television crews arrived just after the fire department and before the Belvedere police. The fire captain, angered at the glare from the lights, drove the television crews back up the stairs and out of the basement while he rigged a pipe frame to hoist out Catherine Martin, not trusting Mr Gumb's hook in the ceiling joist. A fireman went down into the well and put her in the rescue chair. Catherine came out holding the dog, kept the dog in the ambulance.

They drew the line on dogs at the hospital and wouldn't let the dog in. A fireman, instructed to drop it off at the animal shelter, took it home with him instead.

THERE WERE about fifty people at National Airport in Washington, meeting the red-eye flight from Columbus, Ohio. Most of them were meeting relatives and they looked sleepy and grumpy enough, with their shirttails sticking out below their jackets.

From the crowd, Ardelia Mapp had a chance to look Starling over as she came off the plane. Starling was pasty, dark under the eyes. Some black grains of gunpowder were in her cheek. Starling spotted Mapp and they hugged.

"Hey, Sport," Mapp said. "You check anything?"

Starling shook her head.

"Jeff's outside in the van. Let's go home."

Jack Crawford was outside too, his car parked behind the van in the limousine lane. He'd had Bella's relatives all night.

"I . . ." he started. "You know what you did? You hit a home run, kid." He touched her cheek. "What's this?"

"Burnt gunpowder. The doctor said it'll work out by

itself in a couple of days—better than digging for it."

Crawford took her to him and held her very tight for a moment, just a moment, and then put her away from him and kissed her on the forehead. "You know what you did?" he said again. "Go home. Go to sleep. Sleep in. I'll talk to you tomorrow."

The new surveillance van was comfortable, designed for long stakeouts. Starling and Mapp rode in the big chairs in the back.

Without Jack Crawford in the van, Jeff drove a little harder. They made good time toward Quantico.

Starling rode with her eyes closed. After a couple of miles, Mapp nudged her knee. Mapp had opened two short-bottle Cokes. She handed Starling a Coke and took a half-pint of Jack Daniel's out of her purse.

They each took a swig out of their Cokes and poured in a shot of sour mash. Then they stuck their thumbs in the necks of the bottles, shook them, and shot the foam in their mouths.

"Ahhh," Starling said.

"Don't spill that in here," Jeff said.

"Don't worry, Jeff," Mapp said. Quietly to Starling, "You should have seen my man Jeff waiting for me outside the liquor store. He looked like he was passing peach seeds." When Mapp saw the whiskey start to work a little, when Starling sank a little deeper in her chair, Mapp said, "How you doing, Starling?"

"Ardelia, I'm damned if I know."

"You don't have to go back, do you?"

"Maybe for one day next week, but I hope not. The US Attorney came over from Columbus to talk to the Belvedere cops. I did depositions out the wazoo."

"Couple of good things," Mapp said. "Senator Martin's been on the phone all evening from Bethesda—you knew they took Catherine to Bethesda? Well, she's okay. He didn't mess her up in any physical way. Emotional damage, they don't know, they have to watch. Don't worry about school. Crawford and Brigham both called. The hearing's canceled. Krendler asked for his memo back. These people have got a heart like a greasy BB, Starling—you get no slack. You don't have to take the Search-and-Seizure exam at 0800 tomorrow, but you take it Monday, and the PE test right after. We'll jam over the weekend."

They finished the half-pint just north of Quantico and dumped the evidence in a barrel at a roadside park.

"That Pilcher, Dr Pilcher at the Smithsonian, called three times. Made me promise to tell you he called."

"He's not a doctor."

"You think you might do something about him?"

"Maybe. I don't know yet."

"He sounds like he's pretty funny. I've about decided funny's the best thing in men, I'm talking about *aside* from money and your basic manageability."

"Yeah, and manners too, you can't leave that out."

"Right. Give me a son of a bitch with some manners every time."

Starling went like a zombie from the shower to the bed.

Mapp kept her reading light on for a while, until Starling's breathing was regular. Starling jerked in her sleep, a muscle in her cheek twitched, and once her eyes opened wide.

404

Mapp woke sometime before daylight, the room feeling empty. Mapp turned on her light. Starling was not in her bed. Both of their laundry bags were missing, so Mapp knew where to look.

She found Starling in the warm laundry room, dozing against the slow rump-rump of a washing machine in the smell of bleach and soap and fabric softener. Starling had the psychology background—Mapp's was law—yet it was Mapp who knew that the washing machine's rhythm was like a great heartbeat and the rush of its waters was what the unborn hear—our last memory of peace.

JACK CRAWFORD woke early on the sofa in his study and heard the snoring of his in-laws in his house. In the free moments before the weight of the day came on him, he remembered not Bella's death, but the last thing she'd said to him, her eyes clear and calm: "What's going on in the yard?"

He took Bella's grain scoop and, in his bathrobe, went out and fed the birds as he had promised to do. Leaving a note for his sleeping in-laws, he eased out of the house before sunrise. Crawford had always gotten along with Bella's relatives, more or less, and it helped to have the noise in the house, but he was glad to get away to Quantico.

He was going through the overnight telex traffic and watching the early news in his office when Starling pressed her nose to the glass of the door. He dumped some reports out of a chair for her and they watched the news together without saying anything. Here it came.

The outside of Jame Gumb's old building in Belvedere

with its empty storefront and soaped windows covered with heavy gates. Starling hardly recognized it.

"Dungeon of Horrors," the news reader called it.

Harsh, jostled pictures of the well and the basement, still cameras held up before the television camera, and angry firemen waving the photographers back. Moths crazed by the television lights, flying into the lights, a moth on the floor on its back, wings beating down to a final tremor.

Catherine Martin refusing a stretcher and walking to the ambulance with a policeman's coat around her, the dog sticking its face out between the lapels.

A side view of Starling walking fast to a car, her head down, hands in the pockets of her coat.

The film was edited to exclude some of the more grisly objects. In the far reaches of the basement, the cameras could show only the low, lime-sprinkled thresholds of the chambers holding Gumb's tableaux. The body count in that part of the basement stood at six so far.

Twice Crawford heard Starling expel air through her nose. The news went to a commercial break.

"Good morning, Starling."

"Hello," she said, as though it were later in the day.

"The US Attorney in Columbus faxed me your depositions overnight. You'll have to sign some copies for him . . . So you went from Fredrica Bimmel's house to Stacy Hubka, and then to the Burdine woman at the store Bimmel sewed for, Richards' Fashions, and Mrs Burdine gave you Mrs Lippman's old address, the building there?"

Starling nodded. "Stacy Hubka had been by the

place a couple of times to pick up Fredrica, but Stacy's boyfriend was driving and her directions were vague. Mrs Burdine had the address."

"Mrs Burdine never mentioned a man at Mrs Lippman's?"

"No."

The television news had film from Bethesda Naval Hospital. Senator Ruth Martin's face framed in a limousine window.

"Catherine was rational last night, yes. She's sleeping, she's sedated right now. We're counting our blessings. No, as I said before, she's suffering from shock, but she's rational. Just bruises, and her finger is broken. And she's dehydrated as well. Thank you." She poked her chauffeur in the back. "Thank you. No, she mentioned the dog to me last night, I don't know what we'll do about it, we already *have* two dogs."

The story closed with a nothing quote from a stress specialist who would be talking with Catherine Martin later in the day to assess emotional damage.

Crawford shut it off.

"How're you hittin' 'em, Starling?"

"Kind of numb . . . you too?"

Crawford nodded, quickly moved along. "Senator Martin's been on the phone overnight. She wants to come see you. Catherine does too, as soon as she can travel."

"I'm always home."

"Krendler too, he wants to come down here. He asked for his memo back."

"Come to think of it, I'm not always home."

"Here's some free advice. Use Senator Martin. Let

her tell you how grateful she is, let her hand you the markers. Do it soon. Gratitude has a short half-life. You'll need her one of these days, the way you act."

"That's what Ardelia says."

"Your roomie, Mapp? The Superintendent told me Mapp's set to cram you for your makeup exams on Monday. She just pulled a point and a half ahead of her archrival, Stringfellow, he tells me."

"For valedictorian?"

"He's tough, though, Stringfellow—he's saying she can't hold him off."

"He best bring his lunch."

In the clutter on Crawford's desk was the origami chicken Dr Lecter had folded. Crawford worked the tail up and down. The chicken pecked.

"Lecter's gone platinum—he's at the top of everybody's Most Wanted list," he said. "Still, he could be out for a while. Off the post, you need some good habits."

She nodded.

"He's busy now," Crawford said, "but when he's not busy, he'll entertain himself. We need to be clear on this: You know he'd do it to you, just like he'd do anybody else."

"I don't think he'd ever bushwhack me—it's rude, and he wouldn't get to ask any questions that way. Sure he'd do it as soon as I bored him."

"Maintain good habits is all I'm saying. When you go off the post, flag your three-card—no phone queries on your whereabouts without positive ID. I want to put a trace-alert on your telephone, if you don't mind. It'll be private unless you push the button."

"I don't look for him to come after me, Mr Crawford."

"But you heard what I said?"

"I did. I did hear."

"Take these depositions and look 'em over. Add if you want to. We'll witness your signatures here when you're ready. Starling, I'm proud of you. So is Brigham, so is the Director." It sounded stiff, not like he wanted it to sound.

He went to his office door. She was going away from him, down the deserted hall. He managed to hail her from his berg of grief: "Starling, your father sees you."

Jame Gumb was news for weeks after he was lowered into his final hole.

Reporters pieced together his history, beginning with the records of Sacramento County:

His mother had been carrying him a month when she failed to place in the Miss Sacramento Contest in 1948. The "Jame" on his birth certificate apparently was a clerical error that no one bothered to correct.

When her acting career failed to materialize, his mother went into an alcoholic decline; Gumb was two when Los Angeles County placed him in a foster home.

At least two scholarly journals explained that this unhappy childhood was the reason he killed women in his basement for their skins. The words *crazy* and *evil* do not appear in either article.

The film of the beauty contest that Jame Gumb watched as an adult was real footage of his mother, but the woman in the swimming pool film was not his mother, comparative measurements revealed.

411

Gumb's grandparents retrieved him from an unsatisfactory foster home when he was ten, and he killed them two years later.

Tulare Vocational Rehabilitation taught Gumb to be a tailor during his years at the psychiatric hospital. He demonstrated definite aptitude for the work.

Gumb's employment record is broken and incomplete. Reporters found at least two restaurants where he worked off the books, and he worked sporadically in the clothing business. It has not been proven that he killed during this period, but Benjamin Raspail said he did.

He was working at the curio store where the butterfly ornaments were made when he met Raspail, and he lived off the musician for some time. It was then that Gumb became obsessed with moths and butterflies and the changes they go through.

After Raspail left him, Gumb killed Raspail's next lover, Klaus, beheaded and partially flayed him.

Later he dropped in on Raspail in the East. Raspail, ever thrilled by bad boys, introduced him to Dr Lecter.

This was proven in the week after Gumb's death when the FBI seized from Raspail's next of kin the tapes of Raspail's therapy sessions with Dr Lecter.

Years ago, when Dr Lecter was declared insane, the therapy-session tapes had been turned over to the families of the victims to be destroyed. But Raspail's wrangling relatives kept the tapes, hoping to use them to attack Raspail's will. They had lost interest listening to the early tapes, which are only Raspail's boring reminiscences of school life. After the news coverage of Jame Gumb, the Raspail family listened to the rest.

When the relatives called the lawyer Everett Yow and threatened to use the tapes in a renewed assault on Raspail's will, Yow called Clarice Starling.

The tapes include the final session, when Lecter killed Raspail. More important, they reveal how much Raspail told Lecter about Jame Gumb:

Raspail told Dr Lecter that Gumb was obsessed with moths, that he had flayed people in the past, that he had killed Klaus, that he had a job with the Mr Hide leather-goods company in Calumet City, but was taking money from an old lady in Belvedere, Ohio, who had made linings for Mr Hide, Inc. One day Gumb would take everything the old lady had, Raspail predicted.

"When Lecter read that the first victim was from Belvedere and she was flayed, he knew who was doing it," Crawford told Starling as they listened together to the tape. "He'd have given you Gumb and looked like a genius if Chilton had stayed out of it."

"He hinted to me by writing in the file that the sites were too random," Starling said. "And in Memphis he asked me if I sew. What did he want to happen?"

"He wanted to amuse himself," Crawford said. "He's been amusing himself for a long, long time."

No tape of Jame Gumb was ever found, and his activities in the years after Raspail's death were established piecemeal through business correspondence, gas receipts, interviews with boutique owners.

When Mrs Lippman died on a trip to Florida with Gumb, he inherited everything—the old building with its living quarters and empty storefront and vast basement, and a comfortable amount of money. He stopped working for Mr Hide, but maintained an apartment

413

in Calumet City for a while, and used the business address to receive packages in the John Grant name. He kept favored customers, and continued to travel to boutiques around the country, as he had for Mr Hide, measuring for custom garments he made in Belvedere. He used his trips to scout for victims and to dump them when they were used up—the brown van droning for hours on the Interstate with finished leather garments swaying on racks in the back above the rubberized body bag on the floor.

He had the wonderful freedom of the basement. Room to work and play. At first it was only games— hunting young women through the black warren, creating amusing tableaux in remote rooms and sealing them up, opening the doors again only to throw in a little lime.

Fredrica Bimmel began to help Mrs Lippman in the last year of the old lady's life. Fredrica was picking up sewing at Mrs Lippman's when she met Jame Gumb. Fredrica Bimmel was not the first young woman he killed, but she was the first one he killed for her skin.

Fredrica Bimmel's letters to Gumb were found among his things.

Starling could hardly read the letters, because of the hope in them, because of the dreadful need in them, because of the endearments from Gumb that were implied in her responses: "Dearest Secret Friend in my Breast, I love you!—I didn't *ever* think I'd get to say that, and it is best of all to get to say it *back*."

When did he reveal himself? Had she discovered the basement? How did her face look when he changed, how long did he keep her alive?

Worst, Fredrica and Gumb truly were friends to the last; she wrote him a note from the pit.

The tabloids changed Gumb's nickname to Mr Hide and, sick because they hadn't thought of the name themselves, virtually started over with the story.

Safe in the heart of Quantico, Starling did not have to deal with the press, but the tabloid press dealt with her.

From Dr Frederick Chilton, the *National Tattler* bought the tapes of Starling's interview with Dr Hannibal Lecter. The *Tattler* expanded on their conversations for their "Bride of Dracula" series and implied that Starling had made frank sexual revelations to Lecter in exchange for information, spurning an offer to Starling from *Velvet Talks: The Journal of Telephone Sex*.

People magazine did a short, pleasant item on Starling, using yearbook pictures from the University of Virginia and from the Lutheran Home at Bozeman. The best picture was of the horse, Hannah, in her later years, drawing a cart full of children.

Starling cut out the picture of Hannah and put it in her wallet. It was the only thing she saved.

She was healing.

CHAPTER

60

ARDELIA MAPP was a great tutor—she could spot a test question in a lecture farther than a leopard can see a limp—but she was not much of a runner. She told Starling it was because she was so weighted with facts.

She had fallen behind Starling on the jogging trail and caught up at the old DC-6 the FBI uses for hijack simulations. It was Sunday morning. They had been on the books for two days, and the pale sun felt good.

"So what did Pilcher say on the phone?" Mapp said, leaning against the landing gear.

"He and his sister have this place on the Chesapeake."

"Yeah, and?"

"His sister's there with her kids and dogs and maybe her husband."

"So?"

"They're in one end of the house—it's a big old dump on the water they inherited from his grandmother."

"Cut to the chase."

"Pilch has the other end of the house. Next weekend, he wants us to go. Lots of rooms, he says. 'As many rooms as anybody might need,' I believe is the way he put it. His sister would call and invite me, he said."

"No kidding. I didn't know people did that any-more."

"He did this nice scenario—no hassles, bundle up and walk on the beach, come in and there's a fire going, dogs jump all over you with their big sandy paws."

"Idyllic, umm-humm, big sandy paws, go on."

"It's kind of much, considering we've never had a date, even. He claims it's best to sleep with two or three big dogs when it gets really cold. He says they've got enough dogs for everybody to have a couple."

"Pilcher's setting you up for the old dog-suit trick, you snapped to that, didn't you?"

"He claims to be a good cook. His sister says he is."

"Oh, she called already."

"Yep."

"How'd she sound?"

"Okay. Sounded like she was in the other end of the house."

"What did you tell her?"

"I said, 'Yes, thank you very much,' is what I said."

"Good," Mapp said. "That's very good. Eat some crabs. Grab Pilcher and smooch him on his face, go wild."

DOWN THE deep carpet in the corridor of the Marcus Hotel, a room-service waiter trundled a cart.

At the door of suite 91, he stopped and rapped softly on the door with his gloved knuckle. He cocked his head and rapped again to be heard above the music from within—Bach, *Two- and Three-Part Inventions*, Glenn Gould at the piano.

"Come."

The gentleman with the bandage across his nose was in a dressing gown, writing at the desk.

"Put it by the windows. May I see the wine?"

The waiter brought it. The gentleman held it under the light of his desk lamp, touched the neck to his cheek.

"Open it, but leave it off the ice," he said, and wrote a generous tip across the bottom of the bill. "I won't taste it now."

He did not want the waiter handing him wine to taste—he found the smell of the man's watchband objectionable.

Dr Lecter was in an excellent humor. His week had gone well. His appearance was coming right along, and as soon as a few small discolorations cleared, he could take off his bandages and pose for passport photos.

The actual work he was doing himself—minor injections of silicon in his nose. The silicon gel was not a prescription item, but the hypodermics and the Novocaine were. He got around this difficulty by pinching a prescription off the counter of a busy pharmacy near the hospital. He blanked out the chicken scratches of the legitimate physician with typist's correction fluid and photocopied the blank prescription form. The first prescription he wrote was a copy of the one he stole, and he returned it to the pharmacy, so nothing was missing.

The palooka effect in his fine features was not pleasing, and he knew the silicon would move around if he wasn't careful, but the job would do until he got to Rio.

When his hobbies began to absorb him—long before his first arrest—Dr Lecter had made provisions for a time when he might be a fugitive. In the wall of a vacation cottage on the banks of the Susquehanna River were money and the credentials of another identity, including a passport and the cosmetic aids he'd worn in the passport photos. The passport would have expired by now, but it could be renewed very quickly.

Preferring to be herded through customs with a big tour badge on his chest, he'd already signed up for a ghastly sounding tour called "South American Splendor" that would take him as far as Rio.

He reminded himself to write a check on the late Lloyd Wyman for the hotel bill and get the extra

419

five days' lead while the check plodded through the bank, rather than sending an Amex charge into the computer.

This evening he was catching up on his correspondence, which he would have to send through a remailing service in London.

First, he sent to Barney a generous tip and a thank-you note for his many courtesies at the asylum.

Next, he dropped a note to Dr Frederick Chilton in federal protective custody, suggesting that he would be paying Dr Chilton a visit in the near future. After this visit, he wrote, it would make sense for the hospital to tattoo feeding instructions on Chilton's forehead to save paperwork.

Last, he poured himself a glass of the excellent Batard-Montrachet and addressed Clarice Starling:

Well, Clarice, have the lambs stopped screaming?

You owe me a piece of information, you know, and that's what I'd like.

An ad in the national edition of the *Times* and in the *International Herald-Tribune* on the first of any month will be fine. Better put it in the *China Mail* as well.

I won't be surprised if the answer is yes and no. The lambs will stop for now. But, Clarice, you judge yourself with all the mercy of the dungeon scales at Threave; you'll have to earn it again and again, the blessed silence. Because it's the plight that drives you, seeing the plight, and the plight will not end, ever.

I have no plans to call on you, Clarice, the world

being more interesting with you in it. Be sure you extend me the same courtesy.

Dr Lecter touched his pen to his lips. He looked out at the night sky and smiled.

I have windows.

Orion is above the horizon now, and near it Jupiter, brighter than it will ever be again before the year 2000. (I have no intention of telling you the time and how high it is.) But I expect you can see it too. Some of our stars are the same.

Clarice.

Hannibal Lecter

Far to the east, on the Chesapeake shore, Orion stood high in the clear night, above a big old house, and a room where a fire is banked for the night, its light pulsing gently with the wind above the chimneys. On a large bed there are many quilts and on the quilts and under them are several large dogs. Additional mounds beneath the covers may or may not be Noble Pilcher, it is impossible to determine in the ambient light. But the face on the pillow, rosy in the firelight, is certainly that of Clarice Starling, and she sleeps deeply, sweetly, in the silence of the lambs.

ALSO AVAILABLE IN ARROW

Red Dragon

Thomas Harris

The novel that launched Hannibal Lecter's legacy of evil.

Sexual hunger; demonic violence; sinister logic – the lethal components of a deadly formula driving a psychopath in the grip of an unimaginable delusion; a boastful killer who sends the police tormenting notes; a tortured, torturing monster who finds ultimate pleasure in viciously murdering happy families, and calls himself . . . The Red Dragon.

'The best popular novel published since *The Godfather*'
Stephen King

'Completely gripping' *Time Out*

'Something out of the ordinary for strong nerves and stomachs, an intricately crafted chiller' *Observer*

arrow books

Hannibal

Thomas Harris

Seven years have passed since Dr. Hannibal Lecter escaped from custody, seven years since FBI Special Agent Clarice Starling interviewed him in a maximum security hospital for the criminally insane. The doctor is still at large, pursuing his own ineffable interests, savouring the scents, the essences of an unguarded world. But Starling has never forgotten her encounters with Dr. Lecter, and the metallic rasp of his seldom-used voice still sounds in her dreams.

Mason Verger remembers Dr. Lecter, too, and is obsessed with revenge. He was Dr. Lecter's sixth victim, and he has survived to rule his own butcher's empire. From his respirator, Verger monitors every twitch in his worldwide web. Soon he sees that to draw the doctor, he must have the most exquisite and innocent-appearing bait; he must have what Dr Lecter likes best.

'Worth the wait . . . look no further for the chiller of the year'
The Times

'Readers who have been waiting for *Hannibal* only want to know if it is as good as *Red Dragon* and *The Silence of the Lambs* . . . It is a pleasure to reply in the negative. No, not as good. This one is better'
Stephen King

arrow books